Julian Rathbone is the author of... ...acclaimed *The Last English King*, *Kings of Albion* and the Booker-shortlisted *Joseph*. Along with his last book, *A Very English Agent*, they are all available in Abacus paperback. Julian Rathbone lives in Hampshire.

Praise for *Birth of a Nation*:

'Tremendous fun, as Julian Rathbone plays fast and loose with great swathes of American history . . . He wears his learning lightly and has a disarmingly flippant side. *Birth of a Nation* is notable for the sheer breadth of the material it contains . . . Rathbone finds a succession of contrasting milieus, all superbly described, for his itinerant hero . . . the novel can be recommended without reservation. It has all the ingredients – a likeable hero, a string of feisty heroines, well-drawn locales, dramatic reversals of fortune – of the classic English adventure story' *Sunday Telegraph*

'Clever stuff this. Rathbone writes well, has a vast knowledge of his subject, and is witty' *Herald*

'Julian Rathbone has always set subversively right the things most popular fiction is content to leave wrong. His thrillers are in the fine tradition of Eric Ambler: radical critiques of the way things are, and of the way most thrillers accept that status quo. When he writes novels set in the past, they are reminders of guilty secrets, where the jokes – and Rathbone is often very funny – depend on the gap between high pretence and sordid actuality' *Independent*

'If history, as Marx suggested, repeats itself first as tragedy and next as farce, then Charlie's rollicking version of it is firmly in the second camp' *Financial Times*

Birth of a Nation

A NOVEL

Julian Rathbone

LITTLE, BROWN

ABACUS

First published in Great Britain in September 2004 by Little, Brown
This paperback edition published in August 2005 by Abacus

A CIP catalogue record for this book
is available from the British Library.

ISBN 0 349 11895 7

Typeset in Goudy by M Rules

Printed and bound in Great Britain by
Clays Ltd, St Ives plc

Abacus
An imprint of
Time Warner Book Group UK
Brettenham House
Lancaster Place
London WC2E 7EN

www.twbg.co.uk

For Arthur and Nina

This novel is a fiction within a fiction. It purports to be one volume in a, so far, three-volume apology for his life written by a man who is a spy, a rogue, a coward. In real life such people are not to be trusted – even less so in fiction. I am labouring this point because there are historical figures in this narrative and some historically important events, and geographically identifiable places. If you feel I, or Eddie, have got these wrong, you may well be right. But, if you think it matters, I would add that you have forgotten what fiction is.

Prologue

March 1853

Charlie Boylan, also known as Joseph Charles Edward Bosham, is back in his cell in Millbank prison, sitting at the table they have brought him, knowing that the following day he will be arraigned before the magistrates and formally charged with the attempted, or actual, murder of Thomas Cargill, a Home Office functionary, depending on whether or not Cargill lives through the night. Since Charlie is innocent he is not unduly bothered. He has a handle on the Powers-That-Be which he is confident will ensure not only that he will get off but also that they might at last agree to pay him a modest pension. He has been left with a pile of clean paper and a steel-nibbed pen and inkwell, in the hope that he might be induced to reveal the whereabouts of the cache of papers which forms the main plank of his claim for a pension. The papers are believed to include evidence of a forty-year-old scandal of royal incest and other similarly sensitive stuff.

Charlie, who could be as much as sixty-three years old, is not a pleasant sight. Long, straight, grey hair hangs down on either side of a face that was once good-looking enough though it always carried an ingratiating expression of complicity; his eyes of faded blue water a little, perhaps from the fumes of the candle they have given him; his nose, once discreetly aquiline, is studded with blackheads and pock

1

marks; his thin top lip droops over a once generous, now merely floppy bottom lip, its corners merging into the deep lines etched on either side of a somewhat receding chin. His clothes, a black serge coat over a grey shirt and loose cravat, are old but, for the time being, tolerably clean and deloused. Still, sitting as he is, one is hardly aware of his two most extraordinary physical features. He is very short, about four-and-a-half feet tall, and he has, beneath his clothes, a pelt of furry hair, some of which is quite long, though it is patchy over his buttocks, knees and elbows. Once it was black, with a slightly reddish or gingery sheen: now it is all sorts of shades between dark grey and white. As the last of the few women, who, responding as much to suppressed maternal instincts as to sexual curiosity, have had him in their beds, remarked: he is a silver tabby.

So, there's our Charlie. Or, as he prefers to be called through most of what follows, Eddie.

He pulls the paper towards him, adjusts the position of his candle, blows on his fingers. He lifts his head and hears again the thunder of the surf and sees again the sails of the *Beagle*, hull down, drop beneath the horizon, and with a sigh, dips his pen. The nib scratches on the cheap paper and a tiny spray of ink, which he brushes dry with his threadbare sleeve, flicks across the page.

Since the Voyage of the Beagle *has been fully and well described by the Scientist on board, Mr Charles Darwin, in his extended account published in 1839, I will not endeavour to surpass his efforts but begin the next part of my tale on the day I was inadvertently marooned on the largest of the Galápagos Islands . . .*

Part I

THE GALÁPAGOS

A devil, a born devil, on whose nature
Nurture can never stick . . .

The Tempest, Act IV, Scene i

1

'These finches, sir,' I suggested, as a small flock of the little brown birds zipped away from us in a low fluttering flight, 'are not identical to the ones we saw on Narborough Island.'

'The differences are slight,' young Mr Darwin replied, and strode on briskly, leaving me and his man Covington to struggle a little to keep within earshot, encumbered as we were by the impedimenta of our master's trade, viz. teak boxes with brass handles for the specimens he collected, his hunting gun and a bandolier of made-up cartridges, provisions of ship's biscuit with freshly cooked turtle meat in a soft leather bag with a drawstring and a wineskin filled not with wine but water. He was making for the lip of a crater, some hundred or so feet above us, the way rendered difficult by the overflow of lava that had tipped over its edge. The morning was already far gone and had been spent in prising barnacles from the rocks and pools by the seashore, these being of a shape and appearance altogether different to the knowledgeable eye from varieties commonly found on the coasts of England.

'And yet those on Narborough differ considerably from the flock we saw on Chatham Island,' I added, raising my voice to be sure he would hear me, for Mr Darwin was always ready to discuss and note down differences between species of the same animal or vegetable genera, finches as readily as barnacles.

He was approaching the lip of the crater and his mind, behind its curtain of bushy black eyebrows, within that high magnificent forehead which yet rose to a higher cranial dome beyond it, was concentrated on what he would see when he crossed it. Nevertheless he paused and called back over his shoulder.

'In what respect did they differ, Eddie?'

'Those on Narborough were darker of hue, almost black.'

'Why should that be, I wonder?' he asked himself rather than us, but then pushed to one side the habit of speculation so as to take in the view that now opened before him.

This was striking enough: a vast crater, oval in shape, its longer axis being about a mile and the drop below its lip five hundred feet. The bottom was filled with a small lake, clear and blue, its surface sparkling beneath the sun. The attractiveness of this patch of water was enhanced by the overpowering heat of the day which was approaching noon. Mr Darwin hurried down the cindery slope, setting up a cloud of choking dust that billowed about our thighs as we followed him. He bent his knees and scooped up water in his palm, shuddered, turned his head, and called up at us as we approached.

'Salt,' he cried. 'Salty as brine.'

He wiped his hand on his trouser, and his mouth on his loose shirt, and sat, knees spread, on a boulder of lava by the water's edge.

'Give us a swig then, Syms. That confounded saltiness has left me quite parched.'

Covington, whose first name was Syms, unstoppered the waterskin and passed it to his master, who took a gulp, swilled his mouth and spat, and then lowered it and looked over it. His dark eyes contrived to appear both serious and whimsical at the same time, while his thickish lips above his heavy jaw spread in a half-smile.

'Any ideas, Eddie?'

'About what, sir?'

'The darkness of the finches on Narborough.'

'Well, sir, could it not go like this?' Having started so confidently I felt I must go on. I racked my brains, caught a glimpse of a thought flitting from branch to branch in the undergrowth of my mind. I determined to lime it. 'Perhaps it is Nature herself plays the part of the breeder . . .' Covington looked up at this with a sneer on his face and a scoffing laugh on his lips.

6

'No, let him finish,' said Mr Darwin, ever kindly and courteous.

'The finches on Narborough,' I continued, 'lived among the black rocks of that island. Over the years could it not have been the case that those of paler hue were seen and singled out by birds of prey so only black ones survived to breed? Thus blind Nature makes the selection by using hawks to kill off all the paler varieties. You could call the process Natural Selection.'

Covington let out a yelp of laughter, but Mr Darwin's heavy brows had contracted and he pinched his bottom lip between thumb and forefinger.

'Eddie, you have a daring mind.'

'My father, sir, foster father I should say, was a philosopher, a rationalist, and no doubt I acquired some of the characteristics.'

'By Natural Selection or through example, do you think?'

'Nature or nurture? Why there's a conundrum deeper than why some finches are black and others are not and one my father frequently bothered his head with . . .'

Covington had to stick his oar in here.

'The answer is simple enough,' he cried, 'and should not be contested by any good Christian. God said: "Let the waters bring forth abundantly the moving creature that hath life, and fowl that may fly above the earth in the open firmament of heaven." On the fourth day, I think you'll find.'

'Fifth,' said Mr Darwin. 'The fourth was the two great lights.'

At which Covington sat for a moment or two, muttering to himself, and counting on his fingers like an infant tyro on his first day at Dame School.

The thing of it was, this Covington, a young man, not much more than a lad and country-bred, was in the way of having his nose put out of joint by my presence. He had been hired or taken on by Mr Darwin as personal assistant and general body servant for the duration of the trip, having, I believe, served the family in the past. My emergence on the *Beagle*, from behind the rum barrels in the spirit room, some four days out, and my acceptance by the crew as second cook and bottle-washer, had not impinged on him, but when, a year or so later, Mr Darwin took to making extensive walks over the lands we visited while the ship went about its business of charting hitherto uncharted coastlines, it was a different story. For such was the amount of gear he wanted to have at his disposal, and the collection of rocks and fossils he liked to take back to the ship, it became clear that a second pair of hands, and a second back, were needed. To begin with, being a stowaway and a presumed criminal who would be offloaded when the *Beagle* reached the penal settlements in Australia, I was not much talked to by either of them, but bit by bit I managed to get a word in here, offer a thought there, and so on, and by now Mr Darwin treated us as equals, and indeed seemed to find my conversation more rewarding than Covington's.

Our brief repast concluded, Mr Darwin glanced at his pocket timepiece, looked up at the sun and announced we should move off if we were to examine as much of the island as he had a mind to see. He set off at a good lick, Covington seized the food bag, water bottle and Mr Darwin's gun and left me to struggle behind with the two specimen boxes. Before long they were some way ahead, but then later, on an easier stretch, I almost caught up with them and overheard what perhaps they would have preferred to keep to themselves.

'Yon Eddie Bosham is a rum sort of cove, is he not, sir,' I heard Covington remark. 'I wonder at times if he is truly human.'

'Oh, he is human, all right,' our master replied. 'What other creature could he be?'

'His stature, which is stunted, and his hairiness, put me in mind of an ape.'

'I understand why you should say this, Syms, but I assure you if he is an ape he is a talking ape and if he is a talking ape then we must call him human.'

'Aye,' cried I, 'a talking ape, perhaps, but not I think a doltish dullard.'

They stopped and turned. 'Perhaps, Syms, he has the measure of you there.'

Mr Darwin laughed, and it was clear to me that Covington was quite seriously annoyed but hid all behind his young master's broad back.

Whether or not Covington engineered what happened next I have no means of knowing, but I do believe there were sins of omission if not commission. If he did not actually say to Mr Darwin: 'Sir, I am sure he was taken off on the first boat, there is no need to stay for him', then I make no doubt that he did not press the possibility that I might still be on the island.

For the thing of it was, turtle flesh did not agree with me and, as I have already mentioned, it was cooked turtle flesh we had taken with us and off which we had made a pic-nic. It took three hours before it pressed its complaint against me in such a way that would not be denied, during which we continued to scramble over the lava fields collecting what scraps we could of living matter as well as rock from that barren landscape. At about three o'clock we turned back, heading for the beach called Bank's Cove with about a league or so to cover before we got there, and at that point I realised I must evacuate my bowels as soon as maybe or suffer the humiliation of soiling my trousers. The problem was that in that lava field there was no boulder that thrust itself up more than the height of my knee above the rest, and no bushes, trees or thickets. In short, with a muttered excuse, I left the boxes and scrambled away a hundred yards or so, and over the visual ridge.

What followed was long, painful, noxious and noisome, and left my inner upper left leg not entirely free of faecal matter and no means to clean it. When I moved away some twenty minutes later, I was aware that I was taking the stench with me. Consequently, I completed the walk back to the beach at a slow gait. The boxes, incidentally, had gone and I must suppose that Mr Darwin and Covington contrived to take them. And, of course, once the cove was in sight, they were gone too: the cutter and the captain's whale-boat and the four men who had brought us there. And the *Beagle* herself was already standing off under full sail on her way to James Island some forty leagues away, and I could not imagine that Captain Fitzroy would easily be persuaded to turn her round to pick up a criminal stowaway who had probably, I could almost hear him say it, chosen this lot in preference to being handed over to the proper authorities at Sydney Cove.

So there I was, some four or five days later, reduced to the habits and appearance of an ape, sitting, or rather crouching, on my rock, part musing on the wonders of Nature about me, part wondering was I not wasting my time waiting, watching out for a ship that would scarcely in the time have reached its destination, let alone done its business there and then returned to pick me up. At last with a sigh and a glance at the westering sun, and feeling the chill of the evening offshore breeze about my naked shoulders, I picked my way back to my more sheltered beach where the black sand and grit still held some warmth and the flies buzzed over the remains of a large lizard I had slain and managed to eat part of, raw.

Here's a thought. Several, indeed many, times since the *Beagle* slipped her moorings in Plymouth harbour, I have seen Mr Darwin stripped to his waist and, believe me, he is almost as hairy as I am with a black pelt that swirls up his back and along his shoulders.

2

Make no doubt I was now king of Albemarle, lord of the islands, emperor of the ocean, god in residence. How can I be so sure? Picture me seated in splendour on my basalt throne, carved, ground, smoothed to an amber-coloured shine, fifteen feet above my beach. Around me flutter and flock a thousand finches, splendidly variegated as to colour, feeding habits, size and shape of beak: some feed on the ground and some take berries and seeds from the etiolated bushes, small trees and cacti, which sprout up where a residue of gravel has pooled itself between the cracks in the lava flow. The cactus finches are plain and brown and have dagger beaks, not the wedges of more ordinary finches, and they stab at the thick stems of the dildo cacti, which are shaped like giant erect pricks.

Above them the æther is filled with larger denizens of the air. Out over the bay big brown pelicans cruise in pairs, flapping lazily behind their heavy probing beaks which can scoop up a shoal of silver anchovy in one gulp. High above them three albatross keep station on motionless wings. Meanwhile, swallow-tail and lava gulls squabble at the base of the cliffs over the flotsam remains of a baby seal. Neither species is gull-like in colour, having slate or even blue bodies and dark heads, rendering them difficult to see when they roost on the ledges of the cliffs.

A chapter of penguins passes in front of me, waddling along in their black and white habits, the white dusted with yellow, the black

11

with blues and greens like those that illuminate the plumage of a crow. Over the sea-rounded stones and pebbles they go, hurrying a little more as they approach the runner of lacy spume that edges the margin of the sea. The younger novices push to be in front of their superiors in their rush to get at the silver fish and one topples on to his belly. For a moment or two he flaps his flippers and thrashes his webbed feet as if he were already in the water. By the time he has himself upright again only the very young are surging past him, while his coevals are already transformed into sleek swimmers, as graceful now as they were just previously comical and clumsy.

A whiskered sea lioness arches her flubby neck, lowers the fringed curtains of her eyes and dips her doggy snout before raising her blacker than ebony mask to emit a mellifluous cry. Thus she signifies obeisance and acknowledges her vassalage. To me. Poseidon. Trident-wielding lord of the vast and briny acres. Except I have no trident. This done she claps her flippers, turns, and with muscles rippling below the surface of her fatty back resumes the sea like a cape or gaberdine. With one last bark across her shoulder she flips her fluke, and is gone.

So here I am, sprawling in the little pool I have made myself, now that the heat of day is past, flat on my belly, with my elbows wide, fists clenched to prop up my chin. I kick both feet and as the water swooshes over my buttocks and up my back I feel how the tiny water lizards are cruising there: they make me laugh. And my prick swells deliciously as I roll it in the yielding soft sand. Above my head, eight feet or so up the cliff, a pumpkin vine drifts across the lintel of my cave: a yellow flower, shaped like a trumpet, drops and as it falls a bee circles out of it and lazily loops on buzzing wings until a passing gull snaps and takes it. Sometimes the vine lets go a fruit, and once I caught one as it fell, caught and crunched it, sweet as a melon.

I turn on my back and sit up, knees drawn to my chest, and look out over the sea, hatched with sunbeams, and maybe see in black silhouette a whale go by, breaking the mesh of fire it swims through. Such a sight prompts my mind to drift back to that last conversation with Covington and Mr Darwin regarding the Creator and Creation. It was a subject that exercised Mr Darwin greatly, and often as we trudged through the Argentinian pampas, the Patagonian wilds, or up the topless Andes, I heard him muse on the problems posed by the fossils he found, the time the rocks needed to assume their present contours, and such like matters while Covington stumbled behind misquoting the Scriptures to shield himself from such honest doubt. Sometimes, when he did this, Mr Darwin would scoff at his image of the Creator, saying he was no better or wiser than the Patagonians we had been among some months before, whose chief god was Setebos.

Well, I think to myself, if there is a god, he's not much of one. He's a mean bugger, a spoiler, a bully. Not just the whale, that great Leviathan, he made, and as I think about it my eye scans the world around me, sees the flightless auk, the finch that pricks deep into the dildo cactus for the worms that live there but will not eat ants, and the ants themselves that build a wall of seeds and settle stalks about their hole. He made all these and more, made all we see, and us too. Why? Out of spite. How else? He could not make a second self to be his mate – as well have made himself!

If I were he, and wishing I were born a bird, I could make a live bird out of clay and call it Eddie. I could give myself wings and a hoopoe's crest. I could will me to fly to yon rock top, bite off the horns of the grasshoppers that make such a din through their veined wings, and I wouldn't care a damn. I could break his leg off and if he lay there stupid, I should laugh, and if he didn't beg and weep I might give him three legs. Or pluck the other off, leave him like an egg and teach him he is mine and merely clay.

This does not show he's right or wrong, kind or cruel. He's strong and Lord. I'm strong compared to yonder crabs that march from the mountain to the sea. I'll let twenty pass and crush the twenty-first with a rock, not loving or hating it, just because I choose so to do. So he.

Still, god-like though I am when I choose to be, I still lack one thing after a week of solitary rule. I am referring to man's red fire, no less. I have spent hours clashing together rocks in all combinations: basalt against sandstone, lava against granite, I even tried the larger shells. Once or twice, no, more often than that, I got a spark, but never enough to take on a pile of seed shards, straw, feathers, whatever. Once a leaf blackened, I breathed on it, a tiny thread of red glowed along its outer edge, I blew harder . . . I blew it away! In desperation I scouted the beaches and coves, trawling the wrack, hoping for a wrecked ship's timber still holding an iron hasp, a nail.

Why this desperation? Can *you* imagine eating raw lizard, raw tortoise or turtle? Mussels and oysters, yes. Whelks, just, and even shrimps. The Nips of Nippon I am told eat raw fish for a delicacy, but not I . . . anyway, not those varieties I could easily get. More easy yet were the birds. They were so ridiculously tame. Really. I could walk amongst them with a stick and knock them off their perches, stamp on their heads or smash them with a rock. But I couldn't cook them.

No surprise then that my bathtime meditations were dissolved in the steadily growing hunger for a real, edible meal. Dismissing as bootless considerations of the nature of god, I called my privy council together to discuss the problem. These were: the stable-born Duke of Willingdone, my Lord Slitherpuddle, and Dick Add-it-on, known as Lord Acid-Mouth.

I sat on my throne of basalt and called the meeting to order.

'Gentlemen,' I said, 'the first item on the agenda, the last, and all those between, are . . . man's red fire.'

'Eddie. We know your game, we know what you're up to. Got the measure of you.' This from Duke Willingdone.

'Man's red fire, y'know?' Acid-Mouth nodded his head portentously.

'And why, that's what I ask the House to consider. That's the nub, y'know?' Willingdone's voice rose to a shout, the sort of noise that could turn the direction of a battle or send a train on its way from Waterloo. 'ALL THE BETTER TO COOK US!'

'Oh, I say,' cried Lord Slitherpuddle, and he began to cry in earnest, so the sea filled and a wave splashed against my throne, dowsing me.

Mollification was in order. I applied it with a trowel.

'I would not wish to cook all of you,' I murmured. 'Not all at once. Slitherpuddle on his own would keep me in cooked meat for at least a week.'

'This is too much,' Acid-Mouth, my homely secretary, squawked. 'Give me my Six Acts. Call out the Yeomanry. Read the Riot Act, and send seditious libellers to the gallows . . .' and with these and similar demands, threats and taunts, he set off across the sand, huge front flippers hauling him along with a rowing motion, back ones scrabbling in the sand like those of a man who attempts to push a recalcitrant load through snow.

'Come back, come back,' Slitherpuddle called after him. 'We need a quorum, without a quorum we're fucked.'

14

But Acid-Mouth paid no attention. He was on the sea's margin now.

'Hark, how the dogs do bark,' he hollered. 'Join hands when you've curtsied and the wild waves kissed. Just watch me!'

And he waddled into the lambent wavelets, shook his head as the first broke over it, and for a moment or two his great domed plated shell seemed to be gravity-glued to the bottom, then it floated, like a black islet in the bay. He flopped a flipper, whether in disdainful farewell or merely to add direction to his progress I do not know, and sank away, quite out of sight.

'Turtledum and turtledee,' Willingdone grunted and then fixed me with his baleful eye, clashing his lower beak against his hawk-like upper. 'I've never had a lunch that was free, nor lovelier than a tree. Coming, Slitherpuddle? Give you a bunk up if you like.'

'Where are you going?'

'Cactus grove at the top of the gully.'

'That'll do me.'

His red pouch glowed for a moment then he slithered off his rock, his nails going clickety-click on it as he went. Once on Willingdone's back, he too looked at me, and swinged the scaly horror of his tail. I recalled how Mr Darwin had been much amused by taking a ride on the back of a tortoise.

'Watch your step, moon-calf. Or you'll end up crab meat.'

I watched their progress up the gully. They were very slow. Had hardly gone more than fifty yards before he who made us flapped the blanket of the night and let it settle. Through the darkness I heard Willingdone's roar, made faint by distance and the churning of the waves.

'Try buggeryjars, ma'am.'

3

Dawn in slate-grey mantle touched my brow with greasy fingers. I awoke parched and hungry. On the sand, facing the entrance to my cave, a semicircle of blue-backed gulls watched me with baleful eyes, red-rimmed, the colour of yew berries. The *capo* of them put his head on one side, the better to suss me out, then waddled on spread webs a little closer. The gang followed, closing ranks as the radius of the arc they made contracted. Beyond, the grey sea heaved and rolled like a monster emerging heavily from slumber and at the end of the headland, white water plumed and fell. A ball of thorny twigs trundled across the sand between the gulls and the swirling, spumy hem of the ocean. The wind on which it rode ruffled a few feathers. A rattling, rustling noise above my head: the wind was shredding my pumpkin vine.

'Shit,' I thought. 'There's going to be a storm.'

I straightened creaking, painful joints, stubbed my toe on a boulder as flat as a Dover sole and, hobbling, got myself out from under the rocky lintel. Immediately the wind gusted about me and I hugged my elbows with my hands. The gulls took three steps each backwards, looking over their shoulders to see which would take wing, not wanting to be the first.

Buggeryjars. What could he have meant?

Breakfast I needed. But my stomach heaved at the thought of whelks or barnacles, limpets or winkles. The last pumpkin had gone.

I could club a gull and tear a leg or wing off. Bile rose from my empty stomach at the thought and stained my taste buds with gall and bitterness. I spat yellow.

The storm was rising with the tide, the crash of rollers, the howl of the wind, the blackness of the racing clouds. And of course I was still ravenously hungry. I stayed more or less where I was for an hour or so, either huddled like a womb-bound foetus with knees pulled up, or making a determined start in one direction or the other only to turn back after ten yards or so to resume my sulky crouch in the shelter of an overhanging rock.

But at last, as the storm broke and hurled driving rain almost horizontally so that, even sheltered as I was, it whipped my shins and shoulders, and the thunder clapped and the lightning forked, despair conspired with the madness of the elements to drive me staggering out on to the sand and towards the gully, the one I had followed with Mr Darwin and his cursed Covington. I felt I would be safer inland. I feared my cave would be inundated by the rising sea.

I strode along the strand, hands in my armpits, my eyes watering. My scrotum and prick shrank away, like hibernating dormice in their nest of hair. The gulls followed for a few yards then launched into the air, cruised above me for ten yards or so then tilted to the wind and let themselves be carried up, up and away, over the cliffs, inland. Wind-blown spume and sand stung my shins and thighs.

I turned inland. A storm-tossed albatross slid helplessly down the corridor of wind above me. At least the force of it all was behind me now and at times I felt I was being lifted by an invisible Lemuel Gulliver himself towards the crest.

From the top, from the edge of the plateau of lava that tilted upwards towards the mountains, I began to pick my way over the petrified waves and runnels and lumps. The lava was greasy with rain; there was no shelter from the wind which blew now not from behind but on my side or even took me head on so it filled and ballooned my cheeks if I let my mouth hang open and threatened to dump me on my back. Of course I slipped more than once and sat there while wind and rain tore the tears from my eyes and I struggled to overcome sudden fits of shakes much more violent than mere shivering.

Head down, watching my footing rather than where my feet led me, I stumbled on, occasionally barking my knees on a rock higher

17

than the rest, or using my hands to guide me round obstacles even bigger, and as I did so I became aware that the gale was now taking me from behind, and even the left rather than the right. I glanced up and saw that the granite-hued ocean, striated like black marble with white plumed rollers, pounding out of the swirling murk that veiled the furthest horizon, was still behind me. And as I looked I heard a roar rising to a banshee shriek, punctuated by ear-shattering cracks of thunder; I turned and saw, racing towards me across the barren rocks, that most dreadful of sights, a twister, two thousand feet high, a swaying pillar of iron grey in whose heart the lightning flashed and forked behind the spiralling wall of shrubs, trees, grit, small stones, dead or dying birds it sucked up to its spreading crown. My last memory of it is of being snatched off my feet, of the air being sucked out of my lungs, of being buffeted by the corpses of finches and skewered in the thigh on the barbed beak of a frigate bird before being swung, as if I were the ball on the end of an Argentinian vaquero's bola, into the second circle of Dante's Hell. I don't recall though that I met there Francesca da Rimini or her naughty lover.

Waking moments alternated with hours (days even?) of dream and I cannot now say for certain which was which. However, there was comfort, either in the waking or the dreaming, as of a soft, warm, blubbery closeness, of a tongue, or two, that rasped like a cat's across my body and even in and out its interstices, of a nipple, firm against my cheek but then pushed urgently into my mouth. As time wore on I let my hands and legs wander, pulled back my buried head from such warm damp pillows, allowed my eyes to open to find I was looking into dark brown pools filled with a glassy tenderness. Two fur seals, pearly-grey like the sand I lay on, but mottled on their backs with brown and black, had licked my wounds and scratches, fed me from their soft udders with rich and creamy milk. They cradled me on their floppy furry bellies, sheltered me from the storm as best they could and later from the hot and fitful sunshine. Around us some fifteen or twenty more lay basking, filling the air with their tuneful mooing, bell-like in warning, or soft and extended like a choir of 'cellos.

As my strength returned I gradually became aware of the beauty of my new home. First, the sand. Grey at a distance and when wet from rain or the receding tide; it was paler when dry, and very fine: ground coral and pumice, crystalline too, so that each particle glittered in the sunlight. Where it adhered to my hairy skin it seemed I was robed in light. Then this new bay, new to me. At its widest it was a good half-mile across, but this was not at its mouth, at the opening to the ocean beyond, for it was almost landlocked at low tide by a string of keys or cays linking its two headlands. Yet it was deep, perhaps in the middle unfathomably deep, for it was not your usual sort of bay or cove, formed by the erosion of the restless ocean on one side and by stream or river on the landside, but was in fact a volcanic crater. For all its depth, and the deep intense blue it held except under the most overcast of skies, it was warm, heated perhaps by hot-water springs or the closeness of molten lava beneath the crust of its bottom.

It was this heat no doubt that attracted the birds, sea mammals, abundant species of fish, and round the shallows of the rim a great efflorescence of water-borne flora. Apart from the birds that were already familiar to me, there were doves and hawks, flightless cormorants and ordinary shags, mockingbirds and flycatchers, petrels and blue-footed boobies, and buzzards that swung in slow sweeps, hundreds of feet above us, across the empyrean or hung there as motionless as kites.

Seals and sea lions had colonised the wide band of sand, darker than the rest, that lay on the water's edge and was laved by the tides. They sang and barked to each other, nursed their kittens and their pups and weaned them on sprats and anchovies. Occasionally squabbles broke out between the males over wives or territory but in the main they kept good order amongst themselves, respecting the commonweal of all. Over food there was no call to quarrel for it was there in abundance. As I recovered, my foster mothers encouraged me to go into the water. At first I had named these two good females Tess and Jess, but then when I found they could not tell these syllables apart, I tried again, remembering two ladies I had known in England in years gone by, Maggie-May and Kate, which did very well. Maggie was the larger, more buxom and generous with her milk, Kate the thinner, but by no means thin, and somehow sharper in her manner, the one who preferred to lick me, wash me, groom me, keep me tidy. Maggie also had a distinctive mark by which I could easily tell her from her sister or cousin, namely a yellowish-brown patch in her pelt, just close to her right shoulder, that was shaped exactly like the heart in a pack of cards. It was only about an inch across but the outline so particular and neat my eye always lit on it when I came off her nipple and peered like a baby down her back.

It was clear they took me for one of their own kind and were puzzled at my poor performance as a swimmer and my total inability to manage underwater. But I splashed about and swam a little, though always with one toe on the sand beneath, and even at this depth was able to see abundant different species including shrimps that remained motionless or darted like arrows across the rippled bottom and flat fish spotted like leopards that, by undulating their finny fringes, could bury themselves. Sea horses no bigger than my thumb hung like Chinese lanterns above them, and higher still shoals of triangular silver fish with black bars just inside their leading edges and agate-coloured square fish with yellow fan-shaped fins on their gills and yellow tails patrolled their reaches in squadrons. Beyond these sandy shallows the seabed plunged to a depth deeper than the sounding of any plummet and I kept well away from its edge.

I grew stronger yet and took to clambering over the rocks at the ends of the sandy swathe, and from these I could peer into far deeper and even clearer water where larger puffed-up fish, spotted like guinea fowl, contested the territory with ugly mottled brutes with evil orange-rimmed eyes or fish with hawk-shaped faces or beaks, marked all over by a pattern of hieroglyphic-like shapes. Occasionally a green sea turtle would cruise by paddling its slow flippers or, more briskly, a clutch of playful penguins.

Venturing further yet along these rocks, I reached the outer rim of the bay and here I found beauties beyond any I had yet seen, in the live corals, some pink-and-white striped, with pink tendrils, others in the form of orange daisies, with gently swaying petals like spearheads. And here the fish were yet more brightly and variously coloured, those like parrots feeding off the beds of petrified coral beneath the living, crunching it up and passing it out of their rear ends in the form of the fine white sand that mixed with the volcanic dust on the strand.

Of course, there were horrors, too. There always are in or near the sea, are there not? Having said that, the first fright I had was *en plein air* and on rock. What caused me to start, and almost choose to escape into the water rather than run for it, was coloured like the rock, and craggy like the rock. Iguanas they were. Giant iguanas, nasty enough basking in the sun, but when they hoisted their fat bellies above their five-toed, trunk-like legs, and their tongues flickered and they hissed, revealing uneven grey and black teeth, and exhaled foul vapours, I knew I had come upon the serpents of this Eden.

And, finally, the sharks. There were those whose dorsal fins cruised restlessly outside the crater's rim, ready to snatch a sea lion pup, or a too venturous penguin; but there were also those with huge hammer-like heads and others, ten feet long or more, which basked near the surface so you felt they were lying in wait for you though I never saw them feed off anything but the abundant sea kelp. Nevertheless, maybe it was that Maggie-May and Kate had lost their newborn kittens to these beasts, and that was why they were so ready to make a baby out of me.

And, finally, on the land, under the cliffs, there was a flock of tiny birds, one of the few species I had come across before, though always caged. It was some days before I made their acquaintance for they kept to the moraine of boulders, as far from the sea as they could get, and tutored as I was by my pair of mums, most of my attention was directed the other way. But at last, as the weather moved into a deeply settled period and the lagoon was as still as a millpond, a small group of them fluttered nearer to where I sat gazing lazily but without ennui at the slow unfolding of life in front of me.

They were cheeky little things with striped, masked faces, tiny beaks curved in to their throats and brightly coloured as any of the fish but not more than two inches long in the body and as much again in their darker tails. One hopped very close. I held out my finger for him, like a perch. He flew on to it, his sharp, twig-like little feet wrapped themselves round it, he put his head on one side and spoke.

'Who's a pretty boy, then?'

4

To suggest I was utterly surprised would be an exaggeration. I was not surprised to hear one of these birds speak in this fashion, merely that I should hear it where I was. Naturally enough I had taken them to be native to the island or islands, put there by an all-present, omniscient god (Jehovah, Juggernaut or Setebos, what's in a name?) for our delight and instruction, but not to entertain us with childish chatter. But back in London, in one of the many museums and galleries designed to appeal to the idle and curious that were springing up in the vicinity of Regent Street, even before I left, I had heard caged birds much like these, saying similar witless things as 'Pretty Budge' and 'Where's Joey?'. And now, of course, I recalled what they were and where they came from. They were budgerigars and they came from Australia.

That Old Willingdone had got the word wrong when he said 'buggeryjars', or I had misheard him in the rising wind, either of those I could accept, but why had he urged me to try them in my search for fire? I was soon to find out.

My new friend released his grip on my finger, and fluttered on to the sand behind me. He flew a few feet more, then, when I remained where I was, flew back again, and so on and so forth until it dawned on wits dulled by sun, the heavy milk of my wet nurses, and a general lack of mental stimulus, that he (or she?) wanted me to follow him. His companions joined in the game and soon I was walking and occasionally stumbling through the line of dried weed and scoured twigs and other debris that marked the furthest reach of the sea on to the very soft and very white sand that lay below the cliffs. I heard a warning bark or two behind me and, turning, beheld Maggie-May clearly admonishing me not to stray. She would not follow me as she did not like to be on the dry sand, and anyway she knew by now that on land I could outstrip her as easily as she could me in the water.

Soon I had to skirt large boulders fallen from the cliff and then even climb over them. It was a different world from the shore. There were some limpets and barnacles on the rocks but dried up and I would guess dead, some seaweed which definitely was dead, but there were also thin, hard needles of grass, small cactuses and even little bushes with thickish leaves not unlike tiny holly. Prettier than any of these were several daisy-like plants with succulent leaves, but far bigger than those we are familiar with in England, and brightly coloured. The sun was on them: later I was to realise that without direct sunlight they closed.

By now we were making our way along a track of silver sand winding between black boulders. Whether or not it was man-made or just naturally there I do not know, but it led quite unmistakeably to a deep fissure in the cliff, a triangular hole about fifteen feet across at ground level and reaching an apex some thirty feet up. A cave, but I was never to discover how far it penetrated into the cliff for, ten feet in there was a skeleton. I confess the suddenness of this sight had me back outside and shivering with fright, with the buggeryjars twittering about my head. But curiosity soon overcame these childish terrors and within a moment or so I was edging back in.

Yes, a human skeleton or cadaver, for in places skin like dried parchment remained, and sinews too, and a swatch of hair dropped over one eye socket from beneath an old felt hat, the sort whose rim can be fastened up to make a tricorne. Other remnants of clothing hung about him as a cutaway red coat, faded now to russet, with buttons of brass coated with verdigris, breeches, and a still serviceable pair of black boots. From all this, and from the scabbarded, basket-hilted sword that was attached to his belt and the flint-lock pistol he held in the bones of his right hand across his knee, I took him for a military man, a soldier or possibly a marine . . . but if he was, then I must suppose he was a deserter – or had filched the gear from some honest man. Why? Because by his foot there was a small

23

iron-bound chest, only about eighteen inches by ten and ten inches high, but filled or nearly filled with a hundred gold guineas.

There was one other object which provided an answer to a question that may yet be bothering my readers: a domed birdcage, made from thin cane, and part smashed, lay on its side by his other foot. It was not difficult to conclude that my buccaneer had come ashore with a pair at least of buggeryjars and that they had been the progenitors and ancestors of those that now hopped and ran around my new friend.

Examination of the little chest, and the euphoria which accompanied the discovery of its contents, did much to allay my first childish fears and gave me time to accustom myself to the presence of what was after all no more than a bag of dry bones. By the time I had counted up to a hundred and cursed a situation which had put such wealth into my hands without the means of using it, the inner wheels of my brain had churned on a turn or two to the point where I had realised that a thimbleful of dry tinder in the pan of the pistol, together with the spark when the flint struck the leaf of the pan, could well be all I needed to start a fire on which I could broil the fish Kate and Maggie-May brought me.

Nevertheless I could not restrain a little shudder as I began to prise back my new friend's brittle fingers, and a dizzy-making start when one of them snapped. With the pistol free and snug in my own more sentient fist it was but the work of a moment to pull back the hammer, push up the leaf and pull the trigger.

I damn near shot off my toe. The combination of a particularly well fitting lid over the pan and the exceedingly dry and hot air between storms and sea mists had kept my buccaneer's powder dry for the lord knew how many years. The retort was more of a fright than anything else and sent the buggeryjars scampering into the air outside. And no doubt it gave all the denizens of the beach a start, too.

The rest was easy. Dry seaweed made good tinder, some sheets of paper I found sticking in Blackbeard's pocket, from which time had bleached out any writing there might have been, served as kindling, and within five minutes I had a little fire going, nursed along with twigs and more leaves. I could see that fuel gathering would be a tedious chore so I resolved to leave it at that until I had some suitable fish, fowl or meat to hand.

24

I returned to my foster mothers in as happy a mood as any I had experienced, not just since I was dumped on the island but even going back to the wonderful week I had spent with the original Maggie-May in her home near Plymouth* before being smuggled aboard the *Beagle* in the first place.

Blackbeard? Why not? Some long black hair fringed his chin, so it seemed a good name for him.

There followed a blissful period at least a month long for I saw the moon reach fullness twice, during which I was indeed king of the island.

The moon when full. I cannot describe in a way that will satisfy me the beauty that it now took on. It was huge, especially when it dawned, a magnificent gold fruit hanging in the purple, a sphere, a globe, not a disc at all, a carriage for a goddess whose image or reality was etched on its surface, a goddess excellently bright, armed with bow and arrow, hair streaming behind her, her sleek hounds about her, as, huntress that she is, she chased me, her Actaeon, down the velvet passages of night. And the golden wires she traced, as if with a shuttle, across the surface of the bay, framed in the craggy tumbling of the rocks, and the lightning flashes of green that streaked the wave crests as glassily they broke around my feet.

On nights when she did not shine, or before she rose, I built great fires that crackled like distant musketry, sending pillars of aromatic smoke and sparks whirling into the breezes that billowed them about above our heads; into the cave of shimmering red-hot embers I thrust joints I'd hacked with Blackbeard's sabre from the carcases of turtles, rays, sea bass, eels and squid with heads as big as mine the sea lions brought me, or the fowl I had only to knock on the head where they perched with my new-found pistol.

Nor was my diet now fish, fowl and amphibian only, for following a giant tortoise I found a way up the cliffs and into some scrubland beyond where there were shrubs and daisy trees, and above all cactuses, succulents from which my armoured guide took long draughts of liquor. Especially good was the sap of a plant that consisted of three or four fluted, prickly pillars, segmented by each season's

* See *A Very English Agent*, Chapter 50. J. R.

25

growth, which bore gorgeous white flowers like drooping lotuses with yellow spear-shaped sepals.*

Tentatively at first, and then with more gusto as I savoured the mild sweetness of the oozing stream, I drank with him, my friendly tortoise that is, and found not only an easing of the painful thirst that often plagued me, but also a deep euphoria, a heavenly sharpening of all physical sensations, and, once I had drunk beyond a certain amount, entry into a world where the inanimate became animate, spoke to me, danced and sang for me, and where the animate revealed their true shapes and natures, in a strange anthropic beauty. In brief, my cohabitants of this new-minted paradise took on a nature that was in a way human though left them shaped in many ways like their workaday selves, viz. seals, sea lions, dolphins of many sorts and also gulls, boobies, cormorants, albatrosses, hawks and flamingos.

These denizens of the island and my mind now served me in a hundred ways. They brought me vegetable food, as fruits, nuts, sea plants that, once roasted on the edge of my fires, were crisp and tasty. They swam with me and gave me rides on their backs and indeed one whiskered sea lion did his best to teach me the art and I made some progress though I remained unhappy out of my depth. But he did get me to bask on the surface of the bay with legs and arms spread in an 'X', like St Andrew on his cross, with head right back and the deep, deep blue of the sky staining the white radiance my acquaintance of ten years earlier, the poet Shelley, supposed lay behind it.

What else did they do for me? Maggie-May and Kate continued for a time to suckle me, but when they saw I had other sources of nourishment both liquid and solid, made it plain they had new delights to offer. Taking on the form of mermaids or more precisely nereids, they would lie with me, turn and turn about, with me prostrate on my back, my head between, say, Kate's breasts and the green filaments of her weedy hair about my face, while Maggie-May sprawled across me and mingled the furriness of her skin with mine, so delights beyond the dreams of even the most particular of libertines shook the innermost halls of my soul.

* This description suggests a version or subspecies of *Trichocereus pachanoi*, a source of mind-altering peyote as rich as the more commonly used *Lophophora williamsii*. J. R.

Meanwhile the sea lions and the turtles conspired to build us a palace, a pleasure dome worthy of my rule. They shifted the timbers of wrecked vessels, made canopies and pavilions out of old sails and banners, planted gardens with flowers brought from the inner fastnesses of the island, created water features that tumbled the crystal fluid down steps from pool to pool and planted aromatic trees . . . all I lacked was a marimba-playing maiden. In short, I could truly say I fed on honey dew and drank the milk of paradise.

5

Yet – and what a fool I was – I longed for the companionship the presence of my own sort would bring, and the day came, it was late in the afternoon, when, as I was sat on my customary perch at the end of the headland where the black sea heaved and sighed on one side and the lagoon glowed blue and turquoise on the other, on the horizon appeared a smirch, an intrusion, a three-masted ship, mains'ls and gallants set, almost hull down, inching along that line between the dark Prussian blue of the sea and the lilac of the sky.

She was in no hurry, she gave me time, and I did not need much for I had anticipated this moment by heaping a pile of sea wrack and driftwood on the headland but beyond the reach of tide and storm. It was but the work of a moment to get the whole thing going and a column of smoke rising in the air, black smoke because I included the wodge of fat that lies behind a dead turtle's tail.

Within an hour she was standing off the row of keys that marked the outer edge of the crater, at a distance of about half a nautical mile, and it was by now quite clear to me she was not what I had hoped she might be, that is the *Beagle*. I do not have much of an eye for ships: one three-master a hundred feet long is much like another to me, whether rigged as a bark or a brig. Like the *Beagle* she had whaling boats: there were three slung from davits along her sides, making six in all, identifiable as such, even at that distance, by the sleekness of their outline and the fact that their sterns were not

28

squared off but pointed like their bows. For these and other reasons I formed an opinion that turned out to be correct that what I was looking at was a whaler. And flying from a line behind her spanker was a flag. Twenty-four stars on a blue ground and thirteen red and white horizontal stripes covering the other three-quarters. The Stars and Stripes. Land of the Free. My country 'tis of thee. *Unum e pluribus*. In God We Trust. In short, she was an American whaler.

By now the sun was dropping and it soon became clear that her captain was content to remain hove-to with mizzen set and maybe a sea anchor or two, until the morning light. I let my fire burn down and took myself off to Blackbeard's cave. Why, I was not sure, or did not allow myself to analyse too closely, but I suspect I just felt safer hidden away until I had had the opportunity of making a judgement on what sort of people these were that had arrived on my doorstep. So I drank some cactus juice, gnawed at the well-cooked but now cold meat of a cormorant before snuggling down between the black-booted feet of my old friend.

The morning was as rude a wakening as I have ever had. First I heard the cacophony of a huge crowd of gulls and boobies and such like; then the deeper note of whooping, hallooing men above the snorts, gasps and barks of seals and sea lions; and then the sound of a sea-song:

> *The master, the swabber, the boatswain and I,*
> *The gunner and his mate*
> *Love Maggy, Meg and Marian,*
> *But none of us cared for Kate;*
> *For she had a tongue with a tang,*
> *Would cry to a sailor, Go hang!*
> *She loved not the savour of tar nor of pitch,*
> *Yet a tailor might scratch her where'er she did itch:*
> *Then to sea, boys, and let her go hang!*

Rubbing my eyes and stretching my limbs I hauled myself to the mouth of Blackbeard's cave and looked over the boulders to the silver sands beyond.

Two big men, one of them black, wearing the flared ducks of sailors, but naked from the waist up, were striding through the colonies of fur seals hitting them on the heads with cudgels contrived from belaying pins. The black man's body and face too were networked with a filigree of tattoos. There was, I later learnt, an art in the way they landed their blows, the aim of which was to render the beasts deeply insensible or dead without breaking the skin of their heads. Behind these two came four more who carried the bodies of my loving friends to the margin of the sea, where yet more of their company set about skinning the cadavers (though some, from the way the blood spurted as the knives went in, were still alive) but with great care and skill. Using long knives, once broad but now ground to stiletto-like thinness by decades of grinding, whetting and sharpening, they sliced one long slit from the join of the tail flippers right up to the masks, and peeled back the skin, lined with blubber as it was, to reveal the scarlet muscles and purple, pumping organs within. These were deftly filleted out and thrown into the sea where the gulls that had first awakened me screamed and hollered above them, tearing out strips and chunks, which, pursued by their mates, they carried off to their fastnesses on the cliffs above.

Finally, these Yankee butchers pulled the bones and muscles of the flippers out of their gloves in the way one skins the limbs of a rabbit, thus releasing the pelt. All that remained now was to scrape away the blubber, which was done as deftly as the rest, though put on one side to be rendered down, and there they were: the happy possessors of whole, undamaged skins, the inside leather as soft and supple as a kid's, the outer as fine and glossy a fur as ever graced the white shoulders of a society beauty. Meanwhile, a deep stain of red spread slowly out from this shambles and into the wide lagoon beyond.

Why did the seals not break for it, make for the water, the sea, that was their more natural home? They had pups or kittens to suckle and protect, the men kept between them and the water's edge, on the sand they could move no faster than a human baby walks.

What was I to do? What could I do? I hid.

Slowly the noise abated. At first my aim was to remain where I was, hunched up clutching my knees behind Blackbeard's coat, which was as far as I had yet gone into his cave, planning only to emerge when I felt sure these marauding murderers had returned to their ship and the ship itself was hull-down on the horizon. But presently I was aware of aromas drifting around me: the smell of brewed coffee, and even the tang, I thought, of spirits warmed with it, rum, perhaps, and finally and most telling of all, tobacco, the odours of alehouses, of streets and people, in short of civilisation. I could hear too, though muffled by the splash and drag of wavelets, the rumble of talk, of human talk, and English it was, well, the American version of English. A longing to be amongst my own kind again, however rough and ready, took hold of me and would not be denied.

Then came a distant report, not much more than a pop, but carried on the wind across the keys, across the surface of the lagoon to the men on the beach. I heard a rise in the pitch of their voices, and I felt the sense of bustle and purpose run through the crew. Clearly the bang, a blank cartridge from their one cannon, was a signal that their bark was ready to put on more sail and depart. If I was to beg a passage with them – and suddenly I was very sharply aware that that was what I wanted, if, as I say, I was to take what might well be the last chance for some months or years to get off this island – then now was the time to make a go of it. But before I came out of my hiding place I bethought me of possible vicissitudes ahead and turned back. It was the work of barely ten seconds to scoop up old Blackbeard's money box, but as I turned I came face to face with a small, dark man, who already had his trousers around his ankles and was taking a shit precisely where I made my bed on stormy nights.

'Holy Mary, mother of God, and blessed Saint Patrick now remember me but not for my sins,' he cried. I might as well add at this point, since he figures quite largely in my narrative, that his black hair was streaked with white like a magpie, that he had heavy, thick, black eyebrows, and his brogue was not entirely Irish but had a touch of Liverpool about it. Let's call him Liverpool Irish.

Hurriedly he wiped himself with some of the piled leaves that made my mattress, stood, pulled up his trousers, and produced a sprung clasp knife from the pocket with one hand making the popish cross across his chest with the other.

'Jesus, Mary and Joseph,' he cried, but in a low voice, 'be you an ape or a devil from hell and be that a skelington or the Lord of Darkness, I'll be having that little box you're carrying and be damned if I don't.' And he snatched it from me, folded back his knife, undid his coat with his spare hand, took it off and wrapped it round the box. Finally, tucking the whole bundle under his arm, he stumbled away back out into the sunshine. I followed him.

Two of the whalers were already clear of the beach, their crews pulling on their sweeps, but the other, though off the shingle, was still held by two men in the water while a further three prepared to clamber over the gunwales. Seamus, for that was his name, turned, saw me capering after him, and shouted.

'Hey, boys, see what I have here. Is he an ape or a man, do you t'ink?'

Of those preparing to board the one who was half in, the blackie from the islands, went the rest of the way, the other two turned and waded out of the water, back on to the shingle. Arms akimbo they eyed me up and down, all their attention on me, which was no doubt what Seamus wanted, the better to smuggle that box over the gunwale unobserved.

'Bugger me,' cried the first, a big man with a scar on his cheek, his hair pulled back and tarred in a tail behind his head, 'but I thought yon ape was a man when first I saw him.'

'Sure he's a man. Look how he has the feet of a man,' this from his companion, as big as the first, but this one had a great haystack of hair, save no haystack was ever so unruly. It turned out he was a Swede.

'No Christian, if he's a man.' This from Seamus who had sidled past them and was getting himself and his bundle into the boat while all eyes remained on me. 'Look dat he wear no clouts on him, at all. If man he be then he be a savage and a certificated cannibal, I t'ink.'

One of those in the boat now added: 'With all that hair and no clothes the bugger's an ape, Christian or no.'

'I tell you, those feet he has on him no ape never walked on.'

'He's but a brat either way. He baint no more than four feet and a bit. I seen the apes on the Rock and they be bigger nor he.'

'Yet it is my opinion that his face is somewhat lined and leery, the phiz of an older man.'

I now did a thing that was as stupid as any I have ever done in my life. I don't know how many days, weeks or even months I had been on that island and lived amongst my friends the seals, but during all of that time I had uttered no more than five words of English and they all cursing. But, as you know, I have other languages as well, and I think my addled brain could not decide which to try. To those I had added the rudiments of seal-ish, as how a bark may be moderated to express anger, warning, or hunger, how a grunt could mean hello, or, pitched a little higher, could mean a warmer greeting, infused with

32

recognition and pleasure. And so forth. This is not the moment to give you a lesson in the Phocean lingo. Suffice it to say I now addressed them out of habit with that particular bark which a seal will use to one not of his circle, expressing wary welcome infused with a note of query as a 'howdedo, pleased to make your acquaintance, and whom, may I ask, do I have the pleasure of addressing?' sort of a greeting.

'There. I told you he was an ape. Either an ape or a bog-standard Irishman.'

'Fockin' native dat you are, what do you know about de Irish?' Seamus called from the boat where he had stowed his coat, and the box, under the pile of seal skins. By 'native' he meant native American, one born there of English descent. The two of them turned away from me, making their way back into the water. Panic flooded my veins. I ran behind them to the water's edge, still jabbering like a seal pup that sees its mummy moving further off than it likes and all the time struggling in my brain which, I have to say, was possibly somewhat hazed by my daily intake of cactus juice, to find a word or two of English.

The Swede was the first to note me behind them.

'Hey now, mine frents, see but this critter expresses a strong desire to come wit us.'

The first of them to speak, him with the scarred face, was already in, sitting on the stern thwart, facing the steersman with his oar. The Swede, up to his knees in the limpid water with his big hands on the gunwale beside them, was preparing to give the last shove that would set the keel free of the shingle, before himself clambering into the moving boat. I raised my voice to the sort of plaintive scream young seals make when truly lost or threatened. He turned – Sven was his name as I later discovered – and fastened his huge red hands round my waist, swung me high and dropped me at the steersman's feet, then followed me too.

I landed on their pile of seal skins whose top almost reached the level of the gunwale. For a moment I sat there with my hands spread over my head in a posture I now recognise is often adopted by apes of all sorts when threatened, but then as the boat shot forward raised my head and peeped through my fingers to get, by peering round the steersman's torso and under his arms, a last glimpse of my home amongst the seals.

33

And what a shambles it now was. Bleeding carcases lay across the sands, a dirty smoke drifted up from the fire I had first lit and which the whaling men had kept going for their own uses, and beyond it I noted a pitiful fence of seaweed and cactus, low ridges in the sand in which bedraggled weeds and twigs withered and died, a little chain of pools and mounds such as children make when left to their own devices on a seashore. Were these the gardens and water features, the cascades and palaces of my drugged brain? Were the little piles of coloured or sparkly pebbles and seashells the treasures I had gathered? I must suppose they were, and I felt a dull sort of shame at the primitive, savage wreck I had let myself become. And to think I had allowed myself to be suckled by beasts . . . I shuddered at the thought.

The whaler, powered by four powerful sweeps, sliced across the lagoon and between the keys and in no time at all was bumping gently against the side of its parent ship. As we passed beneath the transom, on which I read the words *Town-Ho*, *Nantucket* beneath the drooping hem of the Stars and Stripes, I heard a deep voice above me, a voice infused with authority.

'I'll have no stowaways aboard my ship, Mr Ericsson. If the blighter can swim toss him overboard, otherwise take him back to the nearest rock.'

'No stowaway, my captain, but an ape. He took a shine to us and I reckon he should come aboard for he's kind of cute and will fetch a dollar or two I'm sure, as soon as we make it back to Nantucket.'

So it was I came aboard the *Town-Ho*. They made some ceremony of it all, entering me in the captain's log as unpaid sea ape taken aboard from the Tortoise Islands, and gave me a pen to make my mark, but I pretended I did not know the use of it and cast it aside at which the captain pushed my thumb with some roughness in the blob of ink I'd made and used it as a man uses the other sort of seal to make a mark with the print it left. At this, and feeling the hold Seamus had on me slacken a mite, I broke free and ran up the mizzen shrouds, jabbering the while and then scratching at my armpit the way I once saw an Italian organ-grinder's monkey do in the Vauxhall Gardens, just before they were cut off from the river by the new railway on its embankment.

Well, some were fooled by my performance and others not and one of those was a young cabin boy not more than ten or eleven years old whose charge I became. This in itself was handy for his main occupation was to help the cook and so he fed me on scraps and an occasional piece of ship's biscuit and jerk, a sort of plain ungarnished pemmican I was to become overfamiliar with in my later travels across the American continent . . . but I must not anticipate. Anyway, this lad spotted one anatomical feature I could not hide, though nothing, once we had established my true nature and in secret were communicating with each other in Christian tongue, would persuade him to tell me what this was.

Years later I rumbled the matter: shaggy though I was I could not conceal from him the fact that my member, by which I mean my pilgrim's staff, ramrod, reamer or Captain Standish, was not the neat pink prodder your average simian boasts but the altogether knobblier affair we humans are blessed with. Be that as it may, one day he challenged me quite simply by offering me an apple from the captain's barrel and refusing to part with it until I had given him a 'please'. But, bless him, he kept mum.

One morning when I was entertaining him with gossip about the great people I had known back in London, such as the Duke of Wellington, Lord Liverpool and Viscount Sidmouth, and the great doings I had been concerned with as scotching rebellion and putting down revolt, together with my exploits on the field of Waterloo, I chanced to ask this bright lad what his real name was, for the men called him 'Ish', 'Come hither, Ish, and scratch my back', or 'Listen here, Ish, fetch me my baccy from under the pillow on my hammock', and such like.

'Ish cannot be what they stuck you with at the font,' I said, 'so tell me your real name . . .'

'Call me Ishmael,' he replied.

Part II

WHALING

And the mighty rencontre is finished by the gigantic animal rolling over on its side, and floating an inanimate mass on the surface of the crystal deep – a victim to the tyranny and selfishness, as well as the wonderful proof, of the great power of the *mind* of man.

THOMAS BEALE, *The Natural History of the Sperm Whale*, 1833

6

You yet may wonder how it was I was able to maintain my imposture for so long, that is over the space of a further six weeks. Well, the answer is . . . not without difficulty. There was, nevertheless, much that worked for me: the support of Ish whose standing on board was improved by his new position as my custodian; the desire of those sailors who had all been at sea for three years for some novelty; and, above all, the physiological accidents a Nature bored with the ordinary and mundane had visited on me at my conception. I stopped growing at the age of eight, at least upwards, though in every other way I was perfectly formed. However, with the onset of puberty other less appealing features manifested themselves. Very slowly, at first it was no more than the usual haze boasted of by the more swarthy of my Iberian friends, I grew a pelt of body hair. It is not long, it is not thick, not in comparison with a dog, a horse, a rat: but long and thick enough for these simple whalers to take it as evidence of my simian ancestry. And at this particular time, of course, it was some weeks or months since my cheeks had felt a razor or my head a barber's shears. Over the years other features had appeared which were collusive to the deception. My bones retained the thinness of boyhood but my frame and other organs grew to manly dimensions, imposing upon my legs and ribs a strain they could not easily accommodate. I thus became bow-legged and deep-chested, both characteristics of the simiadean race.

39

So from appearance alone it was not difficult for these simple, ignorant people to give credence to the idea that I was an ape. They may have sailed round the globe two, three times or more (Scarface, whose nickname was, for reasons I never was told, Fair Trade, reckoned he had done it five times), but they hardly ever made a landfall, and only in answer to the most exigent need, as being unmasted in the China Sea by a typhoon. Back home in Nantucket, they rarely strayed much beyond the precincts of the taverns and whorehouses they spent their earnings in before signing on again. However, they did have some preconceptions, and they were not always as accurate as they might have been. Above all, they were convinced that apes are natural and gifted climbers. Well, some may be, but most are not. I doubt your average bull gorilla is any more adept than I am at swinging about the rigging of a storm-tossed bark, a skill these sailors had off as well as any monkey.

'Show us the way, Panzee,' Fair Trade would holler, chivvying me up the shrouds to the main yardarm.

'Can you jump to that halyard? No, he would though if we had a nana to give him, they love your yeller nanas they do,' cried one Stibbs, who was up ahead of me, and so it went on, and I realised if I were to maintain my deception I should have to come up with some wrinkle that would excuse me from flying about that forest of spars, ropes and canvas like a squirrel. So on about the third day I got myself at the top of the companionway that dropped as steeply as a vertical ladder into the fo'c'sle where the men had their hammocks and let myself slip down the four feet, bumpety-bump, thumping my bum, to the floor beneath. Once there I let one knee buckle and twist under me in as horrid a way as I could manage, and there I sat and hollered, remembering, but only just, to keep an apish timbre to my wordless shouts, until Fair Trade and one of his mates put aside their pipes, for they were off watch at the time, and came to help me.

'What's wrong then, Panzee? Did yer hurt yousel'?'

And I damn near answered, "Course I did, can't you see, my knee is buggered?' but managed in time to scream and jabber as before. And of course when they got me to my feet, I let my knee go again, and so forth, until Fair Trade kindly scooped me up like a child and carried me back on to deck. From then on I hobbled like a lame duck and was never expected to go aloft again.

'Panzee'? Well, Seamus had touched on the bite of the west coast of Africa on a previous voyage, in a Portugee port, and he said that was the word the natives used for the black apes that came into the villages looking for cooked meat.

The *Town-Ho* seemed a sound enough vessel, though prone to take on water somewhere near her keel in ways that defied explanation, though those who knew her earlier history said she'd been struck by a great white whale. The leak had been repaired, of course, but now seemed to have sprung again and it was all hands to the pumps every sundown but not for long.

Town-Ho. A strange name for a ship. One day when Ish and I were hunkered down in the lee of the galley and no one around, I asked him what it meant.

'It is,' said he, 'the cry the masthead man gives in these waters on sighting the Gallipagos Terrapin. "Town" perhaps being a corrupted version of the word terrapin.'*

We had held a westerly course for a week, tracing in reverse what would have been the track of the *Beagle*, had she left a track in that trackless waste, and then headed north and west, looking for the grounds, if that is the right word – it seems wrong to me – of the sperm whale off the coast of Mexico. All this time we saw and did nothing worthy of report. At last, on a transparent blue morning when a strange unnatural stillness was spread over the sea, a great white mass lazily rose in front of our bowsprit, and gleamed like a sheet of snow, where it glistened for a moment before slowly subsiding and sinking from view. Our forepeak watch at the time was another Negro called Jackson who hollered that it was the great white whale himself. All ran to their stations at the davits ready to put down the boats when up it came again, but when it did it turned out to be no whale but a vast pulpy mess, furlongs across, of a slimy, glassy, pearlish colour, with long arms warty with peach-tinted suckers as big as round tin trays. Then, with a low sloppy breathing sort of a sound, it sank away again.

Fair Trade was all for launching at least one boat.

'Hack off one limb and we'll feed off him a week,' he cried. 'The Dagos from Galician lands count him a special good dish.'

* A similar explanation for the name is given by Melville in a footnote to Chapter 54 of *Moby Dick*, so we must suppose Eddie has it right. J. R.

'Only a Dago would eat squid for a week,' countered the mate, and the boats remained inboard.

But then all turned to see what or who was causing a not unfamiliar sound, the rasping, singing note of a harpoon head being sharpened, and there behind us, sitting on the deck with his feet crossed in front of him was that black tattooed savage, whose name was Quodlibbet, or sounded like it, a-sharpening his harpoon.

'When you see him 'quid,' he said, 'then you quick see him 'parm whale.'

And sure enough, the very next day – about halfway through the morning watch with the weather still very calm and still, and an opalescent sort of a mist lingering between sea and sky so there was no horizon though you could see the sun above, a lemon-coloured ball – we heard that cry again, from the fore masthead: 'Tha—a-a she blows, sperm whale on the lee bow, forty fathoms off.'

All rushed with a shout to the side except those who grasped the shrouds and hoisted themselves above the deck and there he was, a gigantic sperm whale, lolling in the water, like the capsized hull of a frigate, his broad glossy back three feet or more above the surface of the glaucous swell, as black as a Hottentot, for all the world like a portly banker smoking his after-dinner cigar, spouting at intervals his haze of briny spray from his hole.

'Clear away the boats! Luff!' hollered the captain in his high, piercing voice and spun the helm down himself before the helmsman could handle the spokes.

But as the boats were lowered, the whale, wanting to keep a little distance until he knew what we were about, swam off, gliding as slowly and easily as if he were a sea lion at most rather than one of the biggest monsters of the deep, scarcely breaking the slow swell into wavelets, yet continuing to do his breathing – for what they do is they come up for as much as ten minutes, and take short repeated breaths signalled by the plume of vapour, and thereby store enough air to allow them to remain under water for an hour or so. For this reason it is of utmost importance to the whalers to get close enough to him to harpoon him within that ten minutes, for when he rises next he may be a league away.

And as the men slid down ropes or clambered out of the ports that were open on account of the heat and stillness of the day, and into the four boats, that had already been dropped, Fair Trade himself gathered me into the crook of his left arm and took me into the lead boat which he always skippered, and Quodlibbet, with his harpoon, and Seamus followed.

'Panzee, you'll bring us luck I make no doubt,' he rasped in my ear and then shot a stream of tobacco juice over my shoulder into the briny before settling me next to himself in the stern, he being the headsman, while Quodlibbet, as harpooner, took up his station as leading oarsman in the stem.

Given the chance I'd have refused the offer, the place, the duty imposed on me, given the chance. Trust me. My preferred way of life has always been contemplative – action frightens me, and I steer clear if I can.

The little flotilla, with Fair Trade's boat the leader, formed a wide spaced arrowhead and moved as silently as maybe, the men propelling us with paddles rather than the noisy oars; nevertheless old whale had maybe caught the gist of what we were about, for while we were still a hundred feet from him up came his tail, forty feet into the air. 'There go the flukes' was the shout, and he slipped below in one long, curving, silent movement.

Stibbs, in the boat on our starboard side, lit his pipe, and beside me Quodlibbet rested on his oar and stuck the lump of cork he'd hacked from the ruin of a fisherman's net back over the razor-sharp head of his harpoon which sat in its crotch on the starboard gunwale.

After the full interval of his sounding up came whale again, and not so far off after all and, at a hundred fathoms, nearest to us so that Fair Trade felt sure now the honour of the brute's capture would fall on him. Our quarry was aware of our presence and possibly of our intent for he surged away from us 'head-up', that is his massive cranium rose from the water so his huge snout and the dome behind it were clear, leaving only his thin lower jaw and his fluted underside to offer any resistance to the water.

'Row, you fuckers, row, row,' bellowed Fair Trade, who was now so possessed by the demons of the chase that he seemed another person altogether, quite different from the kind and even-tempered giant we knew him to be by habit. And all around him, those who could, in any of the six boats, hollered and screamed, and hallooed like banshees, like devils on horseback, like dogs with a view, each according to their nature and the people amongst whom they had been reared, so the Viking cry of the Berserker broke from Sven's lips and the 'Ka-la! Koo-loo!' of your Polynesian warrior from Quodlibbet's, our aim being to be up with him before he sounded again.

Then their random shouts died down and to keep good measure with their four big sweeps and following a beat Fair Trade set going in the stern, they sang and heaved together:

> Away, heave away,
> O, heave away together
> Away, heave away,
> O, heave away, Joe!
>
> King Louis was the king of France
> Before the revolution
> But the people chopped his head off
> Which spoiled his constitution.

Soon we were in the whale's wake and foam broke over our prow, as the boat bucked and reared like a colt in spring, for he knew now we were after him, but was not yet ready to sound again. 'Peak your oars,' shouted Fair Trade, and 'On your feet, Quoddy,' Fair Trade screamed, 'Give it the bugger, NOW!' and thrown true and straight the harpoon shot, propelled only by the sinews of that dusky, tattooed arm yet as certain as a bolt from a crossbow, the line whipping the air behind it, the black staff not deviating, the barbed blade as bright as lightning as it caught the sun for a second. Sharp as it was it sliced into the brute's broad back and held 'socket up' – that is, it was buried in his flesh up to the socket which admits the handle or 'pole' of the harpoon.

A cheer from those in the boats, and from the seamen left on the *Town-Ho*, reverberated across the still deep. The sea, which a moment before was unruffled, now became lashed into foam by the immense strength of the wounded whale, who with his vast tail struck in all directions at his enemies. Now his enormous head rose high into the air, then his flukes were seen lashing everywhere, his huge body writhed in violent contortions from the agony the 'iron' had inflicted. The water all around him was a mass of foam, some of it darted to a considerable height, and the sounds of the blows from his tail on the surface of the sea could be heard for miles.

As soon as he saw it hold, Fair Trade gave the line two turns round the loggerhead in the stern of the boat so, taut as a piano string, it sang in the air not more than a foot or so from where I crouched clutching the rearing sides. 'Stern all,' he yelled, and, as one, his crew pushed on their oars instead of pulling while the line whistled down the boat and smoked as it passed round the logger-head, and smoked again in Fair Trade's hands for all he wore the quilted canvas squares to protect his palms. It was like holding an enemy's sharp two-edged sword by the blade, and that enemy all the time striving to wrest it out of your clutch, for the whale had suddenly disappeared – he had sounded again, and the line, running through the groove at the head of the boat with lightning-like velocity, this time ignited. 'Wet the fucker, keep it wet,' screamed Fair Trade and Seamus, who sat or stood beside the helmsman, caught a dollop of sea in his hat and managed to tip some on the post, and some in the tub which held the coiled two hundred fathoms of line, but on his second attempt lost water, hat and all.

'God damnit,' he screamed, 'did I not pay a shilling for it in a Scotland Road pawn shop these ten years since?'

Two hundred fathoms, four hundred yards, but it was whipping out of the tub and round the loggerhead and through the groove faster than any marlin ever pulled line from a fisherman's reel, and 'Hoist an oar,' he shouted at which signal Stibbs's boat came alongside and just in time 'bent on' the second boat's line. But still the monster sought to rid himself of his enemies by descending vertically into the dark and unknown depths of the ocean.

Despite his burning hands and all, Fair Trade got three more bites of the rope on the loggerhead and, seeing it gave out no more, scooped me up and pushed his way to the stem passing Quodlibbet who was making the same trip in reverse. With the bucking of the boat, the greasiness of its bottom planks, and the thwarts to be crossed with their oarsmen and oars, and the bloodied spray in his face, it was a perilous journey though no more than twelve feet or so, but he made it, put me down on the thwart Quodlibbet had vacated, in front of black Jackson, and armed himself like Hector in front of the gates of Troy with a spear long in length, but with a broad, sharp head or blade that could inflict a terrible, death-dealing wound.

But the end was still a long way off though the harpoon so well thrown by Quodlibbet stuck fast. Maddened by the pain of it our foe surfaced again and thrust on across the swell, churning it the way a ploughshare turns the shiny loam and almost as straight. A continual cascade played at the bows, a ceaseless whirling eddy in our wake. Each man clung to his plank and Quodlibbet, standing now at the steering oar, bent himself almost double, eyes blinded by the spray that swept across the bowed heads between him and his headsman.

'Haul in, haul in,' bellowed Fair Trade, sensing a weakening in the thrashing flukes in front of him, and all seized the singing line, until inch by inch, then foot by foot and yard by yard, he came abreast of the beast's giant flank. Now in went his lance, thrust with a force that would have stopped a bear, pierced a shield, fixed a man to a tree through his chest, and the blood fountained out of our quarry, splattered across our heads, slipped like spilled milk down the sides of those hill-like flanks. The sun played on this crimson cloud in the sea, reflected it off every face so that we looked like savages painted for some hideous ritual. The whale, in its last extremity, gasped more and more for air, sending jet after jet of vapour from its spiracle.

'Close to, get closer,' Fair Trade screamed to his helmsman and Quodlibbet leaned on his oar to bring us back alongside. Now he plunged the lance in one last time, close to the beast's fin, and leaned on it, one foot deep, two, three, so the butt was between his knees and his waist, and he churned it about, almost swung on it, probing, digging, searching. Suddenly the vapour from the wrecked beast's breath-hole turned red and then gushed, as the point and blade sliced the sides of his lungs and maybe the pulmonary vein so he began to drown in his own blood. But not dead yet. In his throes he suddenly wallowed, effecting the 'flurry' many whalemen dread, caused by the whale spinning on the axis from head to flukes, wrapping himself in impenetrable, mad, boiling spray, and at this moment the unspeakable happened.

I must tell you now how every line has two harpoons attached to it, the second ready to be hurled if the first fails to stick or comes loose, and, in the whole commotion and battle that follows the striking with the first, this second can be left, ignored and forgotten, to thrash about. And on this occasion the whale's mortal flurry set up such a bloody tide, almost a wall of liquid crashing over our heads that this second harpoon which had been to the bottom of the ocean and back, struck Fair Trade across the neck and swept him overboard. Simultaneously, the boat swung round through a half-circle, carrying him with it, so it thrust him against not just the whale's upturning belly but the haft of the other harpoon, which was crushed through his ribcage. For a moment his face, twisted in a ghastly grimace, made yet more horrid by the scar on it, appeared like a disinterred corpse's on the surface. They reckoned later, the crew that is, as they smoked their pipes and relived the terrible event, that both whale and headsman had died together, and their souls, bound in one shared but terrible ecstasy, rose to heaven or sank to the bottom of the fathomless deep of the ocean, as one.

Seamus used his clasp knife to cut the line and Fair Trade's body sank away, sucked by a last spasm, passing under that of the giant he had killed.

'Oh, shit!' said I, and in the silence broken only by the slipping and slopping of the dying waves all heads turned towards me.

'Sheee-it!' I added, this time for myself and my changed situation.

7

That evening they all met in the fo'c'sle to decide what was to be done with me. I was clothed in a pair of Ish's ducks he'd grown out of on the voyage and a cutaway jacket with brass buttons, for, as Seamus said, raising his huge eyebrows – "Taint dacent he go about butt-naked, being a man not a monkey.' They put me on top of a half barrel of biscuit in the middle and all crowded round in the tiny space beneath a hurricane lamp that swayed ever so slightly, and very slowly, in the gentle heave of the calm ocean as if the ship were a baby and the waters of the world the womb in which, unborn, she lay while her mother slept.

They were huddled tight, most bent a little, knees drawn up, and all bar the five who were up against the barrel so pressed against their neighbours they could scarce manoeuvre hand or arm to tend to their pipes, or the mugs of rum and lime juice that were passed from mouth to mouth. The dim light, whose source was a lantern above my head, was no more than a red glow through the thickening smoke on their raised faces, on peeling skin, the stubble of cheeks shaved only on Sundays (that day was a Friday), the bruises left by sun, wind and tackle flying in a storm, the scars and broken teeth earned in brawls from Nantucket to Seattle.

Once gathered, they were almost silent for a space with just a muttered apology or a grunt of displeasure as a foot searched for a space to put itself, and through that quietness came another sound, eerie and portentous. The dead whale had been roped alongside, and a thousand swarming sharks feasted on its fatness. Almost often enough to make a rhythm of it they sharply slapped their tails against the hull and if you ventured on the deck for a piss over the side or just a gulp or two of fresher air you could see them, beneath the light of a waning half-moon, wallowing in the sullen black waters, turning over on their backs and flashing the dull white of their bellies as they scooped out huge globular pieces of the whale the size of a human head.

Yet such was the enormity of the monster they fed off they scarce made noteworthy inroads into the rich mines of its blubber – there was an abundance of plunder left for the crew of the *Town-Ho* to haul aboard and render as soon as the sun came up. Meanwhile, I was the cynosure of all eyes, the pole star to which all turned their faces as surely as the needles of so many compasses.

Sven Ericsson was the first to speak, and indeed from then on seemed self-appointed speaker or chair of the assembled crew, perhaps on account of his size which was, if anything, a hand's breadth larger than Fair Trade's had been, but also because of the openness of his character which was not belied by the openness of his face.

'Panzee,' he began, 'is no proper label for a proper man. Vot's your handle?'

'Ay, tell us your name,' they all echoed, nodding wisely at Sven and at each other as if to say, good, here is a man who knows the proper proceedings, how to start the affair with due ceremony.

For a moment I had it in mind to crack on I knew no English, that I might speak to them in Italian, Spanish or French, all of which, being native to none, I know as well one as the other. But there was a growl in their response; they wanted to get on with it, and tactics of delay would, I reckoned, only stoke their anger. Anger? Yes, for no matter they invented charges against me, their main concern was the chagrin they felt that they had been shown up so ignorant as to mistake me for an ape.

'Joseph Charles Edward Bosham,' I replied, 'and happy in your company to answer to Eddie.'

'That you will not,' Sven rumbled, 'a proper formality is to be observed. You will at all times be addressed as Mr Bosham.'

I thought this through for a moment, considering the fact that a yet more proper mode of address could be Viscount Bosham, or Lord Bosham of Bosham in the County of Sussex, these being the style bestowed by a grateful prince upon my grandfather in Rome in 1746, where both Prince and his adherent were suffered at the time to remain in exile following the Young Pretender's tragic defeat at Culloden. But I felt all this would be beyond the comprehension of those before whom I was arraigned and I desisted.

The questions came on now at quite a pace. Why was I on Albemarle in the first place?

'Marooned, sir,' I answered, 'through no fault of my own . . .'

But I was hard put to it to present a convincing explanation of my misfortune as an accident. With many 'ayes, 'tis so, that's how it was', and puffings at their clays, they agreed no honest men would so leave one of their number by happenchance and not come back for him when they discovered he was missing. They must have left me there because I was a rogue, a thief or Jonah, perhaps, and this punishment lit on being as close to death as they could allow themselves without incurring blame for murder.

'Why was you naked, no dacent Christian man goes naked!' This from Seamus who seemed a touch obsessed with the subject.

'Why should I not go amongst my friends the seals and sea lions as naked as they?' I replied, which turned out for reasons I could not find to be rational almost as offensive as the offence itself. Perhaps they objected to my honouring the seals they had slaughtered so freely as possible friends to one of their own kind.

'That is no answer to the question,' Sven growled. 'Try again.'

'I took my clothes off to dry after a wetting and they were washed out to sea,' I half improvised.

That seemed all right and they moved on to the next.

'How came you by your low stature and your furriness.'

'God knows.'

'That too is no answer.'

'It's the only one I have. He knows. I don't.'

And so it continued: a succession of questions, some germane to my status and condition, some merely prompted by curiosity. Before long, what with the exertions of the day behind them, the closeness of the room, the narcotic effects of rum and tobacco smoke, many of them nodded off and to an agreeable chorus of snores the big Swede came to judgement and wound up the proceedings.

'Joseph Charles Edward Bosham,' he pronounced with due solemnity, 'this court convened in the fo'c'sle of the *Town-Ho* on the second of December 1835 finds you guilty of wilful deception of your shipmates. On the matter of whether or not you are Jonah to this ship we temporarily reserve judgement, but consider the loss of our dear friend Fair Trade an evidence that that may be so. On the first count we'll give you a bloody good beating as soon as there is light enough on deck to do so.'

The which sentence was duly carried out.

With the first lightening of the sky to the east four or five of them carried me on deck. I struggled as vigorously as I could until the Negro Jackson gave me a hearty belt across the mouth. They hoisted me into the foremast halyards and spreadeagled me there, tying my wrists and ankles and stretching me as tight as they could so the middling parts of my body hardly sank in over the deck at all. Next they thrust a wedge of jerk into my bleeding mouth so I might not cry out too loudly, and finally Sven took up his stance behind me with the tarred end of a rope in his hands and proceeded to give me the thrashing he had himself decreed.

You know, it was not so bad. I was a soldier for a time in Duke Willingdone's army and have seen malefactors die across the breech of a cannon as they took a hundred lashes from the cat; I have seen men bleed almost to death from the crisscrossing network of slashes left by the cuts of a sergeant major's cane. Indeed, I did not writhe enough to satisfy them and Seamus when he took over from Sven called for them to pull down Ish's ducks.

'His back's so hairy, he does not feel it like he should but on his bum, 'tis not so much.'

Tell you the truth, the first ten or so I took on the buttocks carried a sort of pleasure as well as pain and I hoped none behind me would be aware how, in front of me, Captain Standish was like to justify his name.

I kept mum because I was gagged, and fixed my mind on the still gently heaving swell of the iron grey ocean. Beneath me the giant whale still wallowed to the motion of the ship and sea, not quite in time, but rising before the ship and then dropping away before she came down too, with the creak of the ropes that held the carcase alongside and the slurp of the black waters squelching up between. He must long since have ceased bleeding, even from the gouged-out wounds the sharks had left, but still his blood hung in the water

51

around us, browning and purpling it rather than painting it red. A few sharks still cruised about but aimlessly and satiated, and on went the beating, thwack, thwack, thwack . . . thwack . . . thwack. Slower as the Irishman's arm grew tired.

'This is bloody nonsense.'

It was the dark voice of the Negro Jackson.

'You lemme have a go,' he went on. 'I goddamn know about beating the way none of you lots do, I bin proper beaten, un 'undred times, you give me that goddamn rope an' I'll show you.'

And sure enough he laid two between my ribs and my bum which fell as exact as they could in the same place and carried on with a will the others did not seem to have.

But hardly had he got going than a shaft of sunlight blazed like a fiery lance from across the waters ahead of us, the clouds I had been looking at turned purple, red and gold in as little time as it takes me to write the words, the sky turned blue and the ocean too. A bell rang, fast beats, the mate blew his whistle from the poop deck, orders were shouted and bare feet pummelled the boards behind me, and I was left to hang forgotten where I was.

Sven and another big man whose name I did not know – I think he was a Scotsman – climbed down the side of the boat and out on to the whale himself, though both with lifelines still attached, and went to work severing the brute's huge head from his body, this being a herculean task for, in contradistinction to almost all other mammals, a sperm whale's neck is the thickest part of his body. First they hooked it with a giant hook, flown from a block suspended from the maintop and lashed to the lower masthead of the mainmast. Then, they used big, sharp, long-handle spades with blades shaped like broad leaves and as sharp at the edges as razors, but even with these it took a good half-hour, perhaps an hour even, I can't tell, before the great skull was loose. Still attached to the hook it was swung to the stern of the ship where it hung half in and half out of the water, made buoyant on account of the quantity of spermaceti oil held in its case.

That done, Sven and the Scotsman now carved out a strip of blubber about three feet broad and a foot and a half thick and four or five feet long, though not severing the further end, all in all in just the way a gardener might lift turf from a grassy lawn. Another big hook was lowered from another block swung next to the one already in use for the head, the which Sven and his mate now threaded or pushed through a hole they had made in the strip of blubber. Passing through the blocks the line ran down to the windlass which ten or more of the sturdiest members of the crew now began to turn and struck up a work song or shanty while they did so, Seamus giving them the verse and all joining the chorus.

> *O, poor old Eddie Panzee*
> *Panzee, boys, Panzee!*
> *O, pity poor Eddie Panzee*
> *Panzee, boys, Panzee!*
>
> *Though Panzee was no sailor . . .*
> *He shipped aboard a whaler . . .*
> *Though Panzee was no beauty . . .*
> *He could not do his duty . . .*
>
> *So they gave him nine and thirty . . .*
> *Yes, lashes nine and thirty . . .*
> *O, cap'n being a good man . . .*
> *He took him to the cabin . . .*
>
> *Now Panzee he's a sailor . . .*
> *Chief mate of that whaler . . .*
>
> *He married the cap'n's daughter*
> *Panzee, boys, Panzee!*
> *And sails no more upon the water*
> *Panzee, boys, Panzee!*

Which, no one will deny, was fancy improvising on Seamus's part and so much was it liked it got took up and I heard a version sung in a 'Frisco whorehouse, some twelve years later, but with the name *Panzee* corrupted to *Ranzo*.

Slowly they began to peel the blubber off the whale, while down below the two giants with their spades cut along the lines they had already started. Slowly, under the influence of this tearing pressure, the great carcase turned and the two men kept pace with it, as if on a gigantic treadmill, until the blanket of blubber, thus freed, reached the block. Now it was severed at last from the creature it had warmed through Arctic seas as well as the tropical ones we were within, hauled on board and fed into the blubber room. But even while this went on a second hook was established in the tag end of the first blanket piece, and all the time the birds wheeled around, cackling and screaming, and the sharks continued to infest the waters, occasionally taking vicious blows from those spades so those unhurt would turn on their erstwhile friends and relations as they bled and crush them up, out of reach of the weapons, in their hideous mouths filled with rapacious teeth.

At about the time the next strip was begun I managed to spit out the wedge of jerk, and I had to work my mouth to get the juices flowing again, so dried up was it with the salt and so forth. Then, when the third strip was under way, I became aware of a presence behind me, a darkening and chill presence stood between me and the still-low sun.

'A sight, you will agree.'

Glancing over my shoulder I was able to get enough of him in focus through the corner of my eye to recognise him as the captain of the *Town-Ho*.

8

I had seen him about the place but rarely away from the poop deck. He spent most of his time in the cabin below it and in the adjoining chart room. He was tall, well-built, with a big-boned look about him and always wore a black coat and yellowish nankeen trousers with a tall hat, except when the wind was blowing up a gale, at which time he resorted to an oiled-skin affair with flaps and a tie below the chin. Most of his orders came through the mate, but that they were his there was no doubt. Although he looked like a small-town physician or preacher on account of his clothes and the general severity of his countenance, he clearly knew his duty and the means by which he would carry it out, as well as any other sea captain.

'Certainly,' I replied, 'a sight.'

He gripped my right palm, tethered as it was to the shrouds, in his left hand.

'Tom Gardener,' he said. 'You have the advantage of me.'

'Joseph Charles Edward Bosham,' I replied and I squeezed his hand in response. He withdrew it, the formality having been completed.

'I am afraid my crew have not treated you as well as they should.'

'The fault is, in part at least, my own. I should not have practised on them a deception so childish it never occurred to me it would wear for more than a day.'

'Well,' he went on, 'you do not cease to surprise them, and me too, I should add.'

'How so?'

'Your stature and your pelt are curious in themselves. That you should turn out to be, what shall I say, well spoken, is yet more odd.'

I felt a touch of chagrin at this, and shrugged or rather wriggled my arms and legs which, due to my situation, were now causing me more distress than my poor back.

'My physical attributes are a sport of nature and could have occurred in any family. I could equally well say that your manner of discourse is not to be expected amongst seafaring men, unless they be commissioned by the King. Or President.'

'Perhaps.'

Silence fell between though not around us. The squealing of ropes through blocks, the creaking of timbers, the shanties of the men, the cacophony of the sea birds continued unabated. He had put me in a quandary. By elevating my social rank to something comparable to his he had almost precluded the petition I was longing to make: that I should be cut down from my ignominious and painful position. It was now surely up to him to make the move. That he was as much a gentleman as one can expect a Yankee to be was now not in doubt: his manner of speech which was hardly tainted with a Yankee drawl at all, his easy but not hail-fellow-well-met manners all indicated as much. One does not put such a person under an obligation to one by insisting on a favour they should have perceived and prevented.

'Quite a sight,' he repeated at last.

'Indeed yes.'

At this point the fourth blanket of blubber was hitched up and began to climb inch by inch towards the main yardarm. The carcase continued its slow revolution, like an orange peeled by a lazy giant, revealing a sort of thin, translucent skin beneath, through which could be seen the beast's monstrous ribs and internal organs.

'It was a noble creature,' I added, more out of a desire to keep the conversation going than for any other reason.

'Noble be blowed!' said in a matter-of-fact sort of way, not obviously contentious. 'I am not sure in what nobility may be said to exist, but it does not, I think, reside in the nature of a brute without feelings or reason.'

'I had in mind its size, its strength, its courage perhaps. Its freedom to cruise the ocean seeking its own satisfactions. Like a monarch.'

'Mr Bosham, your manner and mode of address and so forth had led me to believe that in spite of your appearance you might be a person with whom one could have a rational conversation. But you are now talking rubbish. That creature was an insensate machine, cruising the ocean as you say, to maintain itself alive and causing the death in doing so of a million other creatures. It was no more noble than the sharks or scavenging birds that now invest it.'

'So, there is no reason at all to feel regret or even guilt that one has slain, or caused to be slain, so nob . . . um, grand an animal.'

'Certainly not. Neither regret nor guilt has anything to do with the case. Pride, perhaps, or at any rate satisfaction in seeing to it that a difficult task has been achieved as efficiently as possible might be allowable.'

'Efficient . . . ! One of your men was lost, one of the best of your men.'

'One calculates for such losses. They are an inevitable part of such an enterprise. I might add this is not a calculation I have made. It is part of the equation formulated by the people who set it up. Thus and thus much expense, thus and thus much loss, or risk of loss, against the possibility of a substantial profit. In so far as I am a paid functionary I too am part of this equation. I also happen to be an investor in it, one of five people, but that is by the way.'

'And this equation actually did include as one of its terms the possible death of an operative, an employee?'

'Of course. To formulate it otherwise would have been to deny the possibility, indeed the probability, of such an event happening. You must be aware, Mr Bosham, that whaling is a dangerous activity likely to cause not just the death of whales but what one might call collateral losses amongst whalers.'

He paused to extract a panatella from a case he withdrew from an inside pocket of his coat. He bit off the end and spat it into the sea. Next came a lucifer. He struck this on the hard wood of one of the small blocks that secured the shrouds, shielded the flame with his palm, sucked smoke in and let it out.

'In point of fact the equation includes total loss of the ship and all hands, including me.'

I coughed helplessly as the smoke passed beneath my nostrils.

'And how will the loss of Fair Trade affect your equation?' I asked, once I had recovered.

'On the debit side of the ledger, very little. We shall have to raise the wages of the man I choose to appoint as headsman in his place, should we choose to continue hunting whales. However, I suspect that this latest, being such a sizeable brute, will just about complete the filling of our lockers. On the credit side there will be the gain of his rations, the fact that there will be one man less to pay a bonus to, promised to the men if we make a good sale of our cargo . . . and so on. It's finely balanced so not a matter of great concern either way.'

'His widow, children?'

'If there are any, and they can prove they are, they will be paid his wages due to yesterday morning once we are returned to Nantucket.'

'Which will be when?'

'If I elect to go straight back, six months or so.'

'Back round the Horn and up the east coast of the southern cone. But what else can you do if your lockers are full?'

'I have a mind to try the settlements on the west coast. Ecuador, Peru, Chile, down to Valparaiso. If we can shift what's in the holds we may come back out here for more.'

'Won't there be a risk in that? Carrying coin or bullion from your sales?'

'The Bank of New York has an office in Valparaiso,' he said, and he wandered off towards the poop, the better no doubt to survey the progress that was being made in what the whalemen call 'cutting in', leaving me to survey the scene from almost as good a vantage point since my position was, in spite of my low stature, a foot or so above his.

By now the whale was three-quarters peeled and as the process approached the flukes and the narrower parts of its body, it proceeded more quickly until a sudden though less than fulsome cheer broke out below me, a weary cheer, perhaps tainted with sarcasm. I heard the clatter of Captain Gardener's shoes on the ship's decking, as he ran past me to lean over the side a yard or two nearer the bow than I was, a yard nearer the flukes of the whale which was now on its back. The sword-like spades had laid bare in a final humiliation the whale's genitals and anus. It was the anus and colon that had attracted the shouts, jeers and cheers. It was at these parts that the captain now directed an expectant and animated gaze.

A blow with the spade, a twist, and an almost surgical opening of the last feet of its digestive tract revealed that it was impacted with a deep grey substance, marbled with darker lines, of a soft consistency like uncooked dough, enough of it at least to fill a hundredweight coal'sack. And it gave off an overpowering, sickening smell that I have only ever encountered before in the field latrines of large armies. In short, what I and all the others were looking at and recoiling from was unevacuated sperm whale shit.

They hoisted it aboard in buckets and filled a barrel and a half with it. Within two days the odour had shifted to a peculiarly sweet and still somewhat nauseating, earthy odour. Once ashore it would be dissolved in hot alcohol from which solution it would throw brilliant white crystals: ambergris. In this form it sells to parfumiers, classy cooks and quack doctors for twenty-five shillings an ounce. What we were looking at was two thousand two hundred and forty pounds sterling less the fairly minimal cost of processing it, and the loss of some of its weight.

The sun began its swift descent to a dark horizon and the black smoke rose through the rigging and the listless sails as the work of rendering the blubber down to oil got under way, using big cauldrons brought up from below for the purpose. What was left of the beast was at last set free from its bonds and allowed to drift astern. Only the head remained and even then, making use of the last moments of daylight, the men were bucketing out of its interior the spermaceti oil that it contains and without which the finest machinery required by our new industries cannot work. Meanwhile the cadaver flashed like a marble sepulchre, a vast, white, headless phantom, round, on and above which the sharks and sea vultures, unrestrained now by human presence, thrashed and screamed as it moved on into the night.

But one last horror remained. Just as it passed beneath our counter it slowly turned over and by some strange quirk of fortune the body of Fair Trade broke free from where it had perhaps been suspended by the line in the waters beneath it. For a moment his face, made ghastly by the depredations of the sea and the sharks, leered up at us and then the birds descended, shrouding him with beating wings. That sight, and the smell of the whale's shit, will stay with me until I die.

As the corpse of the whale drifted away astern beneath its scavengers, clouds, the outriders of a tropical storm of some intensity, began to thicken over the western horizon and the sun set with an ominous blaze of colour. It caught the *Town-Ho* on its outer edge and swung her as if she were the whistling object on the end of a child's string in a wide quarter-circle that took us relentlessly into the under-belly of Mexico. But all that began at dawn the next day. Meanwhile, Captain Gardener personally cut through the ropes that still held me to the shrouds and, holding my hand in his, took me back to his cabin. There he proceeded to bugger me.

'For a lot of the day,' he panted, 'when not supervising the cutting in of the whale, I have had your buttocks more or less presented to me. Your overall hairiness too has excited in me a more than intel-lectual curiosity. You won't refuse me this harmless pleasure.' By now he had divested himself of his black coat and nankeen trousers, and his prick was up and pointing to two o'clock, 'Because if you do I'll send you back to the fo'c'sle, where they are already carousing on rum as a reward for their efforts during the day, and not just one, but a gang of them, will be looking for further entertainment. Be pleased to kneel on that chair.'

He had a cup of fresh spermaceti oil to hand which eased the ini-tial discomfort and no doubt added to his pleasure. And yes, indeed, my hirsuteeity did enflame him, for throughout the act, which he repeated thereafter whenever his duties on deck during the storm allowed him to come below, and indeed at other times once the storm had ceased shaking us and dropped us much in the way a bored puppy finally discards an old slipper, he ran his fingers over my torso and hips and thighs, teasing the hair and sighing at the tactile delight it gave him. I have known women to be taken with me on this account but this was a new experience.

The storm raged for several days; I really have no clear recollec-tion of how many, and in spite of the way we were pitched and tossed, and the waves crashed against us, in spite of stomach-churning drops and dizzying rises, and all the rest, I was not seasick. I never am. I recall poor Mr Darwin was seasick whenever the *Beagle* ploughed into the open sea and did not recover until we had dropped anchor in some sheltered bay or port. Whatever.

On one occasion when Captain Gardener was seeing to our safety on deck, I took the opportunity to scout round his cabin. It was not big, twelve feet by ten perhaps, with a fine but simple mahogany table and matching chair with a hooped back, a tallboy, and a narrow cot, on which I managed to get some sleep when the captain was away, though not when he returned. After the usual had been done I was then given a blanket and a corner on the floor. Against the bulwark by the door was an upright case holding six old Tower muskets, securely locked in a rack. There was also a large sea chest, also locked of course, but I found the key in one of the drawers in the tallboy. In fact, I knew it was there because it was in that same drawer that Gardener kept his reading glasses, wrapped up in a drawstring chamois leather pouch. Once or twice, when perusing a chart in the chart room, he had asked me to fetch them for him.

It was something of a treasure chest. There was a small sack of United States silver dollars, there were exchangeable notes issued by the Chase Bank and the Bank of Boston, the indentures signed by the crew, a copy of the agreement between the owners and the captain, a captain's certificate, and so on and so forth. There were a pair of percussion-fired pistols in a fine case and powder and ball to go with them. A somewhat crudely painted miniature of a severely dressed woman with a scarf over her head caught my eye: on the cedarwood backing a label read: 'This is for you, Tom, to remind you that your Betsy awaits your return, confident that by God's grace you will resist all the temptations that assail those that go on long voyages, signed, your Betsy.' Well, I thought, if I ever meet you, Betsy, I'll have a tale to tell . . .

But most extraordinary of all was a much smaller chest snug in the corner of the larger. It took only a moment of close attention for me to be sure that it was indeed old Blackbeard's chest that I had last seen being smuggled aboard the whaler by Seamus, and thence on to the *Town-Ho* itself. How came it here, in the captain's chest? I never did find out but in the end supposed the villainous Gael had brought it to the captain for safekeeping, knowing that if it were to be found in the fo'c'sle his mates would force him to share the contents . . . which remained as they were when I first saw them: a hundred gold guineas.

Meanwhile, on deck and above it in that awesome cage of canvas and ropes, the crew struggled to keep us afloat. There were casualties. Stibbs, the headsman of the second whaler, was lost overboard from the end of the main yard as he and others struggled to take in the last reefs on the biggest sail. And the black, Jackson, had his arm broken. It wouldn't mend, went gangrenous and on the day we first saw the

61

coast of Mexico, with the sun shining on still ferociously tossing white horses, Sven, who also acted as ship's surgeon, cut it off. Jackson died under the shock of it all.

After the flummery of a burial at sea, conducted with Bible and prayer book by the captain, he came below, with a face as long as a donkey's.

'I have to tell you, Eddie,' he said, 'the only choice they are leaving me is to keelhaul you, so slowly you must drown in the process, or make you walk the plank.'

'Oh shit!' I cried. 'Why?'

'They take you to be a dyed-in-the-wool Jonah, on account we have lost three men since you came aboard and have had to run with as bad a tempest as any we have seen, and in waters not known for them at this time of year.'

'Oh shit!' I repeated. 'And what's your view of the matter?'

'I favour the plank. Your death is not thereby an absolute certainty. You might even suffer Jonah's fate and be swallowed by a whale to be spewed up on a friendly coast. Or I could assert my authority and insist we sail up the coast for a day and a night which, by my reckoning, and with this following wind, will take us to a harbour, where we can put you ashore. This port of call is in fact a necessity, since we have lost a couple of sails in the storm and that damned leak near the keel seems to be letting in water faster than ever.'

'Do that, Captain Gardener, please do that.' I am not ashamed to write that by now I was on my knees, pleading like a slave in a painting of old Roman times.

'What is the name of this port?' I added as an afterthought.

'Acapulco.'

'That will do, that will do nicely,' I said, though I had never before heard of the place.

The day and the night duly followed without incident save that Gardener called a meeting of all and told them he would put me ashore at this port we were heading for and there was to be no more talk of Jonahs, keelhauling or plank walking. He had me a couple of times during the last night and seemed quite melancholy at my imminent departure, though I cannot pretend that he actually offered any gratitude, let alone expressions of a more tender feeling.

The mate, a character I have not described to you, mainly because I hardly ever saw or spoke to him – he was a dour Geordie from Wallsend – came below just after dawn to report that we were three leagues off the entrance to the harbour and with a light following wind should be approaching the roads within an hour or so. Gardener pulled on his trousers, his coat and his tall hat and went on deck to supervise the last stages, and after fulfilling certain obligations to myself I followed him and stood near him on the quarterdeck with the mate and helmsman beside me. My presence there, clad only in Ish's second pair of ducks and an old patched shirt of Gardener's, drew an ironic cheer from those of the crew who saw me, but my attention was more firmly fixed on the panorama that was scrolling out in front of me, the next stepping stone, I hoped, to my eventual return to these shores.

The sea was going with us, rough and pure, with long dawn rollers advancing, rising and crashing down. Between us and the shore the sea teemed with life: there were dolphins, a small pod of grey whales, crowds of sea birds, and several small fishing boats from which men in wide-brimmed straw hats with conical crowns cast lines with apparent success for catches that included at one end of the scale mackerel and dorado, to a man who, after great labour, hallooed and waved his hat on bringing over his gunwale a small marlin.

At this moment we experienced a truly wonderful phenomenon. The *Town-Ho* sailed straight into a hurricane of immense and gorgeous butterflies, swooping seawards as if to greet us. It was as though clouds of multicoloured autumn leaves, but far more brightly coloured, were zigzagging overhead, brilliant in the morning sunlight, before endlessly vanishing astern.*

The men began to show some signs of friendship towards me, prompted perhaps by feelings of mild remorse that they had treated me so badly.

"Ello dere,' cried Quodlibbet, 'long time we didn't see you, Eddie.'

'Ah sure he kept snug enough troo dat storm, didn't yer, yer ol' rogue,' said Seamus with a grin that showed teeth newly broken.

And dear Ish himself came alongside.

* In *Under the Volcano* Malcolm Lowry describes a similar scene when the heroine, Yvonne, arrives in Acapulco on a steamer from Los Angeles. J. R.

63

'Are you all right, Eddie?' he asked. 'Will you be all right amongst the heathen Injuns of these parts?'

'I'll be all right,' I answered. 'I've taken care of that.'

Even Sven gave me a curt nod and a gruff 'Mornin', sailor!'

By now we were passing round the first of what I had taken to be islands, leaving both on our starboard lee and a wide, almost circular bay, calm, and the water emerald in hue, opened up in front of us. The mountains that hung like a backdrop stood out clear and magnificent in the limpid morning air and the sun, already high enough, cast long, deep, purplish-blue shadows down their riven, almost orange flanks. Since we were clear in the middle of this bay, there was a great deal of luffing and helm-upping, and haul away there and let it out here, all that sort of thing, which, even after all the ocean-going that has been forced on me, I cannot pretend to understand. We turned to port through a hundred degrees or more and the town and harbour opened themselves up to our view, while the further side of the northern island, shaped like a long tooth protecting them from all the ocean could do and revealing itself to be not an island but a peninsula with an isthmus rising to high fissured cliffs, lay along our port side.

On the right-hand side (for let us now drop all this nautical blarney as at last we see the prospect of terra firma ineluctably upon us) was a small castle within Vaubon-style fortifications, and then looping round below it a not insubstantial little town and port, with quays, warehouses and twin church towers with domes on top, so like the ones I had known throughout my childhood in Salamanca, I felt quite a lump of nostalgia combined with a sort of wistful joy rise up in my breast. And at last it dawned on me: I really would be all right, for had this not been, only ten years earlier, not Mexico at all, but New Spain, and did I not speak the language like the native I, to all intents and purposes, had been, until the wars plucked me from my first homeland?

With sails down all but the spanker, two whalers were dropped to tow us into the quay where an hour or so short of midday we were duly moored and a gangplank in place.

'Right, Eddie, off you go,' barked the captain.

'What? Just like that?'

'Just like that, Eddie.'

But he took my hand, very briefly, down by my side, and squeezed into my palm one of my gold guineas.

As I walked down the gangway, somewhat awkwardly, indeed feeling a certain internal discomfort, the whole crew of them leant over the side and gave me one last jeering cheer.

And one of them, I'm not sure which, called out: 'Take care, our Eddie, they're all *loco* in Acapulco!'

The natives looked at me with some wonder and curiosity, but not enough to stir them out of what I was to learn was their customary midday torpor, and I headed for the nearest narrow alley, where, once I was sure I was well out of sight of the *Town-Ho*, I relieved myself of my burden.

Forty stacked gold guineas, wrapped in the fine little chamois leather bag the captain kept his reading spectacles in, made a cylinder about eight inches high and less than an inch in diameter. About the size of Gardener's Captain Standish.

And if you can't guess where I had hidden them then you don't know the answer to the old riddle: 'Where did the monkey put the nuts?'

Interlude I

End of March 1853

'Francis Buff-Orpington.'

'Eh?'

'My name. Francis Buff-Orpington.'

'Ah!'

Joseph Charles Edward Bosham, aka Charlie Boylan, preferring at this moment to be called Eddie, stands up from his table, with its two piles of treasury stationery, the smaller one written on, the other virgin and still tightly stacked. He sets down his steel-nibbed pen and wonders whether or not he should offer a hand to the young gentleman who has just been shown in by the duty screw. The young gentleman is tall, very thin, is wearing a coat whose cuffs, both at his wrists and his ankles, are too short. He has an eager sort of a face, with an eager sort of an expression as if nothing would be too much for him, as if he has no desire in the world but to please whomever he is with.

He does not, however, offer his hand, but walks over to the high, barred window, with its shallowly arched top edge, and looks out. He is tall enough to do this. Eddie is not.

'Lovely day,' he offers. 'Breezy but not cold. Daffodils and all that sort of thing.'

'Really?'

'I say, I'd better tell you why I'm here.'

Eddie waits. Head on one side, expectant, but not too expectant. He's not in good shape. His hair has grown during the three weeks of this particular incarceration, and is now lank and greasy. His clothes have a shabby, unpressed, rather grubby look to them. His bottom lip droops even more moistly than before. The cough and the phlegmy nose that besieged him in Pentonville have returned and the evidence glistens on his coat sleeve. His voice when he speaks is hoarse. And, frankly, he smells – the prison odour of sour sweat gathered in the unwashed crevices in his armpits and his groin has returned all too quickly.

Francis Buff-Orpington clears his throat and continues.

'Eff Oh chappies washed their hands of you. You're back in our court. The Aitch Oh, don't you know. And I'm, um, to handle you.'

Eddie twists on his stool to face this gangly youth.

'Handle me?' he rasps. 'How's that then? I'm here, on remand, charged with attempted murder, which won't wash, waiting to be released when the magistrates come to their senses and realise there is no case to answer. So what's this handling lark?'

Eddie, as always, can assume what tone, manner, he likes. He can be a toff or a wheedling, mewling member of the *lumpen proletariat*. He can assume the deportment and style of a scholar or the idiocy of an oaf. Just now he is a bully, sensing that this very young man, this very minor tyro from the Home Office, is unsure of his ground, is even uncertain as to why he is there.

'I grant you,' says F. B.-O., 'that the charge of attempted murder will not wash, um, stand up in court, but there is the other little matter. Well, several actually.'

'I'm listening.'

'Carrying a loaded pistol into the House of Commons.'

'Fiddlesticks. An oversight. Three months at her madge's pleasure top whack. I've already been in jug for nearly four. Next.'

'Attempting to extort money from Her Majesty's Government under false pretences, namely claiming you were not properly rewarded for performing certain services thirty years ago which either you were paid for or you did not perform.'

'And getting that to stand up in court will mean making public exactly what those services were. They include political assassination, entrapment of innocent individuals, acting as *agent provocateur*,

67

and saving Her Madge's life on the occasion of the opening of the Great International Exhibition . . .'

'Oh come on . . .'

'The mob will carry me out of the Old Bailey on their shoulders.'

'Oh come on, Charlie—'

'Eddie.'

'I beg your pardon?'

'Just now I have a whim to be referred to as Eddie. Edward is as much one of my forenames as Charles.'

'Oh, very well. Eddie. For reasons of national security the trial may be held *in camera*—'

'*What?*' Eddie makes the word rhyme with 'twat', such is his surprise and simulated anger. '*National Security?!?* What in the blazes is that? That's a new-minted concept! Is it come to this? Are we Austrian? Have we become a tinpot German state? Is this *China* that you set the security of the state above the freedom of the individual? Oh Milton, thou shouldst be living at this hour. John Wilkes, where are you? Will Cobbett, we need you . . . I actually met old Cobbett a couple of times, you know? Mad as a hatter. Racist too – hated blacks.'

'He's mentioned in an earlier part of your memoirs. Which brings me to why I'm here.' Buff-Orpington unglues his rather droopy back from the wall by the window, simultaneously extracting a sheaf of papers like those on Eddie's table from his flat case, specially designed to carry documents, quite the latest thing for civil servants. He plonks them down on the table with some force so that a couple of sheets of unused paper rise off Eddie's stack and float to the floor. Eddie bends to pick them up and almost falls off his stool.

'Steady on, old chap.'

But the young civil servant has recovered some poise. Really, this Eddie is just as wretched a creature as his superiors have told him he will be.

'This stuff,' he says, injecting a new and quite hard note into his voice, 'simply will not do. You have written a hundred pages or so in a deuced crabby hand and not a word of it pertains to what you should be telling us. All this *stuff* about the Galápagos, whalers, and now Mexico . . . it's not what we want from you at all. Frankly, old chap, you have lost the plot!'

'I'll get round to it, squire, I'll get round to it. I promise you.'
Recognising a change in the weather Eddie hauls in sail, puts up his
helm and sets off on an altogether more emollient tack.

'But what are you playing at? Why should you think we might be
interested in your prurient fantasies regarding seals and the captain of
an American whaler—'

'Look, squire. All I'm aiming at is background. Corroborative
detail. Adding verisimilitude to an otherwise bald and possibly
unconvincing narrative. The better to show you that I am penning
an honest account . . . What I was up to since I stowed away on the
Beagle, that was the commission Mr Elliott gave me—'

'No, sir. Mr Elliott was speaking for the Foreign Office. Your commission now is simple. Either you tell us where you have hidden the
documents which you claim might cause embarrassment to the
Queen and possibly her government, whose servant I am, or you
produce a digest of what is in them. That is your commission.'

'But that's just the point, ol' chap. Some of what is in them papers
is my memoirs, penned over the years, often when the events were as
fresh in my mind as like yesterday—'

'Eddie. You know what we want. Just do it.'

'A bottle of gin and a steak pie would . . .'

But F. B.-O. is already knocking on the cell door to summon the
turnkey to let him out.

'Mr Cargill was always very accommodating in such matters when
he visited me in Pentonville . . . Oh, shit. Fuck.'

For the lanky not-so-civil servant has gone.

Poor Eddie looks forlornly round his cell, at his hammock, at the
four brick walls painted in a light shit-coloured tint, the too-high
window. In a corner he has stacked the books that were on the table
when he arrived, provided by the Society for the Promotion of
Christian Knowledge: a prayer book, a hymn book and some pamphlets. In another corner he has placed his wooden platter, his tin
pint mugs for cocoa and gruel, a saltcellar and a wooden spoon.
There is a utensil like a pudding basin for pissing and shitting in, and
a piece of soap. Finally, against the wall opposite the one with the
hammock, is a wooden washing tub.

No wonder he is happy to spend the daylight hours contemplating
and recording an adventurous, colourful and even exotic past,
embroidered by the unconscious skills memory always employs.

Grateful that Mr Buff-Orpington, in spite of everything, has left him with the means to continue his story, he picks up his pen again, smooths the top sheet which he has retrieved from the floor. Lost the plot, has he? Well, maybe. Perhaps a new start is indicated. He is aware that he has just spent thirty pages on his account of his experiences on a whaler and his arrival in Acapulco. At this rate he'll not catch up with himself in thirty years, supposing he lives so long. Resolving to be more brisk, he sets pen to paper . . .

Part III

MÉJICO

Poor Mexico, so far from God and so close to the United States.

PORFIRIO DIAZ (attr.)

9

With my pouch of gold in one hand and my single guinea in the other I now sauntered away from the quays, taking a direction I reckoned would bring me to the cathedral. I remembered enough about Spanish towns to suppose that there would be a square thereabouts, and in that square a bank, and, Acapulco being a port, a place of exchange. Not that the streets I was in in any way resembled the centre of a Spanish town. These were roughly cobbled but with many gaps and loose stones, narrow, and tilted inwards to a hollow spine, an open sewer, or cloaca that failed to carry the detritus of the lives of those that lived in them to the harbour and the sea. There were slices of melon rind, rotting vegetables, mule and donkey shit, and a fair amount of the human variety too. The smell was horrible and the swarms of flies also. It was not all unmitigated squalor. Tropical plants hung from pots in the embrasures. Parrots gossipped and strutted back and forth in cages and for a time a small flock of pure white doves tumbled through the humid air above me. Not all the odours were distasteful either: some were sweeter than those that rose from the effluent in the middle of the street – tobacco, spiced cooking, coffee and the alluring aroma of chocolate.

Dogs barked as I passed, an emaciated white and yellow cat mewed at me and responded with the tribe's usual easy come easy go affection when I tickled its chin. And from one house came the sounds of clapping to a guitar or two, castanets and a drum, beaten *con moto*

73

with the palms of the player. There was Spanish there, and Flamenco, but also a more Dionysian beat which I took to have come from the native Indian music. How to describe this music in one word? Latin-American seems to me as good as any.

As I approached the centre the buildings rose to two or three storeys with balconies on the higher floors and the street became cleaner since here it was not left to gravity to disperse the muck but to road sweepers with carts. Again the balconies were hung with flowers, and on one or two of them ladies, whose olive shoulders rose from clouds of lace and chiffon above voluminous crinolines, strummed in melancholy fashion on mandolins. Occasionally a door left open revealed beyond the grills a glimpse of patios cloistered with wooden carved columns, where fountains played and caged birds sang.

Presently, for all that a hot and steamy lethargy hung over everything, I became aware of a susurration of feet behind me, of chattering, and high-pitched but subdued calls, directed, I realised, at me. I turned and found I had attracted a small cloud of urchins who closed in on me like flies. These had nothing Iberian about them except black hair. Their faces were dark, with high cheekbones, and a sort of sculpted look to them, their eyes also dark and somewhat oriental in cast. They wore rags, square, patterned cloths whose corners hung between their knees and which were supported on their thin shoulders by means of holes or slits through which their heads were thrust. I doubt a simpler garment has ever been devised. Round their loins they wore ragged trousers to their knees, or cotton skirts, and those whose feet were not bare wore open shoes, sandals really, made from woven dried grasses. And they chattered and almost sang in a sort of high clickety language which owed very little to Spanish though I could hear some Andalucian in it.

I later learnt just why my appearance had stimulated such interest. It seems their religion taught them that a certain god had visited on the world a terrible hurricane from which few survived and those who did were turned into monkeys. Now my arrival came barely two days after just such a hurricane had swept through and past the town, and so I was supposed to have been in the eye of it and . . . turned into a monkey!

It was not long before we came to a stone archway which might once have been part of a town wall, before the town spread beyond it. At the end of the street which threaded it I could see a sunlit square with tall palms and, hoping that one at least of this tribe might advise me how to find what I was seeking, I turned on them.

'*Buenos días*,' I called.

They almost froze, transfixed. I tried again.

'*Buenos días*,' louder this time.

''*Días . . . 'días, 'días*,' came back at me, but uttered hesitantly. After all, who would expect a monkey to give you the time of day in the language of your masters?

I fixed my eyes on those, dark, liquid, deep amber, heavily fringed, of a girl who stood towards the front of this little crowd and seemed a little older than the rest. I guessed she was there to look after one or more of the smallest. She was the one who had answered most confidently, which was why I had picked on her, and on account of a lively beauty that emanated from her. She wore a shift above her skirt, rather than the square of stuff the others affected, and a shawl over her glossy hair which was woven into a plait that ended in the small of her back. Round her long neck, nestling above her sparrow-like clavicles, there was a string of what looked like chunky white beads. She was about my height, not more than an inch more.

I directed my speech at her, in Spanish of course.

'I need a barber,' I said, 'a tailor, some food and drink. I have money but not in the currency of your country so first I need a place where they buy gold.'

She gave me a long, slow look, her dark eyes expressionless, during which one of the urchins, a small boy of about four years old, came to her side, and, taking her thin brown hand, stood as close to her as he could with the thumb of his other hand in his mouth.

'Show me,' she said. Her voice was sharp, but not high-pitched.

I opened my palm, keeping my thumb on the guinea I still held in it. The gold glinted seductively. She turned to the others.

'¡A la *chingada!*' she snapped.

I was not then familiar with the expression which is definitely Mexican though couched in a Spanish sort of a way. It means 'fuck off!'.

This her small cohort, except for the limpet-like brat at her side, duly did, not literally, of course, but grumbling and with frequent sour looks over their shoulders as they went.

She thought for a moment or two more, then gave a tiny shrug of her bird-like shoulders. 'Come!' And she went before me through the arch.

Almost immediately she was accosted. There was a tiny *cantina* just inside with a small table and a wooden bench from which a large man unfolded himself into an upright position as we appeared. He was wearing what had once been a flamboyant uniform, dark blue with red facings, but was now shabby and grubby, the coat undone so that the larger side with froggings flapped in an unwieldy way beneath tarnished silver epaulettes. As he stood, his long, low-slung and heavy but empty scabbard clanged against the table leg. His face was crimson with broken blood vessels, his beard full and dark with streaks of grey beneath the remains of his latest meal. 'The fuck, Juanita, where do you think you're going?' A gravelly voice, lots of phlegm, some of which he hawked on to the cobbles a yard from my feet.

'Taking this foreign gentleman to Don Alfonso. He has a gold coin he wants to change.'

'That's no gentleman. That's a monkey. Has the circus come to town?'

'Take care, Don Pepe. He speaks good Spanish. He came off the Yanqui whaler and he really does have gold. So, he's a gentleman.'

The policeman, civil guard, whatever, began to button his coat. 'I'll take him.'

'¡A la chingada! He's mine.'

And she set off down the street with determination, still dragging the urchin with her. I paused, gave Pepe a shrug and a grin, to which he responded with another gob, and followed her.

We passed a few shops now, all closed apart from a greengrocer's watched over by a somnolent figure hunched up at the back, his sombrero pulled over his face. Amongst the serried ranks of vegetables and fruit, many of them exotics I could not name, he had . . . oranges. These were irresistible and I snaked out a wandering hand to filch one, but he must have been peeping through the latticed straw of his hat brim, for his lean, brown but strong hand flashed like a striking cobra and caught my wrist. Followed a brisk exchange between him and Juanita which ended when she gave him a small bronze coin. This bought three of the fruit and we walked on more slowly, shedding strips of the peel as we went. The first lick of my fingers during this process to remove a trickle of juice was like stepping from one world to another, so strong was the burst of euphoria that went with it.

I was on a boat no longer. The earth was solid beneath my feet, the shadows did not sway in my path. I was eating food as fresh as that morning's dew, and the whole mind-altering experience was amplified beyond even this as we strolled into the square.*

It was rectangular, the further end filled with the façade of the church or cathedral, the west door with a screen of tumbling *putti* surrounding a *pietà*, *La Nuestra Señora de Soledad*, done in plateresque style, beneath two twin-domed towers.

A gravelled walk bisected the vista, an avenue of palms above hedges of hibiscus in bloom, rose, red and white. The other three sides, including the one we had penetrated, were colonnaded with low arches resembling a cloister, but with more shops, offices and such like in the recesses. It was towards one of these that Juanita now directed our footsteps.

On a lintel, painted in cursive black lettering, decorated with curls and curlicues, were the words '*Don Alfonso Fereira y Guitierrez, Comerciante en Oro, Plata, y Piedras Preciosas*'.

Juanita lifted a bronze knocker and banged it back with a sound like a pistol shot. Six sleepers roused themselves from their day beds behind the square pillars and formed a little half-circle behind us. We waited. She fired off another shot. Again we waited.

'Come on out, you dirty old Israelite,' she shouted. 'It's Juanita from the harbour and I've got a gent off the whaler came in this morning with gold to sell.'

The gate of the judas slid back, and, darkly, because it was silhouetted against the bright sunlight filling a patio beyond, a head appeared. I could make out a skullcap, a lot of beard and two dark eyes that glinted out of deep, circular sockets. 'Be off with you, Juanita. That's an ape, not a gentleman.'

'Show him your gold,' she hissed at me.

Again I lifted my palm, but carelessly so that those behind saw what was in it. This produced a collective sigh from the toilers and mendicants, and a sort of suggestion that they might move in on us. Juanita held up her head, straightened her back. They could not see her face but they retreated. I began to feel it was a lucky moment, the one when she decided to accompany me.

---

* Acapulco was destroyed by earthquake and tidal wave on 31 July 1909. I cannot find any records confirming what it was like before then, but we must assume Eddie has it about right. J. R.

'Did you come by it fairly?' old Don Alfonso croaked, still maintaining his defences behind his very solid door.

'Paid off this morning,' I said. 'I shipped aboard at Valparaiso and this is what I have earned.'

'Why do you go about looking like the old man of the mountain?'

'Because he can't buy clothes or the services of a barber until you've bought his gold, you silly old cow.' Clearly Juanita felt it was time to get things moving.

Bolts squealed, locks grumbled, the door creaked and swung open. A huge Negro, seven feet tall and built like Hercules, fastened it behind us. We followed the old man across the patio – myrtle, roses, orange trees, a fountain, goldfish – to his office on the other side, and the Negro, who wore leather pantaloons with two pistols and a knife stuck in the red sash, followed us to Don Alfonso's office. Whitewashed walls, polished cabinets and bookcases filled with ledgers, a sturdy table equipped with brass scales, an ebony inkstand with all the accoutrements, a high-backed chair behind it and two three-legged stools in front and a large and sturdy chest, hooped with iron and secured with heavy padlocks, behind. Not a cobweb or spot of dust in sight. Now that we could see him in the clear sunlight, Don Alfonso was revealed as a neat and dapper man, old, granted, with a lengthy beard, yes, and an everlasting cold on his chest, but the beard and his long hair clean and neatly trimmed, his gown, made out of a very fine lightweight crimson velvet, spotless.

He took my guinea, unfolded the arms of wire-mounted spectacles, stuck them so they rested on the tip of his nose which was long, but not particularly Jewish.

'An English guinea,' he said. 'A spade guinea. No longer legal currency and too many of them about to be collectible. But it was honest coinage and if this is not counterfeit I'll buy it.'

He placed it in the left-hand tray of his scales and added small weights to the right-hand one.

'Spade guinea? What does that mean?' I asked as he busied himself.

'The shield on the obverse is pointed at the bottom, giving it the appearance of a spade. They were among the last guineas to be minted.' Using tweezers, he placed a last scruple or whatever on the tray and the two sides came to rest exactly level with each other.

'One hundred and thirty troy grains. Exact. Why should a Yanqui captain pay you in old English gold?'

78

I shrugged. He fixed me with an eye like an auger.

'It's not the only one you have, is it?' and his gaze switched to my cylindrical pouch which I still held tightly in my right hand. 'I'll give you a rate. Four of those to one eight escudos gold piece. And I won't buy less than eight of them.'

He held out his left hand. I put the pouch in it. He loosed the drawstring and tipped out the forty coins in a little shower of gold.

'Holy Mary, Mother of God,' said Juanita and crossed herself.

Carlos, still attached to her skirt, crowed and crowed, like the very bird of dawning himself. He knew a good thing when he saw it.

The deal was soon done, and I walked off with my somewhat detumescent pouch in one hand and a small bag made from coarser leather, containing two large gold pieces each worth eight escudos and a small handful of silver and bronze in the other. Don Alfonso came out into the patio but no further.

'Shalom,' he murmured, as the Negro led us back to the big door.

'By how much do you suppose he profited from the deal?' I asked Juanita as we skirted the pool.

She shrugged. 'He gave you three-quarters of the value for your gold. That's fair enough.'

I supposed she was defending her choice.

'How much did he give you?'

'Eight reales.'

The afternoon had moved on and the town was waking up. Quite a procession formed behind us as we proceeded round the *zócalo*,* made up of beggars, the unemployed, children and a few housewives or servants of the better-off burghers, come out to buy the makings of their evening meal. A group of itinerant Indians in multicoloured blankets and woollen peaked hats tootled on panpipes backed by a guitar and a palm-struck drum in one corner, and in another waiters straightened tables and chairs in front of the Ateneo, the club where men of intellectual pretension met to discuss the latest novel by Madame de Staël or Georges Sand to reach their shores.

Our first visit was to a tailor who sold me a decent linen shirt, pantaloons of white cotton with a broad leather belt and, best of all, a black coat, waisted, with short tails behind. Next, a cordwainer fitted

* Mexican for 'plaza'. J. R.

79

me up with a pair of serviceable boots. Across the square a barber shaved me and cut my hair. He also fitted me out with a wide-brimmed hat woven from dried Indian maize leaves and with a long leather cord. At each establishment Juanita was given a tip or commission, sometimes in silver, more often in bronze. Finally, as the municipal lamplighter went round the square lighting the large oil lamps set in each archway, we took our seats at the outside table of a small restaurant almost next to the Ateneo.

A waiter hovered for our order.

'Potato soup, grilled marlin and a bowl of fruit,' she said, and at that moment Acapulco went *loco*.

A crowd, similar to the one that had followed us, debouched into the square. From the middle of it all a sudden musket shot, fired upwards so that the smoke puffed above their heads and a small shower of sparks marked the descent of the wadding, shattered the air. Doves and pigeons clapped their wings and swirled into the violet sky. The crowd parted and in the midst of it, even at the distance of some fifty paces or so, I saw and identified those enormous eyebrows and that silver-streaked dark hair.

'Dere he is, d' fockin' bastard, lemme ged at him, leave off of me, let me gedadim! No! Dat's not what oi'll be doing. Gimme tat piece of yourn, Quoddy and let me blow his brains out.'

'Oh, ¡*mierda!*' I said.

Behind him, amongst other members of the crew of the *Town-Ho*, Quodlibbet, with his hair standing up like the crest of a giant bird, handed Seamus a second musket.

I touched Juanita's bare shoulder.

'Do you think you could find me somewhere to hide?' I asked.

'Cost you!'

'Naturally.'

She stood, took my elbow, and we scarpered, leaving little Carlos screaming behind us.

The oil lamp shattered above him, spilling glass and flaming oil on to the table, and the square again reverberated to the sound of the gunshot.

10

To cut a long story short, she hid me in a hay loft, took more of my coins and returned a couple of hours later with a plate-sized slab of dough – not the soup, fish and fruit I had been preparing to feast off.

Bootless to recount what my feelings and thoughts were while I was waiting for her. They were what you'd expect. But one fear kept recurring. I knew very little about Juanita, but one thing I did know was the wily way with which she always had her eye on the main chance. If Seamus outbid what she thought she could get out of me, then she'd betray me, and she'd not bother with a Judas kiss either.

I counted the chimes from the church clock against a general muted hubbub of the town coming to life after the long hot day, and shortly after the stroke of ten she was back. My eyes were now a touch more accustomed to the darkness, and I could just make out her head in the gap above the steps, and her movement, stooped below the eaves, across the floor towards me. She thrust the floppy sort of a pancake thing into my hand.

'What's this?'

'*Tortilla.*'

Potato omelette it was not, but a large disc of unleavened bread with a slightly bitter taste. Still, by then I'd have eaten crow, granted it had been cooked. Considering what I went through on Albemarle, maybe uncooked, at that.

She prattled on as I chewed away. 'There's ten, fifteen maybe, of them roaming the town after you. They have four muskets and one of them, he seems to be leading them rather than the Irishman who fired at you, has two pistols—'

'Can't be! He's the captain. Captain Gardener . . .' but then I bethought me – after all it was from his chest I had taken the gold. But would he leave the *Town-Ho* for that, with her holds and lockers almost filled with a cargo of blubber, spermaceti oil and ambergris? Why not – the Geordie mate and a guard of ten or so men would keep her secure.

But there was more reason than that, which Juanita now revealed.

'Their ship has a leak, and the shipwrights won't begin work on her without they're given gold in advance at least to cover the materials. So you see. They have to find you. And they will if you stay here. Here in Acapulco.'

Overcome with hopelessness, I groaned. 'I didn't take all their gold. There's plenty left.'

She shrugged. 'Anyway, they're here and they're staying here.'

'What shall I do?'

'Go to the city. Mexico City. It is so big no one will find you there . . .'

Now, and all through what followed, she spoke with a sort of quiet quickness, a personal urgency – she had, as they say, her own agendum.

Meanwhile, I racked my brains for what scraps of the geography of the New World might be stored within.

'How far? How long will it take?'

'The mule trains take three weeks; one left the day before yesterday. You can catch up with it.'

'How will I know the way?'

'I'll come with you.'

'You will?'

'If you pay me.'

'Of course.'

'And first you must give me three of the escudos that Don Alfonso sold you.'

'Why?'

'So I can buy a mule or a pair of donkeys to carry us.'

The geography was coming back. Mexico City. Head north and east and I would come to Louisiana. New Orleans. Cotton boats. A

82

passage back to Liverpool . . . My heart sang at the thought. I delved into the larger of my bags and came out with the coins she'd asked for. One of the gold pieces, each worth eight escudos, had been changed at the tailor's so that left one, but with a lot of loose change there as well. And of course I still had my thirty-two English guineas in the smaller bag.

'Juanita,' I said, 'I'm trusting you.'

'It's mutual,' she replied, took the coins and was gone again, pulling the trap door to behind her.

The clock struck midnight and a short while after I was aware of a dull, warm light coming up through the gaps in the floorboards. Someone with a lantern had entered the stable below. I tried to peer through the largest crack, but it was not large enough. I pressed my ear to it but could distinguish little of the bargaining or whatever was going on beneath me, except that it was between Juanita and a man with a deepish voice. After ten minutes or so he departed and she came back up the steps.

'Right,' she cried, and her voice rang with glee at what she had done and the prospect of what was coming next. 'I have bought the mule and the saddle and tack that go with it. Come on!'

'What, now? With six hours still before the sun comes up?'

'Of course! Do you want our departure to be observed?'

No! I forced stiffened knees to do what was required of them, and winced as the bones in my back cracked as I got up. Almost I fell down the stairs. Then: 'My bag. The one with the Mexican . . .'

'¡Estúpido! I've got it here.'

'Of course you have.'

Out in the alley there was a little more light than there had been, an orange half-moon on its back was just clearing the foothills to the east, before setting out across the sea. She led the mule out on to the cobbles, snorting and shaking his head.

'Meet Chiquito,' she said.

But chiquito, very small, he was not. He was a bloody great brute, eighteen hands, I'd guess, black shading to a dark, glossy brown, with enormous but upright ears and huge teeth. He was saddled up with a sculpted affair of rock-hard leather, as big as a throne with a low back and a pommel like a mushroom-shaped harbour bollard. The stirrup leathers were hidden in fringed, woven cloth. Juanita tightened the broad girth straps, raised the stirrups which were as big as buckets.

83

'Up you get.'

She held the reins as I tried to clamber on board. I failed. Chiquito stamped a hoof and struck a spark. Juanita, using the pommel and the back of the saddle as handles, almost floated on to his back.

'Follow us.'

I tagged on behind but, fearful of losing them in the darkness, took hold of the beast's long, plaited tail, advisedly keeping to the side in case he kicked out. He did, and missed. She dug her heels in and took us down the alley past more stabling to a tiny square with a pump in the middle. It had a low wall round it. Doing as I was told, I climbed on to the wall and tried again, with a little more success except that I ended up behind the saddle, looking out over the massive spread of the creature's buttocks. Juanita looked round at me then pulled herself forward against the pommel.

'¡Tonto! Turn round, and get yourself into the saddle behind me.'

Chiquito did not like it one bit. He sidled away from the pump and rubbed himself against the wall of the nearest house as if trying to dislodge me. However, even though at one point I was on my knees clutching the raised back of the saddle, I managed to clamber over it, and sat at last behind Juanita. She gave the brute another kick, pulled his head round, and as we moved off I almost fell sideways the other way. She sighed.

'You'll have to hold on to me. Put your arms round my waist.'

I did. She was so thin, yet so strong, it was like clutching the trunk of a young mountain tree, a silver birch perhaps.

We followed a track, straight at first since it marked a boundary between fields, and partly metalled. The moon rose higher and brighter behind us. We went through orange groves whose outer branches almost met in front of us, and whose globes of gold gleamed like lamps in a green night. I could have reached out and plucked them. And thorny pomegranates, odoriferous fig trees, and other fruits I could not put a name to then, but one, with plum-sized fruits many of which had dropped and were crushed, gave off a pungent smell like that of tomcats, but sweet. I asked Juanita what it might be called.

'Guava, tonto!'

Then came plots of Indian corn with melons growing between the serried stems and small fields of lower-growing vegetables, beans, peppers, perhaps, or animal fodder. Stands of palms stood at the corners of the holdings which were hedged with cactus or low, tumbling

walls covered in vines and creepers. An owl floated by and a fox signalled his presence with a bark before trotting busily across our path.

Presently we began to drop a little, even zigzag, and we could hear
the rustling flow of a steady stream. Banks of opalescent mist formed,
shivered, grew more persistent as the river, a sheet of white gold,
appeared through the purple darkness of the trees. The track met a
wider road which followed the river up and away from the town.

Juanita flung out her thin brown arm in front of us and turned her
head towards mine.

'Méjico,' she cried.

Her voice throbbed with longing and triumph together. She, we,
were on our way.

'Carlos,' I asked. 'What about him?'

'Carlotito? *What* about him.'

'Shouldn't you be looking after him?' I remembered that we had
last seen the poor little chap sitting in front of a table where burning
oil flickered over broken glass, and the crack of Seamus's musket
still echoed round the town's *zócalo*.

'Why?' She thought for a moment and then again turned her
head, this time with disdainful incredulity in her dark eyes. 'You
can't think he was mine!'

'No. Of course not, but—'

'I was looking after him for my aunt.'

'And she—?'

'Making fuckee-fuckee with your sailors.'

'Not mine.'

Chiquito clopped on, not fast, but steady, rhythmical. We were to
find he could do that from daybreak to dusk and even through the
night.

Dawn was as sudden as lightning out of a clear sky. Not that direct
sunlight reached us for some time, but where there had been a darker
darkness, a jagged mass against the lapis lazuli of the night sky, inlaid
as lapis lazuli often is with patines of bright gold, there appeared as if
in a theatrical transformation scene such as you might see at Drury
Lane, two huge peaks. Reddened by the sun, then gold, one of them
a thrust-up arch of the earth's crust, a gigantic, even at that distance,
bow of vertically fissured rock, was evidence of the titanic forces

that shaped our planet, many, many (if you will believe such *scientists* of today as Sir Charles Lyell, friend of Mr Darwin) millions of years ago.

Immediately there rose around us an unearthly symphony of sound. Close to there was birdsong, echoing across the river, trills, arpeggios, with appoggiaturas and other ornaments far beyond the reach of even the most gifted of coloraturas, then the cackle of parrots trailing their long vermilion tails across the bushes, and, right up close, sucking up not the nectar but the tiny insects that had got there first, a purple and green hummingbird, its wings a grey haze in front of the blossom it served. It was a chorus sliced and slashed with screams and hoots and squeals, and yet, from far, far above, the mewling of eagles calling to one another across the limpid depths beneath them could be heard.

Ahead of us a small grove of leguminous trees, filled with big black hanging pods amongst their feathery leaves, swayed and bent as a troupe of white-hooded monkeys swung like clowns through their boughs; a tiny deer, its pelt spotted like the sun flakes of the forest, danced tiptoe across our path. Suddenly Chiquito checked, head up, huge ears laid flat along his skull: a snort, and a most uncharacteristically uncertain whinny followed. The jolt brought Juanita awake, for she had been dozing, leaning into me, so my head was on her shoulder and my cheek warm against hers – I had been content to leave her so, for Chiquito seemed to know the way, and there were, in any case, no choices to be made.

'*¿Qué?* What is it?'

'*¡No sé!*'

Instantly alert, she narrowed her dark eyes, sat up dead straight, slowly scanned the riverbank and the forest, sniffed the air. Then she froze, except to bring her mouth a little closer to my ear.

'Jaguar,' she breathed, making the 'j' a long-drawn-out guttural sound, and almost a glottal stop on the 'g' so at first I failed to understand what the word was.

But then a looping, swinging movement of something very dark in a dark tree about ten paces ahead of us and twelve feet above us caught my eye, and slowly I made out the presence that had brought about Chiquito's petrifaction.

A long, glossy, black shape, marked with ebony mariposa spots, lay along the sturdiest of the forest giant's lowest limbs, and from that sweeping tail I had seen first to the hard anvil shape of his head which was set between small, rounded ears he was a full four or five feet long. He lifted his cheek from the back of the paw where it had been resting, bared feline fangs and the deep crimson of his throat in a low snarl.

'It's all right.'

She could have fooled me.

'He's already eaten.'

I sensed the downward cast of her eyes and saw at the foot of the tree the quarter-eaten carcase of some cloven-footed beast of the forest. Chiquito was not so sure and would not pass. Juanita kicked him, shouted, swore with obscenities I had forgotten since my boyhood in a Castilian village and others, no doubt Mexican, whose meaning I had yet to discover. But that wise mule had no intention of walking under a bough that supported a predator known to take not just mules but full-grown horses, too.

Eventually, and with a characteristic '¡A la chingada!' and moving in as unlady-like a manner as you can imagine, Juanita swung her long brown leg over the high pommel and slipped to the ground. Picking up rocks the size of monkey skulls, she proceeded to bombard the jaguar, together with taunts and high, brittle shouts of command, and in between throwing them she pranced in the air, spread her legs and arms, seeming to make her thin body twice the size it was.

We were terrified, Chiquito and I.

I was ready to gather the reins in my hand, turn Chiquito round and gallop all the way back to Acapulco, and I am sure he would have been all too ready to do my bidding.

But jaguar was puzzled. Cats have expressive faces, and I'd say consternation was the emotion he was experiencing. Cats will always bolt from the totally unexpected, though when the first spasm of fear has receded, their boundless curiosity may prompt them to return to work out what it was that had frightened them. But this one was not yet ready to do that. As the third rock thudded into his neck, he turned, and slipped in one long, lithe, fluid movement from his station and, with scarcely a rustle of leaves and no cracking of twigs, was gone into the undergrowth like a black shadow of nothing.

'There,' said Juanita, turning back to us with a little stamp of her bare foot, and pushing a damp lock of hair out of her eye. 'What's the matter with you two? Left your balls at home?'

Well, that was certainly true of poor old Chiquito. As for me, without actually checking I guessed mine might have shrunk up out of their little bag back to where they had initially come from.

She swung up into the saddle and when I tried to put my arm round her waist again, she sat forward with a disdainful wriggle.

'Keep your cowardly hands to yourself,' she said, so to remain reasonably secure I had to twist my arms behind me and get a grip on the saddle's high back. Off we went again.

After a time I grew bored with her grumpy silence.

'So,' I said, 'you have an aunt. But what about a mother and a father?'

She was brisk, matter of fact.

'Never knew them. A year after I was born my father was shot during the revolution against Iturbide.'

That made her about thirteen years old.

'And seven months after that my mother died with her sixth baby. I was the only one that lived.'

'I'm sorry.'

'Why? It happens. I said I never knew them. I grew up doing what I liked because my aunt had too many of her own to take care of to look after me properly. I do whatever I want to do, and now I am going to Méjico to make my fortune.'

She gave Chiquito a kick as if to get there quicker.

An hour or two went by. Intermittently the sun shone directly on my back, and in spite of the hat I had bought at the barber's in Acapulco and which, due to its long leather cord, I had managed to keep attached to me albeit for most of the time on my back rather than on my head where its brim would have been a nuisance, I began to sweat and feel dizzy. As we approached what looked like a junction of tracks with a narrower one than ours going off to the right, I realised I had to satisfy two contradictory needs.

'Juanita,' I moaned. 'I must shit and eat.'

'Gringos,' she sighed. 'No balls at all.'

Nevertheless she pulled Chiquito into a stop, got down, and even reached up a hand for me.

She pointed to the bushes by the roadside. 'In there.'

Well, I was not about to go far in. This was jungle, you know? Snakes, scorpions and tarantulas as well as jaguars. What I produced was not healthy. Effluent rather than shit, and very noisome. Which was her reason, Juanita said later, for taking Chiquito twenty yards or so up the lesser track away from the main one, though I believe she also wanted to put a distance between us while she too had a piss at least.

She was sitting on the bank almost out of sight when I came out and I crossed the main track to reach her.

'Give me your hat,' she said, getting up as I approached, 'and keep an eye on Chiquito,' who was now relentlessly tearing leaves off a bush and crunching them up.

I did as I was told. It was becoming a habit.

She was some time and I was beginning to get worried as well as hungry, but she came back eventually with my hat piled with fruit and nuts, almost all of which were strange to me. However, they made a fair enough breakfast though most were small and sour, not being cultivars but wild. I sat beside her and we munched away, spitting out peel, stones and pips until suddenly she froze, with a yellow date-like object halfway to her mouth.

'Someone's coming. Four of them. Up the hill. Come on!' And she pulled me off the bank and behind the buttress-like outgrowth of a very tall tree. I was beginning to protest: why hide? They would be bona fide travellers, surely? They might even have some Christian food with them, like bread or what they called tortillas. But she shushed me and presently I heard, too, the beat of horses' hooves in a steady trot, though how she knew there were exactly four of them defeats me to this day.

And then there they were. For how long could we actually see them as they went by? Ten, fifteen seconds? Long enough.

A mustachioed, unshaven brigand was in front, cluttered with a bandolier of cartridges, a sabre, and with a gun across his back, then Seamus, with his silver-streaked hair streaming behind those eyebrows that looked like the foam in front of the prow of a speeding ship, next Captain Gardener himself, both armed like buccaneers, and finally, swaying in the saddle more than the others, and very red-faced indeed, the civil guard who had made us stop when we entered the inner part of the town only the day before, and whom Juanita had addressed as Don Pepe.

Well, they went by without a glance in our direction, not exactly galloping, but very definitely in a considerable hurry.

'¡Mierda!' said I.

'Oh sheet,' she agreed, giving me a grin to show that she had made out what the word meant.

11

'We cannot go on as we were,' she went on.

'What do you mean?'

'They will catch up with the mule train. They will be told no one has seen us. They will come back looking for us.'

'What shall we do then? We can't go back to the town.'

'Of course not. We will take this trail.'

'Do you know where it leads?'

'It's the old trail. Shorter than the new one, but not wide enough for carts. If we're lucky it'll bring us out ahead of the mule train.'

I shrugged. There were questions to be asked. Had not the plan been to join the train rather than travel on our own? But I acquiesced and followed her back to Chiquito. She joined her hands low in front of her and managed to give me a bunk-up. We were on our way again.

Too narrow for carts? That should have warned me.

Immediately it became clear that, having left the bed of the river, this new trail was going to climb far more quickly than the one below had. It snaked, it zigged, it zagged, it hair-pinned. The slope across which it traced these manoeuvres became steeper and steeper to the point where one wondered how it was trees could still grow on it. Some indeed had given up, and their crowns of roots angled out from the stony, crumbly earth. Within two or three hours the species changed, too. The giant hardwoods of the jungle gave way to trees that were known to me from my boyhood and youth. Indeed, arbutus

90

with white, waxy flowers hanging in small clusters, juniper and sweet chestnuts put me in mind of the deep valley of the Batuecas in Spain, twelve leagues or so from Salamanca.

At this point we could still occasionally see the river, a thin, bright ribbon, meandering far below us between the darkness of the forest canopy and the piled crags beneath, but in the early afternoon we crossed a ridge and left it all behind us. The trail now debouched on to a wide expanse of long grasses and flowers through which a small stream gurgled and warbled and which supplied fodder for two long-horned, brown milch cows, stolidly grazing and tended by a young man. Beyond him was a roof of steeply pitched bamboo, or possibly stalks of Indian corn, from which rose a tenuous thread of lavender-coloured smoke. 'Thank God,' I said. 'We should be able to buy ourselves a decent meal and maybe lodging for the night.'

I was aware that Juanita's lips tightened.

'We'll get food if there is some already prepared, but we'll not stop the night here,' she said, growled really, the way a crossed cat does.

The boy, cowherd, stared at us across the grasses, but said nothing, though I called out a cheery '¡Hola, buenas tardes!' as we passed. He was perhaps fourteen years old, but tall for an Indian, being thin, and straight, with dark red hair that rose wirily from his forehead like a lion's mane. He was naked and his skin was a reddish leathery colour, his body, like that of an underage Spartan ephebe, well-formed for his age and size.

The cottage was the survivor, together with a small barn, of what had been a cluster of low stone buildings, now tumbled and ruined, perhaps by earth tremor or even a big spreading fig tree that had grown up amongst them. A woman, short, dumpy, in black with a grubby white headscarf, was standing in the low doorway beneath a grey, cracked beam as lined as her countenance. Her face was sculpted, heavily boned, teak coloured. She said nothing as we dismounted, but turned away through a beaded curtain and into her den as we approached.

'Una bruja,' Juanita whispered, and took my hand. Hers was icy.

Bruja? Witch. I felt myself shudder. Nevertheless, hunger sat on my shoulders like the Old Man of the Sea and drove me through that curtain.

A step down took me into a small, dark room lit only by the daylight that struggled through cobwebs covering a small, square hole set into the undressed stone. Facing me was a low fireplace in which smouldered the stripped cobs of maize that fed the thread of smoke we had seen. Primitive cooking implements leant against the wall of the wide chimney. The centre of the room was occupied by a long, scrubbed wooden table, marked and hollowed in the middle in a way that suggested it also served as a chopping board. Along one wall, under the hole that passed for a window, there was a makeshift bed of lashed withies with a sack filled with grasses, and at the end of it a small pile of unstripped corncobs. One last thing is worthy of remark. In the darkest corner, on my right as I entered, was a pile of what, in the gloom, and at first sight, I took to be large, round, grey stones. I took another look.

They were skulls.

The crone turned and faced me. 'Eat?' she asked. 'Drink?'

I tried to moisten my suddenly dry mouth and lips, but no meaningful sound emerged. She took my silence for assent and began to bustle about, in a slow but purposeful way. From a shelf she took down a misshapen bottle and a tin mug. She poured a colourless liquid from the bottle into the mug, and as she did something white, about two inches long and more or less solid, dropped from the bottle on the flow of the liquid. Then she took a wicked looking kitchen devil and sliced a fresh lime in half. Now she came up to me holding the mug and the half lime in her hand. Close like that I could smell her. Dirty yes, farmyardy perhaps, and sort of old, but not unwholesome. She put the mug and the lime on the table, and pulled towards her a large glazed earthenware jar, took my hand, and smeared a good spoonful of grey, sweaty crystals from the jar across the back of it. Then she picked up the mug and the lime again.

'Eat the salt,' she growled.

I did, and gagged on it, yet it filled a need and I licked my hand to get up the last traces.

She handed me the lime. 'Squeeze it into your mouth.'

The sharpness struck like a snake, the fragrant but bitter freshness lit my senses as if it were a handful of snow.

'Now drink.'

I made a mistake. I looked into the mug. There was a fat, white grub drifting above the bottom.

Her voice rose, peremptory, almost a squeak. 'All of it!' and I felt a prick in my stomach: the kitchen devil. I drank.

A glorious cataract of light, warmth, energy flooded my gullet like a rocket going down instead of up and burst like an exploding star in my stomach. Waves of euphoria rushed from its epicentre along all the rivers of my body reaching to my finger and toe ends, making the hair on the back of my neck start like the fretful porpentine's. Oh! I cried, and oh! again.

'Saint Margaret,' she croaked from behind me, 'Saint Margaret, pray for us now and at the hour of our death.'

'Oh yes,' I sighed. 'Oh yes indeed.'

And her knife clattered to the floor as Juanita hit her on the head from behind with my bag of gold.

Gold's heavy, and she got a swing on it as if it were lead shot in a sock, an equaliser.

Juanita took me by the hand and led me back out into the sunlight.

'You really are a *coño*,' she said. I'll not translate that, in case elderly people sensitive to words with sexual content should come across this account. But I should point out that in Mexico *coño* is particularly applied to people of Spanish origin which is what Juanita took me to be. 'Why didn't you wait for me?'

'Why didn't you follow me?' I mumbled, tripping on a stone, so she had to grab my elbow to keep me upright.

'I had other things on my mind.'

She led me up to Chiquito. 'Get on his back. You'll be safe enough there.'

Fortunately there was a handy bit of tumbled-down wall to help me on the way.

'And put your hat on. You don't want to get sunstroke.'

'Where are you going?'

'Unfinished business.'

And somewhat jauntily she sauntered off, pulled a feathery frond of grass as she went, sticking the moist end in her mouth. She disappeared behind a ruin in front of the giant fig tree. The lower branches dipped, heavy with green leaves and purple fruit, like a fancifully devised candelabra. Six heavily beaked, black-masked scarlet cardinals flew out of the top, and I saw a reddish arm come down through the heavy leaves, fig leaves indeed, to catch her hand as she reached up. A warm breeze carried the scent of figs towards me. I turned away. I have my sensitive side you know, and resolved to make the most of the gradually fading euphoria left by the witch's brew.

Presently the earth moved. A very minor shock, such as are fairly prevalent in that part of the New World.

Ten minutes or so later she came round the ruin again, looking at the ground but with a cat's quiet smile on her face which was slightly flushed as was the skin between her throat and the top of her shift. She climbed up in front of me, handed me a fig scented with sex, shook the reins, gave Chiquito a kick, and we were off again.

'That was nice,' she murmured. 'I don't think he's ever done it with a woman before. I showed him. Wild thing.'

When we were about halfway across the meadow, she turned in the saddle and gave a wave, high above her head. I turned, too. The red-skinned lad was standing on the ruin beneath the fig tree. He waved back.

'Made my heart sing,' she added with a sigh, and then set her face resolutely in front of us.

But half an hour later he was back with us and now with some scraps of garment on – patched, belted trousers whose frayed bottoms ended between his knees and his ankles, and stuck in the belt a short but serviceable looking sheathed machete on one side, a leather bag on the other. But far more extraordinary was what was on his head – a sort of crown of upstanding plumes, a bright iridescent green in colour, with some gold, edged with shimmering crimson. A handful of similar feathers decorated the spear he was carrying, just where the leaf-shaped head joined the hickory haft. Finally, his torso and face were marked, painted, with broad lines of zigzagging white paint or clay. The whole effect was decidedly comic.

He looked up at Juanita, and, even though he must have been running quite fast to catch up so quickly, spoke rapidly in their rattling language. She turned to me.

'He's a bit mad,' she said, 'but he wants to come with us. All right? He knows the way better than I do.'

We continued to climb, the three of us now. I remained on Chiquito's back, Indian held the reins in one hand, close up to the bit, but always remained behind the beast's eye so Chiquito was given to understand that he was the leader, he was setting the pace, could pick his own way through the boulders and fallen branches that littered the ground in front of him. Juanita walked on the other side of

Indian, close to him, often with her head on his shoulder where the unevenness of the way permitted it, and held his hand at all times. They chatted away quietly, in their clickety, sibilant tongue.

The forest of scrub oak with occasional mature trees merged into woods of pine through which scarves of mist gently drifted. Looking behind us I realised that we were above much of the cloud which now, as evening encroached, was shot with glittering gold beneath the beams of the sinking sun, or a lustrous lilac where the shadows of the mountains fell across it. But most wonderful of all were the plants that grew on the trees.

The first we saw was a wonder in itself, a clump of broad, succulent, dark green leaves, as big as a large man's fist and out of it, growing on a long drooping stem, a chain of brilliant white flowers, each with three petals above and a sort of tongue below, white I have said but with a centre of deep crimson and purple. Soon there were many of them, some on almost every tree, and then it seemed the trees only existed to support them, maybe as many as thirty or forty on a single trunk, each tree festooned with blooms. As the light thickened they took on an unearthly glow, hanging like small lamps in thousands.

Well, eighteen years ago there was no English word for them, but now our Natural Scientists have found one: orchids. Although many species exist as small plants growing on marsh land and chalk all over the damper parts of Europe, they go by the names common people gave them and were generally unnoticed by the gentlemen of the botanical societies. That is until Charles Hooker and John Lindley, also friends of Mr Darwin, discovered nobler and more obviously grand examples in the mountains of Assam. Full many a flower is born to blush unseen . . . until someone discovers its collateral relations. I digress. So? As Mr Shandy remarks in the Reverend Sterne's great work, digressions are incontestably the sunshine, the life and soul of reading.*

Onwards and upwards. The pine forest thinned. Lichen-covered rocks heaved themselves like whales out of coarse grass. The mountains, very much nearer now, reared up above us, with steep scree below climbing to the huge arched cliff face, a segment of the earth's skin, that soared between us and the peak beyond where streaks of snow lay like muslin in the shallower of the fissures. There was a

* Well, not quite, although Eddie has the gist. The exact quotation may be found in Chapter 22 of Book One of *Tristram Shandy*. J. R.

strong wind up here, driving the mist and clouds between us and the rock face, slicing us with a chill as cold as a knife. I could see how the trail followed the edge of the scree, then zigzagged up it, before losing itself in a serrated edge, a chaplet not of thorns, but rocks. Then over to our left, dropping into the far distant ocean, the sun sank. For a time it continued to light up the sky, turning high cloud first into liquid white gold, then ruby, and finally a deep purply black as solid seeming as the rocks themselves though the empyrean beyond and above still retained an aquamarine luminosity. With it gone, the chill bit even deeper.

'Chiquito will need all his strength and all his skill to keep his footing from now on,' Juanita said, after a brief confabulation with Indian. 'You must get down and walk behind him.'

I looked down at her, stared unbelievingly into the dark pools of her expressionless eyes. Clearly she meant what she said. With heart beating and feelings of chagrin and fear breaking loose in my head, I dismounted.

'If you want you can hold his tail again. He won't mind.'

As it climbed the scree the track – you could hardly dignify it as a trail any more – became even more narrow, barely four feet across. Looking down if one dared one was forced to wonder how and why the stones remained motionless on such a steep slope. Surely they should slip and slide into the wide basin that now opened up below us, a basin rimmed by that cirque of crags that looked far more impenetrable than any fortification built by man? Indian urged us on. I wanted to go back. But he was determined, it seemed, to get us to the point where the scree and the trail hemmed the rock faces while we could still see. Personally I didn't want to see anything – certainly not the backs of the eagles or vultures that cruised below us. Then came the cloud which gusted about us on the back of the wind. At first I thought it was a snowstorm, a flurry of tiny flakes no bigger than midges but as thick as a swarm of locusts, but it was simply icy droplets of water.

Now I could make out the angle on the shoulder of the mountain, where it met or broke up into the saw-edged cirque and the track crossed the ridge. It seemed to promise a sort of hope as the wind plucked our clothes, making them into sails that could carry us into the abyss . . . but what lay on the other side?

We were almost there when, such is the way with sunsets in those latitudes, suddenly all was dark, almost pitch-black. I could hardly see the broken surface we were meant to be walking on, what rocks were at my feet, though a false step would certainly have sent me tumbling down in a fall more horrid than one through empty air. With Juanita walking behind Indian, level with the beast's shoulder, I took hold of Chiquito's tail, as instructed, trusting the wisdom that says mules are more intelligent than horses, believing that if I did slip I would still be moored to the mule, but almost immediately he missed his footing, and the flick he gave with his rear hoof to re-establish his balance threw up a stone against my shin. I stopped to rub it with one hand, but kept hold of that hank of plaited mule hair with the other, hopped a couple of times, lost my footing and was dragged the last few yards to the col, the gap in the ridge, and the blackness of rock opened into the pool of darkness that was the sky . . .

Indian clicked and hissed at us.

'He says there's a cave five paces away, where we can spend the night,' Juanita said, as she helped me to my feet again.

It was not what I'd call a cave. More a sort of overhang about eight feet long, three feet high and about five deep but with the roof sloping down at the back. They pushed me into it and then busied themselves disencumbering Chiquito of his saddle and so forth, and discovering various useful objects, such as six tortillas, a leather bottle and a couple of blankets I had not realised were there, rolled up in a package under and behind the saddle. How they managed all this in what was to me almost pitch-darkness, with a precipice yawning at their side, I don't know. But they did.

We ate a little, drank lukewarm, tannic water, and then rolled ourselves up as tight and snug as we could, with Juanita in the middle, and I tried to sleep. It wasn't easy. The floor was a litter of gravel, rock and other less pleasant things as, I discovered in the morning, dried turds, presumably human. My companions seemed determined to indulge in intimacies that dragged the blanket off me so I almost froze; later they chattered incomprehensibly. And, of course, by what must have been getting on for the middle of the night judging from the moonlight which was by then spilling around us in spite of that inadequate overhang, I found I needed a piss.

The sight that met my eyes, as I performed the task frail Nature had imposed on me, was both exhilarating and terrifying. The moon was very bright for at that altitude there seemed to be no mists or earthly exhalations between us to dull its light. Facing west and south I could see how the mountain ranges we had crossed tumbled in irregular, descending, black ridges to the ocean itself, which seen from that height, was a more vast expanse than ever it appears from less Olympian viewpoints. It was silvered and chased like that wonderful shield of Achilles, casting back to the sky and the moon such light as lit up her dusky half so one could imagine the brightness of everything was enhanced by reflections thrown to and fro as between two mirrors.

I buttoned up and faced the other way and this was when the terror struck. How often have you seen the swooping and climbing mountain cirque linking two massifs above a deep and black cauldron-like basin and wondered at the hugeness, the weight, the solemn magnificence of it all? But have you also considered the forces of ice and wind and so forth which, through countless millennia, have shaped that broken crown? Well, I had not, and what it was that terrified me as I turned and moved a few steps to the north and east was the discovery that this ridge of teeth was by no means as substantial as I had thought. Not to labour the point any further, at the level on which our track appeared to cross it, it was no more than six feet wide and above that level tapered to a thinness only inches thick or less. One has heard such formations described as razor-edged. Well, that, pretty precisely, is what this one was. But that was not in itself the cause of fear. On the western face scree and rocky debris climbed almost to the roots of the teeth. On the other the rock faces plunged, shadowy and black, into a visually bottomless pit, untouched by the chaste goddess behind. My head swam and I clutched at one of those giant shards, and prayed that I would not prove to be that last straw on top of aeons of decay that might make it topple.

At this moment a stone skittered behind me and the sound was followed by that steady spring-like rush so typical of a young and healthy woman's micturition. I forbore to look round until it had trickled back to silence. Juanita straightened in front of our overhang and took the three steps that brought her to my side where she linked her elbow with mine.

'He's *loco*, you know?' she said, giving her head a slight nod backwards towards our resting place.

'How so?'

'He says he is Quetzalcoatl, come back to save our people.'

'Eh?'

'The god of the sun, lawgiver, wind god, messenger, even, for Christ's sake, the road sweeper. He writes the book of fate and he invented maize; he taught humans how to ferment maguey so we can get drunk. Like Jesus he went into the Underworld and saved all the humans there. Those feathers he wears are the Quetzal bird's, so that's who he is but he's also a snake and a river. The Feathered Snake. I ask you!'

'So?'

'He says he was hidden away in that cottage we found him in by a priest or some such to save him from the Christian god and that old hag was set to look after him and teach him the secrets of the universe and so forth. And that the prophecy was that when he came of age a young woman who is also a goddess would come and kill the witch and together they'd go into the land of the Maya, south from here, and lead an army to throw out the gringos.'

'You didn't kill her. The witch, I mean.'

'No. I didn't think I had.' She chewed her thumb. A cold breeze had got up and gusted about us. She pulled her cloak closer round her arms. 'But he says I did.'

I sat down in the lee of one of those rocky teeth, caught her hand and pulled her down beside me.

'Will you do what he wants?'

'What, go and live in the jungle with a load of uncivilised losers? Mind you, he's good at fucking. But that's not everything, is it? There's more to life than fucking. No. I want to go to Mexico City. That's where it's all happening.'

That's a relief, I thought.

'Well then. That's what we'll do.' And I squeezed her hand.

'He won't let us.'

'How can he stop us?'

'He's got a spear and a machete. He'll kill you and kidnap me.'

We listened to the wind for a minute or so. Then, together: 'He's asleep now . . .' 'Couldn't you hit him on the head like you did with . . .'

We looked each other full in the face. Her eyes were large and expressionless. Then we both stood up and she had a rock in her right hand and I had one in my left . . .

12

We approached our destination from the south, that is dropping through rolling countryside, with the two great volcanoes, the Great Warrior, with its thread of smoke climbing into the sky above it, and the Sleeping White Woman, Popocatepetl and Ixtaccihuatl, snowcapped and wreathed with cloud, that image of the perfect marriage under an almost pure morning sky. Far above us a few white clouds were racing windily after a pale, gibbous moon. Enormously high, too, some vultures were waiting, more graceful than eagles as they swung there like singed papers floating from a fire.

In front of us the arid, dusty plains we had crossed filled up with cactus farms and stands of maize stalks. Even before we could see the city its presence was marked by a dark, purplish haze lying in banks above it, for it was now the depth of winter and very cold, and fires were burning in every house and often on street and alley corners as well. I cannot be sure what the date was except to say that we were somewhere between the Epiphany and Lent, but, I would guess, still a day or so short of Candlemas. The year? 1836.

A fortnight earlier we had caught up with and passed the mule train from Acapulco, and a little later had passed another, and now we saw a third ahead of us. The city survived through the winter months on produce brought in from the coasts or picked up on the way, such vegetables as onions, potatoes, coconuts and so forth as do not perish, bananas and oranges picked before they ripened, and flocks of goats, sheep and cattle on the hoof. As we approached we passed through fields laid out in squares and rectangles, intersected with irrigation ditches but now mostly under the plough, especially nearer the walls, as if the inhabitants worked outwards cutting down and carting in the maize stalks as they died, for fuel and maybe fodder. Far away and to the east the silvery grey surface of a large, shallow lake reflected the dull grey of the sky. The traffic thickened as we got nearer: carts carrying produce in and carts carrying refuse out to dumps above which kites and similar scavengers cruised in vast flocks. Ribbons of shanties began to appear along the roadside, hens and cockerels scattered in front of us, emaciated dogs drifted listlessly in front of Chiquito's hooves, children eyed us sullenly from sack-covered doorways, thumbs in their mouths. The smell was much the same as that of most large cities: a potpourri of horse shit and human faeces but characterised by the local diet and fuel, in this case broiled peppers and squashes, and green smoke from the stalks and leaves of maize. Eventually we came to an arched gateway set in a mud-brick and stone wall some twenty feet high, rudimentarily battlemented. We passed through unchallenged and into a street wider than I had expected, and straight, almost you could call it an avenue on account of the stunted and pollarded trees that lined it, the houses quite grand, and many faced with stone carved in rococo twirls and arabesques with fancifully wrought balconies. Juanita now called to Jorge to halt for a moment, while she looked around, eyes lit up with wonder and excitement.

'Méjico,' she cried again, and one would have thought she was in Paris or London, or even Madrid, such was her approval of what she could see.

Jorge? Yes, he was still with us. You didn't imagine that we, Juanita and I, actually knocked his brains out, did you? Quetzalcoatl as was, but now plain George, divested of his plumes, but clad in a more serviceable leather coat Juanita had bought for him with my gold. And, such was his devotion to her, admittedly rewarded as it was with her favours on most nights, he had walked the whole way at Chiquito's neck and saved our lives too from brigands twice, and once from a fer-de-lance snake which, attracted by the warmth of our bodies, had slipped between us as we slept.

Where should we lodge? Could Chiquito be stabled? And, most immediately, was honest Christian food to be obtained rather than the mashes of thrice-cooked beans and chilli sauce served in tortilla envelopes that seemed to be the staple sold by street vendors from wheeled stalls. Was this the only diet of the inhabitants of this smoky, dirty Wen?

There are few questions in life that gold will not answer. On the way we had all but exhausted the escudos sold to us by Don Alfonso Fereira y Guitierrez, but by the middle of the afternoon Juanita had negotiated the sale of five more of my guineas though at a rate less advantageous to us than Don Alfonso's and in an office less well appointed than his. Indeed, we had to resort to what was little more than a cupboard in the cellarage of a broken-down town house with peeling stucco and boarded-up windows in order to make a transaction which was conducted by a skeletal *mestizo* with greasy grey hair, clad in a moth-eaten gown with huge cuffs from which only the cracked nails of his fingers protruded.

The market, when we came to it, was on the point of closing, which meant the stallholders were loading their unsold produce on to the backs of donkeys while old women, bent double with weakness, disease and age, scavenged at their feet for what had been dropped or discarded as unsaleable. We found a *cantina* that was filling up as the few with money to spare came in off the square for their main meal of the day. Jorge tethered Chiquito to a rail and we took a table from which we could keep an eye on our patient friend. Presently, and without asking us what our preference was, for there was no choice, an Indio lad, no more than seven years old and with a weeping sore on his lip, plonked down in front of each of us bowls filled with half a cockerel floating in a tepid, greasy gravy, garnished with shrivelled green chillis and a lump of grey bread; yes, bread at last! Needless to say the meat was also grey, stringy and tough as well. It was cold. And not the stew only. The sky had turned as grey as the bread and meat, there was no glazing in the window which we sat under so we could keep an eye on our mule, and a flurry of wet sleet gusted across the cobbles outside and even over our table.

Juanita, her elbows on the boards, chewing on the wing bones of her bird, leant towards me after first slapping away from her sleeve the importuning fingers of a beggar woman. She fixed my eyes with hers which had adopted the expressionless look I had come to associate with deception in her, or at least a hidden purpose.

'So, Eddie, what next?'

'Somewhere warm to sleep,' I suggested.

She shrugged.

'And tomorrow?'

'You know I aim to find my way back to England.'

She grimaced, at a loss as she always was when I mentioned the country which, of the three that I could claim as my own, I consider to be the one I am most native to. At a loss because she had not the least idea what I meant by that word.

'How?'

'It lies across the ocean. I shall need a ship. A passage on a ship.'

She waited, chewed on, wiped her small and pretty mouth on her sleeve, pushed a lock of black, glossy hair off her forehead, and drank from the cup of soured milk she had asked for.

'Can you find the ship you need on the lake?'

'No, Juanita, I cannot. I can cross the mountains to the east, to the port of Vera Cruz whence I can certainly get to the American port of New Orleans. And from there I can sail to England.'

'Or,' I added after a moment's further thought, 'I can go overland to New Orleans.'

She returned to her wing, slowly feeding the small bones out of her mouth and into her fingers.

'So you will not be staying here for long.'

'No longer than I need.'

Truth to say, I was not much impressed with what I had seen of Mexico City, albeit it is the most populous town in all the Americas.

Quite delicately she wiped her fingers on the crumb of her bread and ate it. She glanced at Jorge and muttered something in their bastard lingo, pushing back her chair and standing as she did so. What can she be up to? I wondered, with a sudden presentiment of impending loss. Then she put the leather drawstring pouch we had been using as a communal purse on the table in front of me, leant across the greasy bowls and kissed my forehead.

'Adiós, Eduardo,' she said, and was gone, with Jorge behind her.

I made as if to follow but a large man interposed himself between us and insisted I should pay what the three of us owed. He had an eye patch over one eye with a scar running beneath it and out the other side, while his good eye was the wandering sort that appeared to be focused on a space beyond my left shoulder. He had a butcher's knife stuck in his belt and I took him to be the proprietor of the

103

establishment. The seven-year-old boy, his son maybe, peeped out from behind him.

'First,' he said, 'you pay.'

A silence spread through the nearest diners. I guessed they anticipated an event that was not unusual enough to be remarkable, but remarkable enough to warrant their attention: namely the extraction from a reluctant diner of the money he owed.

I glanced over his shoulder. Out in the darkening street Juanita was climbing into Chiquito's saddle. I grabbed the pouch and struggled with the cord. But Juanita had pulled it tight and knotted it. By the time my fingers had loosened it they were going, Jorge as ever at Chiquito's neck, Juanita leaning over the pommel to speak to him, moving off into the now almost empty square.

She had left me with ten of my guineas and a good handful of escudos. Which was fair enough. She could have taken the lot.

Hasta la vista, Juanita.

Interlude II

**An extract from the diary of Francis Buff-Orpington,
12th April 1853**

After a somewhat vexing day dealing with a Mr Guppy, of the solicitors' firm of Henge and Carboy, anent the continued incarceration of Charlie (or, as he now prefers, Eddie) Boylan (or Bosham), I was rewarded with a very signal honour: an invitation to attend on Lord P. after suppertime, in the Coffee Room at the Athenæum. A. T. was in the company, bardic and leonine but oddly shy, perhaps because he had only recently been elected; and W. E. G., who was the recipient of much congratulation on his very recent Budget speech which will do much for the poor of this land, especially through the repeal of the Duty on Soap. Lord Brougham chanced by and was, with much jocularity, told he would now have to withdraw the soubriquet he bestowed so recently on the working classes, viz. 'The Great Unwashed'. I was somewhat embarrassed when Lord P. mildly and privately corrected my pronunciation of Brougham as Bruffam. Apparently he prefers Broham. Also present was Bishop S. W., and the philosophical naturalist R. O.*

---

* I should guess these are: the Home Secretary, Lord Palmerston; the Poet Laureate, Alfred Tennyson; the Chancellor of the Exchequer, William Gladstone; the Bishop of Oxford, Samuel Wilberforce; Richard Owen, then Professor at the Royal College of Surgeons, later the chief creator of the National Museum of Natural History; and Lord Brougham, Lord Chancellor under Grey and Melbourne. J. R.

After I had been invited to admire the portrait of King George IV, the last work of Sir Thomas Lawrence (apparently he was taken ill while touching in the star of the Garter on H. M.'s chest), we were served coffee and then got down to what I now realised was the purpose of this meeting.

Initially the conversation flitted around consideration of the recently reconstituted *Westminster Review* and the clique of radicals who appear to be running it under the ægis (suitable word to use in the Athenaeum!) of a Mr John Chapman. Several names came up, including that of a journalist with a philosophical bent called Herbert Spencer; Thomas Huxley, a doctor and ship's surgeon; an assistant editor Marian Evans* who is infatuated with Spencer while remaining the mistress of a Mr George Lewis, a married man; and some others whose names I am afraid I did not catch.

It was R. O. who narrowed the focus of our conversation to one particular subject of concern: apparently this nest of vipers are promoting, with some intellectual understanding, the doctrine of *transmutation*. I confess this puzzled me for the moment: perhaps somewhat overcome by being in the presence of so much greatness and goodness, perhaps too because the fine brandy I had been invited to take with my coffee had momentarily clouded my perceptions, I assumed that they were discussing Transubstantiation, a doctrine which I would suppose the bishop, who is a leading light in the Oxford Movement, would wholeheartedly support. But, in point of fact, it was he who excoriated *transmutation* most keenly.

It would seem, and I am not too sure how well I understand this, that they were referring to speculation that species can somehow change under the force of natural laws. 'Species' being their word for the different sorts of animals and plants, all living things in fact, on Earth, which were, of course, put here in their finished, created, unalterable state by God during the six days of creation. Now, and heaven knows, I am no theologian and no natural historian or, as they say nowadays, 'scientist', and for the life of me I could not see what the fuss was about.

The bishop put me right about that, not because he knew I was confused, but because the strength of feeling he was labouring under could not be denied the relief of speaking out.

* Aka George Eliot. J. R.

106

'God,' he announced, 'actively sustains the natural and social hierarchies from on high. If we allow this overruling Providence to be contested, if we deny this supernatural sanction, civilisation as we know it will collapse. If we allow this transmutation and it is taken up by the querulous working classes, the whole moral and social fabric will be undermined. Discord and deadly mischief will follow in its train. Revolution even.'

'I can't say I see why,' the poet interjected and I was at one with him on that.

'God created everything out of the ideas he had of everything in his mind,' the bishop expounded in reply, 'from polyps and barnacles to that peak of his creation, man, made in his own image. And men were also created each to perform his duty for God according to the talents God gave them. You recall, do you not, the parable of the talents?'

'Um, yes, indeed.'

'You, my dear sir, have a talent for versification. I for theology and also the ordering of a diocese.'

'And the gentleman who served our coffee and brandy?'

'He has a talent for serving coffee and brandy. He did it very well. As an earlier poet put it: "A man that sweeps a floor, and does it for thy laws . . . makes that and the action fine." Something like that. Now, if we interfere with these divinely appointed arrangements and allow Nature, or whatever, a hand in it all, then inevitably there will be people of the lower sort who will say it is not immutable that they should remain there. Whereas we know very well that, as Mrs Alexander's hymn – a saintly woman, you'll agree – puts it: "He made them high and lowly and ordered their estate."'

'All things bright and beautiful,' the poet said. 'But that's not how I see it. Not when I'm feeling down. To me it all seems a vile struggle, Nature red in tooth and claw—'

'Interesting you should say that,' the professor chimed in. 'For the man, a geologist turned naturalist, who is by far the cleverest and most painstakingly hard-working at sifting evidence and so forth that I know, seems to be coming to a similar view. He believes, I have heard him say, that when the survival of a species depends on defending itself from predators, or competition from other predators, or suffers a radical change in its surroundings, the ones that survive will do so because of certain characteristics they hold more strongly than their cousins. Through interbreeding forced on them by the extinction of their weaker brethren, of the sort our sportsmen use when attempting to produce a better racehorse, these characteristics will be further exaggerated to the point where it is correct to say that a new species has appeared—'

'Poppycock,' said W. E. G. 'A racehorse remains a racehorse, else the Jockey Club would not allow it to race.'

'He has good evidence for his views, but so far fears to publish them.'

'Why?'

'No doubt he fears prosecution for blasphemy, seditious libel, whatever crime remains on the statute books that a man we want to silence can be charged with.'

'So he should. What's his name?'

'Darwin. Charles.'

'I know the family. Unitarians. Which is a polite way of saying atheists. He married a Wedgwood, did he not?'

'And wrote a book. *The Voyage of the Beagle*—'

'His grandfather was Erasmus of that ilk,' the bishop chipped in. 'A Lunatic, a member of the Lunar Society. Who held similar views.'

'Indeed, yes,' said the poet, 'and versified them rather well.'

He began to recite, in a voice that was slightly tremulous, portentous, but kept low so as not to attract the attention of neighbouring tables.

> Organic life beneath the shoreless waves
> Was born and nurs'd in Ocean's pearly caves:
> First forms minute, unseen by spheric glass,
> Move on the mud, or pierce the watery mass;
> These, as successive generations bloom,
> New powers acquire, and larger limbs assume;
> Whence countless groups of vegetation spring,
> And breathing realms of fin, and feet, and wing—*

The bishop had had enough. 'It's all balderdash,' he cried, 'utter balderdash.'

And so it continued with each putting in his contribution in different degrees of condemnation, though for the most part Lord P.

* *The Origin of Society*, Canto One. J. R.

remained aloof from the debate, maintaining an ever courteous and graceful detachment. W. E. G. even suggested that if transmutation was going to lead the untutored and unthinking multitude into yet more occasions for sin than beset them now, then that was enough to warrant its suppression.

'But what if transmutation is true?' pleaded the poet, somewhat irritably.

'"Truth", as sinful mortals conceive it, through a glass darkly, has little to do with it,' the bishop exclaimed. 'If a "truth" arrived at by observation and the exercise of human reason contradicts the teaching of Holy Mother Church, and Holy Writ as interpreted by the Church Fathers, then, quite simply, it is not true. Someone has blundered.'

The poet froze for a moment at this, as though inspired, then nodded his head as if squirrelling something away in it.

'Yet,' he said, once he had recovered, 'the study of Nature must give us cause for doubt—'

'Devil-born doubt?' Lord P., with a twinkle in his eye, making one of his rare interventions.

The poet glanced at him gratefully.

'You quote me, sir. In which case you will know how it goes on: "There lives more faith in honest doubt, Believe me, than in half the creeds . . ."'

Shortly after this exchange the meeting broke up and Lord P. did me the great condescension of inviting me to accompany him on the short walk back to his residence.

'Buff-Orpington,' he began, once we had turned the corner out of Waterloo Place and into Pall Mall, 'I must confess I had a reason other than a wish to enjoy the pleasure your company gives me, in inviting you to our little soirée. The activities of the *Westminster Review* set would, thirty years ago, have laid them open to inquiry and prosecution under the Six Acts. Those were in the days when Liverpool's government had to deal with farmers and artisans like Orator Hunt and Will Cobbett, paupers like Leigh Hunt, and madmen like Shelley, people clearly still under the influence of the Jacobins, Spenceans and so forth. Nobodies, but all capable of inflaming the masses to riots and emeutes. But this crew are different. Some, of course, like the woman Evans, come from peasant stock, but others are altogether more worthy, from moneyed backgrounds in manufacturing and so forth.'

He walked on for a spell, hands clasped behind him in the tails of his coat, then turned his head towards me again and gave a short laugh.

'No doubt the Duke had a point when people of this sort first turned up in Parliament and he referred to the quality and style of their hats, but that was twenty years ago and since then they have attained respectability and, more to the point, respect. Some of them even wear decent headgear. What's more we rely, in the House of Commons at least, on their continued support. We must, therefore, be very sure of our ground indeed, before we make any sort of a move against one of their number. In short, I want to have a much clearer idea of what aims these transmutationists have, of what exactly they are about. Are you following me? Do you catch my drift? For I assure you that it is, at the moment, no more than a drift. Not a current.'

'Um, as I understand it, you want to, er, know more about them?' I ventured.

'By God, you're sharp.'

I suspected sarcasm, which he was at pains to render harmless.

'No, I meant no offence, I assure you,' he graciously added.

We walked on, my mind in a turmoil, and passed through the penumbra of a gaslight. Illumination came at the same time.

'You wish, sir, to have them investigated, but you do not wish to appear to have ordered the investigation.'

His Lordship stopped, with his back to the light, so all I could see was the high profile of his beaver and the corners of the stylishly cut collar of his coat, much like a Silhouette.

'Buff-Orpington. You may well be right. But it's not a matter on which it would be proper for me to comment. I see a "bro-ham" approaching, plying for hire, which I will take. I wish you a good night's rest and success in all your endeavours, whatever they may be.'

So. Not returning to his official residence after all, in spite of the advanced hour.

Another extract from the diary of Francis Buff-Orpington, this one dated 15th April 1853

Charlie, Eddie, whatever, is still being very difficult, even though Mr Guppy's application to have him set at large on a plea of habeas corpus was successful. I wanted to have it challenged but the solicitor general, or rather one of his pompous minions in Chancery, had a look at the papers and said we hardly had a leg to stand on, so I was perforce required to sign a warrant setting him at liberty.

But this, of course, was not enough.

He whined at me, on the very steps of Millbank, clutching my sleeve like some importuning beggar with one hand, and every so often wiping his nose on the sleeve of the other. He stank too. Almost enough to mask the fumes rising from the Battersea sewage outfall which, as the weather gets warmer, are already becoming a serious nuisance.

'Oh, Mr Buff-Orpington, surely you will not cast me out like this, homeless and penniless as I am, on the mercies of this merciless city. I aint got a bean I can call my own, Mr Buff-Orpington, you know that's God's truth . . .'

And so on.

Whatever else he is, he is unashamedly Thespian – one moment he'll talk as grand as, well, if not quite a gentleman, at least with the manners and grammar of a country curate; at the next he'll play the wily Dodger, and a moment later a snivelling mendicant, and all, almost, to the manner born. I say 'almost' for there is always a touch more in the performance than is needed to make it credible. It would do across the footlights of Drury Lane, but in broad daylight, on a city street, well . . . it's just a touch too much.

Enough. After wheedling came the threat. Those damned papers. Well, I held him off with a five pound note; he would, he said, have preferred the yellow, by which he meant sovereigns, but took it nevertheless. I doubt I'll get it back. He set off across the Vauxhall Bridge saying he had once had rooms on the other side and he would look around to see if they or others like them were available. I waited long enough to be sure that Will Wiley, one of our best trackers, was securely in tow, and made my way back to the Home Office.

How long will the fiver last? How long before he's back again? Will I get that sheet back?

And the 17th April . . .

Wiley reported. That bastard Eddie got himself well spruced up, almost respectable, and what did he do? He only took all his manuscripts, the

111

full tale he's been writing up, to Albemarle Street where he called on Mr Murray. He's going to try to get it all published! Certainly all his prison scribblings over the last four months, but maybe too some of what is in those missing papers. This will have to be stopped.

And on top of everything else Lord P. caught me in a corridor of the Office, and very discreetly reminded me of the Darwin business. Transmutation and so forth.

My goodness. I've just remembered. Eddie was on the *Beagle*, or says he was. He knows Mr Darwin, is acquainted with him. Might there not be a way here of killing two birds . . . ? Jehosaphat! I'm sure there might be. I'll look into it first thing tomorrow.

Part IV

TEJAS

You may all go to Hell and I will go to Texas.

DAVID CROCKET, on being rejected for a fourth term as
Congressman for Tennessee, October 1835

13

I realised that it would be bootless to attempt to follow them. Even if by some miracle I had chosen the right alley they had made their intention clear: they wanted no more of me than they had taken, and to meet up with them would only invite a repetition, perhaps more painful than the first, of our parting. Mine host, now my warm friend since he had been paid (possibly overpaid), informed me that his *cantina* also functioned on the upper floor and behind the kitchen as a *posada*, and that I might spend the night there. The accommodation turned out to be augean rather than spartan, consisting of a cot behind canvas walls which divided into six a room that would comfortably have slept two. It had not been swept for a year, I would guess, and the jericho not emptied for a week. The straw-filled sack which served for a mattress was home to a small zoo of insects, as was the coarse woollen blanket, but, owing to the proximity of three other human guests, the whole space was tolerably warm, and that was enough as far as I was concerned. I had, after all, been sleeping rough for a month.

I was woken at cockcrow and the description is well chosen. One thing Mexico City seemed to have in abundance was cocks: for half an hour they drowned out all other noises, even the clangour of bells calling the faithful to Mass. I scorned my landlord's offer of breakfast, but decided that the Plaza Mayor might be the place to be if I were to discover what opportunities the city offered. I took directions in

115

the market that was already coming back to life, bought an orange, which I peeled and ate on my way, and set off over the mile or so that I had to cover, most of it on another of these wide and quite commodious avenues that crisscrossed the inner town in a rational grid.

The weather was still notably cold though occasional gleams of sunshine breaking through the racing clouds were hot. Nevertheless, the sight, quite near the centre, of a coffee-house abutting the pavement, with a stove inside, taken with the weight of gold in my pocket, dragged me inside. Here the liveried serving person did look at me askance, until I showed him a palm with a couple of silver escudos in it. He took my order for a bowl of hot chocolate and sugared *churros* without further demur and showed me to a dark sort of a cubicle away from the windows, and next to an elderly gentleman reading a large newspaper – El Diario Urbano.

As I dipped the first of the fluted doughnut strips into the froth that filled the top of the bowl I was startled by a clattering of paper, followed by the swoosh of a crease folded in on itself, all accompanied by a wheezing, sustained sort of a chuckle from behind the newly reconstituted wall of newsprint that now almost blocked out what light fell on my dark little table.

A headline caught my eye: SANTA ANNA THREE DAYS' MARCH FROM THE RIO GRANDE. Santa Anna, the mother of the Virgin? I was still wondering what this meant when the wall of newspaper crumbled away like an inadequate fortification exposed to the force of a sapper's mine from below, and I found I was looking into a pair of watery grey eyes set on either side of a high-beaked nose, which separated prominent cheekbones, a long jawline and an emaciated grey mustachio and goat beard.

'GrrraTHias,' rasped the voice from between thin but moist lips. 'GrrrrraTHias,' said with even more emphasis. 'I have not, señor, heard such a markedly Castilian "TH" these fifteen years. Forgive me, sir, for this intrusion, but I find I have to ask you where you learnt to speak in so proper a fashion. One would guess, from the way you addressed the waiter, and thanked him with a "grrrathias", that you are a gentleman from the old country, were it not that your threadbare appearance somewhat belies that assumption.'

I told myself that an exhibition of affront at his characterisation of my appearance, whether prompted by its lack of gentlemanly quality and Iberian style, would not be productive of anything but ill temper

116

in both of us, and answered as easily as I could that I was brought up within a league or so of the twin cathedrals of Salamanca.

'And you studied at the university? Then you must be a man of learning. Perhaps you attended lectures in the medical schools? I can find you useful employment if that is the case. And . . .' he positively twinkled at me, 'you will forgive me if I say you look as though you could benefit from an occupation that could bring you a modest emolument. Your name, sir?'

'José Carlos Eduardo Boz'am. You have the advantage of me.'

'Miguel Quesada y Saavedra. At your service.' And he reached across from his table to mine, offering his hand. His fingers were long and thin, but his grip surprisingly strong.

In no time at all, it seemed to me, we were walking towards the Plaza Mayor. The nearer we got to the centre the larger were the crowds with more of the better sort amongst them. And my interest in them and everything else around me somewhat distracted me from what Don Miguel was trying to tell me about the employment he was about to procure for me. There were, it seemed, Federales in the northeast of the country who wished to govern themselves while remaining Mexicans. But the government was committed to centralising all, and ruling the whole country from Mexico City. A general had been commissioned, or, since he was President but not actually president (this I admit was confusing), had commissioned himself to lead a column of six thousand men with a score of cannon against these Federalista provinces. Whatever else it was clearly a very minor, insignificant sort of a thing, which was demonstrated by the fact that this general/president had set off some weeks earlier but had omitted to take with him that most important arm of military might, a field hospital.

By now we were in the Plaza Mayor, dominated by the huge cathedral on the east side, an enormous baroque structure, then barely finished, whose older parts already looked decayed and neglected. The square was much enlivened by a group of uniformed children, from an orphanage perhaps, who sang an enchanting if repetitive hymn to the Infant Christ in guaracha rhythm.

> En las guarachas ¡Ay!
> Le festinemos ¡Ay!
> Mientras el niño ¡Ay!
> Se rinde al sueño ¡Ay!

117

Spanish songs celebrating the Nativity are so much more jolly than English ones, are they not?

Don Miguel led me over to the north side of the square where six large waggons, or fourgons, had been lined up, each with six mules, but smaller than Chiquito, and a troop of light cavalry as escort.

The general who was in command (I was to learn that no command of any significance in this 'army' held a rank lower than general), a young man for all that his shoulders were loaded with bullion tassels and his fore and aft hat was huge and plumed, approached and saluted Don Miguel, stamping his boots as he did so that his silver spurs jangled.

'You are late, Excellency,' this popinjay barked, 'but now you are here we can I suppose, depart. I am assuming that the creature at your side is the medical orderly you promised us.'

'Indeed, he is,' cried Don Miguel, and pushed me forward. 'Señor José this and that, newly arrived from no lesser place than the medical schools of Salamanca itself. Don José, this is your commanding officer for the time being, General Don Pedro Castellano de Orjiva.'

Some of what Don Miguel had been saying had penetrated my addled brain. Was this field hospital not bound for the north-east territory? Would this not take me a substantial part of the way towards New Orleans not only at no charge to myself, but riding in a waggon, and presumably paid to be there? Would I not be under the protection of friendly cavalrymen? This was surely a better way of taking a step or two in the right direction than trying to find my way with nothing but my own meagre resources. The 'general' cast a very doubting eye over me, then shrugged and turned away, barking (he was fond of barking) at a trooper with a bugle as he went. The bugle sounded, the troopers mounted, the waggon drivers, two to a waggon, cracked their whips and whistled up a storm through fingers pressed into their mouths, metal screamed on metal, wheels rumbled on cobbles.

I was about to launch myself at the third vehicle as it began to pass me but Don Miguel caught my elbow.

'Don José,' he hissed, 'I have found you a job. You will be paid. I think I deserve a commission.'

I hesitated.

'I may feel bound to inform the general that your qualifications are after all virtually non-existent.'

I rummaged in my pocket, pulled out a silver escudo. Don Miguel's eyes flashed, his thin fist closed on the silvered knob of his cane.

'Pray, do not insult me.'

I fished about for my purse, found a guinea and tried him with that. He was incredulous at first but after examining it carefully, gave me a gracious smile and urged me to climb over the tailboard of the last waggon. Once in I turned to wave at him, but he had gone.

14

I was not alone. Sitting on the bench on the other side and at the further end behind the driver and his mate, beneath the canvas roof, was a priest. He was wearing a large-brimmed black shovel hat, and a black soutane with a leather belt from which dangled the quite large and knobbly beads and crucifix of a rosary. He had a small breviary open on his knees. He was fat, not grossly fat but certainly not ascetic, and his countenance, which was florid, was entirely European in appearance, though not particularly Spanish. He introduced himself as Father Jaime Irregui, or some such name clearly Basque in origin.

'I take it,' he said, once the formalities of introduction were done with, 'you are a doctor-surgeon.'

'Hardly,' I replied. 'In fact not at all. The gentleman who put me in this position was under a misapprehension.'

'I think not. Don Miguel is surgeon general to the garrison of the city. Had he not found you, he would have had to take the position you are now in himself. And that he was loth to do. The rank of surgeon general is normally a sinecure. He was not expecting to have actually to practise surgical skills for which he is probably even less well equipped than you are. In short, you got him out of a hole.'

He bounced from side to side with the motion of the waggon for a moment or two, then continued.

120

'It would seem that between us we supply the wants General-President Antonio López de Santa Anna Pérez left unfilled when he marched his men away.'

He took in the look of mute enquiry I offered him.

'The army left with no priests and no hospital. It is to be hoped they will need neither before they engage the Federalistas and we must hope we can overtake them before that happens.'

To me this seemed an unnecessarily officious attitude. My own hope, indeed desire, was that any fighting might be well and truly over and done with before we came up with it. But then I had experience of the horrors that accompany modern warfare having been at numerous battles, most notably that of Salamanca itself, and Waterloo, both of which I did my best to run away from.

I should add at this point that Antonio López de Santa Anna Pérez was always known as Santa Anna to distinguish him, I suppose, from thousands of Antonio Lópezes, a name in Spain and Spain's colonies as common as John Smith is in ours.

It took us about a month to catch up with the Centralista column in San Antonio de Bexar which we actually reached just a few hours after Santa Anna had himself ridden into the town. During that month we had, after all, opportunity for Father Jaime to exercise his real skills and I those I pretended to. A week or so before we arrived at San Antonio we ran into a Blue Norther. This is a column of cold cloud, deployed into a battle line or front, driven by an icy wind from the mountains and forests of Canada, right across the Great Plains and into Mexico, bringing with it extreme cold and even snow as much as two feet deep. Its approach is marked by a distinct blue line, darker than the normal colour of the sky, stretched across the northern horizon. Temperatures drop to twenty degrees* and the whole phenomenon can last several days.

We witnessed its aftermath after toiling up a very long if gentle slope across what was virtually desert marked only by the strangely branching limbs of large cactuses, interspersed with the more vulgar variety, called *dildos*. We crossed a watershed and began to descend the steeper north-facing slopes which had been exposed to the full force of the freak weather and discovered that the roadside was littered with frozen corpses, inadequately garbed, many still clutching

* Fahrenheit, of course. J. R.

121

their muskets. Father Jaime wanted to say the last rites over each of the first dozen or so we came across, the ice still beaded in their beards, those that had them, the extremities of their limbs blackened with frostbite, but General Don Pedro urged him to condense the rite into one that would do as much for the souls of all as for each individual. It seems Father Jaime was new to the job of army chaplain and was unaware that this was the usual procedure designed to ensure the expeditious transport of a battalion of souls, as readily as that of a single spy, to the foot of the Judgement Throne. Towards the end of the six miles or so over which this broken line of bodies stretched we came across one man who was still alive, though the frostbite on his feet had turned gangrenous. Father Jaime insisted that I should try to save him and I did my best, aping with the saws and knives with which the travelling hospital was equipped what I had seen in the aftermath of the great battles I had served in twenty years earlier. The job I made of it was good enough to convince Don Pedro and the priest that I knew what I was about, for I was as successful in the procedures as most surgeons are – my patient died in agony after I had been at him for ten minutes or so. After that, we all piled back into our waggons and continued on our way. General Don Pedro thought about a thousand had died from the cold. I would guess the number was nearer fifteen hundred.

A few hours later we used a ford to cross a wide but shallow river called, somewhat unimaginatively, the River Big, or *Río Grande*. The spring rains had raised the level and a couple of muleteers who had got out to urge their beasts on through the quite swift current got their backs wet but came to no further harm. On the other side of the river there was a small township called Laredo where we were made less welcome than in any of the townships we had passed through until then. The reason was that we were now amongst the Tejanos, as they were called, who were Federales to a man and woman, both gringos and spics, that is Americans recently arrived and those of some Spanish blood who had been there somewhat longer.

It was at Laredo that Santa Anna split his army into three columns. He remained in command of the centre which marched on San Antonio de Bexar. It took us another seven days or so to catch up with him. He arrived only a few hours before us at San Antonio de Bexar hoping to round up the gang of some two hundred or so Federales, most of them rogues, trappers, failed lawyers and the like, who had occupied the town, which was no more than a village really. Unfortunately Santa Anna's cavalry approached the town slowly and without any attempt at concealment. The consequence was that this band was able to escape into a nearby mission, dedicated to San Antonio de Valero, which lay just outside the town on the far side of a shallow creek, so shallow that it had never been thought necessary to build a bridge across it.

Now that we have actually come up with him, I should also say a word or two about this Antonio López de Santa Anna Pérez, president and general. Tall for a Mexican, he was good-looking in a saturnine sort of a way, with very dark hair brushed or combed forward over his temples. He wore a high-collared uniform at all times, much embroidered with silver and gold and hung about with stars and crosses. In his shirt he had three diamond studs worth five thousand dollars, and he travelled with his own china, silver, including a silver pisspot, glassware and whores. One of these was a thirteen-year-old girl who put me in mind of Juanita but was not so much of a person, as she felt constrained to play the part allotted to her. He had found her in Laredo and brought along her mother as well. Finally there was Ben, his Negro cook, an escaped slave from Louisiana, a tall, taciturn fellow, very black, who wore a flunkey's livery and white kid gloves whenever he was not actually operating in the kitchen. None of which surprised me – I had seen both French, Spanish and English commanders travel in similar style in Spain, though not of course the Duke who always kept things simple.

Not only in this was he different from Wellington for Santa Anna liked to be called or thought of as the Napoleon of the West, having studied all the Corsican tyrant's campaigns. In fact he was quite skilled in the arts of warfare but was badly served by his men who were brave enough but virtually without training being Indios recruited or pressed *ad hoc* for each campaign as it came along.*

To return to our arrival at San Antonio. Santa Anna drew up his vanguard in sight of the mission building, and demonstrated in front of it with a red flag which he continued to fly from the church tower in the town. According to the rules of war this signified a demand for

* Eddie does not seem to be aware that in 1853, when he was writing this account, Santa Anna was once again President of Mexico after spells in and out of office. J. R.

123

immediate surrender with the threat of the garrison being put to the sword if capitulation were not forthcoming. It was answered by a cannon shot, an eighteen-pounder, which was taken as a sign of defiance. Four cannon shells from the Centrales army were loosed off back into the mission compound.

I should say at this point, in case there is any confusion in your mind, that this had all started as a civil war between Federales and Centrales, both sides being Mexican, and remained so as far as most of the garrison of the mission were concerned, as well as in the mind of Santa Anna. This was Mexico. The government of Santa Anna was Centralist, the new constitution was Centralist. The Federalista Tejanos were therefore traitors. Throughout the siege of the mission the Texians, or Tejanos, flew the Mexican flag, the green, white and red tricolour, but with the year '1824' inscribed on the white panel, signifying that they acknowledged themselves Mexican but supporters of the 1824 Federalist constitution. Simple as that. I mention this because a whole sack of misconceptions about the whole affair has been *spun* out of it designed to elevate the garrison to the condition of martyrs, martyrs for an independent Texas, martyrs even for the United States. I lived in the States for more than a decade but it was in the aftermath of San Antonio that I first encountered the easy readiness with which 'democratic' politicians and newsmen twist and corrupt the truth of any situation to reinforce a popular myth. Many more instances were to come and most far beyond, in the way of corruption and mendacity, those an English peer or even a member of the Commons, would dare to perpetrate in the face not of the common people but his peers.

Well, I don't intend to bore you any more on that subject nor with an hour-by-hour account of how things went for the following week, except to say that the Centrales kept up a steady but ineffectual bombardment for most of the time, ineffectual because the garrison had several sharpshooters with long hunting guns and rifles which prevented the small cannon from being brought into properly effective range, and, apart from one twelve-pounder, the besiegers had nothing that could make an immediate impact on the walls of the mission outside of the range of these sharpshooters.

Incidentally, a word may be appropriate here about the weaponry the Centrales used. This consisted for the infantry of Tower Muskets, the old Brown Bess of the British army through Spain, Waterloo and the 1812 war against the American states, supplemented for the light troops with the Baker rifle, an equally important weapon in the old wars. All these were sold on after the wars to emergent nations across the world, but particularly to the rebel states in the Americas fighting first for independence from Spain, then against each other. It was an odd thing to look at these Indios drawn up in columns or trooping their colours and to think of how I might have seen their ironmongery last in use on the plain of Vitoria or the slopes of Mont St-Jean. And the irony of all this was further compounded when I realised that their blue jackets, white bandoliers, white trousers and black shakoes were those of Napoleon's Grande Armée. For how long will this sale of excess or out-of-date weaponry and uniforms from civilised nations to their lesser brethren go on? For as long as wars are fought and money is to be made by dealing in them, I suppose.

On day seven of the siege, February 29th (1836 was a leap year), Santa Anna sent a message into the mission inviting anyone who cared to surrender to come out, but particularly directing his message, which was in Spanish, at any Tejanos who might be there. Under the Rules of War as understood by professional soldiers the world over, this was a magnanimous offer. The facts of the matter are clear. A fortified place which refuses to surrender (and refuse they had, by token of that first cannon shot) can only be taken by storm, whether or not the assault is conducted through breaches in the fortifications. This is absolutely bound to mean that very heavy casualties will be inflicted on the attackers. Not for nothing are those who head up such an assault honoured as the *Forlorn Hope* since all can expect to be killed. Consequently, to avoid this slaughter, a besieged place is always offered the opportunity to surrender honourably, the garrison being allowed to march out with colours flying and bearing arms. If, however, they refuse this offer it is understood that if they are not relieved, and the place is taken by storm, then they must expect no quarter. They will be killed. No prisoners will be taken. This threat is made to avoid the horrors of an assault. It is a pointless threat if it is not carried out. There is a third option, a middling option. The first demand for surrender having been met by defiance, the besieging general can offer the choice of *surrender at discretion*. By this he means the occupying force may march out but take their chances. It will remain in the attacker's discretion what he does with them – he can shoot the lot, imprison them, or treat them as prisoners of war. This offer Santa Anna repeatedly made throughout the siege.

The commander of the mission was a certain William Barret Travis, a lawyer by trade, a renowned gambler and womaniser who suffered from venereal diseases, but nevertheless had been given a uniform and a commission as Lieutenant Colonel of Cavalry by the Federalist convention, then meeting in the village of Washington-on-the-Rio-Brazas some two hundred miles away. That he was not ignorant of the Rules of War is demonstrated by the letter he wrote at the beginning of the siege addressed to the People of Texas and All Americans in the World: '*The enemy has demanded surrender at discretion, otherwise the garrison are to be put to the sword, if the fort is taken . . .*', thus showing that he knew very well the inevitability of what would follow if he refused Santa Anna's appeal for surrender; so there is no room to find excuses for him for failing to realise what he was condemning his men to. And, by the same token, when an honourable man follows the Rules of War and expects his opposite to understand them, he is not to be presented, as Santa Anna and his Mexicans are throughout America, as a cruel and vengeful gang of monsters.

Enough. Several of the Tejanos in the garrison, especially those having families in the town of San Antonio, took advantage of Santa Anna's offer, and left the mission. Santa Anna allowed them to return to their homes. That evening I was called to Santa Anna's headquarters, a house in the Plaza Mayor of the little town. His Excellency was pacing up and down the small room he used as his office, his head bowed, his hands clasped behind his back. It was a pose which did indeed ape that of his cynosure when forced by circumstances into deep thought, but he may well have fallen into it from necessity rather than in imitation. I waited in the doorway, flanked by the two young staff officers who had been sent for me, uniformed almost as grandly as their master. At last he paused, looked up at me, frowned and drummed the fingers of his left hand on the edge of the roughly carved table, covered with maps, papers and quills. His right hand he slipped into the gap of his embroidered waistcoat and this time I did feel the posture was studied.

'Eduardo Boz'am?'

'Your servant, sir.'

'You who fought by the side of the Emperor Napoleon in the most terrible moments of his military career?'

Well, I had more sense than to contradict a great man when his mind and circumstances are driving him on to a conclusion he already has in sight.

'I have a service for you to perform, for Mexico, and for the lives of my soldiers. Indeed, for the lives of the garrison of the mission.'

Protestations that he had but to name it and I would carry it out remained buttoned behind my sealed lips. I sensed that here was a man who dealt in straight talking, who preferred silence when only the obvious would do. He waited for a moment then continued, and continued pacing in front of me as he did so.

'Today some dozen or so people left the mission. Most of them were women and indeed children, the wives of Tejanos who live in this town, or the Spanish wives of so-called Texians. I have questioned them closely about the dispositions within the fort and its resources. And, to be frank, I remain as confused and possibly as ignorant as ever I was. The point is I simply cannot understand why they do not capitulate. There are fewer than two hundred fighting men in there. The walls will not sustain a battering for more than a week. I have eight hundred effectives here now and within a week I shall have a thousand more. I have sufficient cannon to make breaches wherever I want. In short the mission is doomed . . .' – he was pacing about now in a way that became more agitated with every sentence – '. . . so why do they hold on? What do they hope to achieve beyond their own deaths, and the infliction on my forces of severe but unimportant losses? I have two other armies in the field. They have had successes and they will have more. They will ensure that no relief column will come to these traitors' aid. But I cannot leave this tiny garrison in my rear to menace my supply lines. All they will achieve is a tiny delay in the eventual successful outcome of my campaign. Why do they do this?'

He ended on a sort of strangled cry, and gazed at me from wide, almost frantic eyes. In truth he was pale, his face taking on a morbid, ivory-like colour, his forehead sheened with sweat. Since I had no answer, I gave none. He put both hands on the table and leaned forward, face thrust out beyond the glow of the oil lamp that burned there.

'There can only be one reason – their situation is better than we know it to be, for reasons we are ignorant of.' His voice became hoarse. 'They have either more men and better weapons than we thought; they have, perhaps, sufficient spare powder to lay mines to blow up our assault when it comes, but how can they do even this in any significant way without risking their own lives? Do they know of reinforcements on their way to raise the siege? Does that mean that the countless pleas for help this Travis sends out daily with messengers who inevitably fall into our hands are hoaxes to deceive us? Do they have batteries of guns loaded with grape and canister that will blow my men to bits when we attack . . . ? Damnit, señor, they must have something and I do not know what it is!'

He now fixed me with his dark eye, emulating that of a falcon about to stoop.

'But you, Señor Eduardo Boz'am, will find out for me what it is.'

I felt my heart drop into my stomach like a stone. Or a falcon stooping. This could mean only one thing, and I was right.

'They tell me,' this Napoleon of the West continued, 'you speak excellent English.'

He took my silence for assent and continued.

'Thirty mounted men from the town of Gonzales, the Gonzales Rangers, are approaching. Clearly they mean to slip though our lines under cover of darkness. We planned to capture them but now you will join them in the darkness and we will let them through. Thus you will get into the mission and you will be our spy there. You will find out just why the garrison thinks it can survive without surrendering and when you have you will find means to get back into our lines and report to me . . .'

He paused at last, drew himself up to his full height, stepped smartly towards me, silver spurs tinkling, looked down into my eyes, and took my hand in his.

'Do your duty, my man. I know you will.'

Then he stepped back to the table, finished his coffee in one gulp, and marched out of the room leaving me to my fate and the two aides who would see that I went to meet it.

15

Along the creek there were stands of poplar trees, just at that time of year and in that latitude coming into tender, pale green leaf. They put me in mind of an Andalucian ditty an old acquaintance of mine used to sing to his small guitar back in the old days when I was a youth in Salamanca:

> De los álamos vengo, madre,
> De ver cómo los menea el aire,
> De los álamos de Sevilla
> De ver a mi linda amiga . . .

> I come from the poplars, mother,
> To see how the breeze tosses them,
> From the poplars of Seville
> To see my beautiful love . . .

And that reminded me that I would not have been in this situation if I had not bragged to Don Miguel, the surgeon general back in Mexico City, that I had attended the university there. On such absurd junctions does the fate of nations depend.

The sun sank behind the distant hills to the west, leaving them black, though those to the east still reflected red and orange from their dusty slopes. A bat or two appeared with the first stars and chased the midges across the almost stagnant water of the creek; but not for long, for presently it grew very cold with the threat of another Blue Norther in the air. The aides' horses snuffled and stamped and I pulled my cloak as close around me as I could. We waited thus for an hour or so as the moon came up, and could hear across the *meseta* the occasional shouts, a snatch of singing and so forth, from both camps. Then came the jingling of harness and the steady clippety-clopping rumble of some thirty sets of hooves down the slope on the other side, evidence that a troop or so of horse soldiers, the reinforcements from Gonzales, had arrived.

They passed us about forty yards away, just about invisible at that distance as we were to them, but splashing through the shallow water which caught the moonlight.

'Off you go then,' one of the aides muttered at me, and then, when I didn't move, the other pushed the flank of his horse into my Rosinante so the poor beast almost fell over. I kicked it into a shambling trot and followed the last of the Rangers.

There was a moment of confusion as we approached the mission. The only gateway, a ten-foot-wide porte-cochère, was on the south side, which meant they had the choice of taking the long way round behind the chapel on the east side, or the shorter route on the west side which faced San Antonio and most of Santa Anna's smaller batteries. Eventually, following muted shouts from the garrison and to my relief, they took the longer route, and I followed them. But as we approached the south and east corner, which almost abutted on to a small suburb of smaller houses, the dwellings of the poor, Indios mostly, a sentry or watchman on the mission wall heard us and fired off his musket at random, supposing a surprise attack was being mounted out of the narrow alleys. He hit one of the Rangers in the foot, who promptly told him to fuck himself and his mother too, and stuff his musket up his arse while he was at it. All of which convinced the watch that the men from Gonzales had arrived, and so we were let in.

It was an easy enough matter for me to dismount and mingle with the small crowd which quickly gathered around the new arrivals with many shouts of welcome and flaring torches. Since the Rangers were in uniforms of a sort, I kept away from them from then on, and was never challenged except once the next morning and that by a man with sergeant's chevrons who claimed he had not seen me before. I stated without hesitation, having prepared myself for this eventuality, that I had been lying up in a corner of the church with a fever until that day. Then he asked me my name.

I have no idea where I plucked it from.

'Lewis,' I said. 'Lewis Rose.'

In fact many were ill on both sides with the ague or what the Italians call *influenza*, believing it to be caused by the influence of the stars: indeed, within the mission one of the most famous of its occupants was now laid up leaving Travis in sole possession of the command they had shared – namely James Bowie, brother of the man who invented the knife. This Bowie, James that is, knew more about the proper conduct of war than Travis and had recommended entering into a parley with Santa Anna – but Travis had already done irreparable damage by firing his eighteen-pounder and now insisted, the way stiff-necked men with a high opinion of themselves do, that he had intended that shot to be construed the way it was, and he expected to die like a hero together with all the men about him.

Travis, though handsome, was not an attractive character. He was big, bullying, noisy, often drunk and spent far too much of every day as well as all the hours of darkness in the company of a young woman, handsome and lively, called Susannah Dickinson whose husband and baby daughter were also in the garrison. More attractive were James Bowie and David Crockett, who had waived their equal claims to leadership in order that there should be a unified command after the first disputed cannon shot. They made the wrong choice: Bowie out of illness, Crockett in deference to Travis's commission issued by the Texian Convention. Crockett was the oldest of the three, had been a United States congressman, a full colonel in the United States army, was known as a great hunter and something of an Indian-lover. Indeed he had fallen out with President Jackson over the ruthless way the latter shifted Indians off good land, of which more later, if I live long enough to get so far in my story.

The fact of the matter was, a colonel in the US army counted for nothing. The garrison were not Americans. They were, granted, in two minds as to what they were – either Mexican Federalistas, or citizens of an as yet undeclared Texian Republic. Americans they were not.

Crockett wore a hat made from racoon skin so that the tail of the animal hung down his back or flopped over his shoulder. It looked pretty comical to me.

I suppose I should write a word or two about the inside of the mission, now that my tale has brought me to it.

The main structure was an irregular rectangle enclosing a space about a hundred and fifty paces long and at the south end about forty paces wide and at the north end fifty. Most of this area was empty, a trodden earth plaza with a well in the middle. On the west side a loop of the creek ran along the inside of the wall, but carried little more than a trickle. The garrison used it as a pissoire with a canvas cubicle at the exit end for women to use.

Women? Following Santa Anna's invitation to them to leave not many remained. Susannah Dickinson I have already mentioned. She was a big wench but well proportioned, with luxuriant black hair, of which she was very proud, and startling blue eyes. She was only twenty or so while her husband was twice that – a thin, quiet man who kept himself to himself. His first name was Almeron, and I believe his mother was Spanish or *mestiza*. Like many families who had come in from the town they were of mixed blood, part Spanish, part American. Anyway, he knew how to handle cannon and Travis gave him charge of the battery of three guns mounted in the east end of the church where they had broken open the chancel, which duty kept him out of the main part of the mission so he was not much bothered by having to watch Travis getting up his wife's skirts.

The buildings which formed part of the walls and the walls themselves were undressed stone or adobe brick, the stone ochre in colour, the brick somewhat redder. Sizeable breaches were no doubt possible in time but Santa Anna's guns were field artillery not a siege train and his supply of ammunition was low. Nevertheless the top edges had begun to crumble and fall in three or four places, most notably on the north side.

On the south-east corner was the church, with a vestry where James Bowie was laid up. Crockett commanded the triangle behind the earthwork that linked the church to the main wall, while Travis's post was about as far from Bowie as he could get, just below the north-facing wall.

The next four days were spent in as hard labour as I have ever faced, something I am very averse to, not on account of any defect in character but rather the result of a physique which does not allow me to shift dirt with the efficiency and accuracy larger men achieve. Shovels are not made for my size of person. Some of the earthworks I have described were already in place, but the general feeling of the garrison was that the assault would come sooner rather than later, and so while half of the men manned the guns and watched from the ramparts, the other half swung their spades and picks and shovels, digging trenches, piling earth in places where the walls were at last cracking under the bombardment, making internal ramps and parapets, and an internal fortification facing south, covering the porte-cochère with a couple of eight-pounders mounted in it.

Considering there were already the three six-pounders in the earthwork outside the gate and then the four four-pounders that Crockett commanded to their left, and finally the twelve-pounders in the east end of the church, it seemed to me to be clear that Travis expected the main assault to come from the south-east, out of the Indian *barrio* of the town.

The internal earthwork, being in the plaza or compound, was, oddly enough, the most dangerous to work on, for every half-hour or so the Centralistas would lob a shell over the walls from one of their howitzers. Even so these did little harm. We could see them coming, and there was always a minimum of ten seconds after they had landed before they exploded and often much more, since the gunners who laid them were at less risk themselves from premature explosion the longer the fuse they used. All in all this normally gave anyone who was taking the air, maybe strolling and having a chaw or a smoke, time to get to the side or end walls as far from the landed shell as he felt was necessary and wait for it to go off. But this was not so easy when one was encumbered with shovels and the like and possibly with a trench or pile of earth to negotiate and a sergeant or whatever to rail officious abuse at one.

'We', you remark. Well, yes. I have never found it difficult to become one with the people I am with, and the fact that they may only hours ago or less have been my most bitter enemies has little effect. I could make excuses. There is a bond which is quickly formed between men who are being shelled or cannonaded, no matter what their relationship before. But this is an excuse I prefer not to make. It is my belief, borne out over a lifetime of adversity, that those who live long do so by making common cause with the people they are with, and that those who protest most strongly that this is not so are

133

precisely those who are making the most effort to seem to be a friend amongst friends.

So, we worked hard to make Santa Anna's assault as difficult for him as possible, though this did not prevent me from moving about the place as much as I could, noting where cracks were widening along the mortar lines in brick, where a particular battery of pieces was attended to in a slovenly manner, where Spanish was spoken as readily as English. Or American.

The Americans speak a quaint, old-fashioned sort of English, often using forms we no longer bother with, like 'gotten' for 'got' or 'pintle' for 'prick', while the slow drawl they affect can only be heard in England in such backwaters as Devon or Cornwall, or, if they come from the east coast, it is a sort of bastard Irish that no one from Dublin who believed himself to be educated or a gentleman would stoop these days to use. And if they come from certain parts of New York, as the Bronx or Haarlem, there is yet a harsh sort of a Dutchness to be heard that must go back all of a hundred and fifty years.

During my first day or so in the compound I was much puzzled by the mood of the garrison. It seemed to tip like a seesaw from extreme exuberance, fuelled by what they called John Barleycorn and poteen siphoned from a couple of stills someone had brought in from the town, under the influence of which they sang and danced very vigorously, though roughly and without grace, to a penny whistle and a fiddle. The latter belonged to Congressman Crockett, but he played it so ill that he was persuaded tò let an Irishman who had the art take it from him. Others banged rocks on tin mugs for a rhythm and all whirled and kicked like dervishes until they fell down out of drink or exhaustion. They woke in their other, daytime mood, one of sullen, brooding melancholy. It was only after talking to an oldish man who had been a cobbler in San Antonio that I realised both moods were born of desperation. They were in a fix, and they did not know how to get out of it.

'Bowie,' my cobbler friend asserted, puffing at his clay which was charged with one-third tobacco and two-thirds straw or possibly dry donkey shit, 'is all for surrender, but his voice and arguments are not properly heard for he is asleep or unconscious most of the time, and in pain too.'

'Why, what's the matter with him?' I asked, wishing to keep my gossip going, for he fell as quickly to brooding as his pipe did to going out.

'He has the fever. A sort of a typhussy sort of a fever, I'd say. And he'll die of it if the Mexicans don't get him first.'

'And who argues most against surrender, then?'

'Why, Billy Travis, o'course. Anything Bowie says he has to contradict anyway, but he has his reasons too.'

'What should they be?'

I hunkered down beside him, for he was on the ground, with his back to the east wall, getting the afternoon sun on his face.

'"Discretion" is the term. That Mexican devil has said the only surrender he'll accept is with discretion. Which means, says Travis, there's no terms. He can do what he wants with us. Shoot us as we march out, send us to Montezuma's silver mines to rot and die there, anything. Better, says Travis, to fight and die where we stand. Or sit. There's more to it than that though. He were wrong to order that cannon fired when the Mex first appeared, and he knows it. Court martial it'll be and dishonour if he survives. He'd rather die and take us with him. I don't suppose you have a ball of baccy about you, do you?'

I had so too and cunningly in my pocket I eased off a lump the size of a musket ball between my thumb and finger, gave it a roll and produced it in my palm. Cobbler fastened on it eagerly and began to shred it.

'But it's Bowie's opinion this Santy Nanny is a professional soldier and a man of honour and won't kill soldiers in cold blood. Your baccy's a bit on the dark side, aint it? To which Travis counters that Santy Anny has already called us traitors and the penalty for that is death anyway.'

He stuffed the shreds into the small bowl of his clay, blew on his glowing wick and got the pipe going. First a smile of contentment, then a frown pulled his shaggy brows together.

'Damn me! Where'd you get this black stuff from?'

I wasn't, for once, about to tell the truth which would have been to say from Santa Anna's cook, Ben the Negro. His idea. They'd be starved of the commodity in the fort by now, he'd postulated, and I'd win favour if I had some to hand out.

'A pedlar,' I improvised, 'back in . . .' I realised I had to say somewhere east of where we were, since the west we had come through was all in the hands of the Centralistas. And the only town east I could think of was New Orleans itself.

Cobbler was not impressed, not even convinced.

'How,' he asked, 'would a pedlar make a living selling Mexican baccy, which has a duty on it, in a town where wholesome Virginian goes for a penny an ounce? And how come you kept it in your pocket for five hundred miles?'

Shit, I thought. Is New Orleans still that far off?

And he pulled himself to his feet, gave me a long, slow look from his rheumy eye, pulled his long coat around him, and stumbled off up the plaza towards where Travis was supervising the adjustment of an eight-pounder in the north-west corner, casting an evil glare back at me as he went. But just as he, Cobbler I mean, was passing the well, the three o'clock shell landed fifteen paces behind him and trundled slowly after him.

'Watch yourself, shoemaker!' someone yelled.

He stopped, cupped his ear towards the well-meaning cove who had tried to warn him. The shell nudged his ankle, he gave it a glance, jumped three feet in the air and the monstrous engine blew. Blew him to bits.

I was close enough to get some dust in my eye. You know, I've had many a narrow escape in my life and that one was not only from an exploding shell (a similar missile very nearly did for me in a ditch at Waterloo) but also from a tedious and possibly fatal enquiry as to where I came from, how long I had been where I now was, and how come I had Mexican tobacco in my pocket. I guess I could say, as the Duke did after Waterloo, the finger of God was on me on that day.

Mexican. Cobbler had used the word to name his enemies. In other words he did not include himself or his treasonable friends under the heading. So what did he call himself? I had heard enough and knew enough about those men to realise from their accents and the places they referred to as 'back home' that not many of them had been in Texas for more than a few months and some for even less. In short, they were adventurers, often on the run, including a jockey who was also a horse-thief, and lawyers. It is tautological to call a lawyer on the run a criminal: they make so much money preying on the misery of others they have no cause to go adventuring without the law is snapping at their heels. And not only were there men from almost every state in the Union, there were English and Irish too, including a couple of Scallies* who had jumped ship in New Orleans.

Did they think of themselves as Americans? Perhaps. But while a breed existed who were genuinely American, I mean those whose families had settled before the Rebellion, they were, as I was to discover over the next few years, already far outnumbered by those who thought of themselves not as Americans at all, but as English, Irish, Scots and Welsh. And to these, over the next ten years or so, must be added a steady flow from the rest of Europe. And why were they there? Oh, I heard a lot about a freer life, the land of opportunity, the ever-westward moving frontier that brought out the best in men and women, and a lot of like-minded cant. But really they were there to plunder. To steal the land from those to whom it had belonged for centuries, to cut down forests, kill off the buffalo, and make plains of dust out of the rolling savannahs. And above all they would do this on the backs of Negro slaves.

I have survived. I will survive. I have changed sides, I have dodged, and turned, and wheedled and in the end, when nothing else would serve, I have run for it. I have spied. I have, but only rarely and in the utmost exigency, stolen. But I have not plundered.

And while we are at it, Mr Francis Buff-Orpington, 'twas not I that slipped Mr Cargill his daily dose of arsenic. That was his fucking wife.

* Is this an early use of the word to signify a Liverpudlian? Or is Eddie using it simply to mean a person who refuses to work? J. R.

16

My encounter with the Cobbler (I never did find out his name) was the only scary moment I had while I was inside the mission. Those who had been in the garrison from the start accepted I was a Gonzales Ranger: the Rangers themselves took me for someone who had been there before them. I moved about freely, picking up a shovel here, shifting cannon balls, canister and grape there, helping in the kitchen, all the time with ears and eyes open. Food was running low and we were driven to strange shifts to produce edible meals. For instance, it was declared that the last sack of red beans was not enough to feed all. We had cattle: on the third of March ten small steers were all that were left. Some wag calculated that every animal slaughtered freed up a bushel of fodder from which, given a week, a gallon of whisky could be made. A steer was duly butchered and its meat chopped up into small cubes to make it seem that there was more than there really was, and they were tipped into the cauldrons with the beans. I happened to be by when this mélange came up to a simmer and I was invited to try it by a woman called Gertrudis Navarro, a sister-in-law of Bowie, who had married a Tejana, since dead, with their children, of cholera.

I spat. 'Not enough salt,' I said.

But salt was in short supply.

'I find another way to make it tasty,' Gertrudis said firmly and headed out to the convent garden, which abutted the church's north side, took off her white apron and waved it at the Mexicans in their emplacements a mere hundred yards away to signify she was about her business as a cook and not to be shot at, which they respected. Then she filled it, the apron I mean, with chilli peppers and coriander seeds that remained unharvested from the previous autumn.

Simmered thus until dusk it produced a stew that all who tasted it pronounced 'A O-K'.

'What shall we call it?' cried one guy who had given up a useless homestead in Tennessee to be there.

'Bœuf à la Mode de San Antonio de Bexar,' some fool, a lawyer probably, suggested.

'This aint no frenchified slop,' came from a more down-to-earth sort of a character.

'No indeed. This belongs to an altogether more robust way of cooking. Texian for the meat, Mexican for the beans.' This from a tall, lantern-jawed man called Cooper, generally supposed to have been a schoolteacher.

'Tex-Mex?'

And so it went on until Susannah Dickinson, who ruled the roost in the kitchen area, and indeed over the domestic arrangements generally, when Travis's wandering hands allowed her to, intervened firmly.

'Chilli con carne,' she said.

The next morning, the fourth, we were woken by bugle calls, and the sight, clearly seen from the highest of our ramparts, of a large column of men marching into Santa Anna's lines. A thousand men at least. It now seemed certain that the assault was imminent. Travis and Crockett went amongst us urging redoubled efforts to repair and improve our defences, but met only with a sullen, half-hearted response. What was the point? At the best the odds were now eight to one against us. What would be achieved by fighting? Our deaths were assured anyway; all resistance could achieve would be the deaths of some hundreds of the enemy.

A worthwhile achievement, Travis argued, for the Mexican army in its continuing war against Texas would be weakened by the loss of those men. A few hundred will scarcely make much difference, said others. And so on. In corners, away from the main body, many chawed and smoked and argued that Travis, Crockett and Bowie would be executed as leaders of a rebellion, but that did not mean that honest folk whose only desire was to run their own affairs but remain Mexican would be tried and shot. And through all this I was beginning to get the shakes myself and an unpleasant precognition that I might lose control of my bowels. Influenza? Cholera? Funk? Take your pick. But it was certainly becoming a question that needed an answer – how was I to get over the wall and back to Santa Anna with the results of my reconnaissance?

Travis must have got the message that many of his garrison were having second thoughts. Perhaps he was too. And so, an hour or two before sunset, he had a bugle sounded and we all lined up on the west side, against the wall, where we would best be protected from a shell should Santa Anna decide to lob one in. Even Bowie was brought out on a hurdle. Travis kept us waiting just long enough for three or four of the more independently minded among us to begin to question why we were there, before walking out with his big white hat straight on his head, and his uniform, brushed and sponged by Joe, his big Negro manservant, spic and span, and his fist on the hilt of his cavalry sabre. He took up his position alone, in front of us.

'Friends,' he began, then cleared his throat and dropped his voice an octave and doubled the volume. 'Texians. Countrymen. Let's face the facts. We are caught between a rock and a hard place. We can choose to stay and fight, to the death, our certain deaths, or we can surrender with honour, knowing we have done more than any Texian could ask from us, and march out in good order, trusting in the honour and mercy of General Antonio López Santa Anna Pérez, General and President of Mexico. I do not have the right to make this choice for you, but now is the very moment in which each and every one of you must make it for himself.'

He paused. A gruff voice from the rear called out: 'He's right. Let's get the hell out of here.'

And several other voices murmured assent with 'hear, hear!' and 'aye, aye!'

Travis now took a pull at his sabre but it jammed, and he had to hold it out, scabbard and all, to his tame giant Joe, who caught the end of it and pulled against him until the shiny, slightly curved blade came clear. He gave it a swing in the air so Joe had to duck to avoid decapitation, then slowly and carefully, dragging the point for five or six yards, he drew a line in the sand.

'Let all those who are ready to follow me, cross the line I have drawn!' he cried. Great, I thought, the mood of the men has got through to him, he's about to surrender at discretion after all. But there was one young man who was ready to move even more quickly than I was.

Tapley Holland had no doubts at all. He had a new wife, and a well-watered homestead, not far away, up in the hills near San Marcos, and he wanted to get home for the spring sowing. He was straight up and across the line. Twenty or so followed him quickly. Then there was a bit of a pause, and some of those who had crossed the line called out to those who had not and bit by bit the flow grew and became a flood. Soon all one hundred and eighty-nine were across, including Bowie, carried on his wattles, and I was left alone, back to the wall, trying to look devil-may-careish and a touch scornful. Fact of the matter was, I'd worked it out. If they were about to surrender then that was the end of the matter. Meanwhile, what a reputation would I win, and nowhere near the cannon's mouth at that, if I went down in history as the only man in the mission prepared to die there rather than surrender. I'd be a hero for life. The least I could expect would be a triumphant journey to New Orleans and a first-class ticket on the next clipper bound for Liverpool.

Once they were all across Travis and Crockett together came across the now empty space and shook my hand. Well, so they should, I thought. Mind, Travis's heavy ring, gold with a cat's-eye stone, pressed quite cruelly.

'That's all right, Lewis,' said Travis. 'I made a promise and I'll keep it. Get your things and we'll see you have safe passage across the lines.' And Crockett said much the same and shook my hand too.

Well, O-K, I thought, I got it wrong. But it's turned out all right.

'I've no things to get,' I answered.

Travis looked down at me out of his big black eyes, all serious, a man keeping his word, and touched the brim of his hat with his raised finger.

'Be off with you then,' said Crockett, and gave his head a toss so the tail of the animal that formed *his* hat flicked over his shoulder.

I went out through the church but first I had to pass many of the men all of whom had crossed the line in the sand. A lot of them looked puzzled, confused even. There was some murmuring.

'Damned if we aint been hoodwinked,' said one; 'Not a lot we can do about it now,' said another; 'I was bloody sure he meant those who crossed the line marched out,' said a third; 'Stands to reason it dooz,' said a Dorset voice, 'why else ask those who wanted to stay to move?'

But none had the courage to be the first to follow me.

Once in the church a glance to my left showed me the corner where Bowie usually lay and it was but the work of a moment to pick up the most useful object there and hide it under my coat. I climbed over the earthworks that supported the guns at the back of the church and touched my hat to Almeron Dickinson who stood there still, clay in his mouth, looking out across the short space to the hovels across the creek that protected the Mexican lines.

'How did it go then?' he asked, removing the pipe from between his teeth.

'I'm the only one leaving,' I said. 'Why don't you come with me?'

'So long as I see the motherfucker with a bayonet up his arse before I die, that'll be enough for me. Good luck to you though.'

He spat, and replaced the clay.

I pulled out a big white kerchief I'd brought with this moment in mind and as I walked across the space between I heard the Irish fiddler strike up a tune I had already heard several times, one that the men liked to dance and sing to.

> Will you come to the bower I have shaded for you?
> Our bed shall be roses all spangled with dew.
> There under the bower on roses you'll lie
> With a blush on your cheek and a smile in your eye.

But the words that were in my head as I crossed the creek were

> De los alamos vengo, m—a-a-dre . . .

17

Through that night and the following day and night I was made to shadow Santa Anna almost all the time. He planned the assault meticulously, down to the very last detail, such as distribution of ladders, axes and crowbars and the issue to every man of a second flint for his musket; he fired questions at me regarding every aspect of the mission from the inside, its defences and defenders. I told him I thought the north wall was the weakest; that the approach to the church which looked easiest, because of the short gap to cross without cover, was defended by three well-laid twelve-pounders charged with canister and that the six-pounders in the earthen bastion in front of the porte-cochère on the south side were well set too. And, finally, that it was behind the porte-cochère that the last spare cannon, the eighteen-pounder, had been built into an earthwork. The consequence was that he followed my advice and ordered the main assault to be entirely directed at the north wall.

In the midst of all this preparation Santa Anna packed off his child whore and her mother, both Tejanas, back to Laredo where he had picked them up. When Mama suggested a suitable sum to cover the likely eventuality that the poor girl was pregnant he offered marriage, which she was happy to accept until someone unkindly pointed out to her that Santa Anna was married already. He also threatened to have me flogged when I fell asleep in a warm corner of his headquarters as dusk fell on the second night.

143

'Shouldn't you be making your own preparations?' he snapped at me.
?
'You are, are you not, the medical officer of this army?'
Oh shit!

I scurried out of the town house and back into the lines behind the town on the south-west side of it, where most of the bivouacs and tents and so forth had been pitched. They were deserted, the men already having been formed up in columns of attack and marched away to their starting points. Behind the camp was the park where the draught animals were corralled, the food stored and the few wheeled vehicles had been left. It wasn't difficult to find the covered waggons we had come in – they had not been moved since our arrival and even in the dark stood out above most of the rest. I hauled myself up on to the driver's bench of the leading waggon and tried to take stock of my situation.

Across my knees I held the Bowie knife I'd picked up on my way through the church. The blade was about twenty inches long, curved on its lower side to the point and razor sharp; on the upper side it was curved concavely from the point for half its length and as sharp, but then it ran straight and a quarter of an inch thick back to the cross guard. The handle was weighted and heavy to give it balance, and bound with rawhide. It was sharp enough to shave with, heavy enough to chop wood, long enough to use as a sword and broad enough to make a paddle and, when I found it, it was in a rawhide case that smelled like smoked bacon and had a strap. Most of the time I had it slung over my shoulder to hang down my back high enough to be hidden by my coat. It frightened me having it. A man can get into a lot of trouble when people who mean you mischief realise you're armed like that.

I can't walk away from this, I thought. And I can't ride. I thought of the piled canisters filled with old horseshoes and other metal scraps as well as musket balls, and the heavier grapeshot I myself had helped prepare and piled by the cannons in front of the likely places of assault, and I recalled the awfulness of what I had seen twenty-one years earlier at Waterloo, of how my friend Fernando lost a leg at Salamanca three years before that, and of how, only a few weeks back, I bungled the surgery of a poor man afflicted with frostbite in his legs and even vomited over him as he died. I recalled the sheer horrid mess a musket ball can make of a man, let alone a six-pound shot.

Then I felt the body of the waggon tip a little, a board creaked, and I tightened my grip on the knife though I did not dare to turn round. A hand fell on my shoulder.

'You have returned to do your duty. Bless you, my son.'

Father Jaime. Fat as ever in spite of the short commons the army had been on since we arrived (apart from Santa Anna and his staff), complexion as rosy. I was pissed off by the fright he'd given me.

'Shouldn't you,' I growled, 'be down in the lines blessing all those men who are going to die?'

'I've been doing your job for you. It's more important than mine. Come and see.'

I stood up and followed him into the back of the waggon. He lit an oil lamp, whale oil, and hung it from the middle hoop that supported the canvas cover. At the back, just inside the tailgate, he'd laid out the surgeon's instruments: saws, cauterising irons, a small bowl of glowing charcoal with a long-handled saucepan filled with gently bubbling tar, knives and probes. There was a sack of cotton waste on the floor and another filled with old cotton shirts and shifts torn into strips for bandages. A couple of demijohns stood next to them, filled with tequila, and a third which gave off a fruity, heady smell . . . opium dissolved in alcohol, a bit like laudanum, but the ingredients very rough. All lit by that lamp swinging from the roof.

'I've made up cots in the other five waggons. Six to each waggon.'

I suddenly felt very sick at heart, a sort of gnawing, desperate emptiness.

'*Padre*,' I sighed, 'you have no idea how many there are going to be, have you?'

We returned to the front of the first waggon and sat side by side. There was a full moon, but the sky was cloudy for most of the time and she only got a glimpse of us intermittently, but it was a lot warmer, no frost; indeed there was a spring-like balminess in the air. I smoked a pipe with the end of the black tobacco Ben had given me, while the priest chewed on a small sticky ball, which in the dark I took at first to be his own plug of tobacco but which turned out to be opium. There was a lot of opium about the place and no wonder: the *papaver somniferum* grows well on those high plains, cold in winter and hot in summer, and we had already passed many small homesteads with stands of dried-out poppy stalks, their seed cases gashed where the white juice that the air turns into a black gum had been bled off.

'We're in the wrong place, you know,' I said after a time.

'How's that, then?'

'The main attack will be from the north, that's where Santa Anna's men are going to be blown to bits, worse than decimated,* I daresay. The wounded will bleed to death before they get them round to us.'

'We'll do the best we can,' he said, giggled, and yawned.

Presently his head flopped towards my shoulder, and he snored, giggled some more, and snored again, out of his head with the drug. I wondered if he had any left, if I could get my hand into the inner pocket of his soutane. I tried to sleep too. The only part of me that did was my arm. It was completely numb when the bugles started an hour or so later. Father Jaime woke up with a start, looked about him, shook his head.

'The usual practice,' he said, 'is to put a table on which we can perform surgery, outside at the back of the waggon, where we can move about freely. I think that's right?'

Using the tailgate and a couple of trestles, we did as he suggested.

The bugles. They played the *deguello*, the sack, the signal to give no quarter, a soul-tearing call, high and brazen, and the men who played it managed to give it a satanic dancing rhythm. We could see none of what happened, as the first grey light beneath a bank of cloud to the east, facing the setting moon, took on leprous white along its belly. Above it remained black, like the great whale as it lay on its side in the lee of the *Town-Ho* months before. But we could hear it. The bugles, then the shouts, the ¡vivas!. And then the crack of cannon and the rattle of musketry as the long shadows cast by the rising sun through the poplar trees swooped across the mesquite. Smoke and dust rose from the low walls in front of us, caught the sun, and already above them a couple of turkey vultures rode the hot air and swung on black pinions above it all. More would follow as the stink of blood mingled with that of burnt powder.

During all this the priest and I set out our stall like butchers in a marketplace.

---

* Eddie is using the word correctly to mean one (not nine) in ten could be casualties. J. R.

146

As I say, we saw little of it. We did not see how Travis, on the north wall, was maybe the first to fall – with a ball in his forehead; how, not much later, Bowie, unconscious in his fever, was also shot in the head where he lay on his litter. And I suppose, had we been looking, we might have seen Crockett in the earthwork on the south side go down beneath a fusillade of shots as he swung his now useless musket about his head, keeping the snapping Mexicans at bay. That's what one of the wounded told us, though later we heard different. But by then we were busy, though I did glance up somewhere about that time, my attention drawn by a cheer and more ¡vivas! to see the Mexican flag, the tricolour inscribed with 1824, the only flag the mission flew, hauled down. I suppose that at that moment any chance Texas might remain part of a federal Mexico died. It was also the moment when the first domino toppled, setting in train the effect that would take New Mexico, Arizona, Utah and California with it.

In the taking of the mission about one hundred and eighty Texians were killed and seventy Mexicans. Three or four hundred Mexicans were wounded, of whom maybe fifty or so survived. In other words, the combination of loss of blood, trauma, gangrene – and the efforts of Father Jaime and yours truly – killed roundabout three hundred, far more than the cannonades and musketry. More died under Bowie's knife than from any other cause. Several men died wandering around the town looking for us and probably in less agony than those who found us. The first to arrive came on one leg but supported by two of his mates. He trailed quite a lot of the other leg behind him, leaving a track of dark blood in his footsteps, that is the steps of his one functioning foot. A jagged shard of canister casing was still embedded in his upper thigh.

We laid him out on our stall. The reverend fed a cupful of laudanum into his mouth from a vessel with a spout, and proceeded without more ado to saw through the man's thighbone above the shard. But I could already see others making their way across the park towards us in twos and threes or sometimes on their own and realised we would have to work more quickly than this. Taking Bowie's knife in both hands I shouldered Jaime out of the way, raised it above my head and brought it down with all the force I could on the spot where he had been sawing. You have no idea unless you have tried how strong a human bone is, especially the hip bone. My hands tingled savagely with the shock, blood spattered in my face. Who would

147

have thought our patient still had so much in him? I wiped my eyes on my sleeve and struck again. Jaime remonstrated.

'It can't be done, Eddie, you can't do it like that!'

'I can, I can,' I cried and struck again and again into the mess in front of me until at last I felt it give and the heavy blade smashed through splintered bone to the wood beneath.

I reached round, searching for the vessel of hot tar so I could anneal the stub and the shattered bone which was leaking marrow, but when I turned back the body was gone – Jaime had rolled it off the further side of the table and on to the already bloody earth beneath.

'You fucking killed him,' he screamed.

'So say your prayers over him,' I yelled back. 'Next please.'

After that, and following the priest's instruction, I used the knife only on joints, feeling my way into a knee or an elbow, striking home and twisting it about until I felt the sinews and cartilege part, the way you do with the top end of a leg of mutton, separating the hip bone from its socket in the pelvis.

Limbs piled up on one side of our counter, dismembered bodies on the other. Mexicans, Indians all, apart from a handful of young officers, formed a circle around us, some sitting on the floor, many nursing clumsily bandaged and bound wounds like babes in swaddling bands, their dark eyes as impassive and empty as those of steers in the shambles. A passing general organised a detail to take the dead a few yards off, where they slowly began to pile into a long bank three or four bodies deep.

At last, after only an hour or so, the flow dwindled and we could even pause and look around at the beauties of a glorious spring morning: there were small yellow and purple flowers in the grass where it had not been churned up, the poplars were hazed with green, and when the guns fell silent we could hear a bird or two singing. Slowly the crowd drifted or were called away. Distant bugles shrilled again, but to a different tune, small fires were lit and tortillas rolled flat and slapped on to flat stones or hot metal. A lieutenant brought us two cans of coffee and looked around at the mess we had left, at the mess the two of us were. I had never felt so tired in my life. Father Jaime slopped the last of the tequila into our coffee.

The lieutenant wrinkled his lips in what looked quite nastily like a sneer. '¡Qué desastre!' he said.

'War is always a disaster,' said the priest.

'Aren't you going to say Mass?'

Father Jaime looked at the young man. 'Fuck Mass!' he said.

Santa Anna took no prisoners. I heard it said five or six got over the walls but were skewered by a troop or two of lancers that he had deployed out in the plain. I saw just one man walk out and that was Negro Joe, Travis's slave, and three or four women, Bowie's in-laws and Susannah Dickinson with her daughter Angelina. Mrs Dickinson was limping, her ankle having been bruised by a spent musket ball, but otherwise unharmed, which says a lot for the Indio soldiers. Rape is generally considered the prerogative of men who have survived being part of an assault on defended fortifications.

Santa Anna took an instant fancy to Mrs Dickinson – most men did – yet he too kept within the bounds of gallantry. He took her and her daughter into his headquarters, asked them to share his meal, a late breakfast really, for it was still only about nine in the morning. They dined off red-crested quail, known as Montezuma quail on account of their crowns, cooked by Ben. And while they dined, and drank the champagne he had kept on one side for the occasion, El Presidente offered to adopt the little girl and no doubt made even more personal suggestions to her mother. She declined and asked for safe passage to the Texian lines whose outposts were some hundred miles away or more. Santa Anna, wishing to go down in legend as magnanimous in victory, or at least to provide a counter to the ill effects on his reputation of putting the garrison to the sword, assented.

Now, I know all this because I had come in moments ahead of her, summoned to report on casualties at the field hospital, a duty which fortunately was forestalled as Santa Anna, casting around for means to impress the raven-haired, blue-eyed beauty in front of him, managed to command me in an aside to serve them at table.

Susannah did not appear unduly troubled by the fact that she had, that morning, lost both a husband and a lover. Don't mistake me – she was not gay or chatty, but ate sparingly with a quiet sort of dignity, sitting up straight with her little girl on her lap, feeding her titbits from her plate. At one point she looked at me, as I straightened after refilling her glass, her gorgeous blue eyes, more violet than blue, on a level with mine.

'You were in the fort for a time, were you not?'

I assented, wondering a little nervously what would come next.

'But they let you walk out.'

'That's right.'

'And all the time you were a spy?'

'Um . . . sort of.' And I moved on.

Later, when I brought round some almond-paste comfits for dessert, I noticed that Angelina, by then asleep in the crook of her mother's arm, had Travis's cat's-eye ring on a ribbon round her neck. I suppose Travis himself put it there.

When the meal was over, Santa Anna offered her the use of his withdrawing room above stairs where, he said, she might rest in safety. She replied that she would prefer to be off.

'Where will you go?' he asked.

'Gonzales, where we live,' she replied.

'I shall be there in a week or so. I understand Sam Houston has his vanguard there and I'll deal with him as I dealt with this rabble.'

'Then I must go further east. Bowie's relations, his sisters-in-law, want to come with me.'

Santa Anna thought for a moment, assuming again a Napoleonic pose.

'I will let you go,' he said at last, speaking in Spanish and in measured tones. 'But you must tell Houston that he will not be safe until he has crossed the Sabine River into Louisiana. And I'll give you a letter to him . . . no. I'll write to all good Mexicans in Texas, and you can get it printed and handed out.'

She thought for a moment.

Then.

'We can't go on our own.' She looked round the long, low room, at the guttering candles on their silver sconces, her eyes finally fixing on me again where I stood in the shadows I had returned to by the big Castilian-style sideboard. 'I'll take the monkey. He's a survivor. And Bill's nigrah Joe. He's strong. And obedient.'

Yet again Santa Anna adopted the Napoleonic for a moment or two.

'One man is not enough. You cannot count the monkey. In a moment of danger he will be more concerned to save his own skin than yours. You can have Ben too.' He turned to his chef. 'Ben, you go with them. And wherever you go you and Joe can tell the Negroes that I come to free them. There will be no slaves in Texas for as long as it is part of Mexico.' He paused, sat down, pulled pen, inkpot a.. paper under his eyes and began to write. 'Be off with you then.'

And so it was settled and we went out into the small plaza. I was a touch mortified to be labelled 'monkey' when my bravery alone had won the mission for Santa Anna for no considerable loss. If he had launched his main assault on the south side far more of his men would have been killed. I was, however, marvellously cheered at the thought that we would be heading east, and, driven like dust before the Mexican broom, maybe straight into Louisiana and New Orleans.

There was by now an evil stench in the air and three columns of black smoke were rising into the sky above the roofs. I went back to the waggons to collect the few things I had there, take my leave of Father Jaime and pick up Bowie's knife which I considered I might as well have about me since I was to set off into the wilderness with a woman, a baby and two Negroes. The sight that met my eyes was as horrid as any I had yet seen, not more horrid but in its way as horrid. Although the bodies of those we had served had been piled on heaps of mesquite brushwood which had then been lit, this was not enough to deter the turkey vultures. There were now hundreds of them, flocking in from all over, their wings drooping as they came in to land, their big taloned feet stretched in front of them, and then the tearing at flesh, the soft parts, and the squawking and screaming that went with it, the sudden fights between them over the choicer morsels, and the squadrons cruising above, waiting their turn against the virgin sky. With those huge paler wings which they wrapped round their shoulders like nasty old men with overlarge cloaks, they seemed undeterred by the sparse flames and the gusting smoke.

The fires crackled and occasionally flared and popped as an unused cartridge exploded. They gave off a thick, nauseous stench of burning fat – not that there was much of that commodity on the bones of the Indios. A similar pyre was set going inside the mission and another against the north wall. None burnt that well and the following morning, by which time we had bivouacked, the Dickinson party, the Negroes and I, fifteen miles away to the east, the black smoke still besmirched the horizon and the smell lingered about us, either carried on the breeze or clinging to our clothes.

Interlude III

A year ago, a friend of mine, who wishes to remain anonymous but is familiar with the National Archive at Kew, came across a file in the Treasury Solicitor's Papers marked, simply, Transmutationist Enquiry 1853. Knowing of my work on Eddie's manuscripts and related documents, he had the contents photocopied and sent them to me. They had obviously been tampered with and also exposed to various risks, probably during World War II, when much of the archive was stored underground, away from London.

Some sheets had been gnawed by mice and the edges of others were apparently charred. Pages were missing, usually on either side of the charred ones, the implication being that they had been destroyed by fire; others were gone for no immediately obvious reason.

Internal evidence seems to suggest that Lord Palmerston, while Home Secretary, had set up a clandestine inquiry into transmutation theories and their possible use to radical dissidents such as Chartists and other leaders of the working-class movement. More bizarrely, this inquiry also tried to establish that connections between the scientists and philosophers and potential revolutionaries actually existed. In this context the fact that Darwin was making frequent trips to south London public houses in the area still known as Borough, and meeting leaders of the working-class movement, who tended to live and meet thereabouts, obviously caught the attention of the civil servant who seemed to be in charge of this part of the inquiry, namely Francis Buff-Orpington. It will be no surprise then to learn that he employed Eddie to investigate. Eddie duly filed a report which is here reproduced together with part of a preamble probably penned by Buff-Orpington himself.

J. R.

. . . acting on information received, the agent, known variously as Charles Boylan, Eddie Boylan, Edward Bosham and Joseph Bosham, therefore took it upon himself, but at the expense of the Home Office, to haunt the Antigallican alehouse* in Borough close to Borough Road and the Queen's Bench prison. It was on the fourth evening there that his target came in off the street. Boylan recognised him immediately although nearly twenty years had passed since he had been acquainted with him. Darwin was more portly, certainly; what had been an incipient baldness was now more advanced; and his face, still somewhat round and open but with deep-set, large, penetrating eyes, bore the lineaments one expects to be etched by twenty years of remorseless study, compromised by persistent ill health, not to mention the inevitable slings and arrows that even the most fortunate of us cannot escape. Nevertheless, Boylan was instantly sure that this was his man.†

He, Boylan, remained in the darker corners of the principal room of the public house for some time, availing himself of the shadows beneath a timber gallery that gives access to the rooms above. These are hired out as supper rooms, meeting places and private chambers. According to his account the place was busy, noisy with talk, but not in the least rowdy. It is not, in the way these things are usually understood, a place of ill repute: it is, however, a noted meeting place for the more radical of the working class; soirées devoted to self-improvement and study are held there. One discussion group led by a cobbler who was in the Chartist Movement has been studying John Stuart Mill's *Principles of Political*

* A popular name for public houses bought by veterans of the Napoleonic Wars with prize money. J. R.
† In 1853 Darwin was still clean-shaven. J. R.

153

Economy. Mill, as you will know, contributes to the *Westminster Review*.

Boylan writes as follows:

'Mr Darwin was wearing a black hat with a brim, a long brown coat and was carrying a flat leather case, much like those in which students of music carry their scores. Almost immediately he was approached by a short person in a leather waistcoat with a flat hat of the sort worn by costermongers. This person doffed his hat and led him through the tables to the one he had left, where a third person was sitting, a slightly more prepossessing character than the generality of the Antigallican's clientèle, in that he wore a dark matching jacket and trousers and had a well-groomed beard. He stood as Mr Darwin approached, shook his hand, and clearly invited him to sit down on the remaining spare chair. After some conversation during which Mr Darwin seemed not exactly ill at ease, but certainly shy, something was said that changed the mood of all three from awkwardly polite exchanges to matters of serious import to all of them. Their heads almost met over the table: Mr Darwin took a notebook and pencil from his case and began to scribble furiously; the other two became animated and occasionally fell into disagreements that generally ended with a short burst of laughter before pursuing their discussion.

'I judged that I should try to ascertain what the subject of this deeply interesting conversation might be. I also purposed to re-establish my acquaintance with Mr Darwin. Consequently, as soon as a place fell vacant at a table adjacent to theirs, I carried my jug over to it and placed myself within earshot.

'"It was a great loss to the fancy, in my reckoning," the bearded man was declaring, "when, back in the last century, the breeders began to select from their tumblers those with the more handsome plumage and ignored what your tumblers are surely about in the first place, namely their ability, if you take my point, to tumble . . ."

'"Your common tumbler remains a very fine tumbler," the coster-monger asserted.

'"And thus remains, to put it in a nutshell, if you see what I mean, squire, *common*," said the bearded man, turning to Mr Darwin who now raised his pencil to draw attention to the query he had on his lips.

'"What you are saying, Mr Brent, is that breeding for appearance, bred out the ability to tumble?"

'"Just so, squire. Oh yes, they look very fine, very fine indeed, with their almond mottles, blue and back bars, agates and then the selfs . . ."

'"Selfs?" queried Mr Darwin.

'"Self-coloured, squire."

'"I must beg your pardon. Self-coloured?"

'"Coloured all over the same, squire."

'"Ah," said Mr Darwin, and scribbled away.

'"But . . ." interjected costermonger, "there is still your long-faced tumbler."

'"Same story," Mr Brent was dismissive, "breed him for tumbling, he'll tumble. But those that have bred him to show, oh yes, they get the good looks, but he don't tumble no more, do 'e? If you take my meaning."

'I shall not bore you with the rest of their conversation save to assure you that it was directed, at the insistence of Mr Darwin, at the effects of selective breeding on pigeons. At one point Mr Darwin seemed to experience severe stomach pains and withdrew for ten minutes or so to the hostelry's place of easement. The costermonger then told Mr Brent that Mr Darwin suffered from a recurring complaint which led to excessive wind, cramps and occasional diarrhœa. The conversation or debate resumed when he returned. After an hour or so of this Mr Darwin took a look at his pocket watch, announced that he had a train to catch, returned his notebook and pencil to his musicians' case, and attempted to settle the account. Mr Brent was adamant that he should not. I stood also and positioned myself so it was not possible for Mr Darwin to leave the room without he came face to face with me.

'"Mr Darwin is it not?" I cried, thrusting my hand out.

'"Do I know you, sir?" he asked.

'"Indeed you do, sir. But it is eighteen years since we were last in each other's company. I was on the *Beagle* with you."

'He took a step back and head slightly tilted took a longer look at me.

'"I'm sorry . . ."

'"Bosham," I said. "Eddie Bosham."

'"Goodness me, yes. So you are. Of course. How could I forget your, um, forgive me . . ."

"'Small in stature, eh, Mr Darwin? But big hearted, I assure you.'

'By now, no doubt conscious of what Mr Bradshaw's Railway Guide has to say about trains to the Kentish hills, Mr Darwin was heading once more towards the doors and Borough Road. I fell in with him.

"'Call you a cab, sir?" I offered.

"'Not necessary. The Brighton and South East London Terminus* is only five minutes' walk away.'

"'I'll walk with you, sir. I know the area and it is not without its dangers.'

"'I have been here before, and have had no trouble.'

'We walked on. Clearly something was troubling my companion, something he wanted to say but he could not quite find the right words to broach the matter. At last he cleared his throat and plunged in.

"'Left you on Albemarle, did we not?'

"'Not to worry, sir. As you see, I got off.'

"'Fitzroy, Captain Fitzroy that is, wanted to go back for you. Said you were a felon and that you should be put ashore at Botany Bay and not before. I'm afraid that I, conscious of the services you had done me, urged him to leave you on Albemarle to take your chance. I felt that while no one would accuse you of being a gentleman you had a sensibility that would sort ill with that of the convicts.'

"'Indeed, sir, I must offer you my gratitude,' I replied. 'In convict settlements I understand that it is only those who are most fit for the rough life, by adapting to it, who survive. And I doubt if I should have been successful.'

'He glanced at me sharply, and then allowed himself a small but warm smile. 'I recollect sir, that you made a perceptive remark about the finches on the Galápagos. I have often reflected on that. Well, here we are. And I must take my leave of you.'

'We had indeed arrived at the foot of the wide stone steps that carry passengers up to the elevated platforms.

"'I would be most intrigued to hear the outcome of your reflections,' I cried, with some desperation.

"'Would you?" he slipped a pasteboard card from his waistcoat

* Now known as London Bridge. J. R.

156

pocket. "Then by all means call on me at Down House if you are ever in the neighbourhood."

'He gave me the card, shook my hand and began to climb the stairs, then paused, turned, slapped his chest and said, with a note of wonder in his voice:

'"Only those who adapt are fit to survive! By Jove, that's a neat way of putting it!"'

I am now able to put into context the following passage in Eddie's memoir. The report he refers to below must surely be the one above.

I have just returned across the river from the Office where I handed in the report of what I am sure will be merely the first of my meetings with Mr Darwin. Buff-Orpington affected a certain boredom with the whole business, but I could tell he was pleased that I had managed to blag myself an invite to the Darwin abode and looks forward to receiving whatever I can extract from it. It only required minimal pressure to extract from him five sovs, so that was all right. Wonderful after such a long time to be in gainful employment again.

And so, here I am back in Walcott Square, in my front room, looking at a cherry tree in full blossom on the tiny green, a last survivor no doubt of what was all too recently a country orchard. One could argue, possibly Mr Darwin might, that it has been allowed to survive on account of the splendour of its swagged flowers and the sweetness of the fruit that will follow. Thus fitness is not always a matter of strength and brute force, but may also express itself in beauty and usefulness.

Writing that report has put me back into a writing vein so I will take up my pen and my tale again where I left off, following the fall of the Mission of San Antonio, known in history books as The Alamo, which, Englished, means The Poplar Tree.

Part V

TEXAS

Texas has achieved her entire independence and successfully asserted her right to a position amidst the nations of the earth

SAM HOUSTON, President-elect, 25 November 1841

18

It took us a week to walk to Gonzales – we had no pack animal, the three women were lumbered with baggage done up in knotted blankets, Angelina had to be carried on someone's back, sometimes mine, in a woven basket, Indian-style, like a cocoon, and we often stopped to beg food and drink when passing a homestead or smallholding, so all in all we did pretty well to cover more than a hundred miles in the time.

Susannah limped on her bruised ankle for a day or so, but otherwise was not bothered by it. She carried a parasol to shade Angelina and walked just behind Ben and Joe, very much in command, our leader as it were. Both Ben and Joe had been through that country before, but going the other way, so although there was little chance of getting lost they did occasionally argue with each other when the trail bifurcated or became so indistinct as to be uncertain. When they did Susannah cast the deciding vote for she too had been down this trail, and always she was right.

Most of the way was through untouched wilderness, a gently rolling or flat plain, broken by rare watercourses, much like the pampas of the Argentine where I had been with Mr Darwin and the unlikeable Covington, but, since the soil was for the most part a rich black with the consistency almost of very well-rotted horse manure, it was wonderfully blessed with a multiplicity of plants and animals, especially just at that time of year, in the first efflorescence of spring.

From a rise it looked fairly featureless, a great sea of bluestem and other grasses shifting in greenish, blueish tones as a gentle breeze or cloud passed across it, and frequently dotted with the black humped shapes of bison like schools of whales or porpoises gently ploughing a sunlit sea, but more numerous than the denizens of the deep. But when we descended into the plain we found, in my case at least, almost submerged in the taller grasses as I was, the variety of plants that grew beneath them, especially flowers as scarlet poppies, blue bonnets with blue spikes crowned with white spears, and leguminous creeping vines with flowers like sweet peas.

About once a day there was a river or creek to cross, often little more than bayous or barrancas. Along them there were trees that offered shade: oaks, elms, cottonwood and a blossoming tree Ben called hackberry, and by the water itself sedge, wild ryé and reeds, with fish in the occasional pools and waterfowl clucking and scooting across them. There were pecan trees too, some with the previous autumn's nuts still unscavenged on the ground beneath them. In these places we saw grey ground squirrels, white-tailed deer, a couple of times grey foxes, and on one occasion a tabby or spotted bobcat snarled at us from the crutch of a tree. And once, just once, a black bear gave us a fright, but he loped away quickly enough when Ben and Joe shouted and yelled at him.

The heat was a bother in the early afternoon and insects too, and it was cold at night, but we all bedded down together on and under the blankets, with Joe and Ben on the outside and the women in the middle with Angelina. A welcome heat soon built up and we lay on our backs watching the constellations and galaxies, as many as there were flowers in the prairie or more, wheeling their intricate, slow patterns across the blackness of the sky, especially visible before the now waning moon arose.

If there was a god behind or hidden in that fathomless deepness, he was a long, long way off, and I had no desire to hear from him – the glory of the world I was in was god enough for me.

One night Susannah Dickinson lay next to me with Gertrudis Navarro on the other side, but the latter already snoring like one of the Seven Sleepers and she, Susannah, took my hand in hers beneath the blanket and I felt her finger moving up the back of mine where she gently teased the hair that begins there.

'You're a funny little runt,' she murmured.

Well, I've been with enough women to know how apparent mockery can be infused with a touch of coquetry and even tenderness, so I turned my hand over, palm to palm and applied a little pressure, not a squeeze you understand, hardly more than what could be taken as an accident rather than a gesture. But she returned the pressure, then paddled her finger in my palm.

'Where you come from, Eddie?'

'It's a long story,' I replied. 'Italy, Spain, England.'

'I guess they're out east some place.'

'You could say that. Where are you from, Susannah?'

'Tennessee.'

She sighed.

'Almeron came from Tennessee,' she said. 'He was a good man.'

'Seemed so to me.'

'We was engaged, then my best friend set her cap at him so he engaged to her instead. Her dad had a good spread down by the river, and we had nothing much.' Then she giggled, and it was such a sweet sound, with affection and amusement in it. 'But day of the wedding I got up early and followed him into his barn and had him on the hay. He was older than me, widowed already, but he never knew what a young woman can do to a man, so he took me to the church instead. There was nothing for us in Tennessee so we headed down Mexico way.'

And she giggled again but this time more sort of deep-throated. Then she pulled on my hand so I had to turn on my side towards her, and she got her other arm round me and pulled me in close so I had my face near one breast and she led my hand to the other. She sighed again.

'But he wasn't so vigorous, old Almeron. While Travis . . .'

This time I felt her breast rise and she shuddered a little on the exhalation that followed. I glanced up at her and saw a tear spill from her eye, like an uncut diamond in the moonlight. For Almeron or Travis? Both perhaps, who can say?

We lay like that for a moment or two, and I felt her bosom rise and fall, as if she were in some distress, then with her free hand she undid the buttons on the bodice of her dress, and fed my hand beneath it so I could feel the damp warmth of her skin, the generous softness beneath, and her nipple hardening between the joints of my fingers.

163

At that point Gertrudis stirred and called out, in fear and maybe horror. I have to say, so soon after what we had seen in the mission, and so forth, none of us slept well, but were plagued with nightmares.

With great gentleness Susannah now disengaged herself from me and turned the other way towards her baby daughter, but first she murmured again.

'There'll be others,' she said. 'There'll be plenty more.'*

I resumed my contemplation of the stars.

We had two encounters of note along the way. The first was at the biggest spread we passed, twenty miles or so west of Gonzales. Susannah declared that Angelina was suffering from a colic and she hoped to find there a remedy. It was on a rise about three-quarters of a mile above a wide, shallow creek, with the land between all cleared and neatly fenced to an extent of a mile or so on either side of the homestead. The main crop was cotton, but there were stands of maize as well, and up round the main buildings a patchwork of stockaded areas with chickens, steers and pigs, or, as the Texians call them, hogs. We smelt it all before we saw it, the rancid odour of spread pigshit, and something nastier, a sharp, poisonous, chemical smell which put me in mind of Manchester. It emanated from a dark oily liquid two Negroes were using to paint the fencing. It was like creosote except distilled not from coal tar but from a thick black bitumen that bubbled freely up from the ground in certain places nearby. And like creosote it was used to preserve wood from rot and termites.

We had by then passed through a big five-bar gate down near the river, which opened on to the trail, and were about halfway up the track to the buildings at the top, when we heard the clip-clop of a pony coming up behind us. Turning, we saw that we were followed by a small four-wheeler with a fringe on top driven by a big man with a huge white beard, wearing a black coat, a white stock and a low hat.

* Susannah Dickinson became a prostitute, then a whorehouse madame. She married four more times, eventually to a cabinet-maker with whom she achieved respectability. The only picture of her shows her as an elderly, powerful looking woman, clearly a strong character, whose beauty has been transmuted to the sort of grandeur strong women achieve. J. R.

164

He had two comely women beside him dressed in white cotton with bonnets, one with straw-coloured hair and the other a bright gingery colour, and behind him a couple of Negro girls holding white babies. One of these girls looked to be sixteen years old, not all Negro but mulatto, and startlingly beautiful. We made a single file and he pulled up beside us, then seeing one of his Negroes had stopped painting the fence and was gawking at us, he flicked his whip so it cut the Negro's face across the nose and cheek, hard enough to leave not just a welt but draw a streak of blood. Negro turned away clutching his face, then very quickly picked up his brush and got back to work.

'Howdy?' our new acquaintance asked, but gruffly, not a friendly greeting. 'State your names and business.'

'We're very well, thank you, sir,' I replied. 'We are Mistress Susannah—'

'I aint talking to no monkey man. You, missus, the one with the kid, you look like the only properly white person. I guess the other two women are Latinos and that's only a step above being niggers the way I sees it. As for monkey man, I reckon I'll consider you on a par with your nigger friends, but that's jus' my God-given generosity. Could well turn out you lower than a nigger.'

Susannah looked up at him, but in the eye, then turned to us.

'This is no gentleman,' she said. 'We'll take our chance elsewhere.'

And she set off back down the hill and the rest of us followed, though with a bit of a push and a shove between me and Joe, since neither of us wanted to stay in range of the whip.

The track was not wide enough for this bully to turn his rig round, but we could hear an altercation behind us and then the patter of feet in the gravelly surface. It was one of the white women from the trap, the blonde one.

'Please excuse my husband's roughness—'

'Downright lack of manners,' declared Susannah.

'Indeed, it must seem so to you. But we are alone out here, ten miles to the next homestead and another twelve to Gonzales, so James is naturally wary . . . Anyway. We should like to offer you some refreshment and answer any other need you have which is in our power to satisfy.'

So we all turned round and followed the equipage up to the house, during which this woman learnt from us our names and introduced herself as Mrs Emma Smith, wife of James Smith and so forth. And once up there we were sat on a bench in front of the main porch and very soon a Negro woman brought out sweet fruit drinks flavoured with mint, very refreshing but with no alcohol. Mr Smith, it seemed, was against strong drink. And they made a sweet peppermint tea for Angelina. Through all this it became clear that the girl with gingery hair was also to be addressed as Mrs Smith, but in this case as Mrs Edna Smith. And, there being no second Mr Smith around, Susannah asked if one of them might not then be the wife of Mr Smith's brother or cousin.

'No, no,' Mistress Edna replied, 'there is no other Mr Smith.'

'Oh, forgive me. One of you then might be a widow?'

'Not at all. We are both married according to the Mormon rite to Mr Smith.'

'Does this not make Mr Smith a bigamist?'

'Not according to our interpretation of Holy Writ. We were driven out of Missouri where our chief church is, but the practice is becoming more frequent and we have no doubt will soon spread amongst all the brethren.'

This said without a blush as if it were the most natural thing in the world, and we all assumed expressionless expressions rather than offer offence by looking surprised or even disapproving.

Then, after a moment's thought, Susannah made an abrupt interjection.

'Well,' she said. 'I have no problem with that. I suppose your rite also permits a woman who has a mind to it to have two or more husbands?'

Neither of the Mrs Smiths seemed able to approve such an arrangement.

'That,' cried Mistress Emma, 'would make the woman a whore and would be entirely against the teaching of the Scriptures.'

Fortunately, and before the women could get downright antsy with each other, James Smith returned and stood in front of us, big hands on top of the pointed stakes of the picket fence that shielded the veranda we were on from the rest.

'Good spread,' he growled. 'What do you think?'

'Very fine,' replied Susannah, somewhat dryly.

'I aim to add a hundred acres this summer. And a hundred the next, and so on. Corn, cotton, pasture for beef. As far as the eye can see.'

Thinking of the variety of grasses, flowers and timber we had seen and the abundant wildlife, I thought that would be a pity, but of course I kept mum.

'And then there's the bitumen too. I reckon when we find more uses for the stuff, this dirt will become real pay dirt.' He turned to Susannah. 'Make you a deal, lady. Bring your Latino women with you, your niggers, and even monkey man to work the spread with us, and you can be the third Mrs Smith. What do you say, ma'am?'

'I think not, Mr Smith.'

'Not good enough for the likes of you, are we?'

'It's not entirely that. At this time I am more concerned with the fact that the Mexican army is probably no more than two days' march behind us. I think it likely they will take all your stock, and your fodder and corn, and probably your wives and slaves too. Now, if you will excuse us, I'll thank you and your . . . wives, for your hospitality and we'll be on our way.'

And up went her parasol, and off we went again, back down the hill towards the five-bar gate.

We followed the creek south for about half a mile, looking for a place where the women in their short, ankle-high bootees could cross and eventually found a place where the watercourse broadened and became shallower and there were tussocks of bluestem growing up out of it that made stepping places. Swifts racketed past us at shoulder height, snapping up the midges.

On the other side there was a thicket of buckthorn in bloom and a clump of alders, and out from behind it all there suddenly stepped the mulatto girl who had been holding one of the white babies in the trap. She stood in front of us, one hand on her hip, the other twirling a grass between her lips. 'Hi!' she said. Then, 'Mind if I join you?'

She had close-cropped, curly hair, which was the most negroid thing about her appearance, a small but not snubbed nose and a mouth that was full and dark but not protuberant.* Her eyes were large and dark above rounded cheekbones and the thing about them was that they were always alive – with humour or anger, always one or the other. Her limbs were thin but well muscled, her fingers and feet long, her figure neat but womanish. And in colour she was

* If this sounds racist, blame Eddie, who belonged to his age, as I do to mine. J. R.

167

creamed coffee. Altogether she was probably the most beautiful human I have ever seen. She was older than I had thought when I saw her in the trap, probably as much as twenty, but still with that bloom on her that girls can lose by the time they reach that age. She wore a cast-off white, waisted bodice with the bones taken out and a long wrap-round skirt, red with white dots and a cloth of the same stuff round her head like a turban. Susannah, her face shaded by the parasol, eyed her up and down.

'Know you, don't I?' she asked.

'Maybe. Ever been to Morgan's Point? New Washington, some call it.'

'At the mouth of the Rio San Jacinto? I reckon,' Susannah answered briskly. 'Went there with my man to pick up nails and such like, just after we got hitched.'

'Right. I work for James Morgan. Coupla weeks back, no, it must be three by now, General Houston came by and made Morgan a colonel and sent him thirty miles across the bay to Galveston. He left me to run the flatboats up the river with supplies for his army which stayed around not far away. Then, this motherfucker James Smith turned up. He'd always had the hots for me and seeing Morgan wasn't there he kidnapped me. I been up on his spread this last week or so, and I aint made a run for it yet 'cos I'd no one to accompany me. And now you reckon Sam Houston's at Gonzales? That'll suit me just fine.'

Susannah shifted from one foot to the other, chewed her knuckle.

'I aint sheltering no runaway slave,' she said at last.

'I aint no runaway slave. I'm indentured, all legal, see? To Morgan. Ninety-nine year indenture, that aint no slavery.'

Susannah jerked her head back towards the Smith spread. 'He'll come after you.'

'No he won't. Them Mrs Smiths put me up to this. They want me outa here. You can guess why.' And she swung her hips the other way.

'O-K, yellow girl. You can come with us. Leastways as far as Gonzales.' She set off again and our new friend fell in with her. 'What's your name, yellow girl?'

'Emily West. But while I'm indentured then I'm Emily West Morgan. Some call me Rose.'

Once we were moving again I got next to Ben.

'What does she mean "yellow"?' I muttered.

168

'Coloured,' he replied, with a note of disapproval. 'Mixed blood. Mulatto. These parts they call them "yellow".'*

We pressed on across the prairie and saw no one else for the rest of that day save an Indian hunting party, the first North American natives I'd seen, for until we left San Antonio I had always been in the company of soldiers and the Indians kept clear of them unless they had decided on a war party. These were Tonkawas, in Spanish Táncahues, Gertrudis told us, five of them on ponies, one with a musket, the others with bows. Tall, lean characters they were, tanned like red leather beneath black tattoos in patterns broad and bold that rippled when they moved. They were bare to the waist apart from earrings and necklaces made from beads, shells, bones and feathers and their long breeches were soft buckskin. All in all they were handsome and more than a little dandyish; indeed, two of them eyed our women a lot and then put on a little display with their ponies, making them dance sideways, rear up, and so forth. There was no threat in them though: clearly they aimed to impress rather than intimidate.

They asked for whisky and, when they found we had none, lost interest and were soon cantering off in a low cloud of dark dust.

We bedded down that night much as we had on the others, about eight miles west of Gonzales, save that Joe did his best to persuade Emily to lie with him beneath his blanket, which she refused most adamantly.

'I is no slave girl, slave boy. I is a properly in-dentured labouring person and I do not fuck about with no slaves.'

But surely she was once a slave?

'Not since the glorious first of August, 1834. That's the day all slaves was freed where I was born, in Antigua. And first chance I had, 'cos there weren't much work on the islands, I shipped first to Barbados and then to New York and there Mr Morgan found me, and indentured me. So I aint no slave. Now you roll up with old Ben, while I find a corner with the ladies.'

But it had to be on the outside of Angelina, because Gertrudis's sister on the other side didn't fancy being so close to a nigger girl.

* The story of Emily West can be found at www.markw.com/yelrose.htm. Both now and later Eddie has it about right, though there is no tradition that says she was kidnapped by a Mormon farmer. J. R.

169

Some of which explained something about this Emily that had been bothering me – namely that her way of speaking was English, and quite well-spoken English when she chose to. Later she told me her master on Antigua had been an English plantation overseer called West whose owners were called Bertram of Mansfield Park in Surrey or Hampshire, I forget which.* Anyway, she, Emily, was lady's maid to Mrs West, and had picked up her mistress's way of speaking, to some extent. And possibly the name 'Emily' too.

We set off at dawn, because we had no food now and very little water and thought to get to Gonzales before we were overcome with hunger or thirst. The first four miles or so were a slow wander up a long rise, with the sun in our faces, and the ground getting drier and dustier with every step. It was hot and still and no sound but the steady beat of crickets. By about nine o'clock, when we reckoned we had no more than three miles or so to go, we crossed the last ridge and were at the highest point of our walk. We could make out Gonzales in the distance, and the line of trees and cultivation along the bayou it was set on, beneath a haze of blueish smoke from the cooking fires in the houses and so forth, but of more immediate interest were three men on horses hacking up the trail towards us. The one in front, an oldish man, about fifty I'd say, with a week's worth of grey stubble beneath a hat almost wide-brimmed enough to be called a *sombrero*, was wearing a buckskin jacket on one shoulder of which a single epaulette had been sewn, above dark blue cavalry trousers and boots. This turned out to be Erastus Smith, known as 'Deef' because he was deaf. He was a native of San Antonio and had a large Spanish family but was too a convinced Federale, indeed a Texian republican. More important at this juncture, he spoke the local Indian as well as Spanish and was the best spy and scout any general could wish for. I performed similar services for the Duke of Wellington in Spain from 1810 to 1813.

Sam Houston had sent the whole party out that morning (13 March by my reckoning) to see if they couldn't find someone who could vouch for the rumours that had reached Gonzales concerning the events at San Antonio and the whereabouts and strength of Santa Anna's army. Which made us just what they were looking for.

* Northamptonshire, surely. J. R.

Deef turned out to be a gentleman of the old school; he and his men got off their horses and put the ladies and Angelina on them and thus walked us the last miles to the town, a small place of white-washed adobe houses and some clapboard round the usual church with a bell over its main door. Outside there was an improvised sort of a camp sheltering about five hundred men in bodged-up tents and Indian-style benders behind a stockade of newly cut palings. There was a flagpole in the middle with a flag I'd not seen before – not many had – blue with a red star in the centre, just approved by the Convention that had declared the independent republic of Texas a week or so earlier. Men were parading around it, many of them in what the Americans call under-vests and *de Nîmes* blue pants held up by suspenders, for they were still waiting for proper uniforms. They were drilling to bugle calls and words of command shouted by a healthily mustachioed man in full military fig with sergeant's chevrons, spitting and bellowing abuse after each order given. But behind him, on a big horse, was the big man, as still and imposing as the statue of the Commendatore in the opera, Sam Houston himself. Seeing us approach, led by his friend Deef Smith, he must have been tempted to come halfway to meet us, but he knew the effect he would have if he waited for us to come to him.

Though now designated a major general in the Army of the Republic of Texas, he was wearing the dark coat, white stock and shirt, breeches and boots you would expect an unshowy gent to be wearing on Rotten Row in Hyde Park, presumably because no one had had time to design and run up a uniform. He was very tall, over six feet, and, unlike most people of height, not lean and scrawny but heavily built, strongly boned, from the broad dome of his forehead to a strong, cloven chin. His hair was already receding, though he was only about forty-five at the time, but worn long, wavy at the temples and tied back over his collar. His mouth was thin and determined, and his eyes narrow, dark in colour, but very bright, the eyes of an eagle. He sat bolt-upright on his horse, a big white gelding, but at ease, as much part of the animal, while he was on it, as a centaur.

Such was Sam Houston, the commander of the Texian army.

At a gesture from Smith we all halted about five yards in front of him, then Smith took another step or two forward and saluted.

'Deef. You're back early.' Houston's voice was deep, slightly abrasive.

'Sam, er, sir, I'd like to, um, present to you Mistress Susannah Dickinson.'

'I know Mrs Dickinson, Deef. You know darn well I know her. Mrs Dickinson, I take it from the fact that you do not have your husband with you that the Alamo has been taken. You have my deepest sympathy if your good husband was amongst those that fell. You had best come to my quarters and tell me all about it.'

The Alamo? I asked myself. Only a little later did it dawn on me that that was what these Texians called the Mission at San Antonio.

19

That afternoon we ate wholesome food cut from a freshly killed beeve and broiled by Ben on a gridiron over a charcoal fire, while Susannah and Gertrudis recounted to Houston the history of the Alamo, and Houston's face got longer and darker as they told it. There was a rumour had arrived ahead of us that a handful of prisoners, including Crockett, survived but were ordered shot by Santa Anna. We denied it, but Houston was not interested in having it disbelieved.

What was being inescapably borne in on Houston was the fact that his four hundred or so men in their forward position at Gonzales were likely to be faced, before the end of the month perhaps, by an army five or six times as strong. And while he might find and train up raw recruits in the east it was too much to expect that they would march west to join him. So what did he do? He got them out of the camp and the little town, all lined up, and the families that lived there too, and by midnight we were on the move again and thus began what the men came to call, within a day or two of the start of it, 'the Runaway Scrape'. And what lit us on the way was the town of Gonzales on fire, beneath columns of flames and sparks, the frames of the houses standing like skeletons against the brightness and then slipping down as if made out of playing cards. Why? So Santa Anna would get no shelter for his men or stores when he got there – which I thought was a mistake since I knew how he liked his comforts and

173

would probably have relished another little holiday in a decent place before pushing on. But then I'd been on many a campaign in the past and Sam Houston hadn't and knew no better.

Many of the men grumbled at Houston and I began to sense a recurring strain or burden beneath their grumbling.

'He's a coward, they all are.'

'They turn and run, then when you least expect it they turn back, and dang me if you aint lost the hair off the top of your head.'

'It's no way for a man to fight, leastways a white man . . .' and so forth.

'You make him sound like an Indian,' I asserted.

'He be-ant no Injun,' a lad, who had a Newcastle accent and red hair to go with it, replied, 'but he lives and thinks like an Injun.'

'Married to a Cherokee squaw, he is, and lived with them these four or five years they say. Gave up being governor of Tennessee on her account.'

'His real wife buggered off and left him on account of his goings on. That's why he left Tennessee.'

'He were a great boozer and knocked her about when he were in drink.'

'Ay, but his squaw got him off that. You won't see him touch a drop now.'

Off the drink he might have been, but on that march Emily West Morgan was never far from his side.

We crossed the Colorado* and on the thirtieth the Brazos at a place called Groce's Crossing, where Houston heard two pieces of news: the good and the bad. I should say here that while all this so-called war was conducted with tiny numbers and was a scritchy-scratchy, jumbled up sort of a business, it did have one thing in common with the Duke's campaigns in the Peninsula. Thanks to Deef and his scouts Houston usually knew what was happening 'on the other side of the hill'. Well, the good news Houston got was that Santa Anna was still at San Antonio, waiting for the reinforcements to arrive from Laredo, and not likely to move until the end of the month. In other words he was still between a fortnight and three weeks behind

---

* Not *the* Colorado, which runs into the Gulf of California, but a lesser river to the east. J. R.

Houston which would give him time to get his army of farmers, adventurers, rascals and vagabonds into some sort of order, and recruit maybe a few hundred more.

The bad news? As the last of his column, using the small steamboat that was the actual ferry, was boarding, a figure on a pony, with a big hat bobbing from its strings behind his shoulders, throwing up clods of mud behind him because there had been a heavy rainfall, came galloping up the west bank. Deef was still on that side, in charge of the rearguard, and the rider pulled up in a final flurry of wet dirt, and began his report.

We could see how Deef cupped his ear at him, shouted at him to speak up. The poor man struggled on, still out of breath, gasping and panting out his news. The steamer got to the other side under its plume of smoke and by now Houston was preparing to board it rather than wait for its return, but Deef saw him there and urged his own horse, an Indian palomino, into the river. Houston did likewise on his big grey, and the two met in the middle, with the muddy water swirling and eddying about them. And now we could all hear what Deef had to say, for like all deaf men he shouted even when there was no need.

'Houston,' he hollered, 'we have a problem!'

A problem? The only other Texian force, a day's march out of Goliad, had surrendered and, so the rumour mill asserted, was shot – on Santa Anna's orders. Which meant there were now three or maybe four columns of Mexicans, each numerically stronger than Houston's, fanned out across the country but closing in on him. But none nearer than a fortnight's march away, and the nearest of them was Santa Anna who still hadn't stirred out of San Antonio.

So what did Houston, with his problem, do? Nothing. He sent out word that every able-bodied male in the state was to come in to him and join the army. And that's why he stayed put. First because they'd know where to find him, and second because Groce's Crossing was as near the centre of the white population as you could calculate, the north and the west being Mexican or Indian country. But he made damn sure with Deef that scouts were out in threes and fours near each of the Mexican columns and that he'd know how they moved and in what direction and how many miles a day.

And the men came in, in twos, fives, and even tens, and he, and the handful of professionals he had, set about getting them to act like soldiers. Not easy. These men were where they were precisely because they wanted to lead independent, free lives on the frontiers of civilisation. Either that or they were crooks on the run. Or both. But they were rational folk, and could soon see that a squad of twenty working together would always achieve more in a pitched battle than a score of individuals who would follow their own whims and desires and eat and shit and sleep when they felt like it, or just go home if the fancy took them.

But the cement that really bound them, and Houston made sure it was mixed properly to set hard but not too brittle, was his careful fostering of the stories of how the Mexicans had shot prisoners, both the Alamo ones and the Goliad ones, and that made the men mad for a battle to get their own back. Their threats and promises round the campfires were bloody: they'd feed livers by hand to the turkey vultures and crows; they'd smash heads open like walnuts or watermelons; they'd cut the testicles off one Hispanic, a word they shortened to Spic, and feed them into the mouth of another.

But cleverest of all, and I heard him set it up myself one night as I was clearing away by candlelight the meal Ben had cooked for him and his closest intimates, was thus and thus. It was near midnight and he sat in a rocking chair in front of a low cedarwood fire with just Emily West Morgan sitting between his knees with her head in his lap and his fingers running through her short wiry hair. It's in my nature to spy. I can't help it. I made a bit of noise with the last pewter plates, muttered a 'good night' and then silently worked my way under the tasselled moquette cloth that was too big for the table and curtained the sides.

'You know that I've put Jim in charge of Galveston,' Houston rumbled.

'Ye-e-ah,' murmured slowly and sleepily.

'To keep Galveston Bay open. It's to make sure we can get supplies in from the east. And, if worst come to worst, as a back door to get out by.'

'Figured as much.'

It dawned on me they were talking of James Morgan that Emily was indentured to.

'Well, his flatboats take what comes in across the bay and up to Morgan's Point, as near as damn, forty miles.'

This time she just grunted, a sort of 'mmm-mmm', then added, 'We call it New Washington.'

'Which is a fool of a name. Do you know how many Washingtons there are in the States? Morgan's Point is as good a name as any.' Then: 'Don't go to sleep. This is important.'

'Get to the point then, soldier.'

'So far, since he left, all those stores are just piling up there in his warehouses or on his quay, and I make no doubt some already have been looted. I need someone there who his Negroes will listen to and obey. Someone to keep order, make inventories, sort out what's what when I send a request, that sort of thing. You read. You write.'

'Yeah. The Wesleyan School on Antigua made sure of that for us even before we was emancipated. But those American Negroes aint going to listen to me, do what I tell them.'

'I think they will. I'll send a couple of soldiers with you . . . No, Ben and Joe would be better. They'll listen to them. And the monkey too, maybe.'

'O-K, General. You're the boss.'

'That's it then. You'll be gone tomorrow. You can bed with me tonight.'

'Yeah?' Her voice took on an edge it had lacked before. 'Spoken like a true gentleman.'

But when he stood and reached his hand down she took it and let him get her to her feet. Tall though she was the top of her head scarcely reached his chin.

'Show me the way, soldier.'

And he led her out.

There was more to it than I fully understood at the time, and no doubt Houston and Emily's pillow talk had been as much to do with 'grim-visaged war' as 'sportive tricks'.

20

Next morning we made our farewells to Susannah Dickinson and her little girl Angelina, and headed off on an easterly trail, but taking a fork that took us south as well. We took Ben with us but Joe we left behind. Houston had no personal servant and thought the dignity of his position required him to have one, and when he discovered Joe had served in that capacity for William Travis he held on to him. Joe was not pleased with this arrangement – by then he was definitely hot for Emily, like a fourteen-year-old.

Emily strode ahead of us, turbanned head up, her red skirts with their big white polka dots swishing through the long grasses, for the track was no more than three feet wide. With legs shorter than the others', and a burden of years greater than theirs, it was a trial for me to keep up with them.

Quite soon, while the morning still had that lovely early freshness about it, the whole landscape and its nature changed into something very different from the rolling black earth prairie we had become accustomed to. The vegetation thickened, palmettos and swamp cypress swathed with moss appeared amongst the trees and finally took over. The ground became soggy and soon downright wet, cut with sluggish runnels and pools, and though there was a trail, it twisted and turned as if searching out firmer ground whenever it could. Our feet sloshed and sucked and plopped, a rich vegetal mud splattered up our legs, and a rich vegetal smell assaulted our olfactory organs. But this was nothing compared to the wonderful flowers and plants that nodded in the thickets on either side of the twisting trail. There were waxy white bell-shaped flowers, some spread like suns, some spiky, and eye-dazzling reds, yellows and blues. Great clumps of rushes rising from fan-shaped ferns above huge plate-like leaves with frilly edges. Some were evil-looking with spots and stripes, and there were some that snapped up the flies that flew into their narrowing trumpets, some of which harboured small toads.

There were vines that hung like snakes and snakes that hung like vines; one wider patch of water left our ankles supporting leeches like small black fruits, and often we had to walk through clouds of tiny flies that followed us, making black haloes around our heads. But then, just when some horror like a great grub six inches long, horned and segmented like a red Chinese dragon, rose off a leaf, or an alligator snapped its jaws at us before rowing off, swingeing the scaly horror of its tail, a cloud of gorgeous butterflies would flicker past, or a pair of hummingbirds or tiny kingfishers would flash enamelled colours.

As the mornings wore on into the afternoons the sun disappeared behind a black cloud and distant thunder growled. It was very hot – stickily, damply hot. And often with the thunder came rain that swept across the swamps in silvery curtains, rattled on the leaves, and exploded like birdshot on the surface of the creeks which steadily swelled and ran faster, flooding their banks, eddying muddily round the boles of the trees.

We saw more Indians than white folk: once a village of huts behind a round stockade of thorn branches out of which the men came and watched us as we walked round their fields. These were not square or oblong, but concentric following the shape of the stockade, supporting in turn beans, maize, pumpkins, melons and tobacco, at that time of the year mostly seedlings or small plants. And another time, in the heart of the swamp, with a mist hanging over the bayou we were looking to find a way across, we saw a little flotilla of three canoes go by, out of the mist and into it again, crewed by men who stood up in the prows of their boats, stark naked but for a couple of feathers in their hair, their bronze torsos streaked with rain, with spears or harpoons ready to strike at fish, and blowpipes too, while the younger men behind them paddled slowly with no noise at all. They paid us no attention, beyond an expressionless glance thrown in our direction.

The farmsteads and settlements were all deserted, the people having upped their stakes and headed east ahead of us, making for the Sabine River and the frontier with the United States. Only in one small town did we find humans in any numbers. Night was coming on and the town was burning, the smoke climbing into the sky above the prairie, and catching the last rays of the sun behind us. As we got nearer, moving cautiously, for this destruction might have been caused by a party of Mexican troopers, we became aware of beating drums and wailing voices, not confused, but keeping time with each other in rising cries of what we soon discovered was triumph. And I observed how Emily's step lightened and became a dance step, scuffing up the dust around her twinkling ankles, and her buttocks beneath those skirts swayed and sashayed in front of us.

Ben for his part was much disturbed both by the sounds – I can hardly call it music – and Emily's reaction, calling it sinful and against the word of God, and such like. He gritted his teeth for a time and his face took on a severe look. Presently he quickened his pace and strode up level with her.

'Missee,' he said, 'we doan 'av to go down there.'

'You're right Massa Ben, we don't,' she replied. 'No "have to" about it. You stay here while Eddie and I join the party.'

And she paused till I was up with them, grabbed my hand and began to run down the slight incline over the last hundred yards or so to the nearest house, little more than a shack, and not yet burning.

Of course I was loth to go with her, but I have never been able to resist the blandishments of a forceful woman, no matter how often I have been led into dire situations as a result.

We made our way to the tiny square where, in front of a small white clapboard church, some ten or twelve Negroes were banging anything they could find that would resonate, from cowbells to rattling sticks on a washboard. Most powerful of all were two big drums made from skin stretched over flour barrels. The deepness of the sound and the bacchanalian rhythms made my chest vibrate and my soul dance.

One old man with white hair blew searing calls through a battered army bugle and another tootled on a fife. The four women in their midst twisted and swung, arms making windmills of delight above their heads, and sang that wailing chant, and through them all a young lad went with a bottle of rum, passing it from hand to hand.

When it was empty he took it back to a barrel set on the plinth of the well in the middle of the square and filled it up again. The women had raided the wardrobes of their mistresses and were decked out in ostrich plumes, embroideries and gewgaws, while a couple of the men sported tail coats and black high hats. At the back a table had been set out and on it the remains of a feast of broiled chicken and goat, loaves of bread and cakes soaked in molasses.

I headed for that and began to stuff my face with all I could – our food for ten days had been precious short commons – and got talking to an old lady sitting in a rocking chair she'd pulled from the house behind her.

'You ain't no whitey, are you?' she asked.

'Not so's you'd notice,' I answered.

'Mex?'

'Sort of.'

She thought about this, chewed away more or less toothlessly, swigged some rum from a pewter jug.

'Mex is good,' she said. 'No slaves in Mexico. Texas for the Mexicans, eh?'

'Rather,' I replied.

'Kick the motherfuckers back over the Sabine, eh?'

She took a long swig from the jug, then handed it to me. Not wishing to offend I took a good pull on it, choked, gasped and handed it back. Another swig for her, then she stood up, swayed ominously, cackled obscenely and waved the jug so what was left in it sloshed overboard, mostly over me.

'Rebemeer . . . Rebebmeeer . . . Shit! Re-mem-ber the Alamo,' she hollered in triumph and then slowly sank to her knees and toppled sideways.

On cue, the church roof caught and flames like the twisted petal of a swamp lily swathed the little shingled tower. Emily, with her arms round the shoulders of two of the male dancers, paused, and looked up at it and the flaring light played over her shining, smiling face.

I spent the night in a stable as far from the fire as I could get. So far indeed and so dark was the night that once through the door I could not see my hand in front of my face. I was, as I recall, singing London's burning, London's burning in a maudlin sort of way. I tumbled into what felt like a narrow bed of straw and went very quickly to sleep. It was the best sleep I had had for . . . months? Years even.

I woke at cockcrow, the bird of dawning on a beam above my head and so not to be ignored, and almost straight away found my face was being scrubbed by a sort of damp sandpaper. I opened my eyes and looked into the black nostrils of a donkey, whose breakfast I was lying on. Not straw but dried scythings from the prairie, fragrant with immortelles. I needed a piss, and as I took it reflected that, like the stable-born Duke himself, I had been reborn in a manger.

There were two donkeys and a mule. What could have possessed their owners to leave them behind? Well, there were a couple of empty loose boxes too, which may, I supposed, have been where the horses had been stabled. Who knows?

I gave up the struggle involved in trying to lead all three brutes out of the stable at once, but got a halter over my moke's neck and managed to extract him, resolving to bring my friends, once I had found them, back for the others. Out in the cool, fresh daylight, with a mist over the prairie and a bank of smoke on the far side of the village above which the blackened skeleton of the church spire still lorded it, I almost immediately caught sight of Emily making her way more or less towards me. Her feet dragged in the dust, she swayed a little, almost as if she were wading through water across a strong current. Her skirts and bodice were smirched, and there was a wild look in her eye.

'Fuck me, it's Eddie,' she murmured somewhat hoarsely. 'And with a donkey too. Give us a bunk up. Got to get off this earth, it rocks about so.'

But she slithered off the other side.

'Perhaps not then.'

She got hold of the moke's tail and allowed herself to be pulled up the hill to the cottonwood trees where we had left Ben.

'I'll just stretch out on the grass and have a nap,' said Emily. 'Eddie, if you want to keep that moke for yourself, you'd better find animals for me and Ben to ride on.'

Just as we were getting these and some tack as saddles and so forth out of the stable, three of the Negro men came up and stood outside, waiting for us. They didn't look menacing, but not overtly friendly either. Two of them were young, one about my age but properly set up. I seemed to remember Emily had favoured him the night before.

'Where's the woman?' the older one asked.

We told him.

'Woman done told us you is going to fetch up with the Mex army.'

News to us, but if that's what she said . . .

''Cos we'd sure like to come along too, and join them, fight to keep Texas Mex. 'Cos there don' be no slaves in Mex. And if Texas become American then slaves we'll be.'

Well, what could we say?

Emily had plenty to say, once she'd heard them out. She stood on the tussock of bluestem she'd been using as a pillow and gave it to them straight.

'OK. But hear me. We had a good time last night, but no fucking from now on. It'll only cause disputations and anyhow, I aint no whore. I do it when it suits me, get it? You go for me, and I'm taboo, but if I go for you then, boy, you're through. Right? Now the other thing is this. The Mex army aint going to win. Sam Houston is a fly bastard and he'll never let himself be beat. So eventually, in a week or a year, he'll win. Now don't say I didn't warn you.'

That settled, the men, still insistent on joining the Mexican army, went back to the village for supplies, as jerk, some oranges, three bottles of rum Emily made them leave behind, a couple of pistols and a hunting gun, with ball and powder to match. As we set off the older one of our new friends said: 'I'm Tom. He's Saul, and the littler one is Solomon.'

'Is that it?' asked Emily. 'No other names, like I'm West and Morgan?'

'Just Bush.'

'All three of us. We're all indentured to Mr G. Bush.'

'But you aint brothers.'

'No, miss, we aint brothers. I don't know any other name but my grandfather had one he brought from Africa. But it weren't any sort of American language so it got forgot. But I tell you this. When I got to be indentured, when Massa Bush moved from Louisiana and couldn't call his men slaves no more, I had to write my name, but I couldn't so he wrote me a "Tom" and I had to put a cross by it.'

'Me too, me too,' chimed in Saul and Solomon added: 'But mine was a slanting sort of a cross.'

'So,' cried Emily, with her laugh, 'you're really Tom Cross, Saul Cross and Solomon Eks.'

Thus augmented we set off again, taking turns on the donkeys, having loaded the mule with the gear we had humped so far or picked up in the village, which included a big haversack, black, cracked leather and straps, which I found in the stable, and from then on kept my Bowie knife in, and some other bibs and bobs I thought might turn out useful. We continued in an easterly direction, but slightly angled now to the north again and later that morning crossed a waggon road, impacted with broken stone, with a sign that read, pointing to the north, 'Harrisburg', and to the south 'Galveston via the Ferry'.

'We'll be there tomorrow,' cried Emily, and her stride seemed to lighten, her indisposition from the excesses of the night before now almost forgotten.

'Where's that then?' asked Tom Cross.

'New Washington. Some call it Morgan's Point.'

'Shall us meet the Mexican army there and that kind devil Santa Anna?'

'Maybe. But at all events we're to take supplies up the San Jacinto River and the Buffalo Bayou to meet him at Harrisburg.'

And Tom grinned with satisfaction, showing his white teeth.

This left me feeling a touch confused, and when we stopped for a short rest and to eat some mashed corn cakes they'd picked up before leaving, and Emily slipped away into the mesquite for a piss, I followed her and caught her as she came out again.

'Eddie, you're a dirty old man.'

'At my age, Emily, what else? But I wanted to square things with you.'

'So?' Eyeing me warily.

'I thought we were on a commission for General Houston. Not to help the Mexicans.'

'So we are, Eddie, so we are. But always the choice is there. I side with whoever will get me what I want.'

'Which is what?'

Her coffee-butter visage darkened a little, with anger perhaps, irritation anyway, as she smoothed down her skirts. Then she straightened and looked me in the eye.

'With whoever will get me the paper that says I'm a free woman and will pay me my passage from New Orleans to New York. I want to know what it feels to be free. Do you have a problem with that, Eddie?'

'No problem,' I said, and added, after a moment's thought. 'I'm for New Orleans too but the ship I want will take me to Liverpool.'

She scratched a spot on the skin where her breast began to swell above the top of her bodice, then her head went to one side and a small smile lifted the corners of her full mouth.

'I've heard of Liverpool,' she said. 'Young Sir Tom Bertram sailed from Liverpool when he came to inspect the plantation not long after his pa fell off the perch. I thought of it before but it seemed too far and the price of the passage beyond any means I'd get together. Look, Eddie. We're on the same side for now, and in this world that's a rare thing. Let's play it out as it comes, eh?'

'O-K,' I said, and we both spat on our right palms and shook on it.

'Well, for as long as it suits,' she added, and I shrugged my acquiescence.

Next morning, after a couple of hours' walking, we topped a low rise and suddenly the whole vista opened out in front of us, completely changed from what we had become so accustomed to. For a start, three-quarters of it was water, a wide sheet of pale gold reflecting the morning sun above it and hardly a ripple on it. To our left and a league or so away a wide estuary meandered into a bay across which we could make out the low-lying further side, another league or so from the nearer shore. In front of us a promontory on which we could make out quays, with black longboats, the flatboats Houston referred to, moored against them often as many as five deep, and on the quays big timber sheds with shingled roofs. Beyond this a long, thin island stretched out into the wider bay which filled the view right to its further horizon so that you felt it must be the open sea but still as flat and undisturbed as an inland lake.

Pelicans flew across it in long, undulating lines, flamingoes strutted their pink and white along the edges, cormorants and ducks rowed their black penis-like heads in arrowed flocks, and white, black-headed terns plunged their dagger beaks into the bosom of the deep. Small fishing boats hauled in the night catch in their nets and punts dragged dredges for mussels, oysters and huge, plump shrimps.

'Galveston Bay and Morgan's Point,' said Emily. Then she frowned, narrowed her eyes, shaded them. 'Strangers,' she said. 'Gentry, too. There's carriages as well as waggons. We'd better wash up.'

21

And so she did. Coming down from slightly higher ground as we were, she soon found a pool of water freshened by a little stream that ran through it, and screened by rushes and a clump of arroyo willows.

'Tom,' said Emily, 'load that gun of yours and lend it to Eddie. If you have birdshot that will do. Don't ask. Just do it. Eddie, stay with me. The rest of you go off with the animals to that cypress.' And she pointed. Don't imagine a tall Mediterranean tree when I say cypress. These were flat-topped with long, low, twisting boughs like the trunks of elephants. 'Now, if any of you leave that tree, and come close enough to see me, close enough so even Eddie can't fail to hit you, Eddie will pepper you. I'm going to have a bath. Right?'

She led me to the bank of the pond and placed me by one of the willows, and stepped down into the water, holding her skirt above her knees. She unwound the skirt, bundled it and handed it to me. Next, she undid the tiny mother-of-pearl buttons that tracked down between her breasts and shrugged off the bodice, and finally, with a sweeping motion of her hand above her hand, which straightened her body like the trunk of a young royal palm, she peeled off her turban. Pushing through lotus pads into the part where the brook ran quite briskly and reached just above her dimpled knees, she scooped up water in her palms and sluiced her short, black hair and her face. Then, lifting her head and arching her back, she splashed more and more so it ran off

186

her shoulders and down her breasts, way down one side of her back and then the other and over the swelling mounds of her buttocks, which, sheeted thus with quicksilver, put me in mind of the dolphins and seals when they swam so freely in the waters of the Galápagos.

Mr Buff-Orpington, through my long and troubled life I have seen extremes of horror as on the great battlefields of the late wars; I have seen men hanged and disembowelled. I have seen women and babes gashed by the sabres of drunkards on horses in the square of an ordinary English town. And there were horrors yet to come, some very soon. But what I have to say now is that there have been good things as well as bad, and Emily in her pool was as richly beautiful an experience as any other in my life.

'Stop gawping,' she said, and scythed water at me. 'Pass me my clothes.'

Stooping over them she now washed them, rubbing and scrubbing at the marks and blotches three weeks or so of walking, drinking, eating, cooking, and Lord knows what at the village we had left, had marked them with, and occupied with this humdrum but natural task she seemed even more radiantly human than ever. She grumbled a little at the more recalcitrant stains, but stepped at last up out of the water and spread the garments across an evergreen bush sunlit with glossy new leaves and small pendulous white blossoms, an arbutus perhaps, and then sat in the grasses, resting her elbows on her knees.

'They'll be dry enough in ten minutes or so,' she said. 'What are they doing?' And she jerked her head back towards the cypress.

'Smoking their pipes.'

'That's all right then.'

Lying back with her hands behind her head and her knees raised, she smiled up at me.

'Argos,' she said.

'Argus. Argus was a boat and a dog.'

'Argus, then. All eyes.' She laughed a little. 'You make a fine peacock, Eddie.'

I grimaced, looked down over my pigeon chest at my short legs.

'Hardly.'

'In spirit, Eddie, in spirit. All eyes, you see everything but you don't do much, and, truth be told, you're really quite pleased with yourself, aren't you?'

Got my number, then. This time I did smile.

Twenty minutes or so later she declared her garments dry and pulled them on, though the skirt was still damp enough to cling to her thighs and buttocks as she walked. She whistled us up as if she were Diana with her hounds, and set off down the slope towards Morgan's Point. And while we were still several hundreds of yards off and skirting a plot of beans, their haulms just pushing through the ridged tilth, we suddenly heard the galloping of hooves over to our left, shouting, and the crack of a pistol or two loosed off, and round a stand of aspens, new leaves twinkling in the sun, came a troop of lancers. They were led by an officer who, having fired his pistol in the air to no effect but to add drama to the scene, now drew a light-weight sabre, while behind him a bugler tootled a charge beneath the Mexican tricolour his neighbour carried.

And over to our right, at the far end of the raised causeway that separated the fields from the bay, where the warehouses stood, a crowd of men, thirty or so in all, spilled out on to the quays and pushing, shoving, and shouting, black coats flapping, hats falling off, vanished to the further side, presumably into the flatboats we had been able to see from higher up.

By the time we got on to the causeway, these men were poling, punting, paddling five of the boats out into the bay while the lancers trotted up and down the quays. They had four or five pistols between them which they loosed off as quickly as they could reload them, their balls splashing prettily into the water, well short of their targets.

Then back to the left again, more shouts and bugles and the head of a column of infantry came into view. They had one cannon which was brought up to the front, loaded and fired, but it had all taken five minutes or so to bring to bear, and by then the five boats had pulled apart and presented tiny targets. The shot fell between them, and once at least close enough to soak the wildly paddling crew, but the range lengthened, they fired only three more shots and then gave up.

A stillness settled over the scene.

Men stood around; a couple of them sponged down the gun. Lancers dismounted and one led his charger round in a circle, check-ing for lameness. The smoke and smell of spent powder drifted to nothing, the sea birds resumed their matutinal occupations as if nothing had happened. A couple of pelicans alighted on the slaty sheen of the water a hundred yards or so out, and sailed like galleons

188

for a time with wings only partly furled, until a rifleman took a shot at them, and they almost nonchalantly and indeed comically, with their long, pointy but saggy beaks leading the way, splashed and flapped back again into the blue empyrean.

Clip-clop, clip-clop, clip-clop. Six of them, and a bigger flag with yellow tasselled edges this time and the not-to-be-forgotten figure on a big black stallion, his uniform glittering with gold bullion, his Napoleonic side-to-side, big cockaded hat across his head, his darkly handsome face looking down at us, yes, none other than El Presidente Antonio López de Santa Anna Pérez himself had joined us.

'Fucking cunts got away then, did they?' he said.

In Spanish, of course. It doesn't sound quite so bad in Spanish.

Then he turned his horse through a tight little circle, neck arched, whites of its eyes rolling, sweat glistening on its flanks, and brought its head up a few feet above mine.

'Don Edmundo, El Enano,' he said, and touched his hat with his crop. 'Our champion surgeon, the only one I've ever commanded who actually killed all of his patients. Turned up again like a bent peso. Pray introduce me to the goddess at your side.'

'Eduardo, Excellency,' I began, but he cut me off before I could say more, by sweeping his hat off in an extended gesture that left it hanging from his hand against his thigh.

'Señorita Eduardo,' and he made his voice rumble, 'it is with the greatest pleasure that I make the acquaintance of such poise, majesty, and—'

'No, Excellency,' I cried. 'I am Eduardo, she is Emily—'

'Emilia Robaïna y Castro de Cuba,' she improvised, firmly, before sinking into the deepest of curtsies.

'And beauty,' the President concluded.

One of his aides now approached, clicked heels, saluted. 'Señor, I regret to report that the rebels' boats are now beyond the range of our ordnance.'

Santa Anna replaced his hat, shifted his crop from his left to his right hand. The aide took a careful step back beyond the crop's reach.

'¡Tonto! I'm not blind.' His even teeth flashed and he smiled down at Emily. And me too, I suppose. 'They call themselves the Constitutional Convention of Texas and they have written up a grandiose declaration of independence for which I shall hang them. If we have enough rope. They are nothing but a gang of small-town lawyers, farmers and shopkeepers and do not deserve the honour of a firing squad. Well . . .' and he looked around, 'this seems a pleasant enough spot, and those barns and sheds look promising. We'll stay here until we know where that redskin Houston's hiding out. And I see you have a very good cook with you. Perhaps he can knock us up a zarzuela . . .' and he gave Ben a nod before swinging his leg over the pommel and sliding to the ground with a studied grace that was only slightly spoiled by a twist of his ankle on a raised paving stone. Taking Emily by the elbow, and limping a little, he led her away towards the one substantial dwelling place on the quay, a two-storey cabin with glazed windows. I heard him explaining to her how he and his army came to be there.

'This riffraff – I mean the gentlemen at present rowing their boats to Louisiana as fast as they can – were holed up in a town called Harrisburg. I nearly caught them there, but they got out just ahead of us. I burnt the town, of course. Some stupido told me they were heading for the Galveston ferry, and perhaps they were, but when they realised how close behind them I was, they . . .'

And that's all I heard before Emily opened the door of James Morgan's house and ushered him in, leaving us outside.

'Seems like we're back on the side of law and order,' Ben said. 'I'd better go and see what there is around in the way of fish.'

I recalled that a 'zarzuela' is a spicy stew of small fry, very popular in Barcelona.

'I'll help you,' I said.

And as we walked past the house I glanced back and saw how Tom was unsaddling our animals and relieving them of their meagre burdens, while Saul and Solomon were at that very moment being inducted into the Mexican army, trying on blue jackets and black hats under the directions of a sergeant.

Down by the waterside we found the fishermen were already unloading their catch on to the quays and selling them to a handful of men and women who had come to meet them from the shacks and huts that surrounded the warehouses. Most of them were Negroes though some were Indians and most worked for Morgan as lightermen, warehousemen and crew for the flatboats. There was more than enough for everybody, indeed normally these fishermen supplied Harrisburg and its environs, but, due to the war, catches had remained unsold for days. As well as the fresh fish we were buying there were heaps of small fry, some larger fish, shellfish and so forth which the herring gulls were picking over in a sated, bored sort of a way. We ignored these heaps but bought a basket full of fresh silvery fish, some plate-shaped, some long like little eels, and some the big soft-shelled prawns we call Dublin Bay and the Spanish *langostinas*, all fresh and still on the boat a young lad was selling them from. There were tiny octopuses too, clams and mussels. We were only just in time because a quartermaster or some such, with a section of rifles, marched up, drove away the buyers and requisitioned all that was left for the Mex army, the fresh as well as a couple of cart loads shovelled up from the stinking heaps.

On our way back we came upon a little garden at the back of the house where parsley and coriander leaves were already sprouting, and a little branch of small chilli peppers and ropes of garlic, sweet peppers and onions hung on the inside of a shed door. There was also a sack of split dried tomatoes which Ben declared would add just that extra touch to the making of a fine fish stew. We took it all through a back door into a little kitchen and got to work, slicing and gutting while Ben got a terra-cotta pan of water going over the charcoal fire.

And at that point we heard her. Singing. From the upstairs room, and her feet stamped on the boards above our heads.

> *You look like history with gold and stars*
> *Take what you want, you're the god of Mars*
> *You got a column so stick me on it*
> *I'm sighing, dying, don't you stop it.*
>
> *You'll get a promotion though you're lost in action*
> *Let me pull the trigger for the first reaction*
> *Send your troops in a circling motion*
> *Penetrate the centre and bring satisfaction.*

There was a lot more to it than that, but that's all I remember, except that it was sung fast, with rhythms such as no one has ever heard in the salons of Europe or even on the empty floors of barns at the summer solstice. You know, I felt a sort of envy that she was singing for that charlatan in his glittering uniform . . . though I suppose at that moment he was probably as unclothed as he was on the day he was born.

Meanwhile, below stairs, Ben and I chopped and trimmed and soon had a good meal going and above stairs the boards creaked, the bed springs rang like bells, the stew came to a boil, she screamed out something that sounded like 'Hunn-eeee!', we shifted the pan off the heat so it sank back to a simmer, and I guess the same happened above stairs too.

Meanwhile, outside, spread along the quays and in the meadows behind them, the army tipped their fish stew out of cauldrons and on to metal plates and also tucked in.

Santa Anna's army hung about Morgan's Point for the whole of the next day waiting for news of the other Mexican columns and the whereabouts of Houston's rebel army. Our General-Presidente was faced with several problems: he had split his army into four columns, all moving east but spread out. Houston's force was now large enough to take on any of them on its own. However, the thrust inland of Galveston Bay was forcing them to concentrate and Santa Anna was afraid Houston might either disband or make for the Sabine River and friendly territory, helter-skelter, before he could be caught. Santa Anna was also bothered by the fact that very little in the way of news was getting through to him. Deef Smith's scouts captured or chased off any Mexican cavalry that came near, and also caught many of the couriers who carried despatches between his armies.

Even so, by dusk on the second day, he knew Houston had arrived in the still smouldering ruins of Harrisburg, and that his, that is Santa Anna's, brother-in-law, General Cos, with five hundred men, was in the vicinity. Major General Filisola was a further two or three days' march away in the north-west with an even bigger force. There seemed, therefore, to be a possibility that he could either meet up with Cos and engage Houston or catch him in a nutcracker between two or even three forces.

If, Mr Buff-Orpington, you have become sufficiently interested in all this to have found an atlas, you will be wondering where Harrisburg is. You may not find it. That is because when it was rebuilt they also gave it a new name: they called it Houston.

On the evening of the eighteenth and through much of the night it rained. Santa Anna was graceful enough to invite me to join him, Emily and Father Jaime for a few hands of cards. We played by candlelight and it soon became apparent to me that all four of us were cheating. Emily assumed an entirely false ignorance of the games we played, using it as an excuse and appealing to our sense of gallantry when the cards fell badly for her. Father Jaime, who of course welcomed me gladly and as an old friend, offering me his blessing and so forth, dealt himself good hands off the bottom of the pack. The cards were Santa Anna's so he was able to read the system of tiny notches on the edges that revealed what each card was, a system I quickly understood and exploited. But at the end of the day, or rather night, perspicacity and circumspection prevailed, and we all made sure Santa Anna won. He gleefully accepted our paper and then with great magnanimity tore it all up.

'I am,' he crowed, 'ruler of the greatest country lying between the oceans – with this goddess too, what more could I possibly want?'

I suspect he had it in mind that Napoleon too fell for a *mulata*, Josephine of Martinique, whom he made his first Empress. And then, no doubt on account of the fatigues of an already well-spent day, taken with a fair quantity of Napoleon brandy drunk through the evening and the smoking of numerous greenish cheroots, he fell on the stairs and went to sleep. We had to call Ben out of his kitchen to help us get him up to bed. Just as we came back below stairs we heard a stamping of feet and a jangle of spurs and found a young lieutenant saluting and blushing and saluting Emily again and again. He had to see the general, the President, immediately, he said.

'That's not possible,' Emily replied. 'The exertions and responsibilities of the day have taken their toll and he is now in deep sleep from which he has ordered he should not on any account be wakened. Is that not so, gentlemen?'

We all concurred.

'But any message you have for him will be communicated to him at the very first opportunity in the morning,' she concluded, with all the dignity of an imperial consort.

'Well, the fact is, and I don't like to say this in front of a person of the gentler sex but since you have commanded it . . .'

'Do get on.'

'Half the men have gone down with the flux. They blame the fish stews they have had to eat. Unless a cure is found they will not be able to march tomorrow, let alone fight.'

Emily turned to Father Jaime. He coughed, hummed a bit and fidgeted. I intervened.

'When a similar complaint afflicted the British army in Spain in 1812,' I said, 'Wellington commanded that they should be given rice and tea. These were prophylactics he had learned to order the use of on his Indian campaigns.'

Emily was brisk.

'There's no time for that. Opium is the best and fastest acting palliative. I believe there is a quantity in one of the warehouses. A farmer who lives near San Juan, called Thompson, known as Hunter, brought in a sack a month ago. I'll see it is delivered to Father Jaime's waggon early tomorrow and he will dose the sufferers appropriately. Won't you, Father?'

And of course the old fool, who knew no better, assented.

Now whether Emily had arranged for the distribution of tainted fish or whether she was merely being opportunistic, I have no idea. I suspect the latter. She took her chances when they came rather than relying on planning ahead.

With Father Jaime on his way back to his waggon, I stood in the doorway of the cottage for a few minutes hoping to enjoy the cool of the night before dawn, but at the first stirring of a breeze I detected on it a whiff of sweet effluent, rotting shrimps mixed with liquid shit. I picked up a half-finished cheroot, dried off the President's spittle on my sleeve, got a light from the candle and thereby masked the unpleasantness. A moment later I sensed and smelled a presence behind me, heard the rustle of her skirt, and then felt her hand and arm circling my shoulder and the warmth of her breast as she pulled my shoulder into it.

'A word in your shell-like,' she murmured, and suiting the action to the word, her lips alighted like a moth on my ear. 'There will be a battle in a day or so. We must be on the winning side, eh, Eddie?'

'Of course.'

'Problem – we don't know who is going to win.'

'Indeed we do not.'

'So here is what we'll do . . .' and she whispered to me a short list of requests and commands. Finally, she put her hands on my shoulders and turned to me and with her head just slightly bent kissed me first on the forehead and then on the lips.

'I bet you're a sweetie in bed,' she concluded. 'Maybe one night we'll give it a whirl. But now . . . it's back to his nibs.'

22

The next day was spent, under Emily's guidance for she knew where everything had been stacked and what was available, in going through Morgan's warehouses, loading into the army's almost empty waggons all the stuff Santa Anna and his quartermaster general felt might be useful. Flour, grain, sugar for a start; then tequila and cactus beer, bales of canvas for the repairing of tents, all the black powder we could find, and so on. Towards the end it became a bit silly, Santa Anna making us put on a barrel of nails – 'You never know when you might need them' – and then taking them off again when it was found that there was no room for something his army really needed. Morgan's Point served the hinterland as far as San Antonio, including places as big as Harrisburg, with all the homesteads and farms dotted between. And the settlers themselves in turn needed a place to ship out their cash crops like sugar, cotton, hardwoods and the barrels of black natural bitumen they called 'crude'. The two-way traffic was carried in flatboats between the Point and Galveston on Galveston Island at the mouth of the bay, whence New Orleans to the east could be reached and Vera Cruz to the south and west.

Yet, at this time the population of the Republic of Texas was, I've been reliably informed, no more than thirty thousand, of whom nearly half were Indians.

I followed Emily's instructions, which were to find, in a locked cupboard at the back of the third warehouse, a sack made of oiled gunny, filled with a black substance that was squashy, malleable and had a sweet, vegetal smell. The sack was a half hundredweight, fifty-six pounds for size, but weighed more, and I had to go and get Tom to help me. I found him on the other side of the warehouse, sitting on the quay, knees up, gazing out over the still, glowing water. He had his new white shirt on, his blue trousers with suspenders, and his new jacket by his side. But his feet were still bare.

'What you doin', Tom?'

'Jus' sittin',' he replied. 'On the dock of the bay, watchin' all the boats go by. Wishin' I was back in Georgia.'

'Well, get off your arse and come and help me.'

'Ass.'

'Eh?'

'Never mind.' But he got up and followed me to the warehouse, whistling a sad little tune as he came. We loaded the sack into Father Jaime's medical waggon. It was his waggon now, not mine.

'What's in there?' asked the Rev.

'Don' know,' I replied.

'Chinaman,' Tom conjectured. 'Opium.'

'Wonderful. I'll begin distribution to those suffering from the flux straight away. We've almost run out. But that's an awful lot, isn't it? What sort of dose would you recommend?'

Well, Emily had already given me an indication.

'A piece the size of a grapeshot is thought best,' I said. 'To be chewed slowly and washed down with spirits of alcohol.'

At that time there were only a couple of hundred or so sufferers, so dosing them used up no more than a quarter of what we had.

The day wore on, got hotter, the clouds built, the rain came. A detachment of lancers herded in a couple of hundred beeves they'd found out on the grassland. Several were slaughtered and the whole army settled down to a huge *barbacoa* of meat broiled over fifty or so fires, the smoke rising as from Homeric sacrifices into the beams of the setting sun. Needless to say, a lot of this meat was not properly cooked, merely charred on the outside and still bleeding in the middle.

Into all this rode a courier, guarded by five troopers. He demanded instant access to the general, was given it, and blurted out his report.

'Houston is on the south bank of the Buffalo Bayou, up in the corner of the confluence, just by Lynch's Ferry.'

'Shit,' shouted El Presidente. 'If he's aiming to cross we must get there before he can.'

You'll have noted already how reluctant his army was to move. It had taken nearly a month to get them out of San Antonio. Once on the march they were quick, no doubt resolved to get to the next place where creaturely comforts could be enjoyed again as soon as possible, but getting them going was not easy – especially where the living was good. Maybe they weren't too happy at the prospect of a battle either, and word soon got round that that was what they were being asked to march towards. Consequently it was not until late in the morning that the column wound along the bank of the San Jacinto leaving Morgan's warehouses and indeed most of his flat-boats and some of the hovels blazing in the usual way. Santa Anna seemed unable to leave anywhere without first setting fire to it, perhaps because it was what Boney did to Moscow.

The pillars of smoke must have been clearly visible from Houston's tent at Lynch's Ferry, a dire warning of what was on the way. But he stayed put. Perhaps his scouts saw how a hundred or so of our men stumbled along behind the rest in a somnambulant sort of way while, up at the front of the column, others continually broke ranks to relieve themselves of the flux in the swamps that bordered the trail. In short, one quarter of the army had the trots and another quarter was blown on opium.

I didn't see Emily to speak to on the march, nor during the rest of the day. Santa Anna was near the front on his big black with his big flag behind him while she rode in his open carriage with a Negro girl darker than her holding a parasol over her. I was in the hospital waggon at the very end of the column with Father Jaime, and somewhere between Ben, Tom, Solomon and Saul marched alongside their new brothers and companions, ready to fight, let's admit it, for nothing less likely to be achieved than freedom.

At about two o'clock, just as the day began to get steamy hot again, the vanguard (by now Santa Anna himself, and his equipage, had dropped back to the centre) skirted a shallow, stagnant lake which lay between the trail and the San Jacinto and came into a fairly large patch of oak forest, the trees scattered over wild meadow with patches of marsh in it. As they emerged from it they were faced with a spread of open meadow, sheeted with wild poppies and daisies, clouded with butterflies, and a line of scrub oak a couple of hundred yards away, marking a shallow ravine. Out of this came a rattle of small-arms fire and the double crack of a pair of cannon.

Santa Anna ordered up his single gun and returned the fire while his many generals deployed the column into line, positioned to receive an enemy attack. But nothing much happened. The horsemen of both sides loosed off their pistols, ran at each other with lances and sabres, and then the Texians withdrew, taking their cannon with them. No one was killed that I could see, and even our half-dozen wounded were still alive the following day in spite of what Father Jaime and I did to them. Father Jaime continued to dose sufferers from the other complaint with raw opium, washed down with tequila.

After the skirmish Santa Anna sent a troop or so of lancers forward to the ravine, which was no more than a long, straight hollow, its bottom not more than five feet below the general level and the slopes not steep. They reported back that Houston's eight hundred or so were camped at the far end of the meadow in line of battle in front of the trees that screened the south bank of the Buffalo Bayou.

Santa Anna ordered his tent pitched in the centre of his line. Saddles, empty barrels and so forth were placed round the one cannon and, that done, he withdrew into his marquee with its many quartered coats of arms elaborately embroidered on the flaps and its ornately carved poles, taking Emily with him, but not before she had cast a meaningful look in my direction.

I knew what she was on about, of course. As soon as dusk, compromised by the smoke from our fires and the mist arising from the rivers and the swamps, had fallen, I slipped away to our army's right and rear. On reaching the swamp that edged the San Jacinto, I followed the curve of the river back round and thus was able to skirt our outposts, screened as I was by oaks et cetera. Beyond the swamp the river slid grey and almost greasy beneath the deepening sky, giving shape to a scene on that side devoid of any human influence or mark, much as it must have done for millennia before, its surface only broken by the rings, and its silence by the plops, of fish rising for the last flies of the day. Presently, though, I heard the twanging of a banjore and a voice raised in mournful song.

> *Effacing charms of earth's fair well*
> *Your springs of joy are dry.*
> *My soul shall seek another world*
> *A brighter world on high.*

> *Farewell my friends whose tender care*
> *Has long increased my love*
> *Your fond embrace I now exchange*
> *For better friends above . . .*

And as the song faded so did the last light from the western sky, leaving the scene in darkness and night. Using trees and bushes as unnecessary cover, for their eyes were fixed in the darkness on the glowing coals of the little fire they shared, I sidled closer to this picket placed on the extreme of the Texian left wing. And found I was not alone. A tall but bulky figure wrapped in a coat stood between me and them and as the song ended he moved forward and hunkered on the edge of the group. A chorus of frogs broke out from the swamp, kept its croaking cackle going for a moment and then as suddenly stopped. The big man cleared his throat.

'That was a wretched song you gave us.'

Silence. Was this fighting talk? But a branch in the fire fell in and flared and the size of the cloaked man was appreciated.

'Why not? We're in a hole.'

'How so?'

'Santa Anna is at our front. More Spaniards are creeping in on us. We have a river at our back. He'll shoot us if we give in, like he shot Crockett, Fannion and their men. Good cause to feel wretched, I'd say.' And the banjorist cleared his throat and spat in the fire. 'And I doubt not Sam Houston feels the same too. If he's not scarpered on the qt leaving us to face the Mex on our own.'

Silence once more, as if we were all waiting to hear the frogs start up again, or the tramp of Mexican boots closing in on us through the dark.

'Sam Houston may be a bloody fool,' said the big man, 'but he's no coward. He'll stand his ground until they chop him down.'

'Does he not feel fear like us then?' This from another party sitting close. You could see his old face in the glow of his pipe when he gave a pull on it.

'Aye. I suppose so. Sure he's of better mettle than the rest of us, but he feels the same, I'll be bound,' this from the big man. 'But he won't show it.'

'Let him show or hide, I'll bet he'd rather be up to his neck in the Hudson in winter, than here right now. And I'd choose to be with him there if I could.'

'Oh, come on wi' yer,' another voice now chimed in, an Irish one at that. 'No fockin' use being miserable. Gi' me that banjoleer an' we'll have a song with a bit of spunk in it.'

A string twanged in the darkness as the instrument was passed over. Paddy or Mick or whatever, drummed his finger ends on the parchment, struck a chord and was off.

> *Sweet Mary, my darlin', the war clouds are looming*
> *And traitors are plotting to fetter the land.*
> *I go on the morrow when cannon are booming*
> *To join in the battle with liberty's band.*
>
> *With tear-moistened eye-lids, I look through the gloaming*
> *And think of the pleasure that blest us of old . . .*

'What pleasure was that, then?' the old man with the pipe interjected.

'His prick up her ass, Irish fashion,' another chimed in and all fell about laughing lewdly as the song finished:

> *It's breaking my heart is, sweet Mary Malone*
> *With sorrow to leave you, dear bride of my soul . . .*

'. . . why, you're all dirty minded sods, so you are, here take your banjer back before I break it on yer pate. Hey, where's the big man gone, then?'

And indeed he had gone. I saw him stand, because he was between me and the tiny fire, and then melt away in the darkness.

'Gone. Did you not ken who he was?' a Scots voice added.

'Old Nick, I don't doubt.'

'No, yer puir fool. It wor our general. Sam Houston.'

'Never!'

But he was right, and now he'd said it I was sure he was. I crept off after the big man. Sam Houston. A touch of Sammy in the night, then.

23

I followed him down the line. Soon we were clear of the trees and
on the edge of the meadow. The men were grouped in fives and
sixes round small fires like the one we had left, and some had made
benders, Indian-style, to shelter in. There was no moon but no clouds
either and the sky was filled with stars and the ground with starlight.
It was even a touch chilly. A bugle called, not much more than a
quarter of a mile away, and looking that way we could see the glim-
mer of the Mexican fires through the trees of the ravine and above
the drooped and closed heads of the poppies in the long grass in
front of us.

Some of his men recognised him and called out. Some he knew
and called back.

'Hi there, Johnnie. You keep warm now with that cough of yours.
Douglas, is it? My respects to your wife when you get home.' That
sort of thing. And even if the men looked about them, wondering
which the hell of them was Douglas, I don't doubt it cheered them to
think Douglas had the Chief's best wishes.

But, my goodness, it was a pretty thin line. Shoulder to shoulder
and in single file they wouldn't stretch the distance, that was sure.
Two-thirds of the way along it we came to a flagpole, but no flag on
it, a table set out with a chair or two behind it and a lamp on it. No
tent. Just a big oak tree spreading its generous boughs over the rest.
General Houston's Head Quarters. As he came up to it, he suddenly

swung round on me, picking up the lamp and holding it so that its dim light fell on my face.

'Monkey man,' he said. 'Let me see you. Edmund?'

'Edward. Joseph, Charles, Edward. Eddie.'

'You've been following me. Crossed my mind to plug you.' And his hand brushed the butt of the holstered pistol on his belt. 'But I figured you were harmless and here with news of Emily West.'

'News of her, and from her, sir.'

'Okeydoke. Sit down and tell me.'

I wasn't sure what he meant by 'okeydoke' but I did as I was told, moving the chair, a bentwood, to the side as I did so. He sat in the other, which had arms. A voice called quietly from behind him.

'That you, General?'

'Yes, George, it's me.'

'Everything okeydoke, General?'

'Just fine, George.'

He leant towards me, fetched a cheroot out of his top pocket, opened the lamp and lit the cheroot, snaked out smoke, coughed, closed the lamp, leant back with the cheroot clamped in the corner of his mouth and his thumbs in the armholes of his vest. What you, Mr Buff-Orpington, would call a waistcoat.

'O-K, Eddie. Shoot.'

I guessed what he meant by 'shoot'. I told him everything Emily had told me to tell him. That by morning next day three-quarters of Santa Anna's army would have the flux and that by the afternoon they'd be doped up with opium. That Santa Anna was expecting General Cos to arrive with six hundred men . . .

'Four hundred at most,' Houston chipped in.

. . . and that these would be the only truly effective troops against him. However, Filisolo, with an even bigger force, was only a day or so's march away by now.

'Sure. I know that already.'

'That's about it, really.'

He smoked for a bit, then chucked the cigar thing into the grass and stood up.

'Shit,' he said. 'We are in a darn fix. A darned fix indeed. Will Santa Anna move first? Will he attack us?'

'I don't think so. Certainly not until Cos has arrived.'

He paced about a bit, his boots brushing the long grass where it had not already been trampled, in and out of the light of the lamp.

'These men,' and he gestured down the line, 'may not fight at all. Only way to make them fight is give them the choice: fight or give in and be shot by Santa Anna's firing squads. Remember the Alamo. Remember Goliad. They're already vamoosing. Five here, ten there. I've brought them too far from their homesteads, their families, their Negroes. And they're scared they can't beat real soldiers. I have it in mind to burn Vince's Bridge to keep them here but if I do that Cos'll draw off and join Filisolo and together they'll be far too much for us. Even if we have beat Santa Anna first.'

He paced about a bit more, this time going further off, out of the light of the lamp, before turning back. When he came back I put in my tuppence worth. Two cents.

'General,' I said, 'why don't you let Cos through – he'll be at the bridge at dawn – *then* burn the bridge.'

'That's 'zackly my way of thinking,' and he slapped me on the back so I nearly fell over. 'But his men, six hundred did you say, are fresh and well. They aint got the flux. They're not doped out of their heads.'

I thought of beef stew, probably already simmering. Of all the supplies picked up out of Morgan's warehouses, the spirits and beers in Santa Anna's waggons.

'Give them to three o'clock or so. Siesta time.'

'But what if he attacks me first? Soon as Cos has arrived.'

'General, he won't.' I thought of Emily. I imagined that tent. Tents in the sun have a wonderful light inside. I imagined cushions, carpets, silver appointments, crystal glassware. Emily taking her bath in the pool above Morgan's Point. Emily in Santa Anna's travelling hip bath.

'He won't,' I repeated. 'I promise you.'

Still, it was a near run thing. Not the battle, but holding his men together through the morning. Holding himself together. It was a lovely dawn. Clear, fresh, dewy. Birdsong. The poppies in the meadow perking up their bent heads and unfurling their scarlet bonnets. But the men looked like raggle-taggle gypsies or travellers – only a hundred or so had any uniform at all, none had shaved or bathed, or even washed, for weeks. Many had lost their boots or they had fallen apart, and had wound balls of cotton or whatever round their feet instead. They were armed – with their own long-barrelled hunting rifles, accurate, well-kept weapons, but once fired taking a devil of a time to reload, forcing powder, tight-fitting ball and wadding down four or five feet of tubing. They had no bayonets, but many did have the Arkansas toothpick, now universally known as Bowie's knife, many thinking it was the creation of James Bowie who died in the mission at San Antonio. They kicked their fires into life and boiled up cans of thin coffee and a gruel made from cornflour. Then they smoked, squabbled, slept a little more, and as the sun rose higher and the flies and gnats came out they got waxy and downright bad-tempered.

Mid-morning, Sam Houston climbed up into the boughs of his oak tree with his spyglass. He came down in five minutes with a big grin on his wide face.

'That yeller gal,' he cried, 'Our Emily. She's just seen six bottles of champagne taken into his tent. A champagne breakfast,' and he slapped his thigh. Then he went a touch wistful, and looked around him. 'She sure looks purty as ever,' he added. 'All she was wearing was a big cloth wrapped round her. Could have been a tablecloth. Or a sheet.'

The rest of the morning wore on. There was nothing to do. I sat at the general's table for an hour or so and set to thinking about 'yellow' Emily Rose West, found a sheet of paper and began to scribble a bit. She needed a song, to remember her by, I thought. But it was not going well. Then Joe went past, once Travis's personal servant, now looking after Sam Houston, and as tall though not as heavily built as his new master. I've already told you he was sweet on Emily, the way he gawped at her while they were together. We exchanged greetings and then he asked what I was doing. I told him.

'Here,' he cried. 'let me do it. I'll say the words for I have the gift. You write 'em down, for that's the gift you have.'

He paused, scratched his curly pate.

'Lemme see. Right. Ready?'

I nodded, and he set off at great speed, almost chanting as he went. I had a job keeping up with him.

'There's a Yellow Rose in Texas, that I am going to see, No other darky knows her, no darky only me . . .'

Meanwhile, many of the men came up to Houston and begged him to let them attack there and then, or march away. One or the other. They couldn't stand the waiting.

'All in good time, gentlemen, all in good time.'

An hour or so off midday we heard a trumpet call from over the west side, answered by one in front of us. It was Cos's six hundred marching in. The Texians fell silent or grumbled even more. Time to go, most reckoned, while they could. Houston whistled through his fingers and waved up a thin, dark man who had been standing back of the oak tree most of the morning with a small but sharp bay colt. He came over, leading the animal.

'Tell Deef now is the time to do his duty,' said Houston, but quiet. Then louder, as the scout galloped off through the woods beside the bayou, 'Tell the men to kill their beeves, cut and dress them properly, and then broil the steaks over their fires in the good old Texian way. And there's a can of black Jamaica rum for every ten men, to drink with the meat when it's ready.'

'Good'? 'Old'? How could anything in Texas in 1836 be called 'good' or 'old'? Perhaps he meant the way the Indians did it with the buffalo? Well, maybe. Maybe that's what he meant. Meanwhile, the thin, dark man on his spirited pony rode like the wind to Deef Smith, eight miles away. An hour later a distant column of black and yellow smoke climbed above the tree tops and the word got out, just the way Sam Houston wanted it, that Vince's Bridge was burning.

Seven hundred and fifty effectives against well over twelve hundred, and no way out.

The word went round, spread like a slow fire down the line, east and west of Houston's oak tree. 'Shit! Remember the Alamo? That fucker sure aint going to let us surrender. Remember Goliad? Five hundred men in one bed after the firing stopped? And then they burned the poor buggers. Man, it's got to be kill or get killed. Them's the choices.'

'Let's get on with it then. Let's get it over with.'

'Not till I've got my teeth in that slab of rump you got there. Turn it over, why don't you? And pass the can; I aint had my second swig yet.'

And back at the table beneath the oak tree Joe rumbled on:

> She's the sweetest rose of colour this darky ever knew
> Her eyes are bright as diamonds, they sparkle like the dew;
> You may talk about your dearest May and sing of Rosa Lee
> But the yellow rose of Texas beats the belles of Tennessee . . .

And my pencil stumbled after him.

*

East and west I wrote just now, but that's not strictly right. The line was more a matter of north-east up by the San Jacinto, running to south-west with the bank of the Buffalo Bayou behind it, so at about three o'clock, just as the men were swigging off the last of the rum, and fetching the last scraps of meat out of the fires where they had fallen, or the holes in their teeth, the sun was dead over our shoulders and shining in the Mexicans' eyes.

'That'll do,' said Sam Houston, more or less to himself, and with his wide but thin lips set almost in a scowl he heaved himself up into the high saddle of his white horse. He had military boots and breeches, but his own old black coat with a cravat, new style, up under his big chin, no hat. He put the horse into a slow, swinging canter and progressed down the lines, calling out to the men, sometimes by name again, and putting together a sort of a speech, but disjointed because he was moving all the time. Henry Five before Harfleur or Agincourt it was not, but I make no doubt probably did the business as well.

'Remember, my boys, you are fighting for Texas and your loved ones . . . The spirits of the brave men of the Alamo and Goliad call for vengeance . . .', which was a good way of reminding them of what would happen if they lost, 'Avenge the inhuman butchery of that redbanded warlord Santa Anna . . . He boasted he would annihilate the rebel Texians and then wash his hands of their blood in the Sabine . . . We must win or die.'

And his officers followed him, and they chivvied the men up from their fires and the remnants of their dinners, got them into line, a single line it had to be, across the meadow, saw that their rifles were primed and cocked and their Bowies loose in the sheaths most of them carried on their backs, so an arm over the shoulder could pull them out in a sweeping motion for throwing or hacking.

'Right, men. We walk to the trees. We keep station together. Then we run a bit faster to fifty paces from their line and give them a volley, but only when we tell you to and you pick your man like he's a buffalo or a deer and you drop him, and then you go like hell, and get amongst them. Now lads, let's have a tune to keep us in step and together, but not a battlesong, something that will make the bastards think we're having a hoedown after our dinner.'

So it was:

Will you come to the bower I have shaded for you?
Our bed shall be roses all spangled with dew.
There under the bower on roses you'll lie
With a blush on your cheek and a smile in your eye

all over again that they marched into battle with.

However, Joe and I stayed behind for as long as it took for me to get down the next verse of his extemporisation.

When the Rio Grande is flowing, the starry skies are bright,
She walks along the river in the quiet summer night.
She thinks if I remember, when we parted long ago,
I promised to come back again, and not to leave her so.

But then some officious bastard of a sergeant poked at us with his gun.

'I'm on the medical side,' I improvised. 'Medical orderly.'

'Well, it aint here they'll be bleedin' to death . . . MOVE!'

So we upped and followed them, the long line of them, a few horse at either end, with Sam on his big white one still prancing in front. They had a couple of small brass cannon they'd been given pulled by donkeys in the middle, but the ground beneath the grass and such was broken and uneven and the gunners had to lend a hand moving them along at the same pace as the rest. Butterflies dithered up around them out of the long grasses and flowers, and an occasional horned lark, and once a small flock of bluebirds too.

They halted and tidied up the formation in the line of trees and bushes that tracked the shallow ravine, only for a minute or so but enough for us to catch up with them, somewhat against our will. Then a bugle tootled a phrase or two that combined the signal to charge with the rhythm of 'Yankee Doodle', the little cannons cracked, aimed at the one Mexican piece set in the low stockade of saddles and so forth, and they were off:

Sing Yankee Doodle, that fine tune
Americans delight in
It suits for peace, it suits for fun
It suits as well for fighting.

207

It took no more than a couple of choruses to get them to where Houston wanted them, and till then not a shot fired from the Mexican lines. He waved his sword in the air round his head, got his big white gelding to do a pirouette, and, well, nothing like 'as one', but tolerably together, they got off their only volley of the battle. Since the Mexicans were mostly flat on the ground behind their low barricade I doubt it did much except wake them up. Credit where credit is due, they got in a return volley at less than twenty yards – these, though prostrate with flux and dopey with opium, were nonetheless soldiers – and dropped maybe twenty or thirty Texians, dead or wounded. Joey and I were grateful for this, since we could kneel down and tend those not dead. Nevertheless, a spent ball parted my hair and I lay quite flat until Joe told me the shooting was over. These casualties were enough, maybe, to have halted the Texians or caused some wilting of the desire to fight, but they were already too close, already too far gone in their headlong rush, and well before the Mexicans could reload they were over the barricade, tearing it apart, hallooing and catcalling like a bunch of Redskins, and in amongst them, even while most were still trying to drag themselves out of their sickly torpor.

What followed was not nice. Neither side could reload and apart from the sporadic popping of pistols there was very little noise in the first minutes, just the crunch of rifle butts on skulls, the rasping slash of those terrible knives across chests and throats yielding instant gouts of blood, the gasp and grunt men make when involved in tough work like kicking down a building or a tree, or butchering a carcase, but soon these were drowned out by the screams of those mortally hurt, the pleas for mercy, the howling cry of men seized with a fever to kill.

'Come on, fellers, they're only runts, piglets or rats, see that one scamper off, wait till I get him . . .'

'Look at this one I've got here. See if I can get his head off in one . . . Ouch, fucking bastard bit me, take that and that . . .'

'Lookee here. A priest, a fucking fat Roman priest. He's lost one eye already, let's relieve him of the other . . .'

Adiós, Padre Jaime.

The Mexicans, small, dark men from the south of that country, Indians apart from their officers, soon broke once the disciplines of line and movement and drill were forgotten, and, throwing their weapons behind them, scampered into the trees. Some of the Texians now paused to reload and went into the woods as if after game, dropping the fugitives out of the boughs, picking them off in the thickets.

Joe and I now felt it safer to draw a little nearer. We clambered through what was left of the minuscule fortification and headed towards Santa Anna's tent. Half a dozen of his officers in their braided tail coats and cockaded hats were covering the entrance with pistols and swords. The Texians took one look at them, decided they meant business, and hurried on like a wave breaking round a rock. The embroidered flap was lifted and out he came, hopping and stumbling as he sought to pull on the second leg of his trousers. His aides didn't wait for him to get it on. One of them slapped the huge Bonaparte hat on his President's head, and then they bustled him into a little improvised corral where their horses were. Someone hoisted him, one trouser leg still flapping, on to his big black horse, and in a moment they were cantering off the field.

But of course they were trapped and picked up the next day trying to get across that same bridge, now burnt, and brought to Houston as prisoners. Many said he should have executed them, but he didn't, and others who were there said signs of the Craft were exchanged between them and Santa Anna got off because they were both Masons. But that's by the way.

The tent now seemed empty, but none of us was quite ready to enter it. There was a sort of magic over it, a sort of taboo, as if it were a sanctuary, a place only Chiefs or Priests could enter. And before any could summon up the guts to break this taboo up came General Sam Houston, on his horse, a Chief now if ever there was one.

The men around, many hideously splashed with blood, gave him a cheer. They called out, seeking his praise, his commendation.

'Chief, we did it, didn't we?'

'It was shooting fish in a barrel . . .'

And so on.

He gave them a wave, which, and I may be mistaken, had a hint of disdain in it, dropped himself out of his saddle, and pushed through the flaps of the tent. A silence settled over us; we were just a small crowd, twenty or so. Beyond, in the woods and on the lake-side and river bank, the slaughter went on. And then he came out again, leading by the hand our Emily, tall, pale beneath the dark honey of her countenance, still with the big white cloth wrapped round her and tucked in her armpits.

Houston let his gaze move slowly over the little crowd.

'You owe this woman,' he eventually began, speaking slowly, spacing the words, his voice deep and carrying. 'And she has told me how you can pay her. Keep our state, our lone-star state, our republic of Texas, free of slavery. And I'll add to that. Remember her. Remember Emily Rose West, the Yellow Rose of Texas.'

Well, there were a few who cheered but not many. Some at the back even booed. They were fed up with the indenture system, straight slavery was simpler.

'And now,' he went on, 'stop the killing. The Alamo and Goliad are avenged.' And he turned away, issuing orders to his staff, arranging for the surrender of such of the Mexicans as were still alive.

Nearly seven hundred Mexicans were killed at San Jacinto. Nearly eight hundred were captured. The bodies were not buried but rotted hideously through the heat of the nascent summer. The main part of the action, but not the slaughter, lasted less than twenty minutes.

Tom, Saul and Solomon were among those captured. Gregory Bush, to whom they were indentured, picked them out of the compound where the prisoners had been herded and, drunk as he was, and supported by five friends, whipped them until dusk fell. Joe went back to being Houston's body servant, and Ben re-emerged as his cook. Joe finished his song:

Oh now I'm going to find her, for my heart is full of woe
And we'll sing the songs together that we sung so long ago.
We'll play the banjo gaily, and we'll sing the songs of yore,
And the Yellow Rose of Texas shall be mine for evermore. *

* This is perhaps the most convincing evidence that there is a lot of truth in Eddie's account. The version of 'The Yellow Rose of Texas' that he has transcribed here exists on a piece of plain paper, c.1836, and is now housed in the archives of the University of Texas in Austin. My source for this information (I have not, yet, myself, visited Austin) is, as stated earlier, www.markw.com/yelrose. J. R.

Part VI

MISSISSIPPI

The Blues ain't nothing but a good woman on your mind.

JOHN HURT, Blues singer, 1893–1966

24

Well, if I may allow myself a form of speech common amongst aficionados of The Turf, this has been a proper turn-up for the book.* Well done, young Guppy. I find myself writing my memoirs not in a prison cell but at an honestly turned if heavy table in the window of a first-floor room in Lambeth, just south of the Waterloo Station. It is in a new square just run up by a speculative builder called Walcott, and I don't doubt it'll fall down within twenty years, but it suits me now. I have the use of a water closet, or Water-Loo, hence "loo', on the half-landing, and there is a lithograph of the Duke's funeral over the mantel shelf and on the wall facing the window another of the Queen at the Great Exhibition. I should figure in this, robed as a Chinaman, but try as I might I cannot persuade myself that the artist has included me. Never mind. I had to pay a sov for a month in advance and another as deposit on the furniture and so forth, so already that's two of the five sovs I blagged out of F. B.-O. However, I have hopes.

The fact of the matter is that this morning, having first satisfied myself that my tracker was in place, I paid a visit to Mr John Murray's in Albemarle Street. I was not taken upstairs to the front

* An unpredictable event, derived from the term applied to horses which win races they are not expected to win. Since they are therefore not backed by punters they are a source of income to the bookmakers. J. R.

room overlooking the street, but I managed to spin out a full half-hour with a clerk in the downstairs office, and that should be enough to put the wind up Mr Supercilious B.-O.

Meanwhile, there's not much to fill the time and I'm now so much in the habit of it I might as well get on as before and continue these memoirs. Who knows but that clerk might stimulate Mr Murray into taking an interest and if he does he'll want the whole shebang, bang up to date.

Where was I?

Oh yes. Having just made our irrefragably decisive contributions to the battle of San Jacinto, Emily West and I were on our way to New Orleans, Emily now equipped with a certificate declaring her a free woman, neither property nor indentured, signed by Sam Houston and countersigned by Morgan who arrived from Galveston the day after the battle. Between them they also coughed up fifty silver dollars. Yours truly got zilch, to use a Yankee term, except a pat on the back. When I saw the specie they found in Santa Anna's waggon train I asked for back pay as medical officer to the Santa Anna army, but that was not forthcoming. However, I still had what was left of my spade guineas tucked away and, anyway, Emily said she'd support me while we were together: in fact she gave me five of her dollars.

On the way out of the Texian camp, we passed a net bag containing the heads of our erstwhile friends Tom, Solomon and Saul, hanging where G. Bush had put them on a cypress, shrouded with Spanish moss, one swathe of which hung across Saul's face, giving him the look of a comical, bearded old man.

'Strange fruit,' Emily commented, with a grimace and a sniff, and walked on.

This prompted me to quiz her on her recent activities, which had ensured the continuation at least of the indenture system in Texas, and possibly legalisation permitting outright slavery of her own kind within the borders of the new republic, although Houston had spoken against it.

She stopped, turned on me, looked down at me, arms akimbo.

'Number one,' she began, 'American Negroes are neither my kith nor kind. I was born in a British colony and since emancipation can claim to be a citizen of that country. My ancestors were brought to Antigua more than a century ago. I am three-quarters white, at least, and the white blood in me is largely that of the Bertram family, people of wealth and note. What is African in me is Ashanti, which accounts for my height and my beauty, or so I have been told. Royal Ashanti at that. I am no more one of these people than you are, let's say, Irish. All right?'

'Of course. I meant no harm. I just wondered, that's all—'

'Fuck off, Eddie. You're full of shit.'

And she turned away, dropped her arms, and strode on down the track we were on towards Lynch's ferry. With her long legs and my short ones it was quite a struggle to keep up with her. All in all, I felt I had touched a raw place, a place that hurt.

I came up with her on the landing stage where a small crowd had gathered, watching and waiting for the large flatboat to be hauled on its winched rope from the further bank a good half-mile away.

'Number two?' I suggested. 'You began with a number one. What is number two?'

'You still here, little man?' She thought for a moment, amber eyes fixed on the further shore, then looked down and grinned. 'All right. Number two. Survival. More than survival. I want to make something of myself. I coulda stayed on the island, kept house for the Bertrams, even kept young master Thomas's bed warm for him when he come over, but I'm worth more than that. I made a mistake getting indentured to Jimmy Morgan, but I was in New York, close to starving, it was fucking winter with snow a yard deep . . . You know what snow is? 'Course you do. But it was new to me. And he promised two good meals a day down south where it never snows. Well, I know better now. I'm going back to NY and this time it aint going to be me that gets stamped on. I'm going to kick ass, and I've worked out how. Does that bug you at all?'

'No, ma'am. Not in the least.'

'You done some bad things in your time?'

'Of course. Yeah. I reckon.'

'Do they keep you awake at night?'

I gave that a moment's thought, decided we were playing truth and I had nothing to lose by playing along.

'Not at all. When you're in a fix you got to get out of it, best way you can. Least ways, if you want to survive.'

215

'You're right. That's one thing this goddamn country has taught me. When the chips are down and it's either you or the next guy, then anything goes. You just make sure it's him – it's usually a him – that goes to the wall and not you. And it's you makes up the rules, 'cos there aint none until you do. What they call the frontier spirit, I guess. You know, like if it's win or lose you want to win, right?'

'Right.'

'O-K. Here's the boat. We'll hang out together until we get to New Orleans, then if you're heading back to England we'll kiss goodbye and no regrets. O-K?'

'Fine!'

Over three hundred miles, would you believe? Those United States are so fucking huge, the distances so great, and in my travels over a decade and a half I crossed them north to south and west to east, and a whole lot of that on foot. The Girth of a Nation, no less, and one of the biggest on the planet.

Two hundred and fifty miles, covered in a fortnight on foot, in a waggon for a day, on the back of a mule in a mule train for three of them, brought us through prairie and swamp land, cotton and sugar plantations, to Donaldsonville, a small town on the big river, which is what 'mississippi' means in some Indian tongues. We used a couple of Emily's silver dollars to cover the last fifty miles on a riverboat, the *Belvidere*, spelt just so, ox-bowing down the Mississippi to New Orleans which we reached in the early afternoon.

Tiny settlements began to appear more frequently behind the levées – banks raised to hold back the river when it flooded – and occasionally we passed big white houses with colonnaded fronts, set back behind formal gardens, each with its own landing stage, some with elegant steam pinnaces moored or anchored close by with gleaming brass funnels. Negroes plied hoes and such like across huge plantations under the eyes of mounted overseers who carried bull-whips or carbines in the crooks of their left elbows. I borrowed a spyglass from a passing officer of the boat and could see some slaves were manacled and many had a hoop of iron about their necks, so they could be chained if need arose.

A few miles further on these gave way to shanties that lined the river, many on the levée itself, each roofed with a thatch of plantain leaves and palm branches, often with an abundance of scarlet

216

hibiscus and such like along their eaves and a small grove of orange trees or plantains behind. Occasionally a waft from orange blossom penetrated the odours of the riverboat. Old white-haired Negroes sat in rocking chairs on their porches while the younger ones fished with rods from the levée or cast nets from tiny skiffs.

'Not all slaves then,' I suggested, 'the coloured folk, I mean.'

'That's right,' a tall man next to us offered. I'd taken him for a preacher or maybe a lawyer, on account of his long black coat and wide-brimmed white hat but revised my judgement as he let loose a stream of tobacco juice into the sulky brown flood beneath us. He was younger, too, than I had first thought, with a blond moustache and thin goatee beard, a prominent nose and pale blue eyes. 'The Frogs had a law that said any that had French blood in them was free, and so it stayed, even after the Purchase.'

'And then there were a whole host more came from Haiti after the bloody revolution there. Same law applied.' This from a thin, short woman with a parasol as well as a sun bonnet. She wore glasses and had a book always to hand in her reticule so I took her for a schoolteacher. 'It's a bad business, no good will come of it, gives our Negroes false ideas of themselves.'

'I beg your pardon!' Emily turned on her, voice like a blade rasping across a steel.

'Oh, I don't count you a Negro, my dear. You speak like an English woman I met, on the upriver boat, oh, some ten years ago, I guess, but I'll not forget her – a Mrs Trollope,* would you believe it? But a more respectable and educated lady I never met. And clearly you are a yellow, not a black.'

An altercation might now have developed, for Emily had all the susceptibility to anger that those who are uncertain of their situation in society always have when they perceive themselves sold short; however, at this moment, a crescent-shaped vista opened up in front of us along the left bank.

'Best way to arrive,' cried Emily. I couldn't see why. Columns of smoke filled one quarter of the horizon. It put me in mind of

---

* This must be Frances Trollope who travelled up the Mississippi from New Orleans in 1827 with her children, including Anthony who later became the famous novelist. On her return she wrote *Domestic Manners of the Americans*, a best-selling account of her three years in the States. J. R.

Manchester, even though here the fumes came mostly from the funnels of steam-assisted cotton boats getting up power to take them down the one hundred and fifty miles through the delta to the sea, the Gulf, to Manchester itself and its cotton-spinning mills.

Beneath the forest a thicket of masts was revealed. The quay these ships were moored at was all but two miles long and every space seemed taken, with more boats at anchor midstream, and, coming as we were along the bank above the quays, the air seemed dense with poles and spars and webs and cradles of lines and ropes, halyards, sheets and flags, not a few of them the red duster of old England.

Everywhere there was bustle and animation in spite of the humid heat that lay over the water and the city beyond, and as we drew nearer we could see how lines of Negro dockers, slaves and freed alongside each other, swung over gangways with huge sacks on their shoulders one way, while coming off the boats they returned with all manner of goods: furniture, kitchenware, crates of choice wines, tea chests, pianos, ironware and cheap tin trays, and from one ship a herd of a hundred or more hogs, perhaps brought not from the south and the sea, but the prairies to the north. Sugar and cotton filled holds just previously emptied of life's necessities and luxuries. And the smells: the smoke which was part coal, part wood soaked in bitumen, hot steam and metal, tar from the rigging, sewage and the sweet but nauseous smell of rotting shellfish, and the cotton dust that hung in the atmosphere and set me sneezing; animal smells, brewery smells, rotten vegetables and decaying lilies – the dense miasma hung like a blanket, shifting as we moved or as the slightest of breezes shifted it, an æolian harp of olfactory sensation.

'Busy place' was all I could think of saying to our tall, tobacco-chewing preacher.

'So it is,' he grunted, 'and all due to steam.' Yet again he let loose another watery chew, before continuing: 'Twenty years ago it could take a fortnight to get up from the Gulf if you didn't have the right breeze. With a steam tug or your own steam you can do it in a day.'

He pulled his hat over his eyes, and lifted up the big leather bag he had hitherto kept between his booted feet and nodded towards the quay where, almost miraculously, there was a space, a berth. Already the deckhands below us were humping the hawsers over their shoulders ready to sling them ashore.

'Time to go down,' he said, 'if you don't want to be caught in the crowd. Your first visit, is it?'

'Mine, yes, but not my companion's.'

'That what you call her? Not my business, but don't let her hijack you into no voodoo business. See ya!'

And he swayed off towards the companionway with a roll and a lurch, and, as he did, the riverboat let off three long blasts on her hooter, loud enough, where we were standing, to wake the dead.

25

We bounced down the gangplank, me with my black leather haversack which I carried by its straps; Emily with what she had done up in a sheet tied at the four corners, and so on to terra firma. Instantly a swarm of urchins, mostly different shades of black, hawking everything from their sisters to a night's lodging, from slices of unripe watermelon to condoms like chipolata skins made from calves' intestines, closed around us and the other passengers.

'First, we'll get our tickets organised,' Emily shouted over her shoulder, then caught one of the cleaner street arabs, a girl, by one of her short pigtails, tied with little red bows, bent over her and shouted in her ear. 'Shipping clerk,' she cried. 'Where can I find a shipping clerk?'

'I'll show you for a dollar.'

'A quarter.'

'Done.'

And our waif took Emily's free hand.

She led us through the market, through the usual litter of cabbage leaves, squashed fruit, picked over by the hopelessly indigent, and across Decatur, took a right up St Ann past the places des Armes and so across Bourbon. This was where the smart shops were, windows ablaze, jewellery, perfume, gorgeous dresses trimmed with coloured plumes, ostrich and peacock which would not have disgraced the new arcades off Piccadilly and were as brightly lit by the newly laid gas that glowed incandescently in the shops and from brackets on the corners for all it was still full daylight. Thirty-six, Mr Murray, you will remember, was the boom year that preceded the slump of '37 and there was a lot of money about. A few more steps took us to a grubby little office beneath a sign that read 'Jacques Verne, Voyages'.

Emily paid off our guide and we went in: a counter, ledgers, books of tickets, an inkwell, and a tall, cadaverous old man with dark grey skin, who smelt of shit and lavender water. The only extraordinary thing was a rough painting on the wall behind him. It figured an octaroon, whose skull-like face was twisted into an expression that suggested it was meant to be frightening, though the horror was betrayed by a self-mocking twinkle in the eye and the rakish tilt of his high hat. He was wearing a black-tailed coat over striped trousers, carried a black cane with one hand and long cigarillo in the other.

We came out with two tickets for a square-rigged freighter with auxiliary steam, called the *Waverley*, just now loading sugar for New York before crossing to the Lyle dock in Liverpool, and due to sail on the evening tide. Emily stopped on the sidewalk.

'That picture,' she said. 'Baron Samedi.'

'Who?'

'Baron Samedi. Chief spirit of the Voodoo.'

We still had a couple of hours to waste and I said I'd like to see the famous cemetery. We took directions and found our way down two or three narrow streets where guitars were strummed lazily in back-rooms and even an occasional piano tinkled or harmonium wheezed, but always with the ratatatat and a b-boom of syncopated drums, real or improvised, at the back of them. Out in the street limber Negroes in tight pants and with wide-brimmed hats pulled over their sharp and gleaming eyes sauntered with studied nonchalance or struck poses with their canes against the wooden pillars and rails that fronted most of the buildings. They called after Emily, sometimes with frank awe at her beauty, more often offering obscenities with which, Mr Murray, I will not disgrace these pages.

The St Louis cemetery is where bodies are famously not buried but immured in tombs. The place was one of considerable grandeur with avenues of stone structures, many in gleaming marble or sparkling granites, with wrought-iron railings and polished metal furnitures, most in the style of the ancient Greek and Roman temples and some as big as small houses. I was hoping to find the last resting place of Sir Edward Pakenham, the Duke's brother-in-law, who led the Third Division including the 88th the Connaught Rangers, in which I myself was an ensign, at the battle of Salamanca in 1812. Sir Edward commanded the British force at New Orleans in 1815 and was killed in the battle which he lost through his own impetuosity, lacking the sagacity of his noble relation. I tried to explain all this to Emily, but she showed a marked lack of interest, though she was impressed by many of the monuments. Thence, having failed in this endeavour to find his tomb, if indeed it was there, we made our way back across North Rampart Street to where the *Waverley* was moored.

I was pleased to note that the flag on the forepeak, straightened by the evening breeze, was the ensign of the Rathbone Line – three red and white horizontal stripes with a red 'R' in the centre of the white. For a time I tutored children of the Rathbone family at Greenbank, their country house near Liverpool.*

We walked down the gangway – the main deck was on a level with or even below that of the levée, so completely loaded was she – and reported to the second mate, who agreed that there was indeed a cabin, a stateroom no less, waiting for us, on the instructions of the shipping clerk. He took us down a companionway and opened a door.

Stateroom? It was no bigger than one of those Hackney cabriolets which have the door behind, and shoot their fares out, like sacks of coal, upon the pavement. Yet somehow some conjuring carpenter had contrived to fit in two bunks, one of course above the other, each no more than two feet in width, together with a washstand and a bull's-eye mirror for shaving. Emily's bundle occupied most of the floor. Maybe because there was nowhere convenient to put it was the reason I held on to my haversack. There was also the consideration that it held my remaining spade guineas. I rarely resorted to stuffing them away in their earlier hiding place now that there seemed to be no great reason for doing so – how wrong I was very shortly proved to be. There being no purpose in staying there except when we had to, we returned to the main deck and at that moment catastrophe struck.

A small, bow-legged man was coming down the gangway. His skin had the mahogany hue of a sailor and he was carrying a small duffel

* On behalf of the Home Office he was spying on them. See *A Very English Agent*, Chapter 46. J. R.

222

bag on his shoulder. His silver hair was streaked with black and he had big bushy eyebrows. He saw me. He stopped a yard short of the deck.

'Jasus!' he said.

'Shit!' said I.

'Eddie!' he cried.

'Seamus!' I replied.

He slung the duffel bag at me and hurled himself after it. I dodged back, round the mainmast. He came after me. I broke away towards the gangway. Emily gave his duffel bag a kick that pushed it into his path. It caught his foot and for a moment he flew, arms outstretched, legs in the air behind him. I heard the crash of his landing, but I did not see it. I was up the gangplank and almost back on the quay before he hit the deck.

It was evening. It was New Orleans. A Spanish town, a French town – and that all added up to *la promenade*, *el paseo*. Anyone in the town – French, Spanish, Creole, mulatto or black-as-the-ace-of-spades Negro – with a halfway decent dress to wear or a suit that made a statement was walking, slowly but not idling except when they met a group of friends or acquaintances going in the opposite direction. Then they coalesced into an animated, laughing, gossiping, even arguing group. There were parasols and *parapluies*; there were high wigs from the last century and the latest pointed hats out of which ostrich plumes spilled and curly-brimmed high hats; there were rouge and painted lips and fragrances and there were moustaches oiled and twisted into exquisitely exact points above goatees that had been trimmed hair by hair. There was gold and a little silver, encrusted with jewels, intaglios and cameos and powdered expanses of chest swelling deliciously to lacy hems cut seductively low, or shirts that were so white it almost hurt the eye to look at them beneath stocks and cravats that tumbled in artfully disposed folds and valleys . . . and so on, to shoes that must have caused concealed agonies as they pinched, for both sexes, toes in points like daggers. You get the picture.

I ran through it all when I could. I sidled and squeezed. On occasion I hoisted my haversack above my head to facilitate my passage. I begged pardon here, made my excuses there, and occasionally threw a glance over my shoulder to see how Seamus was doing. He lacked manners, the polished approach. He pushed and shoved. He had banged his nose on the deck and the blood ran into his mouth so when he huffed and puffed or swore or pleaded for a clear passage, he spat a little shower of claret droplets. Yet, he gained on me, brute force seeming to be more efficacious than the finesse of my approach. But Nemesis awaited him and the goddesses smiled kindly on me. When he was a mere ten paces behind me, and clearly felt that one ferocious lunge would catch me he bellowed out: 'M'geold, ye varmint, do y'still have me fockin' geold up y' sodomite arseshole?'

... and made a final lunge that almost bowled over a mulatto beauty in a white satin damascene dress that would have graced a vestal virgin and spattered it with blood. Her escort, six feet of lean, tough Negro in a white shirt with a gold medallion and kidskin breeches, caught him by the arm, spun him round and smote him with a fist like a smoked leg of pork, so he, poor Seamus that is, went down like the proverbially pole-axed ox. Now, as well as blood, it was teeth he was spitting.

I sauntered off, letting the crowd take me at its own pace, and I even offered a sort of a half-smile here and a nod there, and tipped my battered old hat once or twice at the more fetching of the ladies, but behind the assumed nonchalance my brain was in a fever. What to do? I could not go back to the *Waverley* for that was where Seamus would be as soon as he had recovered his senses. I could hardly search for another ship to take me in the same direction for he would anticipate that move too. Clearly the best thing for it was to go quite some other way, but where? Back towards Mexico? I shuddered at the thought. A boat south, into the Caribbean? But that would simply take me further and further away from where I wanted to be. Then came the message, loud and clear, a blast on a ship's steam hooter, far louder than was strictly congruent with the size of the vessel. The *Belvidere*. Of course. She had disposed of her cargo of cotton, sugar and timber and her passengers seeking pleasure or employment in New Orleans, and taken on, I imagined, ironware and other hardware, the cloths and clothes, the wines and brandies that the port could supply, and passengers too, rich planters returning to their plantations, young families seeking adventure or at least employment upriver, and above all a host of red-faced, beefy-looking youths and young men, in high spirits and many the worse for drink. And she was about to sail again. And where was she going? Why, north of course, at least as far as the confluence with the Ohio whence I could go east. Almost as good a way of getting there as the *Waverley*'s. I climbed the gangway, parted with my last dollars to the purser who was waiting at the top, and was fortunate enough to be offered the last small cabin on the lower deck.

'Where you heading for, mister?'

'Where would you suggest?' I asked.

He looked at the coins I had given him.

'This'll get you far as Vicksburg. Chow included, but you pay for your booze.'

'Then that's where I'll go.'

I took the key to the cabin, looked at the tag, number sixteen, and turned away and almost bumped into . . . the preacher man, the young man with the dark coat and white hat, and the habit of tobacco chewing.

'Howdy, again,' he cried, and slapped the side of my arm. 'The Crescent City not to your liking then?'

'I had business there,' I improvised. 'And it's done.'

'Where you bound this time?' he continued, following me along the companionway.

'Room, I mean cabin sixteen,' I offered, but he was not to be put off so easily. He laughed but continued to hang on in behind me.

'Take them stairs then, it's on the deck below.'

He clattered down the steps, squeezed with me past a family of what I took to be Dutch farmers from the way they talked, and when the key would not turn in the lock of number sixteen eased it through the wards for me.

'Where you really going?' he tried again.

'Vicksburg,' I somewhat grudgingly replied. I don't like every Tom, Dick and Harry to know my business.

'It's no great shakes,' he expostulated, as he pushed the door open for me, 'but, hell, for two nights, it's home.'

He was referring not to Vicksburg but to the cabin which was in fact a little larger than the 'stateroom' on the *Waverley* and fitted out with some attempt at style. The single bed had a woven, tasselled counterpane, there was a small chest of drawers as well as a wash-stand, and a pretty oil-lamp with a patterned, frosted-glass funnel. On the wall above it hung a gilt-framed engraving of mountain scenery with Redskins in the foreground.

My self-appointed guide held out his hand.

'Charles d'Orléans,' he grinned, giving the words a Frenchified inflection. 'You can call me Duke.'

'Joseph Charles Edward, third Viscount of Bosham,' I replied. 'You can call me Eddie.'

And at that moment the deep rumble that had filled the background rose to a roar, white water cascaded past the porthole, for cabin sixteen was just forward of the port paddle wheel which was turning in reverse, and the lurch of the *Belvidere* pulling out from the quay had Duke grabbing my elbow momentarily for support.

'Maybe I'll see you in the saloon in an hour or so,' he said, repeating the grin. 'Buy you a drink.'

And he was gone.

Throughout all the events I have just described I had managed to hold on to my haversack, which I now placed on the bed or bunk and opened up. Yes, lying at a slight angle across the bottom was my Bowie knife, James Bowie's knife it was, you'll recollect, and my little tubular purse which had once held forty spade guineas and now contained only six, the latest having gone on my ticket to Liverpool and some rags and tags in the way of shirts, socks and a spare pair of trousers Emily had made me buy along the way. Striped they were, grey and black of a sort I had never seen in England, but then it was now well over five years since I had been there and how would I know how fashions had changed?

The sight of these and the recollection of how Emily had chosen them quite brought a lump, as they say, to my throat and a tear to my eye. Would I ever see her again? I doubted it. And though it had not been my fortune to bed her (and a glance in the mirror above the washstand reminded me that there was little in my appearance to suggest such an outcome was to have been expected), I knew I would miss her not only as a cunning and resourceful accomplice but also as a friend. Looking back, Mr Murray, over a long and varied life, I have to say there have been very few, either male or female, to whom I could readily pay that compliment – my boyhood friend Fernando, Mistress Flora Tweedy, Sergeant Patrick Coffey and Corporal Kevin Nolan of the 88th, and Maggie-May who later became Lady Danby which no way prevented her from being my playmate . . .

I digress, now, as I write, and then as I listened to the chug of the engines, the swish of the paddle, and watched through the porthole the darkening banks of the Mississippi slip by. I pulled myself together – if I have a gift it is my ability to do just that, and where would I be without it? – slipped a guinea into my trouser pocket, did what I could with my hair, scraped the sharpest edge of my Arkansas Toothpick over my cheeks and endeavoured to brush down my coat, still the one I had bought in Acapulco six months or more ago, by my reckoning.

Beneath the pearly glow of the western sky the riverbanks were merely a dark line above the slightly luminous glow of the water, and in any case of little interest since this, as far as Donaldsonville where Emily and I had boarded the *Belvidere*, was the reach of the river I had already passed over; I was not therefore tempted to linger outside but went straight to the saloon which occupied most of the top deck behind the twin stovepipe-like chimneys out of which smoke, laced with sparks, was pumped across the wide expanse. However, I could not refrain, as I stood at the stern guard and looked out beyond the almost drooping Stars and Stripes, from reflecting on the way the *Belvidere* scarred the satin of the water in a spreading pair of lines, like the flanges of an arrow aimed at the dark heart of a continent.

26

The freight the *Belvidere* carried was quite largely a human one. The semicircle beneath me was filled with those young males I had seen on the quay, some standing at the gunwales, others sitting, even contriving to lie where space allowed it, on the deck. They smoked, chewed, spat. They were tall, tough-looking men, with rough, determined-looking faces and athletic limbs. Most wore loose, coarse brown trousers, some blue *de Nîmes*, and red or blue shirts with sleeves rolled up above their elbows. For all the dourness of their general aspect they were in good spirits: there was much laughter, some singing, and bottles went round, the bottoms hoisted above their mouths and then thrown into the river. Who were they? It was not until the following morning that their presence was explained to me.

Meanwhile, the slatted doors behind me swung open and shut and emitted a gust of warm air aromatised with cigar smoke and carrying on it the animated chatter of thirty or so customers, and I felt a sudden surge of loneliness again which could only be assuaged by the company of my fellows.

The saloon, at first sight, was a swell sort of a place. At the far end was a curved mahogany counter shielding shelves filled with bottles of every shape and hue a bottle can be but leaving space for a big rococo mirror in the centre: in front of it high stools and in front of them a space of bare floorboards kept empty then, but later used for dancing, and round it, following the curve of the riverboat's hull, tables and chairs. There were oil-lamps fitted to brackets above them and, from the middle of the ceiling, a big candelabra sort of a thing with swooping branches like those of a fig tree, almost a chandelier, hung with large glass or crystal drops that vibrated ever so slightly with the rumble of the engines below. There was much gold leaf too, gingerbread at any rate, and the curtains over the windows were crimson plush, so all in all there was a feeling of warmth, enjoyment and wealth about the place.

It was only on the third or fourth glance that one began to take in the chipped plaster on the raised moulding of the gilt, the finger marks on the curtains, the starred crack in the mirror, the ankle-deep litter of paper serviettes, shells and the casings of hundreds of crayfish on the floor in front of the counter. And almost everywhere there were pools of slippery liquid which at first I took to be drink, but soon realised, as a gob splattered near my feet, were the expectorations of the tobacco-chewing fraternity. There were polished brass spitoons but they were calculatedly ignored and even the runners of carpet round the sides squelched as one walked on them, so prevalent was the nuisance.

I found an empty stool in the corner where the end of the bar met the outer wall, which suited me on two counts: first, it was out of the way and left me feeling unobtrusive, something my calling has trained me to value, and secondly, it overlooked a pair of tables pushed together where the only women who had ventured into the saloon had arranged themselves. There were about six of them, and they had three or four children clinging to their skirts or perched in their laps. I guessed they were individuals travelling unaccompanied who had come together for mutual comfort and protection. One of them I thought I recognised, but could not place her for some time. She was thin, small, wore wire-framed glasses, and held on at all times with both hands to a small reticule on her knees. And then of course I remembered: she was the lady who, on our way to New Orleans, had recognised our English way of speaking and likened it to that of a Mrs Trollope. So that made two, three if you include me, who were still on board even though the *Belvidere* was now reversing her journey. Eventually, and he took his time, the bartender came my way and enquired if I wanted anything. I asked for a whisky. He put a shot glass in front of me and filled it to the brim from a bottle of caramel-coloured liquid. And then he waited, bottle in hand. I surmised correctly that he wanted to be paid.

'I owe you how much?' I asked.

'Two nickels.'

I turned to an old-timer who sat next to me and had already offered me a 'howdy' from beneath his huge and floppily brimmed slouch hat. An odour of garlic and whisky hung about him.

'How much is that?' I asked him.

'Two cents,' he grunted.*

'I'm afraid this is all I have,' I said, and placed my spade guinea on the counter.

'The fuck is that?' demanded the bartender, a large man with a face as liberally carbuncled as Bardolph's.

'It is an old English coin, made, as you see, of gold, worth a sovereign and one-twentieth of a sovereign.' I supposed he would not be familiar with the word 'shilling'.

'Go fuck yourself, motherfucker,' and he took back the shot glass which I had not yet touched. I sighed, looked around and caught the eye of Duke who had just come in and was standing at the other end of the saloon casting a lazy eye over it all. He was chewing on an expended lucifer stick which he now spat out, before sauntering across the room to join me.

'Problem?' he asked.

I explained.

'Show me this guinea then.'

I pulled it out again. He picked it out of my palm, hefted it, squinted at it.

'Give you three dollars for it,' he said.

I was so flustered I accepted, though I felt sure he was shortchanging me. I was right. When I changed what was left at a bank in Vicksburg I got four dollars ninety.

The old-timer rumbled what was going on. He shook his head and said: 'Sometimes you eat the bar, and sometimes the bar, wal, he eats you.'

I had no idea what he meant. Still, I got my drink, which I sipped

---

* Yes, I wondered about that too, but it turns out that until the mid-1850s the only coin that was made entirely of nickel was the single cent, hence in those days that was what a 'nickel' was. J. R.

slowly. It was sweet on the tongue, burned in the throat and warmed my stomach with a claw-like fire. I guess it was getting on for pure alcohol flavoured with burnt sugar.

The evening wore on. I bought a small plate of crawfish and did like everyone else with the shells; I had a couple more whiskies. Duke drifted off after chatting in a lazy sort of way. The noise grew, the cigar smoke thickened, gathering in layers in the branches of the candelabra, shifting like a blue mist when a door was opened. A couple of country folk from Nashville appeared and played banjoes and sang and then were joined by an octaroon who played the small upright piano with them.

You see that girl with the red dress on
Some folks call her Dinah
Stole my heart away from me
Way down in Louisiana.

The big bee sucks the blossom
And the little bee makes the honey
Poor man throws the cotton
And the rich man makes the money.

We travel all over this country wide
Playing music by the hour
Always wear this great big smile
We never did look sour.

Several of the men danced together in couples while others badgered the women to dance with them. Three of them did, but not the prim lady with the spectacles. And just beyond where the ladies were sitting Duke was fooling with a small pack of cards – the three-card trick – and, of course, he was losing to two young lads in check shirts and blue jeans held up with broad leather suspenders. But only loose change. I waited. Sure enough, once he had them believing they could not fail to win, he shuffled the three cards he had been using into the small pack, offered it to one of the lads who shuffled them again and gave it to the second lad who cut. The first lad then dealt five out to each of them and himself, leaving five unused. Duke had not touched them after handing them over.

231

Miss Prim made her excuses and went out.

Duke lost fifty cents on the first hand and twenty-five on the second. Straight riverboat poker, the way the game was made, no frills, no cards changed, none shown, a pack of twenty-one cards, tens to aces plus a joker.

Miss Prim came back. The ladies with children had also left and she chose a chair closer to the game than the one she had had. She took a book from her reticule, and held it up in front of her face, almost at arm's length, as if to get the best of the light on it. The book, I later discovered, was *Hell Bent for Damnation, the Sermons of the Reverend John Spencer*. But what I noticed there and then was that she was restless with it, shifting it in her hand, turning the pages, and so forth, while every now and then her gaze seemed to drift off into the distance.

Or at any rate as far as the five cards the lad in front of her held fanned out in front of her face.

By the end of the third hand I'd figured out what she was doing.

Her left hand, holding the book, supported its back with just one finger. Two fingers of her right hand lay against her cheek, in front of her small, delicate ear. Then the one finger of her left hand was joined by another, and her right hand dropped to her lap. Then the two fingers of her left hand became three, and with her right hand she turned a page . . . and so on. The lad in front of her had one ace, no kings, a pair of queens. And a jack and a ten.

Thus, out of the twenty cards they were playing with, Duke knew where ten of them were, his own and the ones signalled by Miss Prim. This did not give him an infallible advantage, but it sure enough helped. And when it came to his turn to deal I was pretty sure he knew what the six leftover cards were too.

After half an hour the lads, looking pretty miserable, had lost five and three dollars respectively and some change, and declared themselves played out.

There were others waiting to take their place but Duke waved them away. He'd had enough of cards for one evening, he said. That was when I realised he, they, Miss Prim and he, were real pros. He followed me to the bar and bought me a drink to go with his.

'Make'm Bulleits,' he said.

Nice bottle, with the words 'Frontier Whiskey' moulded into the glass. Smoother than the rotgut I'd been having. Three nickels each though. I was just raising the shot glass to my lips for a second sip when my elbow received a nasty shove that knocked the glass against my teeth and sent the amber fluid slipping down my chin. It was the larger of the youths who had been taken by Duke and his almost invisible accomplice. So invisible that this thug clearly thought I was he. Or she.

He turned me round to face him, grabbed the collar of my coat with his left hand lifting me up on to my toes and hauled back his right fist behind his shoulder, like an archer drawing his bow, and looked set to launch it at my face. The carbuncled barman pushed the splayed muzzle of a large but old flintlock pistol against his ear and ratcheted back the claw hammer. Duke intervened, and not a moment too soon.

'Have you ever seen this little runt before?' he asked the barman.

'No, Duke,' said the barman.

'But you have seen me.'

'Several times.'

'So you'd not agree with our friend that Eddie here, for that's his name, could have been signalling to me or anything like that.'

'No, Duke.'

Duke turned to the burly youth whose fist, I was pleased to note, had dropped almost to waist level while his other hand had sufficiently relaxed to allow my heels to find the floor again.

'You were beat,' Duke went on, 'fair and square. Now go to bed and sleep it off.'

His pale blue eyes glittered like chips of ice. Burly youth let go of me, shook himself, spat at my feet, missed, went. Barman poured me another Bulleit. Duke lifted his palm from the counter uncovering a silver dollar. Barman picked it up. He didn't give Duke any change. Payment for services rendered I guessed.

I took a chance and drank the whisky the way they all did, in one big gulp, waited for the boat which, so the spirit told me, had taken a slow turn of a full circle, to resume its normal progress, caught my breath.

'Reckon I'll turn up,' I said, 'or rather "out". Even "in". See ya!'

Weaving through the crowd of dancers who were by now all men, and chucking themselves about in the wildest way, I got back through the doors to the stern guard. The fresh air, tainted with smoke though it was, sent the horizons spinning again and I had to clutch the rail.

I set out on the Odyssean journey back down the stairs to cabin sixteen. A light showed under the door. I was sure I had extinguished the oil-lamp, but . . . The door was not locked. I stumbled through. I was in the wrong cabin. I knew I was because there were three people in it. A small pretty woman in a blouse and long yellow skirt, a very large man in a leather waistcoat and *de Nîmes* blue pants and a very small baby wrapped in a blanket, in the woman's arms.

They were all black. Very black.

27

I backed out.

'Showwy, wong woom,' I mumbled.

The big male reached out a huge hand and grasped my wrist. His head was bald, or shaven, but completely smooth and hairless though contoured with bumps and lumps and hollows. His eyes were infinitely sad and hurt, like those of a whipped dog, the whites bloodshot, the irises as black as his skin. Sitting up straight, as he now was, they were almost on a level with mine. His woman reached out a hand on to his forearm, whether to restrain or support it was difficult to say.

'No, man,' he uttered, and his voice was dark and rumbling, 'you the man we lookin' for.'

'Um, how'sh that then?'

'First you come in an' shut that door.'

I did as he asked, staggering a little as I did so and having to throw out a hand to prevent myself from falling.

'Sit yourself down.' He reached out and pulled the chair that was in front of the washstand round so that I was facing them when I sat on it.

'First off – we was sent here.'

'Who by?'

'The railroad people. You a Brit, aint you? I guess that's why they sent us to you.'

'My father was English though born in Italy and lived most of his life in Spain. I don't think he ever went—'

'So am I. From Kingston, Jamaica. An' that means I aint no slave.'

'Nothing to worry about then?'

'Jus' listen, man. Like I *was* a slave. Colonel Fitzalan was like my owner. An' what the fuckin' bastard did was this. Jus' before 'mancipation act become law he took me an' me mates to New Orleans and sold us off to a Mr Ardingly what has a sugar plantation 'bout halfway between New Orleans and Baton Rouge. And now I escapin', headin' north, with Judith. This here is Jude, my Judith, and that's Esther, our little baby.'

He sat silent now, for what seemed an age, was at least a minute, fixing me with those deep, soulful eyes. I had to say something.

'Ah,' I said, 'you're telling me this Ardingly was a harsher master than Fitzalan.'

Fire took the place of soul in his eyes and he clenched his fists which, since he moved the chair, had just hung until then between his spread knees. His voice when it came was a hoarse squawk of frustrated rage.

'Man, they fucking *owned* me!'

'Ah,' I said – mollifying, I hoped, 'of course. I see.'

Though I wasn't sure I did. The cabin was still showing a tendency to turn like a fairground carousel.

'And if that aint enough, he had this fiancée, like he wants to marry her, and her mother had a fancy for Jude here for a lady's maid, 'cos she's purty and sews well, and he goin' to give her to this old woman. But Jude my wife, see?'

Like you sort of own her? But it was only a thought and I said nothing.

'So. To stay together, we gotta go north. There's a woman in Natches will put us on the Underground Railroad.'

A railroad at Natches? Possibly. But *underground*?

Another long moment of silence, just the steady rumble of the riverboat's engines. Then Judith cleared her throat.

'So we only need your help far as Natches,'* she said. Her voice was soft, gentle, an excellent thing in a woman. Man too, come to that.

* This seems to be how Natchez was spelled in the early nineteenth century. J. R.

236

'My help? How's that then?'

'We Brits. Know what I mean?' Mister took it up again after a look at his woman that clearly suggested this was man talk.

'Not sure I do.'

'Stick together. Right?'

Silence, the boat's engines thudded on. Distantly, upriver I suppose, another boat's hooter sounded a mournful note. The *Belvidere* replied, almost above our heads. I cleared my throat and tried to inject a note of authority.

'Well,' I said, 'before I put myself out on your behalf you must tell me what you want me to do.'

'Give us a safe berth. Just tonight and the night afterwards. That's what the railroad people promised. Two nights and the next morning we tie up at Natches and you'll see the last of us. Not much to ask, is it? And maybe the Lord will bless you for the rest of your mortal years.'

This last was thrown in as an afterthought, a sort of extra gratuity, offered in hope but with little expectation it would carry much weight. He was right there, and I think he sensed my reaction, for there was no more talk of the Lord.

'Taking another cabin is beyond my means. And in any case the purser would surely wonder why I should need it and be suspicious.' I paused. 'Anyway, I'm pretty sure they're all taken.'

'You missing my drift, squire.'

I felt the hair that lies in my neck and across my shoulders, and there is, Mr Murray, rather a lot of it, bristle almost like a dog's and a chill run down my spine, for his tone had changed from the not unmanly wheedling of a distraught man to something more sinister.

'The idea is we should stay here, as your guests. Know what I mean?'

And as he said this, he pushed back the edging of the counterpane and drew from under it my knife, my Arkansas Toothpick, my Bowie.

'Oh shit,' I said, and suddenly I felt a lot less drunk than before.

Early that morning, not long after first light as far as I could tell, we tied up at Baton Rouge. Little I saw of it. Brutus Ardingly Fitzalan, for that was my unwanted guest's name, taking his second names in the customary way from his owners', refused to let me out. His woman, their brat and he had contrived to sleep, head to toe, on the bunk. I curled up beneath the porthole or rather window, since it was square, and of course only finally went to sleep a half-hour before we arrived, when all the noise and bustle made sleeping an impossibility. The infant squawled intermittently throughout the night, Brutus heaved and rumbled and once shouted out, I will not say incomprehensibly though the words were jumbled, for the noise was that of an animal racked with pain and anger. There was a pisspot in the cupboard below the washstand, of which Judith first and then yours truly were constrained to take advantage. The air grew foetid, a cocktail, as the Americans say of any mixture, though reserving the word for the most part for strong drink, of sour human milk, piss, farts and infant vomit.

Anyway, once clear of Baton Rouge I managed to prevail upon Brutus to allow me to leave, though he threatened to quarter me like a chicken if I was accompanied on my return. What finally swayed him, together with Judith's urgings, was the promise of something to eat and drink on my return.

'A jug of coffee would surely be a fine thing,' was the conclusion to the parley. 'And some grits.'

Up the stairs and on the gallery I followed the guard rail round to the front of the boat desiring to feel, breathe and smell the fresh air I hoped to find there. And so I did, and, what was even better, the view that now spread itself in front of me was so extensive, was so much a matter of endless space after the confinement of the cabin, that my heart quite lifted at the sight of it and for a moment the problems presented by my charges (for that was how, almost unwittingly, I was learning to think of them) receded to the back of my mind.

The river at this point must have been all of two miles across and in the freshness of the morning light almost unrippled; certainly the surface remained unbroken, a huge sheet of warm brownish-grey modulating to a whiter shade of pale as it stretched towards a horizon of forest, a line of dark blueish-black, the furthest point as much as three miles away perhaps. The *Belvidere* was chugging along, paddles swishing behind me, on the inside of a long, long bend (there is no part in the entire length of the Mississippi that can be called straight) less than a quarter of a mile from the shore on the starboard quarter. The bank was covered with cottonwood bushes, still immature but backed by slopes of more mature trees of the same species, a sort of round-crowned poplar they are, so called from the fluff that supports their seeds as they drift through the air in early summer; the slopes themselves rode to a distant escarpment of limestone cliffs, or bluffs, which had been carved by the elements into the semblance of the towers and pinnacles of a fairy castle in a children's storybook.

But do not imagine the scene was a peaceful one. At least seven or eight people shared this favoured position on the forward guard, like me enjoying the morning freshness, and down below us the fo'c'sle was a busy hive as the deck passengers sought to get their breakfast together, coffee and grits for the most part (an occasional waft of coffee rose up to our nostrils), or disputed a square yard here and there with those newly come aboard at Baton Rouge.

Then suddenly a cry went up.

"Gator, 'gator,' and three or four dozen of them rushed to the side waving and pointing at what must to them have already been a familiar sight, though one that always may inspire awe: a pair of particularly large alligators at least twelve feet long, perfectly still in the water, their scaly backs like gnarled and crusty logs, and almost exactly hued to match the medium that supported them.

Meanwhile, the bend we were negotiating continually unscrolled like a roll of painted paper revealing new wonders or at any rate objects of interest. First there was a tiny settlement, a couple of sheds raised on piles above the muddy bank only feet from the water's edge. A curl of smoke rose from a stovepipe that pierced the shingled roof of one, while from the other a small boy emerged, waving and hallooing with an urgency that clearly surpassed the greeting any small boy will bestow on a passing boat.

'What's the matter with him?' I asked, turning to my nearest neighbour without properly taking in who she was.

'He hopes we will heave to and take on board wood from the pile you may see stacked behind his dwelling at the forest edge,' came the reply and I realised I had spoken to the lady who, in my mind, remained unalterably Miss Prim, albeit I now knew her to be the accomplice of a riverboat gambler.

'His family are woodcutters,' she continued, 'and they survive by selling wood to passing steamers. However, they rarely stop at such places, fearing to run aground, and preferring to refuel at the major ports. These people survive as far as food is concerned from what they can procure from the forest, so often they are content to be paid in strong drink, or black powder and shot for their hunting pieces.'

The settlement and its small boy slipped behind us, like the alligators, with the swiftness of a dream, and now the focus of attention fell on a cluster of boats, still a half-mile off, but approaching fast what with the current on their side and the power of our engines on ours. And they remained firmly fixed dead ahead of us so a collision seemed inevitable. With our steam whistle blaring and our hooter adding a bass note, we bore down on them. By now we could see the detail of the flotilla which was almost hurtling towards us: it was made up of two pairs of flatboats, each pair roped together, and just behind, since they had overtaken it, a raft of the sort known, as I was to learn later, as an 'ark'. The problem was that all the craft involved wanted to use the part of the river where the current flowed most strongly: the ark and the flatboats because it carried them downstream most quickly, and the riverboat because the faster flow indicated the deepest part of the river. To move away risked running aground, especially as the river here was exceedingly wide, which meant there would be shallows and barely concealed banks of sand and gravel.

In the event we passed each other without mishap but with only a fathom or two to spare separating our portside paddle wheel from the nearer of the flatboat pairs. They were strange, primitive craft, not at all like boats, but more like sheds. They even had square bows and were much bigger than their cousins on Galveston Bay, which were smaller since they required sail or oars for propulsion. These relied entirely on the river current. They were covered with plank roofs whose ridge poles ran from stem to stern, as much as sixty feet, but open to the sides. The first pair was filled with maybe eight hundred stacked barrels of flour over which the crew of six, armed with poles to fend themselves off us if we got too close, had to clamber; the second with live sheep and steers, but with an enclosure near the front in which stood, manacled to each other and the roof-supporting columns of timber, some thirty slaves, men, women and a few children. They looked frightened, as well they might. I doubted any of the crew were likely to go to the trouble of knocking their chains off should we hit them.

As they whisked by, briefly rocking in a most alarming way in the turbulence caused by our paddle, most of our deck passengers rushed to the side and jeered at those in peril beneath them, shook bags of dollars at them, saying they were too late for New Orleans, all the best bargains were gone, while their crews hollered back: 'Hand over that steamboat and I'll take it home for my old woman to make tea in! Stop that boat and I'll light my pipe from it! Let off your steam or we'll all be blown to dickens!' were the more printable comments.

From which exchanges I gathered that our deck passengers were flatboatmen themselves, which led me to question the system so I learned from Miss Prim that the practice was to knock together your flatboat in St Louis or St Andrew's Falls, which was as far up the river as you could go without portage, and, having arrived with a cargo in New Orleans, sell it for its timber to feed the furnaces of the steamboats destined to bring you back.

The ark was a different matter altogether. It was basically a raft with a shed for its owners to live in and an enclosure for their livestock. On this one an old, white-headed man and an equally ancient female sunned themselves and smoked their pipes on a wooden seat conveniently placed between the shed and the enclosure, while behind them a middle-aged yeoman manipulated a heavy steering oar. On the roof of the cabin, which served as an upper deck, two more women sat cross-legged knitting, while assorted urchins and dogs gazed at us and waved from the deck. A proud cock strutted amongst them, flapped its wings and crowed, while a cow in the enclosure, feeling the motion occasioned by our passing, mooed.

'So, who might these be?' I asked my interlocutor.

'Many families like this come from the east,' she began, 'down the Ohio, from Pittsburg, looking for a place to settle. Once they arrive at the lower reaches they will look for a place which looks promising, move house, stock and family to dry land, chop down the forest, open a woodyard and, if they are thrifty and avoid the temptations of idleness and drink, buy Negroes, grow rich, become planters, give their clapboard dwellings a white façade with pillars and their sons a Frenchified name. *Voilà*, they are gentry.'

There being nothing else of interest in sight she turned away, pulling down the small parasol she had been sheltering beneath, and, with a rustle of dark-grey taffeta, was gone. I too left the guard presently and went in search of coffee and grits.

28

I delivered coffee and some sour oatcakes to cabin sixteen and was roundly abused for taking so long.

'You fuckin' took your time! Jude 'ere is parched and near starvin', the brat is squallin' for milk she can't find, you want us all to die? It's the fuckin' black hole of Calcutty in 'ere, man. 'Ere, 'ang on a jiff.'

And he slammed the door in my face, but opened it again in ten seconds, thrusting out the jerry pot.

'Get this dealt with, and bring it back, see?'

To describe its contents would give offence, so I won't.

When I returned with it, having emptied it over the side as discreetly as I might, he stuck the point of the Arkansas Toothpick under my nostrils and swore he'd have my nose off if I tried any funny tricks and I was to be back by midday with more to eat and drink.

'A cup of rum would go down a treat,' was his parting shot.

That done, the day wore on, the hours like the links in a giant chain dragged from the deep by the cogged teeth of a steam-powered winch – I have never known, not even in prison, time drag so.

Not a cup but a bottle of rum, which probably contributed to the awful events that were unfolding, when I returned four hours later. I also had water, some oranges and some johnny, or journey, cake I bought from one of the returning flatboatmen, a Kentucky man with red hair. This time it was Jude who opened the door. Small I am, but she was smaller, the top of her head on a level with my nose, big eyes looking up at me all soulful, the baby in the crook of her arm, its head on her shoulder.

'Bring it in,' she said. 'He's asleep.'

Brutus was lying on his stomach on the bunk, one huge hand trailing along the floor beneath him, the other wrist cushioning his cheek, but with his fingers still curled round the hilt of the Toothpick. He'd taken off his singlet and I could see why. His back was a lattice of raw, scabby stripes, like the marks left by a gridiron on a slab of steak. Suppurations leaked round many of the scabs. I set down what I had brought and got out quick as I could.

As I said, the day wore on, every second relentlessly marked by the drumming of the engines and the fall of water from the wheels. Clouds began to gather ahead of us, and a sultry heat fell over the interminable river like a pall. White smoke too climbed into the air against the granite of the cloud, and flame flickered and billowed a few miles inland above the forest, which was thicker now and heavier, oak having taken the place of cottonwood.

I had a neighbour, a yellow-haired Dutchman with a big nose. Updijk was his name. He found a plug of tobacco, placed it in his cheek like the ape in the story, turned and faced me.

'You heard tell about this cimaroon they says is on board, then?'

'Cimaroon?'

'Runaway nigger. Big feller, big buck nigger, bald as a billiard ball. Lost all his hair but he's got a temper on him. They had him chained to a wooden pillar in a stable after he'd run amok and he pulled the lot down, before breaking the manacle off his leg with a sledge. Took courage that. Could smash your foot if you got it wrong.'

I nodded.

'They reckon he must be in someone's cabin, 'cos they searched all the public parts.'

'Oh yes?' said I, feigning lack of interest.

'Come from Jamaicy, they say.'

'Oh really?'

'Jamaicy is English, they say.'

'So I believe.'

'An' you be English I'd say, from your manner of speaking.'

'More Italian than anything else.'

243

'Oh yeah? All Italians hairy runts like you then?'

'Not all, no.'

He turned to the guard, watched the smoke climbing into the sky for a moment and a big heron rowing the air in front of it.

'Two thousand dollar fine and six months in the calaboose if you help a cimaroon.'

'As much as that! Really?'

Heart thumping and feeling rather sick, I turned away and slowly walked round to the back of the gallery and so into the saloon. The evening not yet being far advanced it was almost empty, with just three or four groups of people, mostly men, sitting at the low tables drinking whisky sours, or, in Miss Prim's case, tea. She had set aside the sermons of the Rev. John Spencer and replaced it with *Peter Parley's Book of Bible Stories* by Samuel Griswold Goodrich. Near her, Duke Charles d'Orléans was playing dice with my friend the red-headed Kentuckian.

They were playing Yankee-Grab. Three dice are used, thrown one at a time. The player with the highest total wins, though a likely loser can drop out after the first or second throws. A one spot counts as a seven. As on the night before, Duke was clearly salting, as they say, the mine. Kentucky Red won a dollar on the first round I watched, lost a dollar, then won three times in a row, putting him a clear five dollars and a couple of dimes ahead of the game. Duke acted all nervous. Wasn't sure he'd go on. Game was a bit high for him.

'I've gambled a bit in my time,' Duke said, 'and I know when you shouldn't buck a winning streak. Well . . . but . . . one more chance to get my dough back, then we'll call it a day.'

And he rolled his first dice out of the dice box. Five.

'Looks good. I'll . . . put in a dollar.'

Meanwhile, I was feeling jittery on account of Brutus and all, and was wondering how the guys who were looking for him would go about checking out the private cabins. Well, the cimaroons had locked themselves in and had the key. All they had to do was keep quiet. The searchers ought to assume that the occupier was out some-where else in the boat, and had locked up behind him. I turned my attention back to the game. With his second dice Duke threw a six. His third dice was bound to take him above the halfway mark, the odds were already on his side. He put in five dollars.

'That way,' he said, 'I'm bound to break just ahead of the game, so if you lose we can call it a day and part good friends after some good sport. What do you say, friend?'

And he rolled again but a bit wildly, so the dice rolled off the table and skittered across the floor to come to a standstill just by Miss Prim's foot. But I got there first. Our heads came together above it. She smelled of Parma violet.

'A six,' cried Duke, but I doubt he could see it. 'But darn it, it don't count off the table.'

'Give it to me,' hissed Miss Prim.

'No,' said I.

'Give them this one then.'

And she pushed a dice into my hand.

'A five spot,' said I, proud that I was picking up the lingo, 'keeps me on your side.'

'Done.'

With an old-Europe bow I handed the dice to Duke. He took it with a question mark on his eyebrow. I gave him a nod. He rolled it. A two. Total thirteen. A two? Had she handed him a dice that rolled twos instead of fives or sixes? Why? Because Kentucky would be rolling it as well. But he left it to last.

He rolled a one, counting as seven on his first throw.

'Already halfways there and better,' he crowed, and bet five which Duke raised another five.

'You won't roll two aces in one hand,' he said.

'If I do, I've won, your five and another five.'

Duke matched it.

Kentucky rolled again. A three.

'Anything but a two, and I've won. I bet twenty.'

Duke didn't push him. Kentucky gave the third dice, the one I'd passed up, the one that he thought could come up with a six as well as a two, a good rattle in the box.

Two.

Kentucky swore. Offensively, so again I won't repeat it. I know the quality, Mr Murray, of the people who read your travel books. But he also tipped the table and in the ruckus that followed Miss Prim and I managed to change the dice back again just in case any question arose, and I also scooped up my five dollars.

The thing of it was, these flatboatmen left New Orleans on the journey home loaded. But Kentucky had lost forty dollars, ten sovs, give or take, and that left a pretty big hole in his profit on the trip.

All this provided a welcome spell of activity, displacing the dreadful anxiety I continued to feel at the thought that I might at any moment be exposed as the accomplice of a cimaroon or runaway slave, with all the dreadful consequences that could follow. The actors in the recent drama were now all leaving the saloon, Kentucky still swearing, Miss Prim and Duke, in different directions but sharing a certain look of smugness, though Duke, presumably on hearing that he had lost five dollars to yours truly, threw me a look of reproval albeit lightened with a rueful half-smile. Left to my own devices there was nothing for it but to return to the gallery and watch the banks of the Mississippi slip by beneath the westering sun.

The scene was dismal. As the distance from New Orleans increased the air of wealth and comfort disappeared and but for one or two clusters of wooden houses calling themselves towns, and borrowing some pompous name, generally from Greece or Rome, we might have thought ourselves the first of the human race who had ever penetrated into this wilderness of bears and alligators. And then, of course, there were more of the single establishments, woodcutters' dwellings. The squalid look of the miserable wives and children was dreadful, their complexion of a bluish-white that suggested dropsy. I have never witnessed human nature reduced so low outside the rookeries of London or the hovels of our lowest peasants reduced to starvation by enclosures and the Poor Law.

It was a great relief, therefore, when a bluff close to the shore rose up ahead of us, crowned with a small town of some neatness and prosperity. The slopes of the hill were spread with copious gardens and orchards of pawpaw, palmetto and orange trees in bloom – their sharp, refreshing fragrance was carried to us on the evening breeze. All in all it appeared like an oasis in the desert.

'What town is this?' I asked, in a general way of those around me.

'Natches.' The name was pronounced by a stern, forbidding sort of a voice from behind me, a voice I thought I recognised.

Oh shit, I thought. This is the town where Brutus and his brood were meant to leave the *Belvidere*. I had, I thought, better go below and see what plan he had for getting ashore unobserved.

I turned and found myself facing the owner of the voice that had proclaimed Natches to me. It was the tall, severe-looking but now more minatory than severe, Purser.

'Mr Boylan,' he continued, using the name I had given him, one I occasionally use when I am bored with Bosham. 'Mr Boylan, you will be aware a search has been conducted throughout the day and all through the *Belvidere* for a runaway slave called Ardingly, probably accompanied by his woman and her infant.'

I put on the English Gent.

'I have heard, from the lower sort aboard your ship, gossip to that effect.'

'Every corner of the boat has been examined, and every cabin. Except yours. Cabin sixteen. It is locked, but a cabin boy who is responsible for keeping that part of the boat clean, has reported hearing a Negro voice within, singing one of their religious songs. Do you know anything about this?'

His tone was, I felt, impertinent. But by now I had seen behind him two figures in a sort of uniform, brass-buttoned jackets, boots and so forth with a pair of holstered pistols on the left side of their broad belts and short truncheons on the right. I assumed they had some official capacity – officers of a court, something of that sort.

'Of course not. But I may say, sir, that I left my cabin at eight o'clock this morning and have not had occasion to return to it since.'

'But you have the key?'

I went through my pockets very quickly, then more slowly.

'Good God, sir, no. It's gone. Let me see. I had it when I break-fasted in the saloon, I remember I put it by my plate . . . My goodness, do you suppose I left it there?'

Purser turned to the marshals, for that is what they were.

'Bring him.'

They took me by the elbows and hustled me towards the stairs to the floor below, with my feet scarcely touching the deck. A small crowd of passengers followed us, no doubt comprised of the idle and curious. As we turned at the top of the steps I caught a glimpse of Natches, much closer now, and the quays along the levée below the hill. Clearly we were close to tying up. Down the steps they propelled me, and along the passage, and as we approached the door of cabin sixteen we all were brought up sharp by a deep voice, tuneful and rich, raised in song, issuing from the other side of the door.

247

Oh let us all from bondage flee
Let my people go
And let us all in Christ be free
Let my people go.

You need not always weep and mourn
Let my people go
And wear those slavery chains forlorn
Let my people go . . .

Purser and marshals froze for as long as it took for Brutus to reach the final chorus, then they put me down and moved towards the door, but as they did so we all heard the key on the inside turn, clickety-click, in the wards. It opened a crack and Brutus peeped out. He saw us and instantly tried to shut it, but the Purser already had his foot in it. A moment of impasse, then it was pulled wide (it opened inwards) and out came Brutus whirling my Bowie knife around his head like a Tartar warrior with a sabre, and with one fiendish swipe he took off the nearest marshal's head as he reached towards the butt of one of his pistols. In my hurry to get out of his way I kicked the severed head so that it rolled under the rail and into the river. Then he leapt on to the rail that made the guard of this lower gallery, swayed there for a moment, still swinging my now reeking falchion about his head, before leaping into the crowd a mere six feet below, just as the *Belvidere*'s side nudged the hemp fenders that hung between.

The crowd scattered in front of him, but forming a semicircle that hedged him in. He feinted this way and that at them – dockside workers, passengers waiting to board, sellers of pawpaws, melons and nectarines – and the cordon bulged away from him but would not break, perhaps because of the press of those securely behind those in front.

Marshal two, beside me, drew his pistols, cocked them and fired first one and then the other. The first ball took Brutus high up in the left shoulderblade. He staggered but did not fall. The second struck the cobbled quay with a shower of sparks and ricocheted into the crowd where it did no good at all to a young girl, not more than ten years old, since it hit her in the eye. Another shot was now fired from the crowd which took Brutus in the chest and laid him flat on his back and instantly the crowd, seeing he had dropped the Toothpick, surged forward, some with sticks and cudgels, some with knives. Over their heads and shoulders we could see from our vantage point how the big, bald, black head rose up and then fell again. How he writhed and twisted and kicked for at least a minute before he was completely obscured by the heads and shoulders of his assailants.

At that moment, the captain, or someone on the bridge, began to play the riverboat's steam calliope, just as he did at each major docking. And those at the back of the crowd, and many leaning over the three wrought-iron guards that galleried the *Belvidere*, found the words.

> My country 'tis of thee
> Sweet land of liberty
> Of thee I sing.
> Land where my fathers died
> Land of the Pilgrims' pride
> From every mountain side
> Let freedom ring! . . .

Odd that the tune should be that of 'God Save the King', or rather, Queen! But I have to say they gave it a much faster tempo than we do.

An odour of garlic and beer assailed my nostrils. I made the half-turn necessary to bring its bearer into view: the old-timer from the saloon. He looked down, the crowd parted, Brutus suffered one last spasm and died.

'Sometimes,' murmured the old-timer, 'the bar eats you – sometimes you eats the bar.' And, like every other man on that damned boat, he spat.

29

The *Belvidere*'s stop at Natches was brief and she was steaming north within an hour of the poor Negro's slaughter, having dropped those passengers who wished to leave the boat and taken on those who had business upriver. She also disposed of or loaded freight, the latter being for the most part fruits of a subtropical nature for the large cities upstream, as Memphis, St Louis, St Andrew's Falls and, up the Ohio, Pittsburgh and so forth, Natches being the most northerly place where such fruits grow in marketable abundance.

As we pulled away from the quay the marshal's head, which had lodged in one of the port paddle's buckets, spilled out and bobbed downstream like nothing so much as a coconut, only to be snapped up by a passing alligator. The sight of this caused much amusement amongst those who saw it. In fact, I quickly detected a febrile sort of a mood had fallen upon the crowded riverboat, no doubt engendered by the stirring if horrid sights most of those on board her had seen, but aggravated by the closeness of the night, a high humidity and, yet again, the presence above of stacked black clouds riven with occasional flashes of lightning.

There was a new band in the saloon with a trumpet, a fiddle and a man who contrived to accompany the others by marking their rhythms on a side drum and mounted cymbal. They seemed to play more loudly even than their predecessors of the night before, and faster, and the dancers whirled each other round with high, whooping shouts and much stamping of boots. There was also a small bevy of dancing girls come on board, a troupe indeed, who claimed to be French but were unable to answer in that language when I used it to greet them. They performed gyrations of a wild, acrobatic and lewd nature which involved throwing up their full and many-layered skirts and petticoats behind them, allowing the onlooker an occasional glimpse of white flesh not normally exposed in public, before crashing to the floor with one leg stretched in front and the other behind. Lobbing emptied whisky bottles into a large bin behind the counter, the barman plied his trade with conscientious alacrity. And in his usual place to the side of the counter, Duke Charles d'Orléans was persuading a 'school' of flatboatmen that they could not lose at Poker, while Miss Prim sat nearby and read her sermons and knitted the air with her fingers as the game grew hotter.

And prancing into all this came a figure, a 'yellow' from his colouring, who chose his moment just as the band began to play and sing a song that might have been written for him, or he had written it himself. Certainly I believe he had paid them to play and sing it as an overture to his entrance.

> I saw Satan when he looked the garden o'er
> Then saw Eve and Adam driven from the do-or
> And behind the bushes peeping
> Saw the apple they were eating
> And I'll swear that I'm the guy what ate the core.
>
> I taught Solomon his little A-B-Cs
> And She of Sheba flashed for me her knees.
> Now you'll say that I'm a liar
> But she said I should go higher
> High enough for her to feel the breeze.
>
> I remembers when the country had a king,
> I saw Cleopatra pawn her wedding ring
> And I saw the flags a flyin'
> When George Washington stopped lyin'
> On the day when Winter followed Spring.

He was wearing a high, white hat with a curly brim, a long-tailed black coat, stovepipe striped trousers and a waistcoat whose front was the Stars and Stripes. His white moustache curled at the ends and a neat white goatee floated below his chin, set off by the swarthiness of his complexion. He carried a cane in his left hand and a thin cigar in the right. Deep-set eyes that were grey like year-old ice belied the bonhomie his surface charm exuded. All in all, he put me in mind of the image of Baron Samedi on the wall of the shipping clerk's office, but an old 'Samedi', the Saturday before last, at least. He cakewalked* like a carnival Negro across the floor, and, with cane-holding hand on hip, posed in front of Duke.

He sucked on his cheroot and blew smoke across the space between them. When he spoke his voice was low and rasped like gravel tipped from the back of a cart.

'Deal me in, Charles,' he said, giving the name a Frenchified slur.

The band fell silent. Duke's face turned white. Miss Prim put down her book of sermons and blinked through her spectacles. The flatboatmen scooped up the few coins they had left and melted into the crowd that was already forming around them.

'Who's this then?' I whispered to the man next to me, who turned out to be the old-timer with the wide-brimmed hat and theories about 'bars'.

'Calls himself Sam,' he growled. 'Maybe Wilson, maybe Vanderbilt, some call him Sam Samedi. If you has occasion to address him call him Nuncle.'

Oh my prophetic soul, I thought.

Duke shifted in his chair, adjusted the low table in front of him, gestured with faux magnanimity to the chair opposite.

'Straight riverboat poker, no frills,' he growled, an uncharacteristic noise, not unlike that a threatened cat might make. 'Pairs, threes and four of a kind, but no runs, or straights as they call 'em up north. No draw. Five in the pot. Coin only. The pot's the limit. Take a seat.'

Nuncle Sam folded himself down, handed his cane to a similarly

---

* The 'cakewalk' was a dance invented by Afro-American slaves to guy by exaggeration the foppish dances current in plantation-owning circles. When performed for the entertainment of their owners (who were probably unaware that they were being 'sent up') the best practitioners were rewarded . . . with cake. J. R.

252

coloured gentleman who had appeared at his elbow, peeled off his white gloves.

'And I get to deal when?' he asked.

'Tonight, I'm in the chair,' said Duke. In spite of his pallor his voice remained steady. He gathered up the cards he had been playing with and, turning, tossed them on to the counter. The barman handed down a new pack in a sealed wrapper. Duke broke the seal, fanned the cards facedown.

'Twenty-one,' he said. 'One joker. Wild card. You want to play with it?'

'Mistigris,' said Nuncle. 'Sure I'll play with it.'

Duke scooped in the cards, shuffled them, handed them across, Nuncle cut them carefully on the table, one hand only, pushed them back. Duke dealt three and then three, two and then two, taking them off the top of the pack without picking it up. They each placed two five dollar coins on the table between them and then picked up their cards.

For the first half-hour they played carefully, according to the chances, bluffing in a minor sort of way, probing each other's defences, as it were, until Duke was maybe fifteen dollars ahead of the game. Outside the lightning forked, the thunder cracked and we could hear the rattle of the rain on the deck above. Then, Nuncle picked up his hand, fanned the cards minimally so only the corners were visible in his palm, folded them close and put them back on the table. His face had frozen, like that of a watchful corpse.

'Ten,' he murmured and pushed the necessary coins and bills forward.

'Yours and twenty more,' responded Duke.

Nuncle took him up to eighty then saw him on a round ton.

Duke turned over three queens, ace high and a ten.

Nuncle turned his over. Three kings, the joker, known by riverboat gamblers as Mistigris, standing in for one of them. He scooped in the pool. I felt a finger on my shoulder, a breath in my ear.

'You have six gold guineas in your bag. Give you twelve back if you let us use them.'

Miss Prim.

I had no money, no cash at all, apart from those six guineas, the last from the Buccaneer's Hoard. I gave it a moment's thought. Did it matter at all when I was at last truly penniless? Would tomorrow be worse than in a week's time? And anyway, if Miss Prim knew what I had in my bag, who else? And how long would I remain in possession of its contents on this shipload of monkeys?

'Okeydoke,' I murmured.

'Your bag is not in cabin sixteen. You'll find it in number ten, just at the bottom of the stairs. Here's the key.'

I felt the coldness of the metal against the back of my hand and took it. Trotting along the top gallery, which was open to the sky, I could see in the light thrown from the boat how the black surface of the river was pocked by the rain like the coat of the black-phase jaguar that had given me such a fright when Juanita and I rode away from Acapulco. On a skin of water at the bottom of the stairs I skidded and almost fell, twisted my knee, but came to rest at number ten. Well, I was in for a shock. The room was the same as mine in all respects, including the fact that it was occupied by Judith and her infant, huddled in terror on the floor, pressed up against the washstand. My bag, with others, was on the bed. Questions rushed at me like runaway horses but I stepped aside, took the tube-shaped bag for the last time from the bottom of my haversack, and stuffed it in my pocket.

'Lock the door,' whimpered Jude.

I did, clambered up the steps, slipped again, recovered, and hobbled back to the saloon.

They had broken off on the middle of a hand, with a heap of coin in the pot, waiting for me to come back with Duke's poke. To pass the time, Nuncle Samedi was singing and dancing again, backed by the band.

> I sit upon a hornet's nest,
> > I dance upon de dead,
> I tie a viper round my neck
> > And den I goes to bed.

> I kneel to de buzzard
> > An I bow to the crow
> And ebry time I weel about
> > I jump jis so!

He came back to the table. Duke bet ten.

'Your ten,' said Nuncle, his even, white teeth, filed to points, gleaming like a shark's between moustache and pointy beard, 'and another ten.'

Duke looked round with desperation. Miss Prim found my hand down by my side, took the purse, tipped out the six guineas, pressed them into Duke's palm. He laid three on the table.

'I'll see you.'

Nuncle looked at the gold coins, the quartered arms of Hanover and Normandy blazoned on the spade-shaped shields.

'Pretty chinks, aint they?' he said, and he turned over, one by one, three knaves and the ace of clubs. As he did so the guy in the band with the snare drum began a slow crescendo. Nuncle left the fifth card face down.

'Alleluia,' said Duke, but quite calmly, and turned over, one by one, the four kings. And reached out his hands, shaped like a curved, upright shovel, to pull in the coin. A gasp from the crowd, standing with awed faces beneath the wreathed cigar smoke, some at the back cheered, the drummer hit his high hat, spilling brass across the crowded room.

'Hold still!' rasped Nuncle Sam, and his voice creaked like nuzzling icebergs. He paused, his right hand laid down his cheroot, and hung in the air across the table. The finger and thumb of his left hand snagged the corner of his fifth card and flipped it over. King of hearts. Made no difference, he was still the loser. But a *second* king of hearts?

You can't do what happened next, not in writing. It was all too quick, just about simultaneous. A single-barrel, percussion cap-sprung derringer, the 'Phila', leapt from Nuncle's sleeve and into his hand and Duke went back off his chair with a crash and a hole between his eyes that spouted blood like a faucet for five seconds then died like a faucet turned off. And he with it. But the ball was still travelling towards him when the derringer flew from Nuncle's hand as a second bullet smashed the humerus above it. Miss Prim had *her* derringer back in her handbag, probably before anyone there had seen it. The shots, coming together as they did, stunned all ears.

A moment or two of total silence fell like a dropped plank falling on grass, then Nuncle Sam, clutching his broken arm with the other hand, began to scream and swear. In spite of the noise he was making I heard a phlegmy throat behind me cleared with a rumbling cough.

'Sometimes,' the voice came, 'sometimes the bar—'

'Don't,' I murmured, 'please don't say it.'

255

30

She had me on my back, the knees of her skinny legs on either side of my waist, bolt upright above me (not the only thing there that was bolt upright, I can tell you), hands braced against the ceiling, the underside of the deck above, pushing herself up and down on that part of me that was upright, like the brass cylinders and pistons that drove the paddle wheels round. Her head was thrown back so I could not see much of her face, but every now and then a tear streamed down each cheek, round her jawbone and down her arched neck. Turning my head I could see Jude in her corner, her eyes wide with fright and wonder, dark, the bloodshot whites gleaming in the gloom which was scarcely penetrated by the light of a single candle. Her infant, mercifully, slept.

She, Miss Prim that is, or rather was, if you catch my drift, was clearly riding on a distant cloud, and not wishing to let her down, as it were, before she was ready to descend, I resorted to an expedient I have used in the past, saying, under my breath of course, the thirteen times table up to one hundred and sixty-nine, and then back down again. Then up again.

Sixty-five, seventy-eight, ninety-one, the rhythm quickened, sweat began to appear between her collarbones and ran between her small but swinging breasts, mingled with the tears, one hundred and four, one hundred and seventeen, a sucking noise from down below like a child pulling on a lollipop, her knees pressed yet more tightly into my waist, my member a pillar of fire ready to burst, one hundred and thirty, one hundred and forty-three, one hundred and fifty-six, she screamed, one hundred and sixty-nine, I let go, she dropped her full weight down and it all happened at once.

Her hands now on either side of my face, her face above mine, her loosened hair tumbled in curtains around us – have I said it was deeply reddish chestnut, shot with gold strands which caught the light from the candle flame? – her eyes serious now, almost without expression as she regained control of her breathing.

'Your hairiness,' she panted, 'is disgusting. Like a pig's, a wild black boar's, glossy black above pink skin.' She ran the fingers of one hand through my pelt, across my chest, squeezed my right nipple, then swung her legs to the floor, stood, wrapped a sheet around her torso, tucking it beneath her armpits, and sat on the bed beside me.

'Duke,' she began (his body had already been dropped overboard, the most usual way such problems are dealt with on riverboats), 'and I were lovers. We were, however, as you discovered, accomplices, and, since in these rough and barbaric places a woman needs one, he was my protector.' She wiped her eye on the back of her hand and sighed. 'I was fond of him. Very fond of him. He was a . . . playmate.' Then she looked down at me. 'I doubt you will ever mean as much to me but I see no reason why you should not perform the other duties he carried out on my behalf.'

She went on to explain that she had a house in Vicksburg, where we would be landing the next day and where she proposed I should stay with her, occupying the place of manservant, for some time.

'It will be necessary,' she said, 'to keep off the river until the furore created by tonight's events has died down. In the meantime I will teach you the card- and dice-playing techniques Duke taught me. Then, when we are ready, we shall work the boats. What do you say to all this?'

Turning my cheek on the pillow I murmured: 'I was planning to travel up the Ohio . . .'

'Speak up!'

I raised my voice.

'My aim is to get to New York, and thence to England. Where I come from.'

'Well, yes. And why not?' She leant over me and pinched my cheek. 'I'll tell you why not. You haven't got a goddamn cent to

257

bless your name with. That's why not. You'll need a hundred dollars spare cash, minimum, maybe two hundred, and if you can find a better way of getting that sort of sum together than by becoming my pardner, you're welcome to try it.'

She reached over my head for a linen and lace nightdress that had been neatly folded on her pillow and was now somewhat rumpled, and pulled it over her head, loosening the sheet as she did so and pulling it off from underneath the nightdress.

'Now, you can get as much on in the way of clothing as decency requires and get back to your own cabin. We are expected to tie up at Vicksburg at about nine in the morning. I shall expect you to help us with our baggage, including poor Duke's.'

'Us?' I asked.

'Us. Deprived of her helpmeet as she is, and the father of her child, Jude has elected not to continue up the Underground Railroad just yet. She will remain with me as my personal servant, hired and properly paid, of course, for as long as she chooses to.'

Again – underground railroad! What could she mean?

Mr Murray, it occurs to me that you will not like to print the opening page of this chapter in a volume aimed at a family audience. Cut or alter it as you see fit, I beg you.

Thus began a sojourn of some six months in Miss Kate Battista's residence in Vicksburg. Battista? Her father had been Italian, her mother Irish. Her mother was brought to bed with her on the boat that brought them from Genoa to New Orleans in 1802, during the peace of Amiens, so she knew neither Italy nor Ireland. Her father attempted to set up a house trading cotton for Italian luxuries, such as statuettes of Michelangelo's David (fully fig-leafed), believing that the peace of Amiens would hold, but of course it did not and his business failed. He died of drink before the battle of Waterloo could mend his fortunes. Vicksburg was founded in 1819 by the Rev. Newitt Vick and chartered in 1825, which was the year Mrs and Miss Battista moved there, setting up a shop where they made and sold what they claimed were the latest European fashions to the daughters of the first generation of planters. However, the fathers soon made money (or rather their slaves did so for them) and were able to order the real thing for their women from New Orleans.

With an elderly and ailing parent on her hands and all the disadvantages of her sex, Kate made shift as best she could. For a time she prostituted herself to a wealthy but old planter, a widower, resident in Natches, but his crop was destroyed one year by the army worm and he was forced to marry again – for money. Kate returned to Vicksburg and on the boat she made the acquaintance of Duke . . . A little later her mother finally succumbed to gin and the dropsy.

Some of this she told me as the cart she had hired on the quay slowly made its way up the slopes of Vicksburg towards the house she had near the top of one of the several bluffs that overlook the town. The house was a small, clapboard affair, but very neat, painted white with a shingle roof, set behind a paling fence and partially sheltered by a large walnut tree, walnut trees being a feature of the district. On the ground floor there were two reception rooms, a study and a kitchen. Stairs set between the two larger rooms climbed to a landing off which opened the doors to four small bedrooms. The whole was pleasantly furnished in simple style, some of it made by a local group of Shakers, the beds covered with quilts made by the Shaker women. It was this community of some dozen souls who had persuaded Kate to become a link, or stage, in the mysterious underground railroad. She explained all this to me as she got a cast-iron stove going (she had left it laid and ready for lighting) on which she set a kettle for tea. Meanwhile, she sent Jude (the infant sleeping on her back, Red Indian-style) out into the garden to pick an armful of roses, having first indicated the jugs she could put them in.

'They know I travel to and from New Orleans in a regular way, and when they know there is a runaway with their people there they forge the papers that say he is my property. I pick up him or her, or them if it is a family, and bring them back, passing them on so they can be sent on their way to the next stage or station on their journey north. The whole business is known as the Underground Railroad.'

'Do they know why you take the boats up and down the river?' I asked.

'Oh, I expect so. But they are too wise to bother about it.' At this her eye moistened a little and she turned away, no doubt recalling her recent loss. Then she straightened her back and turned. 'Well,' she continued, 'what do you think? Will you take on Duke's role? Will you learn his skills, or ones equally tuned to gull our fellow travellers?'

259

I thought for a moment. Then I smiled, I hope agreeably. 'I like this place. I like you. I like your proposal and I think you will find me an apt pupil . . .'

My voice had dropped, a hint of perspiration broke out on my brow, she quickly understood what was on my mind. Her voice dropped too but there was no warmth in it. Indeed, it would have blighted the rosebuds Jude presently brought in.

'Last night,' she murmured, 'will not be repeated. I was in shock. Forget it. That is all.'

And suddenly I saw again the Kate I had first seen. Severe, stiff, perusing her sermons and, for all I knew, marking their content even while using them as a decoy. Such were the contradictions of this extraordinary woman.

That very evening we embarked upon a course of instruction, beginning with *theory*.

We were sitting opposite each other at a round table, walnut, or possibly oak veneered with walnut, she idly shuffling a pack of cards, I, sitting upright, in the position of an eager and attentive tyro. A bright Argand oil-lamp, with the circular wick that causes the flame to reflect itself and apparently diffuse more light for the amount of oil burnt, cast its warm but very sufficient glow over the whole room. And yes, the clear oil it was burning was not whale but walnut.

Her eyes, quite green in this light, picking up the green of the evening dress she was now wearing, fixed on mine and held them. She looked caring, tender and very beautiful.

'Duke, on my advice, eschewed card-sharping. Though we are, were, both good at it. However, playing with a reduced deck of twenty-one cards, sharping is very vulnerable to discovery. As was revealed last night. Moreover, it lays one open to the prestidigitorial skills of one's opponent. Nuncle Sam had already spotted that Duke was playing with two kings of hearts. He palmed one in the previous hand and reintroduced it . . .'

'But his hand was still inferior to Duke's.'

'Of course. But he established to all the onlookers that he had been cheated by Duke which gave him the excuse for justifiable homicide that he was looking for, justifiable that is amongst the gambling fraternity.'

'Why did he want an excuse to kill Duke?'

'An ancient rivalry. They were half-brothers. Nuncle's mother was a voodoo queen from Haiti. Duke's mother was French from France. Their father was a preacher, a gambler too, of course. The only men who could ever reach me were the sons of a preacher man. Yes.' She pushed a lock of red-gold hair off her forehead and I fancied a slight flush had rouged her cheeks. 'For a time the three of us worked the boats and the ports together. But the rivalry got in the way and Duke took me off on his own.'

It was clear from her manner that there was more to all this than she was prepared to uncase. Decisively, but with pursed lips, she pushed the cards together.

'Now. Where were we? No sharping and no marked cards either. It's too easy for a moderately skilled player to pick up on the marks. Two games only, both the simplest. Straight riverboat poker, no draw, pack of twenty plus a joker. Keep it simple.* And Yankee-Grab with dice. By keeping to these two there is no room for disputes over rules . . .'

A week or more was spent not on cards but on sciences of the mind.

'You will not, of course, allow personal feelings, only cold calculation, to affect your conduct at the table. You are, Eddie, a person of some delicacy – no, I shall not listen to protestations – and many of the men who come to the table will annoy, even disgust you with their manners, the language they use and so on. There will be a temptation to humiliate them in front of their fellows. Do not yield to it.'

And finally, after many similar nuggets of practical wisdom . . .

'My sex provides opportunities and at the same time disables me. It disables me because I cannot be seen to play at cards, to gamble, much though I should like to. I cannot enter into disputes. I must not appear to make decisions beyond the purely domestic realm and so forth. However, in the eyes of men, unmarried or unaccompanied women are either saints or trollops. Both roles confer advantages.

---

* This is how the first form of poker was played on the Mississippi riverboats. By the late 1830s many variations, such as draw and stud, and the introduction of straights, flushes and full houses were already being played elsewhere, but the original game survived for some time yet on the river. J. R.

Those enjoyed by the trollop may be more obvious but can lead to unpleasantness. Those of the saint work more slowly but ultimately are just as rewarding. To be attractive to men in a *noli me tangere* sort of a way – you have the Latin?* I thought you would, I can always tell if a man has a classical education . . .'

And suddenly I was aware, even as I felt a self-congratulatory glow, that she had subtly slipped into her 'act', and was flattering me.

'. . . To appear virginal, devout, pure, invites confession, confidences, and precludes suspicions, however well-founded.'

'Hence,' I jumped in, 'the buttoned-up clothes, the modestly dressed hair, the improving, spiritual nature of the reading matter you peruse . . .'

My sojourn in Vicksburg was not entirely devoted to the education of a riverboat gambler. We were now moving into the hottest time of the year, and very hot it could be, and humid too, especially close to 'that ol' man ribber', which, as the Negroes who wished to give an impression of jolly acceptance of their wretched lot, while plotting revenge, revolution, murder and mayhem, were wont to say, 'jus' kep' on rollin'' no matter what the weather. As I have said, Vicksburg itself was situated on slopes rising to bluffs and these continued, forested and partly cleared, for some distance to the east, providing a countryside that was pleasantly wild without being intimidating. Picnics were in order but took two distinct forms, for Kate's dual nature was evident even in this.

Occasionally we accompanied a couple of Shaker families and our fare was simple but nourishing, journey cake and cordials, our talk gentle and flavoured with Scripture, the aim of our pilgrimage to visit homesteads where it was known the occupants were in trouble through illness or bad fortune and to supply their wants. On two occasions, once we were clear of the town, we picked up runaway Negroes from their hiding places in a deserted shanty or a cave, and carried them as much as twenty miles to the next 'station' on the 'underground railroad', a small Quaker settlement that flourished on a creek, surrounded by fields of Indian corn and orchards.

Such were the picnics shared with the Friends.

* For those readers who don't, *Noli me tangere* means 'Be unwilling to touch me'. J. R.

262

One curious thing about Kate now revealed itself to me. Not only did she play two very different parts but she also dressed for them. And often, when she did not have the opportunity to change her clothes, she still managed one significant alteration. When she was with the Quakers she wore her spectacles. And when she went into Vicksburg society she took them off.

The leading families of Vicksburg were, of course, planters and the three most prominent lived in splendid houses above the town. That owned by the Duffs was called Duff Green; Balfour was the residence of the Scottish Balfours; and an Anglo-German family, related to bankers, owned the grandest of all, and the one placed highest on the hill, namely Cedar Grove. Kate was wooed by a widower uncle of the Duffs, some thirty years older than she (she was, as you will have calculated, in her mid-thirties), and also by Wilhelm, a third son of the Germans, who had a withered hand and arm, no prospects, and could not expect to make a good match from amongst those who lived on the hill. Either match would have brought her security and respectability and neither appealed to her ('I have already been there, I have already done that,' was her comment expressed with a wry wrinkling of the lip), but their attentions made her a frequent guest at routs, picnics, 'brunches' and even balls, and I frequently went along too in a role that was above that of a servant though below that of a guest. Thus I tended to hang about on the fringes of the company along with secretaries, bailiffs, overseers and the like.

The society of these people was a strange mix of wanton freedom and strict rules. They rode, hunted and gambled to wild excess, and they seduced each others' wives as a matter of course. However, they also cultivated an exaggerated sense of honour so one was expected to 'call out' one's wife's lover, though generally one aimed one's pistol high, or, if sabres were used, declared honour satisfied with a cut; more serious was cheating, or an accusation of cheating, at cards, billiards, whatever, which usually did end with a death.

Thus it happened one evening, at a ball where the claret cup had been overlaced with cognac and the mint juleps with ninety proof hollander, that Kate, fatigued with the over-robust attentions of Wilhelm, appealed to Montmorency Duff to get the German off her hands. Both men were drunk, a quarrel was quickly sparked, the flames took and before we knew where we were it was pistols at dawn. Kate begged me to go along and remonstrate with them, even to the point, she said, of making it clear that she would neither bed nor marry either, so they might just as well forget her and go home.

The meeting took place in a grove of oak trees on the banks of the Yazoo River, a tributary of the Mississippi, a mile or so out of town. Unfortunately, when their seconds agreed on this rendezvous they were ignorant that hogs had recently been let out over the ground for pannage and all was churned up and muddy, and smelled like a pig farm. No one was going to object for fear of being branded a coward. Yet both men, neither of whom had ever been involved in anything like this before in their long lives, were in a state of bluest funk. Wilhelm declared that he was at a severe disadvantage on account of it being his right hand that was withered and he was right-handed. Since it had been withered since birth this did not wash. Duff declared that with age his sight was dimmed and he could not tell one from another of the party. The only effect this had was to send those who supported Wilhelm a good ten yards further to the side.

I did my best. I delivered Kate's message. Whereupon the referee of the whole business, a lean, saturnine Balfour, declared that if that was the case then neither man had anything left to live for and we could go ahead.

In the event Wilhelm, on turning, slipped in the green and shitty slime, firing as he fell. His ball hit Balfour in the left cheek. Duff, seeing only one target in front of him and that but dimly, hit Balfour in the right cheek. Balfour, with the lower part of his face blown away, died in agony a week later.

Kate and I packed our bags.

31

Leaving Jude to look after Kate's house in Vicksburg, we worked the river for more than eighteen months, nearly two years, mostly going upstream and then back to Vicksburg for short stays, but visiting Memphis and St Louis, and finally going the whole way to St Anthony Falls where, on account of the wheat that grows abundantly as far north as this, flour mills had been built in the twenties whose wheels and grinding stones were powered by an artificial runoff from the falls. The flatboats then loaded the flour and took it downriver to every major town between there and New Orleans, their crews making the return journey on the riverboats. Prior to that, most of the wheat flour came from New York or even Europe and, like the Mexicans, most folk ate Indian corn tortillas instead of bread, proper white wheaten bread being the prerogative of the rich.

A league or so south of the falls a French Canadian called Pierre Parrant built a saloon on the bank specialising in Canadian whisky. Parrant had tiny blue eyes with fair eyelashes, just like a pig's, so he was called Pig Eye and his saloon was known as Pig Eye's.* His eyes were not the only piggy thing about him: he was big, fat and gingery. We arrived there some months after the saloon had opened for business and already a small settlement had sprung up around it, the

---

* Within a decade or so St Anthony's Falls was renamed Minneapolis while Pig Eye's became the twin city of St Paul. J. R.

main feature of which was a brothel timber-built in an ecclesiastical style with a central hall or nave hung with red velvet and cubicles like chapels to the sides. Its customers were flatboatmen come up for the flour, mill workers and riverboat crews, and it did well though trade tended to be seasonal. We spent a fair bit of time in both establishments. However, it was in St Louis that our partnership finally came to an end.

April is a cruel month, as they say in St Louis, on account of it being the month when agues and fevers can strike just when you think their season is past, but for other reasons too – and this in 1838 was the cruellest April of my life.

The trouble started when, just below Cairo, we ran aground while we were at breakfast in the saloon. The riverboat we were on was almost deserted, there having been two cases of typhus fever discovered on board and we and a professional-looking man were the only passengers, though the *Honeysuckle Rose*, as she was called, was well freighted.

'Aground?' cried the professional-looking man in a frock coat who had burst in on us. 'Good heavens, how long shall we stay here?'

'The Lord in his providence can only tell,' answered the captain, 'but long enough to tire my patience.'

A breakfast, a dinner, a supper and another breakfast passed before we got off, during which a couple of steamers tried to tow us off the sandbank we were stuck on. Both were heading upstream with flatboatmen going first to hoe the wheat fields, then bring in the harvest, and finally take the flour from the mills. Eventually one of the larger riverboats came up with grappling irons and all and shifted us clear. Our captain now declared that he'd have to stop at St Louis on account of a damaged paddle wheel. Kate and I briefly debated what to do.

'Tell you the truth, Eddie, I'm bored with Pig Eye's, and I'm ready to get back to Vicksburg. We'll get off at St Louis and get a boat back south,' she said, as the darkie in the bow slung the line and called the depth.

'Mark one,' he shouted, meaning one fathom, six feet of water.

Then . . .

'Mark twain,' meaning two fathom.

And that was enough. The captain sounded his whistle, the paddles churned all the quicker and off we went again.

We reached St Louis in three days in pouring rain, and a pall of smoke, flattened by the downpour, hung over all. Already it was a big sprawl of a city, maybe fourteen thousand in population, and yet in all this there was hardly a building above two storeys, nearly all built out of wood, the streets neither metalled nor paved and now veritable swamps of churned-up mire. Near the middle there was a small, not very significant hill with a brick courthouse and scaffolding nearby which we were told would be the St Louis Theater, but away from this area, which also included churches and a Roman cathedral, so-called, as well as a college, all was an untidy jumble of unplanned streets and alleys, thrown up by settlers or speculative builders with no thought of anything but getting a roof over their heads or the heads of their tenants or purchasers. As a result streets had jogs,* dead ends and varied in width. There was no sewage and the inhabitants pointed it out with pride when it happened that a channel or gutter had been dug in the middle of a street to carry the muck off to the river, rather than against the doorways. There was much talk of hotels, banks, railroads, insurance companies, a gas company, chambers of commerce and even a medical society, but little sign of any of that being forthcoming.

And the reason for all this haste and bustle? Our informant, the same professional man who had been at breakfast with us when the *Honeysuckle Rose* struck the sandbank, gave the answer and much else in a saloon on Main Street that very evening. He was one of those people every traveller dreads meeting, who, on discovering you are a stranger in the neighbourhood, insists on taking you under his wing, leading you to all the 'best' places, giving you the 'lowdown' on where to eat and stay, and points out to you all the items of interest, interest, that is, to *him* and ignores your questions and anything that is of interest to *you*.

He was, he told us, a journalist by trade, not a native of St Louis, for the world was his oyster, he proclaimed, but making a short stay there as he travelled the West, preparing a series of articles for east coast periodicals, particularly the *Democratic Review*.

The saloon was a noisy place with, apart from all the usual trappings, a monumentally baroque ornament set high up above the counter. This was in the form of a tilted shield emblazoned with the

* Right-angled bends. J. R.

267

Stars and Stripes set in front of crossed lances also bearing banners, the whole surmounted by a vast bronze bird with spread wings, talons trousered with feathers, a beak like the machined and polished claw on a hammer, and a head which, through the swirling smoke and dim light, I took to be naked . . . a vulture in short. I should have known better. Its brow was actually feathered, but in white, and that made it a bald-headed eagle. Under all a twisted ribbon floated bearing the legend '*E pluribus unum*'.

And the clientele? Brickies, chippies, hucksters and hustlers; river-boatmen, flatboatmen, dockers and porters; women selling spring flowers and women selling themselves; and pastrymen passing from saloon to tavern to inn with giant trays of their wares. Most of this motley lot had money in their pockets, even if it was only a day's wage.

In spite of the racket this concourse produced, and fortified with a pint of Tennessee whisky we bought for him, Mr O'Sullivan, for that was his name, now launched into a vehement sermon, as passionately delivered as any hellfire eruption of a paid-up evangelical, though largely secular in matter and tone.

'What friend of human liberty, civilisation and refinement,' he began after first evicting a wodge of chewed tobacco from his cheek, no doubt finding that its presence impeded the intake of the Rev. Dan Call's John Barleycorn, 'can cast his view over the past history of the monarchies and aristocracies of antiquity and not deplore that they ever existed?'

So far, I thought, Tom Paine . . . always a seam for your American demagogue to mine. But there was more to come.

'America is destined for better deeds. Is it not our unparalleled glory that we have no remissential . . . reminiscences of battlefields? Our annals describe no scenes of horrid carnage where dupes were led on by emperors and kings to slay one another. Nor have the American people ever suffered themselves to be led on by wicked ambition to depopulate land, to spread desolation far and wide—'

'But Mr O'Sullivan,' Kate, her spectacles on the end of her nose, attempted an intervention, 'the Native Americans, the Indians—'

But her voice was no more than a towhead to interrupt the flow of the mighty river the whisky had undammed.

'We are, my dear, the nation of human progress and who will, what can, set limits to our onward march? This is our high destiny.

For this blessed, blessed mission to the nations of the world, which are shut out from the life-giving light of truth, has America been chosen . . .'

Another slurp negotiated his lips but not without some loss down the lapels of his black frock coat.

'Her high example shall smite unto death the tyranny of kings, hierarchs, and oligarchs and carry the glad tidings of peace and good-will where myriads now endure an existence scarcely more enviable than that of the beasts of the field. And frankly, my dears, we can't do this unless we overspread the continent allotted by Providence for the free development of our yearly multiplying millions. This, my dear friends, is our manifold destiny. No. This is our maniform . . . This is our . . . maniacal manacle . . . our madinest festerny . . .'

Inspiration descended on me like Elijah's cloak.

'Manifest?' I suggested.

'Manifest?' He put his arm around me. 'You're a good friend, Edgar, a very good friend indeed and in need. Manifest it shall be. Let's drink then to our Manifest Destiny, as proposed by herr toast-meister sitting on my right. Left . . .'

And holding the bottle by the neck he tipped the last quarter down his throat, sank to his knees and keeled over on his side.

'Goo-ni, Eileen,' he sighed, and closed his eyes.*

Kate and I shared a room that night, and a bed, and for the second and last time, those pleasures more properly associated with connu-bial bliss. Why this should have been so was in part explained by the pillow talk that followed, though I make no doubt that the glass or two of whisky she took with us had some effect. I also remarked to her that, in a way, like Duke, I too was the son of a preacher man since my foster father had been a Catholic priest, but this did not seem to carry much weight with her.

With my head on her shoulder and my hand on her small breast I asked if this was not the reason, then what was.

'Why, Kate?'

* A journalist with the same name did indeed coin the phrase in an article published in 1845, and came very close to it in an earlier piece printed in 1839. I suppose we should in fairness accept the story Eddie gives us here rather than take it that he read either or both of these articles when they were printed, and used them here as the basis of a fiction. J. R.

'I felt like it. A woman does, at times, you know?'

'But why the two people that you are? At least two.'

She sighed, but she knew what I meant.

'You should understand, Eddie. You of all people. You say you are Italian, Spanish and English. You are a rogue but not a very clever one, and a gentleman but not too good at that either . . .' her voice faded as if she did not quite know how to take the point she was making a stage further.

'And you,' I prompted, 'you are Italian too and Irish. But you are also a saint at times, and at other times a sinner. The difference is that you are expert at both.'

'The difference is,' she murmured, after a long pause, 'that I am American from birth, and you are not.'

'What difference does that make?'

'We Americans do not know who we are. Save the natives.' By this I understood her to mean not the Redskins but the white men whose ancestors had lived on the east coast for a couple of centuries or more, in a place they had been making their own. 'We come, or our parents came, into this . . . void, this emptiness, from countries which had rejected us or we had rejected. And then we choose to play a part. We choose it. In your case, your heritage, albeit eccentric and mixed, European rather than belonging to one nation only, chooses you. It is an ancient heritage. Old Europe. It is part of you. It is you. But we choose. And when we've chosen we put it on, like a cloak or a hat. So it never is part of us, us Americans. But we have to make believe it is, so we always exaggerate, we go too far, we act out our parts to the full, we overact, we are desperate to believe that our parts, our roles, are us. But in the end they are not. So always there is a hollow deep in our souls, an emptiness at the heart of what we choose to be.'

I mused on this and remembered certain settlements we had stopped at to take on wood on the river, or other supplies, or pick up freight or passengers.

'Not true of all immigrants,' I said. 'We have seen villages made up entirely of Swedes, for instance, where amongst themselves they speak Swedish, and they build and grow their gardens and have their religion like Swedes . . .'

She shifted impatiently beneath the coarse, damp blanket.

'But that's what I mean. They are play-acting. They overdo it. They are playing at being Swedish. They are more Swedish than any Swede living in Sweden. And yet they could walk to the next village and have a go at being Dutch. It doesn't mean anything.' She thought for a bit, her fingers squeezing and releasing the top end of the grey sheet. 'And that's why we do nothing by halves. We always have to overdo it. We have to make it real by exaggerating it. We get religion, like at a revival or camp meeting, we have to fall about and have fits; we take the Bible and we have to believe every goddamn word of it; we drink and we don't stop when we're drunk, we stop when we fall over. We make money and we have to make a pile of money; yet if we give some away, we give all of it, we lose it all. We can be anything . . . because we are nothing. So, for a time I play the saint until I am bored with it, then I play the sinner. And that's it.'

She lay there for a moment or two, looking up at the wooden plank ceiling, the shifting light of a guttering candle flowing restlessly over her face, then she briskly turned away from me, pulled up her knees, dragged the covers round her shoulders. I tried to fit myself round her, but she shrugged, almost shuddered, and I lay on my back again.

Presently the tallow candle burned down and eventually out, over-laying the stale odours of the room with the smell of rancid mutton fat.

In the morning it seemed we did not know what to do with ourselves, with each other, with the day, though in fact it turned out she knew well enough; it was just a case of making up her mind as to which of the destinies offered she would take, which part she would play. Through the cold rain we drifted back to the quay. The riverboats were lined up straining at their creaking hawsers as if desperate to surrender to the swollen flood of the river. Occasionally shattered timbers swirled into them, banged once or twice on their hulls like small boys who racket down a street knocking on the doors and then rush on.

Standing beside me, with the hood of her cloak up, Kate squeezed my hand, but when she spoke her voice had a cutting edge.

'It's time you got down to Cairo,' she said, 'and made your way east and north up the Ohio.'

'I've no money,' I said, and I was glad that I could, for I sensed she was talking of parting.

'You've worked for me—'

'With you . . .'

But at that moment I became aware of an odour, an aroma, the smell of a cigarillo, coming from behind me, mingling with those of the river and the rain.

'*For* me, for nearly two years, and all you've had is your keep and expenses. I owe you.' She opened her reticule and pushed about in it before pulling out a leather fold which she pushed into the pocket of my coat, though her gaze was fixed on something or someone behind me, beyond my shoulder. 'There's fifty dollars there. That'll get you to Pittsburg. Maybe a bit further. And here . . . take these too.' This time she handed me two wrapped packs of cards and four dice, one of which I knew was loaded to turn up a deuce four times out of five. 'Now. Be off with you.'

And her gloved hand found my elbow and gently but firmly eased me to the side. I turned and saw him.

The white high hat, the eyes glowing in the darkness beneath it, the vest like the flag, the cane, the cheroot. Nuncle Samedi. Forward he came, with a little dance step that took him round the edge of a puddle. He gave me a nod, and his thin lips between his twirled moustache and goatee twisted sardonically. Then the cane came up and its ferrule touched her coat, just below her left breast.

She gave me a wan sort of a smile and slowly removed her spectacles.

He took her elbow and turned her, and they walked away across the greasy, glistening cobbles, back towards the town, and within a step or two her head leant against his upper arm. She did not look back.

Had she known, the night before, that he was in town? Was that why she bedded me just in the way she had that first night, knowing this would be the last? I think so.

Picking up my bag, I glanced up and down the quay and chose from the boats which were facing downriver the one that was being loaded and up whose gangplank passengers were embarking. No one challenged me. I climbed to the highest guard and looked over St Louis, hoping to get a last sight of Kate. But she had gone.

Whisky and garlic at my shoulder. I turned. Yes, it was the old-timer.

'Tell me, sir,' I asked, 'does this boat go south to Memphis and beyond?'

He looked at me with his rheumy old eyes and answered me with a question.

'Does the bar shit in the woods?'

So at last I knew that the 'bar' that you sometimes eat, but that sometimes eats you, is the bear, the wild bear of the forests that were being carved away from the banks of the Mississippi.

The old-timer touched my shoulder, tipped his hat.

'Wal,' he said, 'uh hope you folks enjoyed yourselves . . . Catch ya further on down the trail.' And he headed for the gangplank.

32

I had a run of genuine luck, as well as the contrived sort, during the evenings of the three days it took us to get as far as Cairo, and I decided I'd hold on a bit longer before heading up the Ohio, east and north. I reckoned I had an income on the Mississippi, and a tolerable way of earning it, and I did not fancy taking my chances of finding such easy pickings in towns like Pittsburg, which, I understood, was a growing coal, steel and railroad town: I had already seen enough of such places in England to know that I do not find them congenial and that I am not fitted to the sort of labour they afford. I therefore decided to stay on board all the way to Memphis, and then perhaps either work my way back upriver or down to New Orleans.

The best-laid schemes, as the Hibernian bard has it, often fail to deliver. After nine months my assets had risen from fifty dollars to fifty-two. The thing of it was I lacked much of what it takes to be a successful gambler. First an accomplice. Secondly, the ability to face down burly natives who had convinced themselves that they were being cheated – and what caused chagrin was that this occurred most often when it was their stupidity rather than my prestidigitorial skills that had brought about the losses which stoked their suspicions.

Prestidigitation? Yes. I'm afraid so, contrary to Kate's advice. The fact was that without her I needed some other support to give me an edge, and I soon took to marking the cards and also occasionally slipping an ace down in between my knees. I also taught myself how to hold a card in the palm of my hand while dealing, and so forth. And, of course, she was right. These practices proved to be my undoing.

February, the first week, the very depth of the prairie winter, 1839 I reckon it was – Mr Murray, you cannot conceive what winter was like halfway up the Mississippi. The sky was interminably and hugely grey and often filled with snowflakes that looked dark until they swirled against the low, dark horizons and glowed with a morbid whiteness before settling on the deserted decks, drifting at the doors to the saloons, rendering the outside stairs and companionways even more treacherous than they normally were. Ice floes were shunted by currents across the black water or piled up in fantastic, jagged edifices against the towheads, sandbanks and snags, or were snared on the bends where they accumulated into heaps from which broken branches and timbers from shattered flatboats protruded like black bones from mutilated flesh. Those that broke free thudded against our prow, for we were heading upstream from Memphis again.

On the banks the woodsellers' shanties seemed deserted, apart from occasional columns of smoke that rose into the still air as their occupants burned their livelihoods in the struggle to stay alive; huge icicles hung from the eaves of their roofs, and from the burdened branches of the trees around them; more distantly, the bluffs and occasional hills climbed to low heights blanketed with snow save where the walls of escarpments and rocky cliffs broke through. The only animals we ever saw were vultures soaring in the grey air, scouting for the carcases of those, whether small birds, foxes, deer, cattle or humans, that had succumbed to the cold. Occasionally we heard the howling of wolves.

Behind windows frosted on the outside by freezing fog and on the inside, in spite of the blazing heat from the stoves set in the middle of each public room, by condensed and frozen vapours, cards were played in several schools throughout the day and most of the night. In one corner, a sharp I had come across three or four times during the previous months had set up the apparatus needed for faro, a fool of a game requiring a portable horseshoe table, a faro box for dealing, a check tray and so forth. Its presence was a nuisance to me since it drew off potential 'mugs', especially as the simpler sort of folk believe it to be impossible to fix, whilst all know that poker and dice games are easily 'riggable'.

Nevertheless, it was faro that proved to be my nemesis. We were some forty miles or so above Cairo, and had just passed the small township on the west bank known as Cape Girardoux. It was about four o'clock in the afternoon, and, as I was soon to discover, what was to be one of the coldest nights of the year was already drawing in. In front of me I had Hans and Schwarz, two huge Germans, brothers it seemed from the similar cast of their features, red-faced, sandy-hair close-cropped, not much in the way of noses, and wide but thin-lipped mouths curled in more or less perpetual snarls. Their hands were huge, joints swollen by a score of years of merciless toil as builders and road-makers, on their way now from the south to St Louis where unlimited work in the trade was promised, even in winter and at winter rates. More frightening than their hands were their wooden-soled boots, studded with nails, the uppers formed from buffalo hide imperfectly tanned which in consequence gave off a strong and vomit-inducing stink.

I dealt one a pair of jacks, ace high, the other a pair of kings and a pair of tens, and myself an ace and a pair of tens. The first dropped out on the first round; the second raised me a dollar. Foolishly I met his stake and raised another dollar. He met me and raised five. A couple of bucks I was ready to lose, but this was too much – I should have to resort to . . .

At that moment there was a shout from the faro table, a cheer from all the players and a loud curse from the dealer. They had reached the last set, the last two cards, and the dealer had misre-membered the order they came in, or whatever, and lost a bundle. My two Germans staggered to their feet to see what was happening: like a stupid sheep, I did likewise, you know, the way you do when you're a bit drunk and very tired, and with the ace between my knees which I was about to bring into play. And at that moment the prow of the ship struck a substantial obstacle and we were all thrown forward. The ace fluttered to the ground, just in front of Schwarz's giant foot. He saw it. He even guessed where it had come from.

I ducked beneath the swing of his fist and legged it. The door on to the deck swung behind me and into his path and it exploded as he hit it into a starburst of glass shards and wooden splinters. I ran forward, slipping and sliding on the icy deck, round to the bowed guard below the captain's bridge, and met Hans coming up the other side. Schwarz was not far behind me. There was only one choice left.

276

I jumped. Fortunately this particular riverboat had only one, stern-mounted, paddle. I did not hit water; neither water nor ice were the first thing I landed on. I landed on the upturned face, white against the blackness of the river, of a drowning Cherokee boy.

I suppose the depth of water was not much more than a fathom or so. At all events I was able to recall enough of the skills the seals had taught me on Albemarle to splash my way to a piece of drifting wood, a stave, I later learnt, of the flatboat the riverboat had collided with. The riverboat surged by, churning up crushed ice at its tail, and dimly in the encroaching twilight I could see, beneath the thin, black column of its one smokestack, the burly figures of the Germans, waving their clenched fists above their heads and no doubt hurling abuse and threats into the wrack behind. 'No doubt'? Yes, for I could not hear them above the din of the engine, the churning of ice and water, and the pitiful screams of those around me. I couldn't even be sure I heard the crack of the single pistol shot as one of them let off a bell-muzzled antique in my direction. I saw the red flaming flash, sparks and smoke though.

I was surrounded by some two or three hundred Cherokee Indians, mostly old men, women and children coming from the east side where they had been herded on to a flatboat which could not have carried more than a hundred souls with any degree of safety. It carried no lights, and was too heavy to get out of the riverboat's way and the riverboat had hit it just about amidships, both tipping it and breaking it in half.

With my fists glued to the stave which remained sufficiently buoyant to support me, and my chin resting on it, I managed to kick myself across the current before it took me much further down the stream, and so into stiller water. Presently my feet touched the bottom and I was able to wade the rest of the way through the ice floes and drowning Indians, some of whom had perished almost instantly from the shock of the cold water, or were dragged down by the fur and hide capes and trousers they wore.

Several score who had already made the crossing stood on the riverbank and others hurried back through the snow to join them from the hastily improvised camp they were setting up a hundred or so yards inland. I could see the crossed poles of teepees silhouetted against the last brightness in the western sky and here and there the glow of a handful of fires whose sparks and smoke already climbed across the pale aquamarine, tinged with rose, which banded the horizon and into the clouds and blackness of night above.

I was surrounded by the impassive Cherokees: the men's faces scraggy, lean, matching the spareness of their hands and wrists, tattooed or painted, and, so far as they were visible beneath their buckskins and furs, their wiry bodies; the women's and children's with high cheekbones, softer skins, bright eyes, necks and wrists hung with beads, plaited, dark hair. Most gave me a glance that showed not a flicker of interest, though some must have been felt, for I was a curious sight, neither one of the white cavalry who seemed to be policing their progress, nor one of their own. Nevertheless, after a minute or two during which they sort of shepherded me amongst their teepees without I hardly knew what was happening, an older woman, whose hair was streaked with grey and whose clothes were as wet as mine, flung a blanket round my shoulders and got me to the edge of the crowd of women and children who circled one of the fires, close enough for me to feel a little of its warmth.

What did they think of me? Who did they think I was? Surely, at first, some functionary of the white people who were the cause of all their distress, though not a soldier, but then, when I made no attempt or request to rejoin my own people, they took me in as one of theirs, if only because, like them, I was despised and rejected. That I was neither Redskin nor Negro was evident, but my stature, the darkness of my colouring, my pelt once it was visible – and that came soon enough for my new friend made me take off my wet clothes and added a second blanket to the one she had already given me – all indicated that I was not a white either, and that was enough to earn me a provisional if muted welcome.

Presently, as night closed in on us, a bowl of thin but hot broth was passed round from which it was made clear that no more than three mouthfuls were the agreed allotment, which, so warming was it, seemed almost enough. Then all, and I followed suit, curled up around the embers, close enough to share a communal heat, and, lulled by the high-pitched keening of those who had discovered loved ones amongst the drowned, we slept.

Interlude IV

Transmutationist Enquiry, 1853 (Treasury Solicitor's Papers): Charles Bosham's Report (continued)

Pausing on the corner of Down House, a rather dull-looking, squareish sort of a house that looked neither old nor recent, though a small wing at the further end seemed newer than the rest, I glanced at the tall pair of windows to my left. It was a bright morning and the sun was upon me, the windows moreover faced north, and so my sight could not penetrate the room they shielded beyond a sill filled with stoppered glass jars. Nevertheless, a circle of dim light shone above them and in it I perceived the deep-set, dark eye beneath a bushy black eyebrow of the man who was about to be my host.

A mirror. And set so that Mr Darwin, when seated at work, but alerted by the crunch of footsteps on gravel, could look up and identify who was about to call on him. This pleased me. I felt we had more in common than I had allowed: like me this man was a spy, one who observed but did not like to be observed observing. Nevertheless he had something to learn about the trade – I should have placed the mirror further back, even at the expense of making it larger, so that it would remain shadowed. I proceeded round the corner of the house to the front door and pulled the bell.* During the space that followed, a

---

* This was 1853: the extension on the north-west side, which involved moving the front door to the spot where Eddie was standing outside Darwin's study, was not added until 1857. J. R.

matter of some three minutes or so during which perhaps the butler checked with his master that he was 'at home' to his visitor, I allowed the ambience of the place to build its presence around me.

The grounds, what I could see of them, were well kept (though the effect somewhat spoiled by the presence of a child's hoop and a doll's perambulator) and hidden from the sunken lane outside by a wall; on this side of the house there were somewhat formal flowerbeds laid out with salvia and well-trimmed rose bushes. The noises that abounded were more exceptional. These consisted on the surface of those made by children in unruly high spirits – screams, laughter, shouts of dissent and so forth, from both the interior and outside of the house – but through them I could also detect the rumbling cries of several, possibly many, doves and pigeons. The common fragrances of the English countryside in early July, as of new-mown hay, roses, honeysuckle and possibly jasmine, were also undercut with something less pleasant: the odour of boiling fowl and decaying flesh.

I felt a tug on my coat-tail.

'Etty is hurted. Georgy pushed her. Need an icky plaster.'

I looked down. A small boy, with abundant curly brown hair, about five years old I should guess, dressed in male knickerbockers beneath a flounced, and rather feminine full smock looked up at me, his dark eyes serious.

'I'm afraid I don't have one.'

His bottom lip quivered and he shook his head. I feared tears and rushed on. 'I am sure Etty will get better. What's your name?'

'Fwank.' Which I understood to be 'Frank'. 'What's yours?'

'Charles . . . or,' recalling the name I was known by on the *Beagle*, 'Edward.'

He shook his head in mild bewilderment, or possibly expressing polite sympathy. 'Don't you know, then? Papa is Charles, so I 'spect you are Edward.'

But at this moment the front door opened and I was confronted with the butler, a tall, well-built character with something of the look of a bishop or judge about him. I handed him a card I had had printed for the occasion (receipt attached, please reimburse promptly).

'Edward Boylan,' I said. 'I met Mr Darwin quite recently. He requested I should call on him if I was ever in the neighbourhood.'

'The master will see you. Please follow me.'

The journey was a short one. He bade me wait in a small hall with a narrow staircase climbing out of it, while he opened the first door on the left. During the interval another young lad, older than the first, emerged from a cubbyhole or large, angled cupboard beneath the stairs. I received a brief glimpse of bent sticks which I took to be accessories for 'croquet', a new fad, and battledore rackets. He glanced at me briefly, his face communicating a touch of shame with a request for complicity supported by a finger to his lips requesting secrecy, possibly directed more at the butler than at me, before vanishing through a glazed door that opened on to an extensive, sunlit lawn with mature trees beyond. The butler coughed discreetly and I passed in front of him into Mr Darwin's study.

My visit was not long but I have trained myself to take in as much detail of my surroundings as I can wherever I go. It was a square room with a chimney piece and a marble-bordered fireplace on the left side wall, and a large bookcase on the right. Between these, two tall sash windows. In the centre a square table and under the window a round table whose body was a revolvable drum so the objects on it could be brought under the 'scientist's' eyes and hands, obviating the need to move them. These included two microscopes, one newfangled, the other older with a single lens, many more glass pots, some part filled with coloured chemicals, boxes containing instruments, and a partially reconstructed skeleton of a bird, bigger than a thrush, smaller than a hen. I guessed, correctly, a pigeon. The larger table was cluttered with open books, papers, writing implements and so forth.

So far much the sort of thing one might have expected but there were two unusual features. The left-hand corner, by the door, was screened off with curtains, while up by the window was a large chair with low arms, leather-covered in black or very dark blue, mounted, I discovered, on free-running casters which allowed the occupant to propel himself about the small place, from table to table to bookcase without having to waste time or energy getting out of it.

Mr Darwin half-rose from the armchair and waved me towards a small upholstered stool between the tables.

'Mr Boylan,' he said, his voice deepish and cordial, 'you were on the *Beagle* and we met a few weeks ago in the Antigallican in Borough. How can I help you?'

I expressed an interest in the collections I had helped to make during our shared voyage, and their history since his return. He talked briefly of how most were now stored and some on public display in various scientifically orientated and learned institutions, but also allowed me to handle some fragments of basalt and pumice collected on Albemarle, explaining how they demonstrated the geologically recent arrival of the islands above the surface of the sea.

I asked him what he had been working on recently.

'Barnacles, Mr Boylan. Barnacles to the exclusion of almost everything else. You will recollect the interest I took in barnacles. It has now borne fruit in a monograph nearly seven hundred pages long which I have just finished. But, of course, that does not mean the labour is over, there will be proofs to be read . . .'

His voice tailed off, and he cocked his head at me somewhat quizzically. 'But you are not interested in barnacles.'

'Er, no.'

'Are you not aware that in one particular example of the class of Cirripedia the male is little more than a set of genitals in a sack? And another has two penises?'

'Barnacles do not,' I suggested, 'play a huge part in the great scheme of things.'

A sort of half-smile, kindly in its wisdom, spread across his face.

'That may be your perception, Mr Boylan. But if you ask yourself why . . . Why and how? What then?'

Silence lengthened between us. I was not about to speculate as to how and why a small mollusc or crustacean would need two of an organ that causes enough trouble in the singular. The noise of children at play became more intrusive. The stairs above that cupboard seemed to have become a highway for elephants. Had they no schoolroom to go to? Did Mr Darwin not employ a dominie to tutor them? I, however, prompted by Mr Buff-Orpington, had done my homework.

'You mean to ask, sir, according to what principles, what laws, these humble creatures mutated so variously?'

'Precisely so, Mr Boylan.'

'Not then, simply a matter of the shaping Hand of God.'

'I think not.' A sort of cloud now erased the smile, though a wistful sort of kindness remained. He went on: 'If he exists I cannot believe he is benign. And if he is not benign I prefer not to find his existence credible . . .' and he cast a glance at a framed daguerreotype on the square table. It was of a female child, some eight or nine years old, wearing a check pattern dress and holding a small basket of flowers in her lap. Her countenance was all Darwin; however, what might have seemed an unfortunate plainness in her physiognomy was alleviated by her poise and the clear intelligence that shone from her eyes. He sighed.

At that moment the door was flung open and a girl who looked to be almost a twin of the one in the picture but with a lightness and more obvious prettiness in the more feminine cast of her features burst in.

'Papa,' she cried, 'I must have a sticking plaster. For my knee. Nurse says it's not bad enough for a plaster but it hu-u-u-urts!' and she hoisted the hem of her dress to reveal to us a knee with very slight scrapes, on which tiny scabs were already forming. To my surprise her father instantly found a roll of sticky tape and pulled a piece the size of a songbird's egg of cotton wool from a ball of the stuff on the round table, all the while manœuvring his chair from place to place to do so. He upended a bottle labelled 'Spirits of Wine' on the cotton wool and* . . .

'This may sting,' he said.

'It does no good if it does not,' the little girl replied solemnly, as if supplying a ritual response to his versicle . . . then he scissored off two strips of tape and fastened them in a cross that held the dressing in place across her knee.

'Run along now, Etty,' and he patted her rear, urging her through the door. We heard her shout: 'See, Frankie, you were wrong. Papa said it was very bad and certainly needed a plaster, so there!'

'Nurse is new to us,' her father now muttered. 'Jessie, who had been with us for so long, could not bear to remain here after Annie died, though she does still visit.' Once more he sighed, then the childish pandemonium receded and he seemed to pull himself together, head on one side again as if waiting for a comment or question from me.

'So, sir,' I ventured, 'you believe that transmutation is the engine that produces these many types of barnacle. Would I be correct in

---

* The use of alcohol and allied spirits to forestall putrefaction in wounds though not in surgery was common from the 1750s, though of course the process by which they worked was not understood until the time of Pasteur and Lister. J. R.

guessing that it is in the direction of a general theory of transmutation of species that your present work tends?'

But this was a step too far.

'These are matters too complex and serious to be discussed lightly. I may publish one day. I may not. But I cannot undertake to talk idly about it, as it were, before lunch.'

'Of course not. But I wonder, sir, if you have made notes, a digest perhaps, of the way you are heading. I should be most interested—'

'That is enough, Mr Boylan.' He spoke quite sharply now, though his countenance remained compliant as ever. 'I must get on with my work. I will instruct Parslow to show you a little of what we are up to before you go, but I'm afraid I must get on.' And he found, and rang, a small handbell which conjured up the formidable butler as surely as the Genius of the Lamp appears for Aladdin in the Drury Lane pantomime.

Back in the hall we were witness to the knickerbockered bottom of the boy I had previously seen, emerging from the understairs cupboard, as he rummaged about inside it. He backed out and faced us, slightly red in the face and running his fingers through his abundant hair. He was about eight years old and his face was somewhat longer than that of the other children I had seen. Perhaps he took after his mother.

'I say, Parslow,' he began, 'all the shuttlecocks seem to have gone. I can't find a single one.'

'Come, Master George, let me have a look,' and George stood beside me while Parslow folded down his large frame and on one knee began to hike everything that was in the cupboard out on to the worn Turkey rug that covered the floor. George looked up at me.

'Do you belong to the Fancy?' he asked. 'You look as if you might.'

'No,' I replied. 'I'm more of a barnacle man myself.'

'You know,' he said, quite earnestly, 'when I was little I thought everybody's papa did barnacles and I was puzzled to find one who did not. That's the story the grown-ups tell, though I don't myself remember saying such a silly thing.'

In front of us a small pile began to grow. There were battledores, coats, scarves for children, quoits, balls of various sizes, a cricket bat and a set of stumps, some old shoes, boots and the new sort of rubberised overshoes called galoshes. And finally, from the very bottom of the cupboard, but now on the outside edge of the pile, a large bundle of papers done up in string, perhaps amounting to five hundred sheets or so, but separately if loosely bound as portfolios with ribbon or whatever.

While the other two rummaged about in the lowest layer of debris I was able to read the top page.

> C. Darwin to Mrs Darwin.
> Down, July 5, 1844.
>
> I have just finished my sketch of my species theory. If, as I believe, my theory in time be accepted even by one competent judge, it will be a considerable step in science.
>
> I therefore write this in case of my sudden death, as my most solemn and last request, which I am sure you will consider the same as if legally entered in my will, that you will devote £400 to its publication, and further will yourself, or through Hensleigh, take the trouble in promoting it . . .*

This, I thought, will do very nicely, even if nine years old. How to get hold of it, though?

'Yoicks!' cried George and triumphantly held up a shuttlecock made of turned wood, crowned with white feathers. 'At last we'll be able to have a proper game.'

'Hang on a minute, Master George,' rumbled the butler, like distant summer thunder. 'All this lot's to be put away first, and tidily too.'

'Oh I say, Parslow, do I have to?'

I intervened.

'I'll help you, Mr Parslow,' I cried. 'Let the boy go.'

'Oh, thank you, sir,' the boy exclaimed. 'In spite of your appearance you are a real gentleman!'

And he was off like an arrow before Parslow could stop him.

---

* This is the opening preamble to the 'sketch' which was eventually edited by Francis Darwin, whom we met at the front door, as *The Foundations of the 'Origin of Species'* and published by the Cambridge U.P. in 1909. Hensleigh was one of Darwin's brothers-in-law. J. R.

Together, but getting in each other's way, the butler and I stacked it all back in the cupboard but you can be sure I left the bundle of manuscripts to last so that it was close to the door and the hall.

'There we are then,' I said at last, straightening and rubbing my back. 'That's done. Now, Mr Parslow, your master suggested you might take me round the establishment and explain to me what he is working on at the moment.'

'Not much I can tell you,' he grumbled, but dutifully set off through the glazed door, which I noticed he did not lock behind him.

We crossed the garden, laid out to lawn, with croquet hoops in place, and the children, two boys and two girls, playing battledore, or rather arguing about who should play whom. We remarked the fine trees to the south, a yew, pine, a magnificent sweet chestnut and up near the corner of the new wing, which was a servants' wing, a fine mulberry tree. Then he led me off down a gravelled walk which bordered a big, open meadow to the kitchen gardens of which the main feature were large, long greenhouses, in which Mr Darwin grew a variety of strange plants and hybridised new ones. A turn through a wall took us into an orchard but with a lean-to building against the wall from which emanated, very strongly now, the smell of boiling fowl, made more obnoxious by the fact they were, it seemed, boiled unplucked, feathers and all, and rendered down until the skin and flesh fell easily away from the skeletons which Mr Darwin then reassembled.

'To what end?' I asked.

'Blessed if I know. He doos say he doos it so he can zee how they differ from breed to breed, but you can zee all that whilom they're alive.' Parslow's manner of speaking shifted into a far more rural mode once he was away from those he considered to be his betters. 'Lookee a' tha' then.'

And he indicated a dovecote some fifty paces away above which a trio of white tumblers were at that very moment doing their stuff against the blue of a perfectly clear sky. 'Shame I zay to boil up such handsome fowl and not even eat'm.'

We made our way back towards the house and I was beginning to despair of ever getting at that cupboard unobserved. The children had now left the lawn but could be heard hallooing in the not too far distance . . .

'Playing at Red Indians, like as not,' said Parslow.

An odd way for children to pass the time, I thought, recalling my time amongst the Cherokee. And at that point we heard behind us the yap of a small dog and there was Mr Darwin, walking along the side of the kitchen gardens towards a line of trees a half-mile or so away on the other side of the meadow with a fox terrier jumping about his heels.

'Always takes his walk at midday. He'll be out now for an hour. Lookee, Mr Whatdoyer call yusel', I have duties right now, making sure cook an' all have the lunch properly on the go, zo if you can see your own way out, I'll be leavin' you here.'

And he set off at a tidy speed towards the servants' quarters.

Not invited to lunch, then. Never mind. I waited until he had passed under the mulberry and through the shrubbery beyond and in a flash was back through the glazed door. The string round the bundle was a bit dodgy, but I managed, got the top portfolio out, turned the whole lot the other way up and was off, back through the front door and out into the lane. Mission accomplished.

Back in my 'digs' in Lambeth I poured myself a glass of Watney's bottled India pale ale, cut a slice of pork pie and spooned an onion out of my jar of pickles before settling down to what the title page declared was *A Foundation*. The first chapter was mumbo-jumbo though appeared to be mainly about the breeding of domestic animals. Common sense in the more lucid passages but even so not a barrel of gunpowder to blow to smithereens the God-ordained way things are. Kings and bishops will not sleep any less deeply on account of this, I said to myself, and wondered if my trip to Down had been worth the time and effort. But I've learnt my way about any extended piece of prose, written for whatever reason. If you want the gist, the book in a nutshell, go to the end. The last chapter of *Bleak House*, which I had just finished in monthly numbers on, as it were, the instalment plan, begins, in Esther's voice, 'Full seven happy years I have been mistress of Bleak House . . .' followed by a résumé of the lives of many of the major characters. Does one need to know more than this? Was it really necessary to take on so much lumber during the previous six hundred pages? And thus it was with the *Foundation*.

It concludes: 'There is a grandeur in this view of life with its several powers of growth, reproduction, and of sensation, having been originally breathed into matter under a few forms, perhaps into only one, and that whilst this planet has gone cycling onwards according to the fixed laws of gravity and whilst land and water have gone on replacing each – that from so simple an origin, through the selection of infinitesimal varieties, endless forms most beautiful and most wonderful have been evolved.'

That should do, I thought. That should do.

Part VII

WESTWARD HO!

To go west, of persons, to die; of things, to be lost, rendered useless or unattainable.

Brewer's Dictionary of Phrase and Fable

33

Since leaving the Texian prairie and swamps, the Indians had been an absence for me rather than a presence, but, now it occurred to me, an absence that was palpable, physical. Their absence from the Mississippi, from the delta to St Andrew's Falls, was real: it was their canoes that should have slid across the glassy flood, their nets and hooks that caught the fishy tribe, their arrows and spears that took for need rather than sport the wild turkeys, deer, and on the prairies to the west the buffalo, and it was their homely teepees, whose skins and poles went with them when the need to wander took hold, rather than the cabins and jetties of the woodcutters, which should have lined the banks of a creek or huddled in a hollow. And no wonder, no wonder at all, they were absent from the brick and clapboard towns with their open sewers, smoke, cholera and vice. But now I was well and truly amongst them, and that absence had become a presence as real as air and water and the stones beneath our feet.

The clouds that had filled the night sky presaged a dawn without frost and something of a thaw, so it was through slush and mud that preparations were made to continue the march west. But first the dead from the upturned flatboat had to be buried amidst much lamentation, accompanied by, on the part of the men, or 'braves', slow and solemn dancing, rhythmic with stamping, syncopated with unison handclaps that reverberated like pistol shots. The US cavalry, mounted, looked on in sullen silence. They were the most professional looking soldiers I had yet seen, hard, lean men, with bronzed countenances, big moustaches, armed with carbines and sabres, and with a six-pounder well to the fore. Throughout the march, which would take a further two months before we reached the area designated, they did the Cherokee no harm that I saw, but it was clear that any resistance or wilful interference with their progress into the West would be met with swift and brutal reprisals.

The ceremonies concluded, the teepees, used on the journey until a permanent settlement was reached, were taken down and folded away. At about midday, beneath a sun that was warm enough to carry a distant promise or memory of spring, the column began to form and I realised it was bigger, longer than I had thought, and more mixed. There were somewhere between two and three thousand souls in it, not including the cavalry, and by no means all were on foot. The more senior braves were mounted on wiry ponies, there were small waggons, some covered, pulled by oxen and mules, and at least three open carriages, well-sprung and with big rear wheels. Perhaps most extraordinary of all was the fact that two of these were attended by Negroes who were owned by the Indian chiefs or heads of the lodges or clans they were divided into. But most, nearly all, walked, and I walked with them.

Walked with a heavy heart for it was towards the West we relentlessly progressed, which the Cherokees look on as the land of darkness and death, and which for me was, at the very least, the long way home. But what else could I do? I had nothing but the clothes I was no longer standing up in since the woman who had given me a blanket refused to let me have them back until they were dry. Not a cent, a penny, nickel or dime. Not even my bag and my Arkansas Toothpick. I could, I suppose, have turned back and sought out the hamlets on the river, but what sort of welcome would I get at Bainbridge or Cape Girardeaux? On the riverboats I had heard how vagabonds with no visible means of support were routinely supposed to be charlatans or hucksters, were tarred and feathered and ridden out of town on a hurdle like Hector round the walls of Troy. With these people, I sensed, I was among friends, and I was proved right.

I soon found the Cherokees were more mixed than I should have thought, many having white blood. The facts were these: their women were by their laws and customs far more independent than ours and were freely allowed to choose whom they might consort with and marry. And it was considered no disgrace, indeed quite the reverse, if they managed to take a white man into their home only excepting those that drank strong liquor, which they abominated. The attentive reader will recall that Sam Houston's second wife was a Cherokee, and she got him off the drink that was ruining his life. However, and on the other hand, the white men, especially those who with monumentally pretentious pride called themselves 'natives', rejected and cast out any man or woman who consorted with the Indians and their offspring, whom they designated as 'half-breeds', who therefore, so long as they remained with their new consorts, had no choice but to join the tribe or clan they had married into. There was, therefore, on the march a sprinkling of white men, and more than a handful of young people and children of mixed blood, all of whom were accepted as Cherokee by their brothers and sisters.

It was not long before I made the acquaintance of one Barnaby Bushyhead, a lad of twelve years or so, three parts Cherokee and one part Scot and nephew of the Reverend Jesse Bushyhead, whose daughter caught pneumonia as a result of being tipped from the flat-boat and died two days later. Barnaby was a sharp lad, and, when circumstances demanded, and it was not long before they did, he taught me the Cherokee tongue which I picked up with some ease on two counts, first because, Mr Murray, as I think I have already mentioned, I was brought up tri-lingual in English, Spanish and Italian, and therefore have the gift, and secondly because the Cherokees had worked out an orthography by which they could write and read their lingo in roman characters which facilitated the process for me very considerably. Indeed, I soon found conversation with Barnaby was easier in Cherokee than the bastard Lowland dialect he believed was English. All of which circumstances stated above meant that it was not long before I was in possession of the facts and history that had led to these poor people's condition.

Mr Murray, I am, am I not, in so far as you are concerned, writing a book of travel, in the spirit of those you have already published with success and acclaim? You will not, therefore, expect me to observe the conventions of a mere *novelist*. I could of course drama-tise what follows, present it as conversation between Barnaby and others and myself, larding it with little interruptions and minor incidents, thus sugaring, for the less discerning or attentive reader, the pill of solid information. I believe that such devices, albeit they would mirror the means by which I acquired the facts presented below, would make them not more entertaining for the reader seeking knowledge, but merely tediously extend the matter through art. I shall therefore present them simple and unadorned.

The Cherokees came from Georgia, in the south and east (which was where no doubt Houston was chosen by his second bride), and had signed treaties some years earlier, giving them rights over the lands which had been theirs for centuries. Unfortunately for them, gold was then discovered in these ancestral homelands; prospectors and investors resorted to the usual Washingtonian strategies of deceit, bribery and all manner of chicanery which have characterised procedures in the District since Independence, and no doubt will continue to do so until the Republic goes the way of Ozymandias. By these means they inveigled discontents from amongst the Cherokee to the capital, dressed them up as true representatives of their people, and had the old treaties reneged, cancelled, torn up. President Andrew Jackson now signed an order requiring the People to be moved from their homeland, lock, stock and barrel, to the land of the Red Man, or, to give it its name in several of the native tongues, Oklahoma, five hundred miles west of the Mississippi. To tell the truth, I doubt Jackson was much bothered about the gold – the seams ran out soon enough anyway – but he was very much concerned with what the Germans call *Lebensraum*, room to live, and it was already his policy to move the Indians as far west as they could be got to make room for the growing flood of white European immigrants who were to be the colonists of his new empire. I doubt he yet used the slogan I had devised for him, *Manifest Destiny*, but that was the core of his Indian policy.

The Cherokees themselves presented an extra sort of embarrassment to the white settlers: they were farmers, lived in houses, had a written language and a form of government more democratic than that of the Great Democracy; many were Christian, and so forth. It all added up to a viable 'civilised' nation which had far more right to live where they did than the hordes who encroached upon them. The excuse to do as one liked with them because they were nothing but mere savages had not even the gloss of appearances to support it.

Jackson was a soldier. He it was who defeated the British at New Orleans in 1815. And the movement of the Cherokees was accomplished with military precision and lack of ruth. First, throughout the summer of 1838, they were rounded up and interned in small concentrated camps. Meanwhile, partly carried out by the army and in part by private contractors, dumps of grain and other necessaries were placed along the four or five routes that were carefully mapped out in advance. And, finally, detachments of mounted infantry and cavalry were designated to accompany each column. No doubt these provisions were made to ensure a trouble-free journey rather than out of humanitarian considerations and in the event the People suffered terribly. The march took six months which spanned the winter; private contractors failed to fulfil their contracts; much of the dumped grain was mildewed, and so forth, and the inevitable crossings of the big rivers that crisscrossed their paths were badly managed. Of the fourteen thousand who started the trip, only nine thousand survived. So much for history. What I experienced was the reality.

This began in the way I have already described with a long, thin thread of humanity winding its way into the prairie through melt and churned-up mud. This was not the prairie of Texas which I had crossed from Laredo to San Jacinto nearly three years earlier, with its frequent wooded creeks, its abundant waist-high grass, and myriad flowers – it was altogether a more dismal prospect rendered, no doubt, even less appealing and hospitable by the season. Looking towards the West, where the sun would presently set, there lay a vast expanse of level ground unbroken save by one thin line of trees which scarcely amounted to a scratch upon a great blank. There it lay, a sea or lake without water, apart from what had fallen as snow, a few birds wheeling here and there, above the solitude and silence. The grass was not yet high, there were bare, black patches on the ground. Large though the picture was, its very flatness and extent, oppressive in its barren monotony, quite o'ercrowed the spirit.

And so it went on, day after day. Occasionally there were dips in the flatness, not the delightful creeks of Texas but noisome swamps filled with rank, unseemly growth and the perpetual chorus of frogs, which in that season filled the pools with spawning couples. We were not the first to cross this waste, this slough of despond. Here and there we encountered a solitary broken-down waggon, full of some new settler's goods. It was a pitiful sight to see one of these vehicles deep in the mire, the axle-tree broken, a wheel lying idly by its side, the man gone miles away to look for assistance, the woman with a baby at her breast, a picture of forlorn, dejected patience, the team of oxen crouching down mournfully in the mud, and breathing forth such clouds of vapour from their mouths and nostrils that all the damp mist and fog seemed to have come from them.

But I was comforted too. At dawn on the second day the woman who had given me blankets and taken my clothes (about whom I confess I had entertained thoughts less than kind, believing she had taken them perhaps to clad a husband or son of her own) sought me out and handed them back. Not only were they crisply dry – and how she had achieved that heaven and she alone knew – they were washed and, in the two or three places where it was necessary, carefully darned with threads pulled from the turned and inward facing hems of the coat. She now attached herself to me, and, having ascertained from Barnaby that she was unattached – I later learnt she had lost a husband to the cholera in the internment or concentration camp* – I accepted her as my companion, and later wife.

Yes! She was the only woman I have consorted with, out of far too many, who could claim that title, if one may accept as a marriage ceremony the strange but jolly celebration that conferred a recognition on us that her lodge considered us a couple bound together by their customs for as long as each of us wished the union to last.

Her name, translated, was Shadow-Tree-Swallow, which no doubt suited her well enough in her childhood and early teens, the bird being a smaller member of the swallow family notable for the dark green gloss on its back and the pure whiteness of its breast as well as the way it flaps and glides in flight. She was still small and was often lively but older even than I, being already in her fifties by her reckoning, with a face lined by hardship and some grief, and her long hair streaked with grey. Her face was sharp with a prominent nose and wide mouth, her complexion dark, but her eyes lively and darting which matched her character which, though settled by the years, remained mercurial. She was wily too. When I showed discontent, for instance, with the food she prepared, she quickly passed over its

* The British are often credited with the invention of the concentration camp in the run-up to the Boer War. It seems the Americans beat us to it. J. R.

preparation to me, which, on the whole, I was content to accept. The exigencies of my life have taught me to be a fair hand in the kitchen. She, however, retained control over the medicine chest, or 'bundle' as they called it, dispensing to her daughters, sisters and nieces angelica, echinacea, motherwort and evening primrose, once they became available with the late spring and summer, for female conditions; burdock, goldenseal and yellowroot for skin wounds, and so forth. But all this is to get ahead of my story yet again, for the solemnisation of our union did not take place until we had reached the Land of the Red Man.

But first there was much misery and hardship to be borne, not the least of which arose from the general mood that had descended on these normally equable and pleasant people. They were sullen, overcome with lassitude, and several simply wandered off into the wilderness to die. They were given to outbreaks of wailing or crooning long, monotonous songs of despair. One could see why, of course. They had been imprisoned in their own land and then driven from it. They had been made to feel outcasts and strangers in their own homes. They sensed, no, they had been told, they were a problem. Above all they suffered from that most corrosive of ailments of the soul, the feeling that they had been betrayed, treated unfairly. This irritated me. Get off your backsides and do something about it, I said to myself. Wear it or lose it. If die you must, at least let it be beneath the slash of a sabre or at the cannon's mouth.

The worst came at the beginning of March with a week of icy rain and driving sleet carried horizontally on the back of gales, dragged south by the warmth of the Gulf, howling out of the High Plains and the wastes of Canada beyond, heading for Texas and Mexico, a storm that would become the Blue Norther whose effects I had witnessed exactly three years earlier. The whole column wound in upon itself and formed a shapeless huddle beneath the teepee skins whose frames could not sustain the winds. Waggons were whisked away, bowling across the flattened prairie or splintering amongst trees and rocks. The roar of the wind deafened, the icy droplets blinded, the cold paralysed. For three days no one ate, for in the wrack no one could find the food. And the worst of it was that this was all beyond the experience of people who for generations had enjoyed the clement climate of Georgia untroubled by weather apart from the occasional twister, most of which passed them by.

But at last it blew itself out, the sun returned and with it some warmth; grass began to grow around us and flowers too. We stayed to bury the dead and then moved on, again with many a cheek bedewed with tears, and, along the way, this trail of tears was marked by the blooming of a small ground rose, white with a gold centre, which marked, they said, each place where a tear fell to the ground.

Eventually we came to a rocky hill watered by two thin streams. The commander of the cavalry signified we had come far enough and two braves climbed it, looked around and uttered the word *tahlequah* which means 'this will do', and that was the name they gave the new centre of the Cherokee nation.

The Lament of the Cherokee

Can a tree that is torn from its root by the fountain,
The pride of the valley, green, spreading and fair,
Can it flourish, removed to the rock of the mountain,
Unwarmed by the sun and unwatered by care?

As flies the fleet deer when the blood hound is started
So fled wingèd hope from the poor broken hearted,
Oh, could she have turned ere for ever departing
And beckoned with smiles to her sad Cherokee?

Great Spirit of good whose abode is in heaven
Whose wampum of peace is the bow in the sky
Wilt thou give to the wants of the clamorous ravens
Yet turn a deaf ear to my piteous cry?

O'er the ruins of home, o'er my heart's desolation
No more shalt thou hear my unblest lamentation.
For death's dark encounter I make preparation,
Oh, hear the last groan of the wild Cherokee.*

* Eddie fails to acknowledge he has here adapted a work of John Howard Payne, who, along with many other white Americans, campaigned for the Cherokees. He was also an actor and writer of operas who performed in London as well as America and was the author of the lyrics to 'Home, Sweet Home'. J. R.

34

Buff-Orpington summoned me to the Home Office today and gave me to understand that he has set up a committee to look into the *Foundation*, and other aspects of Transmutationism. Their report is to be examined by the Treasury Solicitor's Office to ascertain whether or not an action for seditious libel, blasphemy or what-all might be advisable or viable. The upshot for me is that once copies of the *Foundation* have been made and distributed to various experts and advisers as well as the members of the committee itself I will be required to take the original back to Down House and replace it in the hope that its brief wander from home has not been discovered.

So, here I am, yet again with time on my hands and the Cherokee looking in dismay at their new homeland.

The fading foliage of the few, scattered trees was already beginning to exhibit the hues and tints of autumn when, following the guidance of the two braves who had gone on ahead, our train of misery and wag-gons issued from the bed of a dry rivulet to pursue its course across what is known as a 'rolling prairie'. The vehicles, loaded with house-hold goods and implements of husbandry, the few straggling sheep and cattle that were herded in the rear, the rugged appearance and careless mien of the sturdy Cherokee who loitered at the sides of the lingering teams, and the women and children who dragged their feet and stumbled behind the waggons, united to announce a band of people, lost in a wilderness, whose disinclination to go any further was a stronger motive than any other for staying where they were.

In their front were stretched those broad plains, which extend, with so little diversity of character, to the bases of the Rocky Mountains with many a long and dreary mile in their rear. The well-watered and temperate meadows and orchards which had nurtured them for a millennium were now already a memory as of a lost Eden. At this moment, when lassitude was getting the mastery of the travellers, the whole party was brought up by a spectacle, as sudden as it was unexpected. With scarcely more than a bugle call to announce it the cavalry, which had been following us, swung right round in a tight circle and, following their thin pennants, set off at a steady trot, with the sun behind them, back east, back the way we had come.

We were alone, but not for long. In the ensuing weeks three more columns like ours came up with us until, all told, there were upwards of eight thousand, that is eight thousand out of the nation of fourteen thousand that had been interned in Georgia nearly a year before. Six thousand bodies littered the trails they had followed or were washed up on the banks of the rivers they had been forced to cross. The winter that followed brought many more deaths, maybe as many as another four thousand, mostly of starvation and cold, for the supplies the soldiers had left us were meagre and soon ran out and the only harvest available to us was berries and acorns from the scanty forest around, fish from the rivers and a lake, and, the following March, a waggon train of grain and corn put together by well-wishers in the east. Not least amongst the dangers emanating out of the neighbouring hills were the marauding war parties of nomadic Indians to whom the Cherokee were no more brothers than the white men who had brought us. All in all a great slaughter – a holocaust?

Years passed and, with carefully husbanded harvests producing corn as high as an elephant's eye, the damming of rivers to form fish pools, the breeding of more animals from the limited stock we had, and a well-planned and mutually agreed spreading outward of the various lodges and so forth, things could only get better.

Years? Yes. Maybe five or six. Shadow-Tree-Swallow and I got by, and I doubt either of us would have managed on our own. She traded on the respect she was paid on account of her age and her standing as a medicine woman; deprived as I am of bodily strength, prepossessing

looks and the gift of a good conscience, I relied on skills less merito-
rious that I have been forced to acquire, namely those associated with
cozenage, petty pilfering, threats and blackmail. I mastered the lingo
too. Like a native. We worked together. We ate.

Sure, I grew fond of my spouse, and I think she of me, but even
during the careless rapture of our early days and nights together the
pleasures we shared were for me compromised by the sour, unper-
fumed odours of her body, the rank, smokey harshness of uncured
leather that lingered from her clothes, and the fact that everything
she did between the rough blankets, she did by the book. The
Cherokee book, that is. I longed for a well-scrubbed and scented
companion and a willingness to allow me, just occasionally, to be on
top.

The thing of it was that, though I ate and enjoyed domestic comforts and satisfactions, my soul still hungered for city life, for theatres,
the bustle of streets, the changing and making of money, newspapers,
and coffee. I pined for bricks and mortar and slates. I was tired of
living in a fucking shed. I am not a rural person. I am not by nature
an agriculturalist, and when Shadow-Tree-Swallow eventually succumbed to the White Sickness* Native Americans are prone to but
European stock seems better able to resist, the desire to be off became
acute.

But the problem was that I was incapable, and I knew it, of setting
out across that dusty, rolling prairie on my own. I'd be lost in a day.
I'd starve in a week if I were not first scalped, or eaten by a bar or
bear, a pack of wolves, or a cougar. Of course, over the years a handful of white men came our way: trappers, travellers determined to get
to the west coast, prospectors for gold and lesser metals, but for the
most part they stayed clear of us or were gone, having provisioned up
from our stores and reshoed their horses, before I could approach
them. And a sentence or two of conversation with those I did speak
to revealed that they really were not the sort of people with whom I
would choose to go on a walking tour.

Then, one evening, early in June I suppose it was, though it was a
long time since I'd reckoned the days and months in a Christian way,
the right man turned up. The sun was about to drop below the crest

* Probably tuberculosis, though of course it was endemic in Europe too.
  J. R.

of the nearest wave of the prairie, leaving its usual rich and glowing train behind it. In the centre of this flood of fiery light, a human form appeared. It was made colossal by its situation directly above the small settlement where our lodge lived and the length of shadow it cast; but imbedded, as it was, in its setting of garish light, it was impossible to distinguish its just proportions or true character. However, as he walked towards us it soon became apparent that he was a tall man, sunburnt, past the middle age, and at that moment of a dull countenance and listless manner. His frame appeared loose and flexible, but it was vast, and in reality of prodigious power. It was only at moments, however, as some slight impediment opposed itself to his loitering progress, that he seemed to stumble a little and grunt out a low oath. Yet one sensed his person, which in its ordinary gait seemed so lounging and nerveless, concealed those energies, which lay latent in his system, like the slumbering and unwieldy but terrible strength of the mountain bear.

One could make out little of his physiognomy and not just because he stood against the light – his face was covered by a huge and untended beard and moustache which left only the pale blue of smallish eyes and a small nose rendered vermilion by decades of exposure to the elements, supported by regular intakes of spirituous liquor. This massive beard, which curtained his upper chest as well as his face, was for the most part a grubby white but streaked with a gingery hue that suggested its original colouring.

The dress of this individual was a mixture of the coarsest vestments of a 'man of the mountains' (to give the trade of trapper its more dignified appellation), the foundation of which was a patchwork of shabby skins worn fur side outwards beneath a long and trailing blanket coat. There was, however, a singular and wild display of prodigal and ill-judged ornaments, blended with his motley attire. In place of the usual deerskin belt, he wore around his body a tarnished silken sash of the most gaudy colours; the buck-horn heft of his knife was profusely decorated with plates of silver; the marten's fur of his cap was of a fineness and shadowing that a queen might covet; the buttons of his rude and soiled coat were the glittering silver coins of Mexico; the stock of his rifle was a beautiful mahogany, riveted and banded with the same precious metal; and the trinkets of no less than three worthless watches dangled from different parts of his person. In addition to the pack and the rifle which were slung at his back together with the well-filled and carefully guarded pouch and horn, he had carelessly cast a keen and bright tomahawk, collared with porcupine quills, across his shoulder, and all this he sustained with as much apparent ease as if he moved unfettered in limb and free from encumbrance.

I should explain at this point that the 'us' I have referred to was a handful of maybe six male Cherokee all too old to be braves and either widowed or out of sorts with their families. We used to gather of an evening on the periphery of the settlement, a lodge of the Long Hair Clan, to smoke Mary Jane which we secretly grew on the sheltered banks of a creek a mile off, and generally to chew the rag until it was almost dark. But by the evening on which this wonderful stranger turned up we had said most of what we had to say to each other many times over and, as on most evenings, a silence at first sullen had settled over us but then as the weed took hold, we'd grin at each other and occasionally giggle.

'Howdy!' said the Stranger, and 'How!' we all replied.

'Now tell me, could a poor wandering soul, half-starved as he is, not find some chow and maybe a warm place for his head for a night or two?'

Oh shit, I thought, another Irishman.

But in this man's case it was not the harshness of Liverpool Irish in his voice betrayed his origins but the soft vowels, sea-salt laden of the west – Galway perhaps or Sligo. He began again, spacing the words the way you do to a foreigner who does not know your tongue: 'Could . . . a . . . poor . . . wandering . . .'

'It could be arranged I'm sure,' I murmured, though with some hesitation. Apart from attempting, early on, to teach the Cherokee kids some English, I had hardly used my own language for seven years or more.

'Jasus,' our new friend cried, and sat down with us as he did so, 'Sure an' oi'm amongst Christians after all.' Then his face took on a sombre cast. 'Not that that,' he went on, 'is always the good thing it should be. Never mind,' and he leant across and put his hand on my knee, 'if you have a pile of brushwood I can sleep on and a blanket and a pillow for the night, or maybe two, I'll say whatever prayer for you suits your own particular de-minuation, so I will. An' if you have a glass of Firmin's whiskey about you, and a piece of jerk you can spare, so much the better.'

'Food we have,' I replied, 'but being Cherokee no spirits or hard drink of any sort.'

'You don't say? Then I doubt I'll be here no more'n a day, just enough to let the ache get outer m' knees, is all I ask.'

By now I was getting that slight chill, that shudder that comes with meeting someone from long ago, or thinking you do, but you can't place him and anyway a passing resemblance was most certainly at the root of it, and the man not who you thought he was, at all. What really set it off was that amongst all the trinkets hung about him was a well-polished piece of brass plate hung by a leather thong round his neck, with the number eighty-eight with a crown joining the eights moulded on to it. Thirty years earlier I had had my own version of this – the regimental badge of the Connaught Rangers, made to fasten the cross-over of the white shoulder straps.

One of our companions went and got him some corn bread, a piece of buffalo jerk and a cup of water, and then, since it was now dark, and the little fire we had been sitting round burnt low, I took him to the tiny shed I'd lived in since Shadow-Tree-Swallow coughed herself into silence. Fumbling about, I managed to get together the bedding he'd asked for, and in the almost complete darkness heard how he divested himself of his strange accoutrements and embellishments. Then at last I did what I should have done an hour before and asked him his name.

'Patrick,' he said. Well, he would, wouldn't he, I thought.

'Coffey,' he added. 'What's yours?'

'Eddie Bosham,' I replied, with a stammer for the word 'Coffey' had chimed with my strong presentiments, and my heart now pounded my ribs.

'I don't think so. It's Joey, is it not? Joey . . . good night! There'll be much to say in the morning.'

Which left me in a state of mind that was more than agitated, for if anyone reads this who has read the memoirs I penned six months ago in Pentonville, it was my belief that this Patrick Coffey had had his throat cut and then been hanged in a Manchester mill on the day of the Peterloo Massacre.

'No, Joey, you have it all wrong. Did you not look closely at those poor buggers? Believe me, nothing so much alters a man's phiz as having his throat cut and a noose round his neck maybe before he's properly dead. I can't recall I've ever seed a man caught both ways at once, but plenty one way or the other. No. You say the men were Connaughts and they answered to our names, me and Kevin Nolan, but sure they would once they knew money was in it for them. And the night before you saw them only by the lamplight thrown through an open door on to a night-dark street . . .'

'They were singing your song, Patrick. *On Monday I touched her on the ankle* . . .'

'Sure by then every Connaught could sing that ditty. It was just about our regimental march. Easy over, if you don't mind.'

I gave the pan a flip, for it was an hour past sunrise and we were breaking our fast with corn bread and eggs fried in buffalo fat.

'So what happened to you, then? How come you're here?'

'Simple enough. After Toulouse in eighteen fourteen, and that was a fock-up of a battle I can tell you, we was shipped off to Loo-ees-eye-ana. Where we was properly focked by General Jackson, he that's President now, and focking the Injuns as thoroughly as he focked us or so I read in a paper I picked up in Santa Fé. In Spanish, but I still have a good bit of the lingo from the old wars, you know? Good eggs but the Pueblos make better tortillas, pinch o' salt makes all the difference. Anyway, Pakenham screwed up, and got killed for his pains, an' I reckoned that that was it for me, I'd done enough sojering, and after ten battles, and all, bloody lucky to get away with a few scratches and broken bones. So I slung me 'ook as the sailors say, took Welsh leave and scarpered.'

He paused and looked out over the prairie, spread like a threadbare carpet before us, his pale eyes misty, then he pushed the cakey bread round the wooden platter, scooping up the last of the yolk.

'Been wandering ever since. Twenty-five years, is it?'

I thought for a moment.

'Thirty.'

'Bejasus, is that a fact now!'

'How do you live?'

'Dis way an' dat. Mostly on my own, huntin', scrumpin', fishin'. You know, twelve years in the Rangers I was, from drummer boy age twelve. Drillin', marchin', left about, right about, from the front – dress! You know the score. Pre-sent arms! Like part of a machine they have in these new manufactories. Fockin' clockwork. It like went to my head when I got clear of it. Do what I fockin' like when I like.

305

And when the powder and shot get low, or I have a deep desire for a pot of poteen, I trap a beaver or a fox or a marten or two, but mostly beavers, and trade'm, the half on whisky, a quarter on a lady or two, and buy my necessaries, which is little more than black powder and shot, with the change . . . Coupla times I got caught up north and wintered with the Injuns. Crow. Too fuckin' rough for me though their chief was a yellow by name of Jim Beckwourth who started out a trapper. They called him 'Horse'. But mostly I stayed on my own . . .'

'But now?'

'First of all the ladies back home took to millinising in silk not beaver and the price dropped. Then. Well, you know. Gettin' aulder. Mainly it's me fockin' knees, but me hands too . . .' he held them out. Many rings, most silver, a couple gold, fancy designs, but some would never come off now so swollen the joints below them. 'As the man says, I ache in the places where I used to play. And I've a great desire to see my mother once more back in Tralee. She weren't more'n t'irty when I took the king's shillin' so she'll be . . .' his brow furrowed, 'sixty?'

'Seventy, Patrick,' I murmured.

Moisture glistened in his eye.

'So much? When I t'ink of her I see a young woman, lovely as a rose.'

I let a moment or two go by. A mile away or more a huge flock of cranes, maybe five hundred or so, taking a break on their way north, wheeled up into the sky, disturbed by five braves on horseback who thought it a jape to ride amongst them. The mournful cacophony of the birds' hollow bugle call filled the air.

'I'll come with you, Paddy, if you'll have me. I've been planning to head east for a year or more.'

'Who said anything about east?'

'Quickest way home. And last night you came out of the west.'

'I was upwind of you. Old habit. Always arrive on the back of what's blowin'.'

'All right. But east is best.'

'No, Joey. You see, one thing I have to do before I leave is see the Pacific.'

'It's just the sea, Paddy. The ocean. No more than that. Believe me, I've seen it.'

'The Pacific. Caint leave without I see it.'

'Your mother, Patrick. She'll be a year older, at least, if we go that way.'

'Don't call me Patrick. Sounds like a priest. Father Patrick. Paddy'll do fine. Joey . . . The Pacific.'

'Not Joey any more. Eddie.'

'The Pacific, Eddie?'

I stood up, stooped, picked up a flint and threw it into a bush. A mockingbird I already knew was there started up out of it and headed west before settling twenty yards off.

'The Pacific, Paddy.'

35

The pale moon was rising above the green mountain,
The sun was declining beneath the blue sea;
When I strayed with my love to the pure crystal fountain,
That stands in the beautiful Vale of Tralee.

She was lovely and fair as the rose of the summer,
Yet 'twas not her beauty alone that won me;
Oh no, 'twas the truth in her eyes ever dawning,
That made me love Mary, the Rose of Tralee.

On the far fields of Spain, mid war's bloody thunder,
Her voice was a solace and comfort to me,
But the cold hand of death has now torn us asunder
I'm lonely tonight for my Rose of Tralee.

'And were you never back in Ireland, never in Tralee, after you joined the Connaughts?' I asked as the last phrase echoed across the hills we were in. Paddy had a good tenor voice, would have filled a small theatre, though rough now on the high notes. We had begun the climb out of the plain the day before, patches of short-grass prairie and near desert with sagebrush, beginning to look dowdy and ochre with daisy-like sky-blue immortelles peeping through.

'Sure I was in Ireland. But only ever at the depot in Wexford or getting well legless in Dublin's fair city.'

Six weeks we had been walking and riding, and it was about the fifteenth time I had heard 'The Rose of Tralee' and the twentieth time I had asked him why he'd never been back to see his Ma. By now I was riding on a donkey we had found browsing off tumbleweed in a dried-up gulch. A cloud of flies nearby had led us to her owner, a Franciscan friar who had lost the skin off the top of his head. Considering he had probably been tonsured we wondered why his murderer had bothered.

'What did they do that for?' I asked Paddy. 'A friar doesn't carry anything worth a dime save maybe his breviary. Even their crosses are wood.'

He scouted about a bit, read the signs like any Indian tracker, and came back.

'Water, I reckon, Eddie. Injuns never carry any – matter o' pride they'll know where to look. And it's pride says they're wusses if they ride a donkey.'

So I took the moke, which I called Paquita after one I'd had back in Spain when I was a lad, and that one had taken me over the Gredos Mountains safely so I thought maybe this one would do the same for me in the Rockies. But a moment or two later I had my doubts.

We breasted a rise, coming through scattered pine trees growing out of loose shale, and came to a halt with Paddy at Paquita's shoulder . . .

'Oh shit,' I said.

The hillside dropped steeply away down to a valley maybe five miles wide, then blue hills began to climb up the other side but instead of tailing off in the lilac heat haze to a distant but low horizon, they went on climbing. And climbing. Until they were mountains. We were still a good twenty miles off so they weren't that high in the sky, but my goodness you could see they were big, especially one, set just off centre from where we were standing. And all capped with snow, in August; no, not capped . . . cloaked. And they made a chain, a serrated barrier, as far south as we could see and as far north.

'Paddy,' I said. 'Let's go east. It's not too late to change our minds.'

But his bright blue eyes were gleaming through the shrubbery on his face, like he'd seen the promised land. He reached back and put his knobbly, beringed hand over mine where it rested on the saddle pommel.

'I love them mountains, Eddie,' he said, and his voice was hoarse with the emotion of it.

'And the ocean's on the other side of them?'

'That's right.'

'How come you've never seen it, then?'

'Eight hundred miles the other side, Eddie.'

'Oh shit,' I repeated. 'How long will it take us?'

'Three, maybe four months.'

I sighed. I felt sick in my stomach and very, very tired. Thirteen years since I left England. Ten since I got off the Galápagos. And we were still heading the wrong fucking way.

'Look,' he cried and flung an arm out to our right. 'Waggons.'

A long, low line of dust like a pencil mark across the valley bottom was just inching its way into view round a bluff. I'd say it was as much as six miles away and a thousand feet or more below us.

'Coming out of Las Vegas.* They'll reach Santa Fé midday tomorrow. We'll be there ahead of them. By nightfall.'

And so we were. Santa Fé stands in the valley of the headwaters of the Rio Grande, with Mount Truchas, the big one we'd seen from the foothills, less than ten miles away to the north. It was a bustling little town of adobe huts huddled in twisting alleys for the most part, but with one big brick building, the palace of the governors, for this was the capital of New Mexico. New Mexico at that time stretched north right up to San Francisco and beyond and from the Pacific to the Great Divide. On the outskirts there were larger adobe buildings that looked like mission churches but were warehouses. Why? Because ten years earlier or a bit more, an enterprising man called William Becknell established the Santa Fé Trail all the way from St Louis, across prairie, desert and forest, hostile Indian country, and made the fortunes of many. Farming implements from the new iron and steel foundries back east, all manner of European luxuries from pianos and Fabergé eggs to guns came in. Furs, silver and salmon pickled in barrels went out.

Paddy, who was older than me by half a decade if not more, and much worn down by the exhausting life he'd led marching to and fro

* No, not *that* one. J. R.

across Iberia and then the same across America, took himself off to a room at the back of a taverna, where I also stabled Paquita, and left me to enjoy the fleshpots. These were not inconsiderable. Thanks to the Trail it was a boom town. The centre was filled with tavernas, cantinas, gambling dens and what-all. Pressure oil-lamps flared above doorways and over tables, guitars and banjos duelled it out as did fla-mencos and hoedowns, heels clattered and clogs, flounced skirts whirled and ostrich feathers. The smells of decently cooked food, redolent with spices, which I'd been a stranger to for a long time, drifted through low doorways filled with beaded curtains . . . and of course I didn't have two nickels to rub together.

Then, there, leaning against a doorpost, dressed like a Spanish gypsy and smoking a cigarillo, I saw her. Or rather I felt her, felt her gaze on me, for she had recognised me first but when I turned, her eyes fell, fringed by lashes that may not all have been her own, though I remem-bered hers, even at the age of twelve or thirteen, had been luxurious.

Her hair was piled up and held by a silver comb; her filipino shawl was gaudily embroidered exposing brown shoulders; the bodice of her dress plunged so almost one felt one could see her navel between full breasts; her leg was thrust out and ankle-booted to enhance the curve of her calf muscle: in short I would have passed her by as a lady of the night I had not the means to make use of.

Then she looked up again and the twelve-year-old I had forgotten for ten years giggled just as she had then.

'Eduardo. Eddie. ¿Como se llama? I forget. But it is you, is it not?'

I took a deep breath and let it out as a long, four-syllabled sigh.

'Ju-an-ee-tah.'

She took my hand, drew me closer and kissed my forehead, then stood back and ran her fingers across my head.

'You stink,' she said. 'When did you last have a bath?'

'It was a cold one. In the Mississippi. I'm not sure how many years ago.'

'Come on, we'll go to my room. I'll have them send up some hot water.'

'I can't pay.'

She grinned. White teeth.

'I owe you, remember?'

Indeed she did. She and Jorge Quetzalcoatl riding my mule with my gold in their pockets out of the Mexico City market.

'Anyway,' she went on, 'It's my place. I can do what I like.'

So, she was more of a madam than a whore, indeed had three of the latter in her care, together with a cook, a barman who did duty as minder too, and a couple of young girls who were apprenticed to the trade but in the meantime served table and cleaned up. One of them – she looked a lot like Juanita all those years ago – brought in jugs of hot water which she poured over me as I sat with my knees up in the wooden bath, built like a small tarred coracle, in Juanita's room. Hung with red plush, with chairs and a black ottoman inlaid with mother-of-pearl, lit by metal lamps with coloured glass that she said had come from Morocco (Birmingham, England, I reckoned), it was sumptuous. An incense burner with a chip or two of ambergris, the origin of which I resisted revealing to her, perfumed the heavy, warm air. We ate lamb chops, and I mean lamb, with *patatas bravas*, and sherbet made from mountain snow carried down by fleet-footed Apaches, flavoured with lemons picked from a tree that grew in the little courtyard behind her establishment's kitchen. It made a change from the scrawny pigeons or jack rabbits Paddy generally shot or trapped for our suppers. And then she put me to bed on goose-down seconds before I fell asleep anyway, and I slept away the night and a lot of the morning. My only regret is that I have no memory of whether or not she shared it with me.

Over the meal and at breakfast of chocolate and *madalenas* she was brisk.

'I'll pay you back what I borrowed. It served me well; the first capital that kick-started* my whole enterprise. I won't pay you interest because you would not have invested it. But first you must tell me how you got here.'

Where to begin?

'I came on a donkey from the Cherokee settlement in the Indian Territory. With an Irishman I first knew thirty years ago. Patrick Coffey.'

'*El Anciano*. We all know Paddy.'

I told her we were walking to the Pacific, which Paddy wanted to see before returning to Ireland.

'I hope he's waiting for me,' I finished.

---

* 'Kick-started'? Like a motorbike? But you kick a mule into motion as well. Anyway, it is apparently the phrase she used. J. R.

'Well, find him. And when you have the pair of you can do me a favour. I have to meet two men. A business meeting. I want you to be there and witness everything that is said and remember it. In case there is any dispute later for there'll be no signing of documents. They'll be here about midday, coming in with the waggon train. Now, while I get ready, you can go and find Paddy and, when you have, bring him back here.'

I found him right enough, in the *taverna* I had left him in, having a late breakfast which had started with fresh fruit, and had reached a second course of his favourite fried eggs with corn cake soaked in syrup. He had his own jug of coffee which he was somewhat reluctant to share with me.

'The full American breakfast,' he purred. 'Only the holy mother knows when I shall next start a day with a meal like this.' I told him what I had been doing and what I had undertaken to do, how Juanita had found me again after nearly ten years.

'Ah, me boyo, that'll be Doña Juanita Luciente de Aragon y Castilla, the uncrowned queen of Santa Fé. If she's a friend of yours you're a made man. You'll not be wanting to traipse around wi' old Paddy if you're in with her.'

Far from it, I told him, I just wanted to fulfil the favour I had promised and then we would be on our way.

He took his time mopping up the last of his eggs and finishing his fourth mug of coffee, but when he had, we got Paquita out of her stable where she had been munching on real oats, and made our way back to Juanita's. On the way we heard, from out on the edge of the town, a great noise of rumbling wheels and screaming axles, lowing oxen, the whooping of their teamsters and the cracking of rawhide whips. There was a crackle of musketry too as they let their pieces off into the air above them. Paddy did not have to tell me that the waggon train had arrived, but he did anyway.

Juanita had changed from the dishabille of a bedroom robe and undressed hair she had affected earlier and was now unbelievably smart in the latest morning fashions of a high-bodiced black moiré dress with hourglass waist and small bustle with a large bow. Her feathered cap was set on luxurious curls, all of which I supposed were hers though not all now attached to her scalp in the way nature intended. She carried a reticule embroidered with jet beads and a small black parasol.

313

'I am,' she said, 'as my weeds suggest, by way of being a widow. Quetzalcoatl believed that if his heart was removed with an obsidian knife he would be reborn the next day with the rising sun and the nation of Aztecs would rise up and acknowledge him as their lord. He persuaded a follower to perform the operation, the first act of which was a success. Not so the second. What I owe you, Eddie . . .' and she handed me a small but weighty purse that chinked authentically. I was gentleman enough not to check the contents there and then.

We followed her to a cluster of adobe godowns on the outskirts of the town in front of which one of the waggons had been parked, its wheels and running gear painted red, its beds a vivid blue, and its roof white canvas streaked with the ochre dust of deserts. Porters, one might almost say dockers for the waggons were the merchant ships of the continent, were unloading wooden cases and carrying them into the largest of the godowns. A group of ten or so half-naked Indians, tall, lean, tough, with heads shaven apart from tufts and ridges of hair like the crests on ancient helmets, armed with guns as well as bows and arrows and tomahawks, stood aside and let us enter.

This particular warehouse was built like a chapel with a single vault but inside was nothing but a large, empty space lit by high unglazed windows. Two men left the apse, as it were, and walked towards us.

'I believe Mr Coffey is already acquainted with these gentlemen,' la Doña Juanita announced. 'Mr Bozzam, let me introduce you to my business associates, Captain John Fremont of the United States Army Topographical Corps and the noted explorer and guide Mr Christopher Carson.'

'Mostly,' the latter, a thickset man of smallish stature, with a square, severe sort of a face, growled, 'I goes by the name of Kit. Kit Carson. Pleased to meet you, sir. Paddy. Good to see you in such good shape.' And he shook our hands with a grip that could have strangled a rattlesnake. Probably had, in its time, at that.

'Shall we get down to business then?' Juanita made a command of it rather than a question.

'Not until you have told us why these gentlemen are here,' Fremont interjected. He was a saturnine sort of a man, tall, thin and dark with a large but well-kempt moustache and beard and eyes that glowed in the gloom beneath the forward pulled brim of his hat, which, like his suit, was quality and black.

314

'I am,' replied Juanita, 'but a poor, weak woman doing business with two men who have . . . reputations. I fully accept the need which is upon us of putting nothing in writing. Fine. But should we later dispute amongst us who agreed to do what, then I require two witnesses who will—'

'Take your side, madame?'

'Not at all, John. Who will avouch the truth of the matter, is what I was going to say.'

I should have said that between us all communication had been in Spanish. Now, however, she was using English and I swear I have it down as accurately as memory allows. Her accent though was very markedly Spanish and gave a wonderfully seductive inflection to the determination which infused her speech.

Fremont gave us a long look, and then slowly, from an inside pocket, produced a thin, tooled-leather case of cheroots. He lit one, blew smoke into the dusty air.

'Paddy, I know,' he said at last. 'But monkey man . . . ?'

'Really, John. That will not do. Mr Coffey and I have known Mr Bozzam for a long time. You must take our word regarding him. We trust him. You should do so too. He is a man entirely without principle but his heart rules his head. He will not betray his friends.'

Fremont looked at Paddy who hesitated for a moment and then nodded slowly.

'Sure, I'll vouch for him,' he said at last.

I felt honoured. Honoured by thieves as a thief perhaps, but . . . honoured.

'Right. Let's get on with it,' Kit Carson said, and lifted a short crowbar from the top of a stack of crates.

Wood cracked and nails flew. The crate seemed to be filled with wood shavings, but he delved into it and pulled out a handgun, the like of which I had never seen before. It was long-barrelled, and had an elegantly curved but weighty butt, but between the two there was a revolving cylinder with six chambers. Carson lifted it, pulled back the hammer, and as he did so the cylinder turned. He pulled the trigger. Nothing happened.

'Bum,' he said.

'It's not loaded,' said Juanita. 'Open that smaller case over there.'

It was filled with small canvas bags, each big enough to hold, say, a largish cat. She pulled one out, loosened the draw string.

'Here you are,' then, as Carson fumbled, 'here let me. First the cap . . .' a small copper disc, 'then the powder . . .' a cartridge of stiff paper, 'and finally the ball. Tamp them up firm, turn the chamber, and do the same again.'

Carson took it from her after she'd loaded the second chamber, and, more than a touch more awkwardly than she, filled the remaining four. Then he held it out in front of him, supported his wrist with his left hand and fired. The ball smacked into the adobe wall ten yards away and the report stunned our eardrums. He fired the remaining five off, making a circle. Bang-bang-bang-bang-bang. A piece of adobe, the size of my hand, dropped to the floor.

'Shit,' he said. Then, 'That is one hell of a gun.'

'Which takes six times as long to load as a single-shot pistol,' Fremont remarked, with his dandyish sneer – an officer if not quite a gentleman. 'I've seen them back east. A Texas Ranger with twenty men armed with them took out a hundred Comanche, back in '34. Walker his name was.'

Carson turned the gun over in his hand.

'Colt, it says. Samuel Colt. Tell you what, though. I'll carry two of them, and when I've fired off one then Federico can be loading it while I fire off the other.' And he grinned down the nave (as it were) and a young lad, very pretty with a mop of black hair, a shirt, cut-down twill trousers and bare feet, whom I had taken to be one of the teamsters, grinned back at him.

'You know,' I said, 'it shouldn't be too difficult to make a cartridge which held all three components in one case. That would make reloading much quicker.'

But the others, either deafened still by the reports, or just not giving much attention to 'monkey man' ignored me.*

'How many do we have?' Fremont asked.

'I have two hundred in this shipment,' Juanita replied. 'I can get you four hundred more. And fifty thousand ball, cap and cartridges. Early in the spring. And it'll cost me twelve thousand five hundred dollars. Which you have not got.'

'Not yet.'

'But this is what I'll take for them. The franchise, a full monopoly

---

* Oddly enough, it took fifteen years, until 1860, before the manufacturers got round to doing just this. J. R.

on every whorehouse in California for fifty years. I'll take ten per cent of the gross and make sure they're decently run.'

She looked at Paddy and me.

'Got that, fellers? Engraved in your heads like the ten commandments Moses brought down from the mountain top?'

We nodded. My head felt as heavy as if the tablets were inside it. But we nodded.

'Cannon?' asked Fremont. 'Artillery?'

'Not possible.' Again Juanita was brisk. 'Too big to be done clandestinely. You can't box up cannon.'

Fremont turned to Carson.

'We need cannon. Castro has artillery at Monterey. There's an arsenal at San Diego.'

'Well, I guess that means Hans Sutter, then. He's got a battery of Muskovite guns.'

'I suppose it does.' Fremont sighed. 'Fucking Swiss cheese.' He turned back to Juanita. 'O-K. You have a deal.' Back to Carson. 'We ought to winter up reasonably close to Sutter, say on the San Joaquín. Can we get there before the snow cuts in?'

'If we get a move on. Take us three months to get over the mountains. Ten weeks if we get a move on.'

Paddy stirred himself, coughed and spat.

'We'll come with you.'

Yes, I thought. To see the Pacific. And then we'll entirely retrace our steps. I had it in mind to suggest I stay in Santa Fé and he could pick me up on his way back through, but by now they were acting busy and carrying on as if that was all decided, so I kept mum.

As we walked back down the nave, I noticed empty niches in the walls.

'This place is mighty like a church,' I remarked.

'It was,' Juanita replied, her face darkening. 'Seven years back, just after I got here, we had a go at what these . . . *burros* are trying now. Set up our own republic, Hispanics and English-speaking together. Cut off the governor's head, which was a mistake, but he was a brute. The army came up from El Paso and Chihuahua. No contest. The US weren't interested because we'd declared for our own country and constitution. The Mexicans locked the ringleaders and their families up in here with fifty Navajo, each of whom had a grudge and a tomahawk. Twelve months later we built ourselves a new church nearer

317

the plaza. That's it. But it explains why we're all being a bit careful right now. So, Eddie, don't go blabbing about what you've seen and heard today. All right?'

By now we were at the big double door, sunlight falling in like a spilled sack of golden grain. I looked back into the gloom and shuddered. The Alamo, San Jacinto, alligators on the river and black men in chains, the Cherokee trail of tears. What a country. What a fucking country. And the *Town-Ho* harvesting shit from the gentle giants of the deep. The sooner I got out the better. But no! First, the ocean.

On our way out the Indians fell in behind us. Turned out they were Delawares, Fremont's personal bodyguard.

36

Because they wanted to meet up with the Swiss Sutter we had to head north and, anyway, Fremont had arranged to rejoin his party at Bent's Fort.

If you look at a map you'd say the obvious route was to head towards Los Angeles, go round the southern end of the Sierra Nevada and head up the big valley to San Joaquín. Well, half the expedition did that, but Paddy reckoned we should stay with Fremont and Carson, 'like keep an eye on them for Juanita' he reckoned, and anyway they'd be quicker, even though they aimed to go through the highest part of the Sierra Nevada, passing the lake the two of them had discovered the previous winter, which they called Lake Tahoe. Well, at least, I thought, they knew the way. They reckoned it was about fourteen hundred miles and at twenty miles a day would take seventy days, say, for good measure eighty, we'll be there by All Saints'. So, we headed north out of Santa Fé, not west at all but north of east up the last bit of the Santa Fé trail, and got to Bent's Fort in ten days or so where the rest of Fremont's party had arrived, he having gone on ahead to meet Carson. We were over a hundred strong now, well-armed, lots of dogs, twenty mules carrying food, pots and pans, various instruments such as a barometer which could be used to tell us how high we were in ways I don't pretend to understand, guns including Colt six-shooters. And a whole load of other stuff I won't bore you with listing. Except there were a lot of what I took to be a clumsy sort of tennis racket. When I asked what they were for, they told me they were snowshoes. Which left me feeling a touch uneasy. As did the thirty or so horses beyond our immediate requirements – food on the hoof if we got snowed in, spares if the ones we were riding went lame or got the glanders, or so one of the mountain men told us.

All the men were civilians, but many had been troopers or rangers, some bandits, jailbirds on the run, whatever. A dozen or so opted out at Bent's Fort and headed back down the Santa Fé Trail: on the way from St Louis they'd found the discipline too tough. Looking over them all on the day we left Bent's Fort, middle of August, you had to wonder: who was going to believe a gang, a squad, a band like this were the necessary accompaniment of a topographical expedition commissioned to map the Great Basin of Nevada?

'Sure, nobody doubts what they're for,' said Paddy when I put this to him. 'We're off to liberate California from the Mexicans. Question is – do we keep it for ourselves or give it to Uncle Sam?'

'And what's the answer?'

'No one knows, Eddie. I suspicion they'll play it by ear. But I guess that deal with Doña Juanita means they hope to keep it for themselves.'

At which moment Fremont, up the front, loosed a round off out of his Colt and we all swung into motion with as little ceremony as that.

Almost immediately we split into two parties. A Lieutenant Abert, the only other military man amongst us, led thirty or so south down the Arkansas, aiming to get round the south end of the Sierra, east of Los Angeles, before heading north, the route I favoured. Fremont and Carson led the rest of us, including the Delawares, up the Arkansas and west. After a couple of days we stopped near a village of Pueblo Indians we didn't mix with since they all seemed to be dying of the scarlet fever.

The skies were wonderfully clear at night; there was a good moon which set early leaving the heavens filled with stars and other celestial bodies. These were an important component in Fremont's tool bag. By focusing the optical instruments he had, which could measure angles, on fixed stars like Polaris, and tracking those that were not, by recording the culminations of the moon and so forth, he was able to determine the longitude and latitude of where we were. He then consulted the two pocket chronometers he had with him and was thus apparently all set to plot the position of each dominant feature we passed, especially mountain peaks. Barometers were used to measure their height, but of course had to be carried to the top; as also did a pan and means for making a fire, for the other way of measuring altitude was to take the temperature at which water boils, that is at two hundred and twelve degrees* at sea level and proportionally less the higher you get.

All of which no doubt had its uses and maybe is of interest to the more 'scientifick' of your readers, Mr Murray, but at the time served only to slow our progress west and give credence to the fiction that we were merely a map-making expedition.

Paddy much preferred to walk than ride on a horse, and on account of the fact that to fall from the back of a small donkey rarely causes injury whereas falling from a horse almost invariably does, I stayed with Paquita. This meant by the end of a day we were often as much as an hour or so behind the main party, but we were rarely any more than that since they stopped quite often for Fremont to set up what he called his 'portable transit instrument', or to reshoe a horse, or to wait while the Delawares, having seen signs of an Indian presence, scouted ahead to ascertain to what extent they were hostile.

We'd followed the Arkansas through the Sangre de Cristo mountains, right to its headwaters in a giant cirque overlooked by four massive peaks, all some fourteen thousand feet high. Two small tarns, five miles apart, black with the depth of their waters, marked the source of the Arkansas to the south and one of the last tributaries of the Colorado to the north. Between the two then, we stood on the Great Divide – from one side all rivers ran south to the Gulf of Mexico or east to the Mississippi, on the other they ran south to the Gulf of California or into the desert where they dried up. Moreover, at this point we had left the United States and were once again under the flag of Mexico.

For a day or two we followed a river which, emerging from its gorge, continued to drop steeply until we came into a vast meadow where it joined the Colorado River. We followed the often precipitous descent of this great river into the second week of September. The meadows broadened and became plains and above a confluence

* Fahrenheit. J. R.

321

with yet another tributary we made use of a wide and shallow passage, passable at that time of year, before what rains fell in that place descended. We now headed north by north-west, crossed a lower range of mountains and, at the very beginning of October, came upon a vast desert area in which two lakes, between which we passed, featured in a strange, flat landscape whose surface was crusted with salt, which was also a feature of the brackish water of the lakes. What river beds there were were now dried and Fremont commanded us to use the water we had with the greatest care. The only vegetation seemed to be sagebrush and tangleweed and for much of the space there was little enough of that. It got worse. We set out across a hundred miles of lunar desolation, frazzlingly hot at midday and freezing at night, with glimmering saltpans and no water at all.

At the worst stage, six of the spare horses were killed and we were invited to drink their blood. One mouthful was enough to make me retch up the meagre, bily contents of an empty stomach. We had water, barrels of it, in a couple of covered wagons, which Fremont set his Delawares to guard. Two rough characters from Pittsburg, who had been nothing but trouble, tried to get past them. Their scalps were nailed to the tailboards of the waggons as a warning to the rest of us. And all this, I constantly reminded Paddy, because of his irrational desire to see the Pacific.

Eventually a range of mountains, hitherto veiled in haze, appeared to rise at dawn, dominated by one snow-clad peak above the rest, and Fremont allowed us to broach four of the barrels. We plodded on all through the day across land as flat as a table, featureless, the only vegetation a low, coarse, soured grass that the animals would not touch, and those mountains, with the one twin-peaked, snow-capped massif in the middle, seemed almost to recede in the shimmering heat haze.

'Well,' I remarked to Paddy, 'with that and nothing else in front of us, at least we can't get lost.'

'Which is why it's called Pilot Peak.'

As the evening cooled and the sun settled behind it, it suddenly stood out clear, bold and solid, and, just as if we were mariners at sea, a low flight of a small flock of birds slipped along on pointed wings above the grass, almost like sheerwaters they were, maybe a variety of quail, heralding the possibility at last of vegetation, vertebrates other than snakes or lizards, and . . . water. The sun blazed from behind the Pilot, and glowed along a low, thin bank of cloud above it, and then its light went out, and darkness closed swiftly over us like a drawn blind.

All through the night the animals were restless, so much so that I thought we were attacked by Indians attempting to steal them, but in fact it appeared they could smell water and fresh vegetation coming off the mountain which was still ten miles away. In the morning when we set about forming up after the usual milkless coffee and grits, a dozen or so did break free and went galloping off over the last of the salt flats. No problem, though; they were waiting for us, cropping the shrubs and the sweeter grass in the first rises of the mountain.

There now lay ahead of us close on four hundred miles across the Great Basin. For three weeks ranges of mountains, running more or less north to south like ribs, interrupted vast plains which for the most part were sagebrush and bunch grass though with patches of semidesert. And full desert, though most of that lay south of our route which for a lot of the way followed the Marias River, now known as the Humboldt. The watercourses, trapped between the Sierra Nevada and the Rockies and running out of both, were at their driest but frequently spread into shallow lakes and marshes in what declivities and basins there were within the Basin.

One respite from this sameness came when we first set eyes on the Washoe Indians, truly Noble Savages who moved about their small settlements of dome-shaped brush huts in an almost natural state, even in late autumn wearing no more than a necklace, a hat, and in the men's case a minimal thong and in the women's very brief skirts of woven grasses. Often they didn't bother with either. They were tall, with bright eyes, easy movements, an aquiline cast to their features, lean, well but not obviously muscled. They viewed us with detachment rather than suspicion, as passing phenomena of little importance to their lives which were spent in hunting antelope, the copious rabbits and waterfowl, to catch the last of which they used cunningly made decoys. The women also gathered berries and on the mountain slopes pine kernels. All of these they dried and stored, the meat as well, to keep them through the winter which was already showing itself with occasional flurries of sleet, and frost at night.

Then at last the day came, in the first week of November I should guess, when we realised the mountains we were scaling, whose peaks rose out of pale shale loosely clad in pine on the east-facing slopes, were higher and deeper than any we had encountered since the Great Divide. Moreover, it began to snow in earnest, great heavy flakes drifting out of an unblemished grey sky.

We crossed a col and still the mountains and snow filled the air and the Great Basin was at last hidden from us. We were in the Sierra Nevada.

37

Four months later, on a clear, bright Californian morning in early spring, before the high fog set in, Fremont announced that we were on the move again. The rains were over, the hills were green, but beyond the hills you could still see snow on the high mountains. We were in the San Joaquín Valley, maybe sixty miles south of Hans/John Sutter's Fort and about the same east of San Francisco, in the heart of that long, wide, fertile strip that runs from way north of Sutter's Fort and the Sacramento River, right down to Los Angeles. And, apart from the rain and the fogs and mists, it was as good a place outside a decent-sized city in which to spend winter as you could want. Indeed, even in winter it was a sort of paradise, the climate almost always temperate, the valleys verdant and rich with edible food and small game, and, where the few settlers had cleared the land, plots filled with salads and beans of all sorts. Most lovely of all were the oranges and lemons just at that time of year coming to ripeness. One wag told us that in California it never rains water, only orange juice.

Fremont and Carson had done the route through the mountains before, so they had known the way – past Lake Tahoe, through the Truckee Pass, and we made it to Sutter's Fort by the second of December. Now at this point Patrick Coffey and I should have left them and headed down to the 'Frisco Bay and the Golden Gate so my mad Irish friend could see the Pacific and leave us free either to take a ship round the Horn or, when the snows went, go back the way we had come.

But no. He hadn't walked unaided since, when coming through the mountains, still on the eastern side, he'd lost a foot. He'd taken a fancy to sliding some of the way on a bit of an old door we'd found in an abandoned hut. A 'toboggan' a couple of mountain men who were with us called it, using the Indian word they'd picked up, but I'd call it a sledge. Even though it didn't have runners. Anyway, it careered off the path we were on, which those up front were making for us through the snow, and pitched him against a rock with enough force to break his leg just above his ankle.

The sledge now became a hurdle to drag him on, with Paquita pulling when we hit a bit of an uphill slope. A Scottish arsehole who said he'd studied medical matters at Edinborough fixed it with splints and such like, but when we got into deep snow Paddy began to howl with the pain of it.

Carson came by just as we were getting set to do the business, looked down at us from his horse.

'Stay your hand, master barber,' he barked, then turned to Federico, his Mexican bummer boy who always rode pillion behind him, and told him to go back to the waggons and fetch a bottle of whisky. This cheered Paddy up no end, and after a half-pint had been poured into him he was ready for anything, even me with a knife and saw I'd borrowed. Needless to say he had a song for it too.

> And it's no, nay, never, no, never, no more
> Will I play the wild rover, no, never, no more.
>
> I'll go home to my Mammy, confess what I done
> And I'll ask her to pardon her prodigal son
> And if she caress me as oft times before
> Then I swear I will play the wild rover no more . . .
>
> And it's no, nay, never, no nay never no more
> Will I play the wild rover, no, never no more . . . Ouch!!!

Well, I took his foot off, smacked hot tar we'd got ready on the stump, and he hardly flinched through his drunken stupor. We set off up the mountain, after the others, still dragging him on his sledge, and when he came round it was a case of 'Where's my fuckin' foot, Eddie?'

'Paddy, it's two miles back where we left it.'

'You'd no right to leave it, sure you did not. Now by Holy Mary, blessed Joseph and all the saints if you won't go back for it, I will.'

So, we unhitched him from Paquita and back I went on her, arriving just in time to see a fox having a chaw on the damn thing, but she left it after I'd thrown some stones at her. I wrapped it up in my scarf and took it back.

Paddy bought another whole bottle of whisky off Carson, with a piece of the money Juanita had given me, and tried to pickle the foot, by washing it in liquor and then wrapping it, still in my scarf, also soaked with whisky. Then he changed his mind about keeping it and asked me to give it a decent Christian burial. Which I duly did, clearing a drift of snow beneath a redwood, piling rocks and grit on it and then the snow again.

It took him a long time to learn to walk properly, dot-and-carry-one, so, as I said, Fremont had us on the move again before we got to the ocean.

Leaving the little palisaded fort we'd made for the winter in an orange grove whose fruits had ripened all through the mild winter months, golden lamps in a green night as the poet has it,* and plenty of other fruits, pulses and salads, we set off in a south-westerly direction towards Santa Clara, Salinas and Monterey. Coming through the Devil Mountains I reckoned we could see a sea mist over the ocean, but Paddy insisted this was not enough; he wanted to be on the beach itself.

That day a troop or more of Mexican cavalry, with a six-pounder gun, began to track us in a less than friendly manner, and when we were halfway down the Salinas Valley an officer with a larger detachment and another cannon appeared across our path which was winding through a grove of oak. He came forward with a flag and a bugler and made his pitch.

'By order of the Commandante General Don José Castro I am ordered to inform you that by trespassing in these valleys and directing your steps towards the coast you have breached the permission granted to you to explore and map to the south-east including the

---

* *Bermudas* by Andrew Marvell. J. R.

Mojave Desert. I am hereby empowered to rescind the aforesaid licences and require you to withdraw from Mexico immediately.'

Although their numbers were not greatly in excess of ours, they were better equipped and mounted, and those cannon were a real consideration. With a face suffused with black anger, Fremont raised his right arm and with a gesture that combined disdain with impatience wheeled us all round and set us back the way we had come. This put Paddy, Paquita and me directly in front of the muzzles of those gleaming brass guns and for once we did our best to keep up with the rest as we climbed back into the mountains. Fremont stopped for a couple of days in a fortified position in the Gavilan hills, but seeing the Mexicans meant business pushed on north.

Short of walking all the way back to the Great Divide, the quickest way off Mexican territory was to head north for the border with Oregon, at that time under Hudson Bay Company laws and disputed between Britain and America – but definitely not Mexican.

On our way we passed through Sutter's Fort again, this being about the third week of March, 1846. However, Fremont and Carson, though clearly in cahoots with Sutter, did not linger, for John Sutter, although a Swiss by birth, a Californian by choice and an American if he had to be, was in fact an accredited official of the Mexican Government which had given him a huge grant of excellent land on the Sacramento River. Consequently he was not yet ready to enter into overt alliance with Fremont in the presence of Mexican troops, even though he had his own battery of cannon, bought from Russians, a large and well-fortified fort and a body of labourers, mostly Negro and Indian.

Sutter was a big man with huge moustaches, a high forehead, deep eyes though somewhat baggy underneath. He was of a melancholy disposition, or at any rate prone to introspection, had a thick Swiss accent and an imperfect command of English which led men of action like Fremont and Carson to take him for a fool even though he had amassed a thousand and more head of cattle, sheep, pigs and fields of corn and groves of citrus, all farmed according to the best Swiss principles of organisation, neatness and order. Manufactories for cooperage, gunsmithing, blacksmithing, carpentry, a distillery, added to his wealth together with four thousand sheep, looms to weave their wool, twelve thousand acres of wheat and eighteen ploughs and he sold barrels of pickled salmon for twenty dollars each.

While Fremont and Carson with their small army headed north, Paddy being once again quite grievously knocked up, we, Paddy, Paquita and I, elected to remain at Sutter's Fort where Paddy was well looked after though I was required to help in the kitchen and occasionally wait at table. Over this I remonstrated with Sutter's major-domo, a Negro, pleading that I was the scion of a noble race and should sit with our host and his family, who had only recently joined him from Switzerland after an eighteen-year separation. To no avail.

A week after Fremont's departure we had a most significant visitor. He arrived towards evening with a train of three mules and three Mexican *indiano* servants. He introduced himself as Archibald Gillespie, American citizen, travelling in Van Winkel Kentucky bourbon whiskey, but as soon as I had shown him into Sutter's reception room he unbuttoned his coat and revealed the buttons and badges of a United States Lieutenant of Marines.

'Although I appear to be a regular officer,' he began, in a suitably conspiratorial tone of voice, with frequent glances at the door and windows as if seeking out eavesdroppers, 'I belong to a small secret agency, attached to the Secretary of State's Department, whose function is to forward the interests of the United States abroad in situations where secret operations are required.'

'Spies and espionage,' Sutter remarked, setting a lucifer to his meerschaum pipe. 'Assassinations?'

'Indeed not!' Gillespie was shocked. 'Clandestine Intervention Abroad is the limit of our brief.' He went on: 'Now, I have important despatches or rather messages for Captain Fremont, and I should be grateful if you could tell me where I might find him.'

'For vy should I this be telling you? That I am an officer of the Government of Mexico you are knowing, I tink.'

At this Gillespie fixed his eyes on me, pursed his lips and gave his head a slow sort of a shake.

'Eddie,' Sutter, having given the matter a moment's thought, also turned to me. 'Please to be leaving us.'

So, I buggered off, but I already knew my way round some of the fort's little secrets, and got myself into a sort of wine closet off the dining room next door where an inadequately plastered chink in the adobe allowed me to catch most of what was said. The gist was plain. War between Mexico and the States was about to break out on the Texian border to settle a dispute over the Rio Grande frontier, but this was merely a pretext.* President Polk, who had replaced Jackson but believed even more ardently in Manifest Destiny, was prepared to send an army as far as Mexico City itself to persuade the Mexicans to give up not just California, but Arizona, New Mexico, Nevada and Utah as well. The letters to Fremont instructed him to carry out that summer what had been planned all along – that is to raise the Stars and Stripes and rally support from the immigrants. It was expected that most of the Hispanic settlers would join him too – they got little from the Centralistas in Mexico City apart from tax bills and had no say in the administration of what they thought of as their country.

Sutter hummed and buzzed, coughed and made kissing noises with his lips through all this and only half jocularly threatened Gillespie with arrest, summary trial and execution for inviting him to act in a treasonable way. Gillespie took this seriously and replied that one day, if not that year, California would become part of the States anyway and when it did Sutter needn't expect to have his deeds to thousands of acres of prime agricultural land† recognised by the new legislature. Finally, Sutter bellowed for me and I returned to the reception room. Which, I have to say, was quite a grand room nicely tricked out with red plush drapes, gilt-framed portraits, good solid furniture and a silver flower bowl in the middle of the rose-wood table. Granted it all had a Spanish feel to it, but none the worse for that.

'Eddie,' he barked, 'where is Captain Fremont being?'

'Up the Sacramento into Oregon,' I replied.

'Tomorrow this gentleman to him you will be taking. You may go. Thank you.'

---

* Maybe the first but certainly not the last time the US has used a pretext to start a colonial war. J. R.

† Sutter lost all to squatters during the '49 Gold Rush, and after years of litigation got none of it back – the US courts refused his claim ostensibly because some Mexican bureaucrat had omitted to countersign some of the deeds, but probably because he had not been sufficiently ardent for California to join the Union rather than become an independent state. J. R.

Oh shit, I thought, and went and told Paddy everything I had heard.

'Bogger that,' he cried, coming out of his sleep, 'I'm staying here. I'm through with traipsing about mountains leastways till my leg's better. Tell me, Eddie, whoi did you have to make such a butcher's mess of it,' he added, for maybe the fiftieth time.

38

It was on, I think, the fourth day or so out from Sutter's Fort that we became aware of the Modocs. A bluff overhanging the river had forced the trail and us upwards and we could see down the way we had come into a wild meadow maybe half a mile away, still green and lush and enamelled with the flowers of early summer, but scarred where the five of us had beaten our way through the tall blue grass. The Indians were following where we had gone before. We had seen them scouting along the riverbank the day before and taken them for a hunting party, but now, because they were so clearly and literally on our track, their purpose seemed more sinister. Moreover, scanning them through Gillespie's binocles,* I was able to assert that they were a war party.

'Those stripes painted on their faces,' I almost whispered, 'their bows and arrows, their tomahawks, I know the tribe. They are reputed cannibals . . .'

'What can we do then?' cried Gillespie.

'One of us must go ahead as speedily as possible, alert Fremont and bring him back to join the rest of us.'

For a moment I thought I should have to prompt him, but at last he sighed and announced the obvious.

'Eddie, I suppose it has to be you.'

* Sic. J. R.

Fremont had announced that he was going no further into Oregon than the foot of the Klamath Falls, which I reckoned could not be more than ten miles further upriver. In this I was mistaken; it was more like twenty and I didn't spot the smoke of his campfires until about midday the next day. Returning with him, we found Gillespie, four days after I had left him, a half-hour before nightfall, in a circle of rounded rocks the gaps between which he and his three men had filled with branches and brush. There was no sign of the Modocs. Fremont demanded to see the despatches but Gillespie had destroyed all the official ones before going into lower Mexico for fear he would be searched and their treasonable nature revealed. However, he had learned their content first which he now imparted to Fremont. There were, though, actual letters from Fremont's father-in-law, Senator Benton. As you will know by now I have over the years developed my own clandestine skills and I managed to have a read of them before we got back to the fort.

Their content was plain. The despatches Gillespie communicated orally informed Fremont that war would break out between the States and Mexico in June of 1846. Captain Fremont was requested to proceed to Monterey with his men and there establish a bridge-head so US Marines could disembark unchallenged from a US navy frigate, hoist the Stars and Stripes and claim California. This was a matter of great importance since it was expected that, once hostilities were under way in the east, the British might try to take advantage of the situation and themselves claim California on the grounds that it was first discovered, and claimed under the name New Albion, by Sir Francis Drake, before the Spaniards had reached this far up the coast.

Benton's letters, however, were a different matter. They urged Fremont to go ahead with what had already been proposed between them and set up an independent republic which it was intended would become the family's fiefdom. Benton promised that enough politicians could be bought in Washington to make recognition of the new state possible. But a second letter was less sanguine and warned Fremont to side with the States if American intervention looked to be too strong.

All this was in the first week of May so there was not much time left for him to make his dispositions. Nevertheless, that night brought a diversion upon us. We were attacked! The first any of us knew of it was that Kit Carson was woken by a thud beside him as he slept – he woke to find his neighbour within the circle of rocks had a tomahawk buried in his head. The attackers were driven off but not before they had filled the body of one of the Delawares with arrows, leaving him mortally wounded.

Daybreak came and with it a dispute. Carson and Fremont believed the attackers were the Modocs, but the Delawares claimed they were Klamaths from the lakeside above the falls; they insisted on avenging their dead comrade and nothing Fremont could do would dissuade them. The consequence was that we had to make our way to the lakeside and there slaughter and burn the residents of a small village, men, women and children, an event that sickened me on account of the contingencies that surround rape, the slaughter of babies and the collection of scalps.

And above all this and beyond it, the sunlight painted ephemeral diamonds on the surface of the lake, the peaks, still snow-capped, floated against a virgin-blue sky. Do not suppose that this was a matter of one band of savages against another, the Klamaths against the Delawares. Fremont's men were as wild with lust and killing as any Redskin and the hunt quickly became a fatal game of hide and seek, though still spiced with danger: Carson would have been taken with an arrow had not Fremont, on the back of Sacramento, the big black charger Sutter had lent him, ridden down the Klamath warrior who had drawn his bow at the mountain man.

Once all the Klamaths had melted away and the Delawares were satisfied with their haul of scalps, we set off back down the river towards Sutter's which we reached in the middle of the third week in May. There I found that Paddy had gone – no one was too sure where. Some said Yerba Buena, which was the more commonly used name for San Francisco, others said Monterey. Of course, it could be either or both – what he wanted was to stand on the very shore of the Pacific: once he had done that he would turn back east heading for Ireland and Tralee. What should I do? Look for him? Head back east without him? And then too there was Juanita's commission to us to consider, to keep an eye on Fremont and Carson and make sure they were doing what they could to fulfil their part of their bargain.

Certainly they had already got full value out of the six-shooters, though Carson had nearly lost a hand with one of them. The thing of it was no one had told him that the combination balls and cartridges ought to be greased. Without this precaution it was possible for sparks to fly out between the cylinder and the barrel and set all six rounds off at once. This duly happened to him and he had to fling the pistol from him to the ground where it hopped and banged like a jumping jack though spewing out bullets as it did so.

As usual, my mind was made up for me for Fremont chose to use me as a messenger boy and, well, not to put too fine a point on it, spy, for the whole country was in turmoil with no one knowing too well what was happening. When I say in turmoil, that's an exaggerated way of putting it. Apart from Indians, north California was a wilderness in those days, almost uninhabited, with not more than seven hundred or so Anglo settlers and not that many more Californios outside the very small towns like 'Frisco and Monterey. I understand that since the gold was found, of which more anon, the population has increased a thousandfold. Anyway, no one knew whether or not the Mexicans could bring a real army up from the south to crush any revolt and whether or not the United States would make a resolute intervention. And everybody was doing their best to back both horses at once so you never knew whose side you were on or who were your allies.

What did Fremont do? He decided to test the water. He knew there was a party of some twenty newly arrived immigrants in a village called Sonoma some sixty miles west of Sutter's Fort, that they had no means to support themselves and after a hard winter were desperate and he sent me to talk to whomever I judged to be their leader. I was also to talk to the Mexican authority in that area, a Don Mariano Vallejo, a general, but like most Mexican generals, a general without an army. I arrived on the thirteenth of June, still transported on Paquita's back, and soon picked out a William Ide and a William Todd as leaders of the pack; I then managed a brief parley with General Vallejo in the adobe hut, the largest on the tiny plaza, which served as his residence and also as a small arsenal. We drank three bottles of sour white wine he'd made himself the previous autumn from some local wild grapes and I listened to how he wanted nothing more than to set himself up in viniculture on land he could be sure he would be allowed to keep. His ancestors, farmers back in Extremadura, had been famous for their wine, he assured me.

I returned to Ide and Todd, and on my instructions Todd set about making a flag which incorporated a bear which looked like a pig, a single star and the words 'Republic of California'.* Shortly after dawn some of the men cut down and trimmed a fir tree, planted it in the plaza and then ran up the flag. Ide appeared, and with a flourish of his hat declared himself President of California, and on my prompting they all gave a good three by three cheer. Then they called on Vallejo, expecting him to offer resistance, but no, he came to his front door and told them he was on their side. Some of the men wanted to loot the Presidential Palace, hoping to find arms, but Ide grandiloquently declaimed: 'Choose ye this day what you will be! Are we robbers or conquerors?'

I returned then to Sutter's Fort; Vallejo came with me and reported what had happened to Fremont, Sutter and Carson, who now had every appearance of being a cabal or junta leading the new state. But they remained cautious. Fremont rode over to Sonoma and was perhaps not too impressed by what he saw; however, reports continued to come in of a steady gathering in villages of both Californios and immigrants, declaring a wish to be rid of Mexico, but avoiding the main question – independence or eventual statehood in the United States? And the most divided were the triumvirate itself, leaning first one way and then the other but never all three the same way at once. Clearly an independent republic with them at the head would make them unbelievably wealthy and even powerful: the alternative, though, would confer a sort of legitimacy on the new state, and security from reconquest by Mexico or being taken over by the British.

It was, in fact, a close-run thing. Fremont sent me to Monterey, then the most important port in California and a naval station too, to find out for him how the land lay. He followed more circumspectly on his big black horse with over two hundred men now, most properly armed and showing some signs of being a disciplined fighting force. The first thing I realised as I entered the adobe walls on July the sixth was that the place appeared near enough deserted – there were no Mexican soldiers in the fort and the people were hiding in their houses. And no Mexican warship at anchor off the

* Todd's aunt, Mary Todd, was, or later became, Abraham Lincoln's wife. Lincoln and Darwin were born on the same day – 12 February 1809. Small world . . . real life has as many coincidences as Eddie's narrative. J. R.

quay either. I took a room in a taverna, which was also a brothel, overlooking the harbour but did not avail myself of the wares, being somewhat out of sorts with all the travelling I had done and a meal of not quite fresh sardines. I had a disturbed night filling the jericho with a nasty, fishy effluent and was woken at dawn from the heavy sleep that comes just before daybreak to those who are poorly, by the sound of a single cannon shot. Peering through my dormer window I saw the arrival of a frigate under full sail, gliding out of the swell and into the glassy water that is sheltered by the peninsula with its groves of turkey oak and, higher up, huckleberry bushes. The flag on her stern peak was the Stars and Stripes. I dressed as quickly as maybe and was down on the quay in time to present myself as Captain Fremont's representative to Commodore John D. Sloat of the US Navy's Pacific Squadron just as soon as he was put ashore with a platoon of Marines and under the guns of his ship. All doubts were thus resolved and any inclination to form an independent republic vanished like the thin early morning mist which had conferred on the frigate a sort of magical, mysterious glamour.

There was a glamour, too, about the ceremony held at midday on the battlement of the small fort that overlooked the town, for it was there, in front of a double rank of Marines, with a twenty-gun salute fired from the ship below, with Commodore Sloat in a plumed fore and aft hat and a silvery sabre held upwards in salute, that the Stars and Stripes was hauled up the flagpole.

> Oh, say can you see, by the dawn's early light,
> What so proudly we hailed at the twilight's last gleaming?
> Whose broad stripes and bright stars, through the perilous fight,
> O'er the ramparts we watched, were so gallantly streaming?
> And the rockets' red glare, the bombs bursting in air,
> Gave proof through the night that our flag was still there.
> O say, does that star-spangled banner yet wave
> O'er the land of the free and the home of the brave?

A big moment perhaps. Even though a midshipman's round, peaked hat blew off and went bowling down the quay and over the sun-spangled water. From ocean to ocean, from shore to shore. Manifest Destiny achieved. No need to go further, we're there. North, south, east or west, home is best! Know what I mean? *Birth of a nation?*

39

'Near run thing'? A British frigate, the *Collingwood*, arrived later that afternoon. Had it been there twenty-four hours earlier history might have been very different with Canada extended down the coast from Oregon to San Diego.

A couple of days later I stood on the quay with a British officer, one Fred Walpole, and we watched Fremont ride in at the head of his little army. It was the last time I saw him, this spare, dark, active-looking man dressed in a blouse and leggings and a felt hat. His Delaware Indians were right behind him as usual and the rest, many of them Negroes and others as sunburnt as the Indians, made a show of trying to march behind them. Kit Carson was there. I told Walpole that Carson was as well known in the prairies as the Duke is in Europe. Most wore fringed deerskins, and they had a small brass cannon they'd picked up somewhere, probably from Sutter. I slipped away. I thought of bumming a lift on the *Collingwood*, which, one way or the other, I assumed would eventually return to England, but Paddy was still on my mind. Out of friendship I felt the least I could do was make an effort to find him first.

It took a bit of time. I met people who'd seen him. After all, as I mentioned some way back, there were no more than seven hundred immigrants in the whole area, not counting the Californios, so a tall, well-set-up old man with a once gingery beard and only one foot stood out and remained in the memory. He'd been seen in Monterey.

But a German called Steinbrook or some such name who ran the tavern on the quay told me that Paddy in his cups had expressed a desire to go down the coast a short way to a forested headland called Big Sur, where the surf was reputed very strong and he had a fancy to see if it matched the rollers that came in off the Atlantic and on to the sands of Galway Bay. So I went down there and did indeed find surf such as I had never seen before, not even on the Galápagos, roaring in twenty feet high and more, exploding on the headlands in great spouts of foam, rushing into the coves like the Scots Greys at Waterloo.

I also stumbled on a weird group of about seven or eight English and French men with five women one would have called 'bluestockings' save they were all starkly naked. They claimed they were living as Nature intended according to principles laid down by the philosopher Jean-Jacques Rousseau and equally mad 'thinkers' who followed him. They lived in shacks made out of fir branches and survived on clams, mussels and the eggs of sea birds. They wore no clothes, copulated freely and in full view and in positions I had not thought to encounter outside a whorehouse. Only their use of our mother tongue and some French distinguished them from the naked Tierra del Fuegians I had met ten years earlier when the *Beagle* visited Ponsonby Sound.

'Are you happy?' I asked one whose name was Henry.

'Of course we are,' he replied, while the wind blew through his matted hair, brought up gooseflesh on his upper arms and shrivelled his balls. 'We live as Nature intended, therefore we must be happy.'

There was no answer to that, though there was to the other question uppermost in my mind.

An old man answering Paddy's description had stayed with them for a couple of days but had declared himself disgusted by their way of life and quite soon taken himself off into the hinterland. I was not surprised. There is an Irish Catholic prudishness beneath Paddy's easy-going ways. I, however, stayed with them for nearly a week but soon tired of their diet which too closely resembled what I had contrived to survive on on Albemarle, not to mention the discomfort occasioned by being made to expose my pelt, albeit they envied it, to the elements that were far more severe than they had been on my island home.

Eventually then, towards the end of August, I came to Yerba Buena or San Francisco, at that time a tiny fishing port and trading station on the horn of the lake-like bay, huddled beneath the steep hills that crowd behind it and shelter it from the ocean. It was not surprising that it was so poorly inhabited: some freak of Nature to do with the size of the bay behind the narrow passage they called the Golden Gate caused sea mists to form round noon every day. These blanketed out the sun and cast a cold dankness over everything and, with the plaintive call of gulls and so forth, put one in mind of the souls of drowned sailors. It was a common saying about the place that summer in 'Frisco was worse than winter* anywhere else, though they assured me that winter itself was balmy and sunny.

And almost immediately I came across Paddy. He was sitting on a bollard smoking his pipe, on a timber quay they called the Embarcadero from which to his left fishermen cast nets and lines and to his right a small, steam-assisted boat was loading goods from Europe, brought all the way round the Horn, to ferry them across to the settlements on the other side of the bay.

'Hi, Paddy,' I said.

He looked up, wiped rheum from his fading blue eye, thumbed down the ash in the bowl of his pipe and put it away in his pocket.

'Hi, Eddie. I just about gave up on yer. But here y' are.'

'What you doing, Paddy?'

'Just watching the ships go by. Thinking of Tralee and how bloody far off it is.'

I had heard these words before or something very like them, damned if I could remember where.†

'Time we were going then.'

'Aye.' He leant down to his side and picked up a boot built round a wooden foot and ankle which he began to strap on to his stump. This boot and the one he wore on his real foot were new, ankle-high, soft reddish leather, what they call, I believe, cowboy boots. 'Cobbler fixed me up wi' this. Don't work too bad.' And he stood up, set his arms akimbo, and did a little clog dance.

---

* 'Summer in San Francisco was the worst winter I have ever spent ...' Mark Twain. J. R.
† From Tom, at Morgan's Point, on the bank of Galveston Bay, Chapter 22. J. R.

And it's all for my grog, me jolly jolly grog,
All for my beer and tobacco.
Well, I spent all me tin on lassies drinking gin
And across the western ocean I must wander.

Where are me boots, me noggin' noggin' boots?
They're all gone for beer and tobacco
For the heels they are worn out and kicked all about
And the soles are looking for better weather.

I'm sick in the head and I haven't gone to bed
Since first I came ashore from me slumber
For I spent all me dough on the lassies don'cher know
Far across the western ocean I must wander . . .

I linked my hand in his elbow as we headed towards the little steamer.

'Paddy,' I quizzed him, 'what did you make of the Pacific then, when you saw it?'

'Not a lot. Sure you was right. It's just another big spread o' water you can't drink.'

'So you're ready now to make the journey back home?'

'Reckon so. Aye, why not?'

Interlude V

An extract from the diary of Francis Buff-Orpington, 18 July 1853

'Ye shall hear of wars and rumours of wars'* . . . so says the Evangelist, and today has been no exception. It seems that a note from the four neutral powers overlooking the dispute between Russia and the Sublime Porte has been rejected by Constantinople with the support of Lord Stratford, our ambassador, <u>though our government was one of the signatories</u>. A very strange state of affairs indeed. Moreover my Lord Palmerston, though strictly speaking as Home Secretary it is not his concern, has spoken forcibly in Cabinet in favour of the Ottomans' continued resistance to the Russian demands. So the possibility of war looms over us just at that point in the year when we all pack up and go into the country – indeed most have gone already and it is unlikely the Houses will sit again before November. Presumably that means nothing will be decided until then.

Boylan's (or Bosham's) reappearance with 'two lovely black eyes' following his second visit to Down, was thus put very much into perspective as the trivial affair it is by matters of truly serious import. Indeed, I have to say it figures in my mind even less than the walking holiday I have planned in the Mendips combined with a visit to

* St Matthew, Chapter 24, Verse 6. J. R.

my Galsworthy cousins in Wells where I hope to renew my acquaintance with second cousin Vicky.

Looking back I see that I did not make a note the day before yesterday that the manuscript of Mr Darwin's *Foundations* had been returned from the copyists. Well, it was, and yesterday I handed the original over to Boylan instructing him to use his skills to return it in such a way that its disappearance for a brief time should not be discovered. And this morning, almost as soon as I had sat in my office chair, he was admitted – spitting with mortification and rage.

Apparently he had gained access to Down House very easily simply by walking round to the back and admitting himself through an unlocked french door which opened into a vestibule where, as I understand it, there was a closet where Mr Darwin kept manuscripts for which he had no immediate use. And while he was returning the portfolio his presence was discovered by a small child called Frank who immediately raised the alarm with a piercing shriek.

Mr Darwin was out. Boylan had chosen his time to coincide with the daily walk the geologist is wont to take that coincides with the final preparations for lunch which the butler supervises in the kitchen. However, the din raised by the child was powerful enough to come to the butler's attention (his name, according to Boylan, is Parslow) and he arrived on the scene before Boylan could extricate himself from it. He assumed, quite reasonably I thought, that Boylan was there to take rather than return the portfolio and having wrested it from him, engaged himself to apprehend him. Boylan, foolishly perhaps considering his dwarfish stature, resisted and the whole matter degenerated into fisticuffs. Boylan claims that he 'gave as good as he got' which I doubt; however, having struck Parslow on the shin with a croquet stick he was able to make good his escape.

Boylan presented me with a receipt of eight pence for a pound of beefsteak which he said he had had to buy to alleviate the swelling and pain, but I refused to countenance it, merely paying his rail fare and the agreed five guineas for his services.

I think I should take Miss Galsworthy a small present but I am not sure what would be appropriate, nor whether I should make the purchase here in Burlington Arcade or wait until I get to Wells . . .

Part VIII

EASTWARD HO!

East, west, home's best.

40

My head aches and a drowsy numbness pains my sense, as though of some dull opiate I have drunk . . . well, of course, that is just what I have done, and if I shut my right eye (my left is shut already) and listen to what is going on behind them I fancy I might hear nightingales. Fuck Parslow. Fuck B.-O. Fuck Darwin, come to that. Not to mention Fwankie. Fuck the whole fucking tribe of Darwins.

That wanker B.-O. is pissing off to the country with all the other sodding toffs. Have I got enough to live on before they get back? I doubt it. Though I doubt I'll live anyway – the whole fucking town stinks of shit in this heat, especially near the river, and the cholera count goes up every day. The toffs used to bugger off because of the plague. Now it's cholera.

I wonder sometimes, is it worth going on with this memoir, this *travel book*? But how else am I going to get my hands on the chinks I need to pay the rent and buy a pie every now and then? If John Murray in Albemarle Street don't take it on, well then there are others. Chapman and Hall in Piccadilly did *American Notes* by the same man as wrote *Bleak House*. But I fancy Murray of Albemarle Street. After all it was on the Galápagian island of Albemarle that my observations on finches sparked off Mr Darwin's transmutational theories.

There we are. A Gordon's and water, not too much water, and another swig of Doctor Collis Browne, and I feel a touch cheerier.

Where was I? Looking for Paddy on the Pacific littoral. Right then. No! Done that. Heading east was the next thing.

After a bit of a discussion about it all we decided to make for the Lake Truckee Pass Fremont and Carson had taken us over, hoping to get over before the *Sierra* got to be *Nevada*, which was usually reckoned to happen round what the Americans celebrate as Thanksgiving Day, the twenty-seventh of November. However, we found the steamer had sailed so instead we got a fisherman with a skiff to take us, including Paquita, who didn't like the experience at all and had to be blinkered, across the Golden Gate. But he wasn't ready to take us that day, so that's why we had another night on the dock of the bay where I lost most of the money we had in the one tavern the village boasted. And while I was losing it was when I heard a longshoreman with a banjo singing:

> *Now Ranzo he's a sailor . . .*
> *Chief mate of that whaler . . .*
> *He married the cap'ns daughter*
> *Ranzo, boys, Ranzo!*
> *And sails no more upon the water*
> *Ranzo, boys, Ranzo!*

My song, I thought, the one Seamus made up for me before we fell out all those years ago on the old *Town-Ho*. But this wasn't all. Next morning when we came out on to the quay we found a little market had sprung up, a couple of trestle tables with fish laid out on them and crabs still live with their claws tied up, a two-wheeled cart selling garden produce, fruit and such like, an old man and an old woman raising cash by attempting to sell off furniture they'd probably lugged in a waggon all the way from Philly or New York, and, at the end of the line, an Indian woman selling furs.

She was old, with straggly grey hair supporting a topknot with a single gull's feather stuck in it and, in the way of her kind when separated from her tribe and kin, resolutely sullen and silent. The furs were short-haired, some old and raggedy, some quite new, and mostly as far as we could see (they were stacked one on top of another) sea lions, seals, and sea otters. Three had been made up into jackets.

'Them mountains are going to be danged cauld,' Paddy remarked. 'Try one on. Could save yer life.'

So I picked one about my size out of the pile, silvery-grey, mottled with brown spots, and slipped it on. It fitted over the clothes I was already wearing like a . . . like a glove.

'Dere yer go then,' and he turned to the squaw and began to bargain with her.

'No, Paddy,' I called, my voice suddenly hoarse. 'I can't wear this.'

'Whoi-iver not.'

I'd seen how one of the markings, just below the shoulder, was a perfect heart shape, like in a pack of cards. I felt a buzzing in my head and my palms began to sweat.

'I just can't. That's all.' And I began to slip it off.

'Too late. It's paid for. Come on, Joey. The poor critter what grew it has no more use for it. He'll be glad it's keeping some other body warm.'

'"She",' I said. 'It came from a she.'

And then I thought, maybe Paddy's right. He usually is. So I kept it and she did keep me warm, right through the mountain snows and ice and over the Plains.

Thanks, Maggie.

Once across the Golden Gate we used the last of what we had left to buy a sway-backed, spavined, knock-kneed old nag for Patrick and together we ambled off keeping to the coast of the Bay, getting lost in the swamps and river mouths, because we couldn't afford any of the ferries, looking more than a little like the Don and Sancho, though Paddy was neither as thin or as old and I am not fat. Plenty of time then, we thought, even though it was, what with one thing and another, the end of August before we got to Sutter's Fort. We were also delayed by a week or so spent with some tribelets of Ohlone Indians, who had inhabited the whole Bay area until the Spanish missions got in amongst them fifty or so years earlier. The ones we shacked up with were on this tongue of land between the ocean and the Bay and had so far been ignored. Well, of all the paradises I came across in America, this was the most paradisiacal.

On the coasts of the Bay the marshlands supported huge flocks of sea and water birds, geese, ducks and waders, and shellfish were abundant everywhere. On the ocean side there were huge colonies of seals and sea otters and at the right times of year the estuaries boiled with salmon. The land rose from the waters' edges in gentle rises into meadows where elk and antelope roamed and grizzly bears and mountain lions too. Higher still, though not yet mountainous, there were rabbits, quail and foxes, while giant condors cruised the unfathomable spaces above.

And we were welcomed because we were not Spanish. We had no guns, no whips, no chains, no crosses or breviaries. We did not kidnap the children and baptise them. They did not yet know what we could do, that, like Sutter a hundred miles away, we could drain the marshes, graze cattle and own the land.

Well, I could go on, but I won't. Enough to say I was ready to stay. But not Paddy. He had his Rose of Tralee to get back to. And anyway, as he said: 'Don' be an idjit Eddie. How long do you think this will last?'

'My lifetime, Paddy.'

'Yor fockin' jokin'. In five years' time, less, they'll be working for wages, like the poor sods on Sutter's. They'll be as bad treated as any Irish between Limerick and Dublin. And yon Sutter's a good man. For a fockin' landowner. Most of his sort are a focking sight worse. Oim Oirish, I know.'

So we left the last of the Ohlone. I knew he was right. Because one night we were having as much of a chat as we could with one old codger who'd run home from the mission and knew a bit of Spanish and we got to talking about wars.

I'd told him the Ohlones couldn't fight, and he took umbrage.

'We're always fighting,' he said, puffing his pipe inside this sort of a basketwork sort of a hut he'd invited us to. 'We love a fight! We had a war back in the early summer. Over water rights to a spring, down on the edge of the forest over there.'

'Who won?'

'The other guys. One of our men got an arrow in his thigh, so we said, all right, you want the water that much you can have it. Soon as anyone gets hurt we stop. I mean, what's the point?'

Paddy was right. We were in a backwater of history that was about to be flooded out, and a day or two later we pushed on to Sutter's Fort on the Sacramento and got there within ten days.

Sutter, tearing himself away from the intrigues that still rumbled on concerning the future of California, thought we were mad.

'You are mad,' he squeaked, his voice fluking up as it sometimes did when he was particularly keen to make a point. 'And for why I shall you be telling. Number one. You have no money. You must take provisions with you, mules to carry food to feed you at least until you get to Bridger's Fort if not Fort Laramie. Two, Indian guides . . . there are being no signposts out in the desert, you know?'

'But that's just the thing Captain Sutter, sor,' Paddy replied as forcefully as he dared. 'We do know. We followed the route with Captain Fremont and Mr Carson, this last spring . . . We do know the way, sor, at least as far as Bridger's and from then on it is well marked, if not by signposts then waggon tracks—'

'And how will you be seeing these tracks? Under a foot or more of snow and ice?'

Paddy was surprised.

'There will be snow on the plains as well as the mountains?'

'Of course there bloddy will.'

'Come on, Paddy,' I interjected. 'Back in eighteen twelve there was snow on the *meseta* in Spain from November to February, sometimes March.'

'Zo. It is money you are needing and the pretty flowers in the desert. You work here for me until the thaw begins, and you will have both.'

And that was the nub of it. All his white men, and a fair number too of his Indians, had gone down south with Fremont to fight the Mexicans and even with the winter coming on he was short-handed. But he was right too.

'Come on, Eddie,' said Patrick, making a last-ditch attempt. 'We'll go back to 'Frisco, or maybe Monterey, and work our passage back on a ship.'

'You aim to go round the Horn the wrong way or are you going to make it a Round the World tour? You aim to climb the rigging with one foot?'

'I can cook.'

'Either way it'll take you a year.'

'We'll walk across Panama.'

'And die of yellow fever.'

'Come on, Paddy, he's right,' I repeated and I turned to the Swiss farmer. 'You see, sir, he wants to see his mother in Ireland before she dies.'

'Ach so!' A cloud seemed to drift over the red face in front of us, and then passed with a shrug of his big shoulders. 'Well, we must be looking after him. Making sure he comes to no harm before he leaves. Look. Go and be seeing Jim Bartleby, my foreman. He'll fix up work for you and agree a rate that neither of us will like . . . which means it will be a fair one!' And he roared with laughter, though I sensed there were still shadows in the corners of the room that had not been there when the conversation began.

So, Paddy and I worked for Sutter, at Nova Helvetia, which means New Switzerland and was what he now called his fort, through the winter of '46–'47. It was hard graft to begin with, especially for Paddy, until Sutter took him up on the cooking. Not that he was a good cook. Quite the reverse. What he had the knack of was making a stew of barley, wheat and potatoes seem more nourishing for less in the material way than you would have thought. And one way he did it was this. Sutter was in the habit of tipping the resulting mash in hollowed out log troughs for his Indians to do the best they could with like pigs. But Paddy insisted they had wooden platters and bowls, and horn spoons like the rest of us. The result was less food wasted, less food cooked and doled out, and the Indians happy to think they were dining like white folk.

As for me. Well, I'm an educated man though it's not something I draw attention to unless it serves my advantage, but Sutter soon found I could prepare a contract or find the holes in a land deed better than he could with only a smear of English butter over the rye bread of his Swiss-German. And I can add and take away without an abacus.

Old Sutter had a reputation for treating his Indians better than the other settlers did. Certainly he was a lot better than the missions. But even he took to beatings and executions by firing squad when the natives got uppity and he ruled by dividing – tribe against tribe – and by having an inner bodyguard of well-fed, privileged braves who'd go after horse thieves and, when they caught them, stick their heads on the stockades. He'd send the daughters of the men he killed as presents to his neighbours to be concubines. All in all, he qualified as well as anyone else to be at the heart of darkness that riverboat arrowing up the Big River had pointed towards.

41

You know I have lived more than most at the still centre of great historical events that have reverberated down the long corridors of time long after I left them, and the thing of it is neither Paddy nor I had much of an inkling of what was going on around us during that long winter. And long it was. For a start the snows began more than a month earlier than usual. Through October we could watch and measure the progress of a white pall of snow down the steep slopes and peaks twenty miles away, at first well above the tree line, dusting the already almost white of rock and scree, cliff and escarpment, with a brighter shade of pale. Then following what seemed like a whiteout lasting several days at the end of October, the cloud lifted and we could see that the darkness of marching fir and pine had been obliterated as surely as the rock. There were other signs of a bad winter too. Bears and wolves were reported in the upper valleys, condors and bald-headed eagles cruised above meadows, and when the storms blew themselves out the strings of smoke from Indian encampments clambered up the cold, still air from winter quarters far further down the valleys than was usual.

Even before the snow we had a foretaste of the horrors to come with the arrival of a Mr C. T. Stanton of Chicago and a Wm McCutcheon from Missouri. Stanton was a stocky sort of a man, in his mid-thirties, not more than five and a half feet tall but very robust. Well-spoken, though, and lettered too. Some three weeks earlier they had left a large party in the eastern foothills of the Sierra Nevada, on the western edge of the Great Salt Lake Desert, the crossing of which by the Harrison Cut had cost them lives and beasts. Their waggons were much reduced by damage and loss of oxen and they had very little left in the way of food, the party consisting of a waggon train of some eighty or ninety souls, women, children and old people as well as the young and fit. Stanton and McCutcheon's mission was to cross the Sierra ahead of the main party, pick up what would be needed to get them across the mountains before the snows set in and take it back the way they had come.

Sutter, though brusque with them, was nevertheless generous.

'Happens every year,' he bellowed. 'Take seven mules, all the corn-flour and jerk they can carry, and two of my best Indians, Lewis and Salvador.'

Paddy, standing behind him, cleared his throat, and spat.

'We'll go with them, sor.'

'The fock, you will.'

'We knows the way, sor.'

'No better than my Injuns. You'll just be two more stomachs to fill.'

'Only as far as where these people are. After that we can go on east. Leave the Injuns to bring them back here. What you say, Eddie?'

'Grow another foot and I'll come with you.'

'Fock off, Eddie.'

But he stayed. This time.

McCutcheon had been somewhat knocked up by the journey so after a couple of days' rest Stanton and the Indians went without him.

Well, the next thing, as already mentioned, was the storm at the end of October, lasting several days, which dumped maybe six feet of snow across the passes, a full month earlier than expected. And on the first day of the storm the third man from what, following McCutcheon's way of talking, we already called the Donner Party after the family that had initiated the train, stumbled into New Switzerland.

This was James Reed. He was tall, good-looking and well-built, dark-haired and of ruddy complexion. At first sight he seemed a ruffian, as who would not who had struggled for so many miles through gorges and over passes and with no support but his trusty hunting gun and a limited supply of ball and powder. But worse than the damage to his physiognomy caused by frost and sun were the scars, scarce healed, and still in part suppurating, that marked and even *indented* his forehead, the top of his head and his shoulders. It was no wonder then that a half-day in his company had to pass before I recognised in him, as one does who himself shares them, the qualities of a Gentleman.

The first clue was the way he spoke an English which was a strange mixture of North Irish and something European – we later learnt Polish. Originally a liberal landowner in his own country, he had been driven into exile by the Russian overlords and had settled as a young man in Antrim before migrating to the States. And it was no doubt his gentility, a sort of quiet reserve that can be mistaken for an assumption of superiority, that contributed in some measure to the dreadful way he and his family had been treated by the Donner faction.

To put it briefly, just on the western edge of the desert he had become involved in a silly dispute regarding the use of teams of oxen to get the waggons up a softly sanded rise. His antagonist was an out-and-out ruffian called Snyder, a connection or friend of the Donners, a man of rough manners with an ungovernable temper. Snyder, enraged by a comment of Reed's that had been intended to be conciliatory, began to beat the Polish aristo about the head with the weighted handle of his bull-whip, causing the wounds whose scars still so grievously disfigured him. Mrs Reed had intervened, herself taken a blow to the head, at which Reed had drawn his knife, yes, the Arkansas Toothpick, and stuck it fatally between Snyder's ribs.

The outcome was that the Donner faction decided to banish Reed, drive him out much as the Israelites drove the Scape-Goat out into the wilderness, leaving him with no means of support except the aforesaid gun, shot and powder. In many respects, though he would have liked company and better supplies, Reed reckoned this was no bad thing. Nothing had been heard of Stanton and McCutcheon and such was the deteriorating condition of the whole band he had already been advocating that a small party should follow in their footsteps and seek help ahead of the train. Consequently, he took tearful farewells of his wife and children and set off into the whiteness of the mountains ahead.

In spite of all he had suffered and the general debilitation of his condition, Reed, like Stanton before him, availed himself of Sutter's generosity and quickly gathered together mules and non-perishable supplies. McCutcheon was now much recovered and early in November, before the first week was out, they set off up the passes away from Johnson's Ranch, the last place on the west of the Sierra occupied by white men not savages. However, they had left it too late and, frustrated by the huge quantities of snow that continued to fall through the month, were back at Sutter's by the 21st.

What their eyes had seen and the dangers they had faced now convinced them where Sutter's experience and arguments had failed, and they spent the rest of the winter travelling the Bay area, raising charity and preparing to make the crossing as soon as the thaw commenced.

And now I should mention just one occurrence which took place on Reed's return at the end of November. He was sitting in the big kitchen or cookhouse which Sutter's white men used, trying to pull off his boots in front of an almost red-hot stove. It was a struggle in which both Paddy and I assisted. The problem was exacerbated by the fact that these heavy boots, constructed of thick leather now no more malleable than wood, had initially been too big for their wearer, and he had remedied this disadvantage by folding up newspaper to make an insole. However, a combination of all the evils inherent in walking and climbing several thousand miles, through extreme heat and cold, had caused his feet to swell.

Well, I need not detail all the exertions needed to remove the offending (and indeed offensive) footwear except to say that they were eventually successful.

Mr Reed sighed out Polish thanks to the Virgin and Saint Crispin, I looked around for the means to wash my hands, while Paddy, straightening out the newspaper also called upon the Holy Mother, Joseph, Jesus and all the saints to bless him while he perused the crumpled, yellowed, but still largely legible sheets.

'What's this then?' he cried. 'Famine in Ireland? Sure there's always famine in Ireland.' But he read on with surprising ease, for he was far more literate than one would expect, particularly favouring verse if he could get hold of some. 'T'ousands dead, especially on the west coast, Galway de-pop-ulated. Total failure of potato harvest second year running . . . what's d' date of this rag then?' and he pushed and pulled at it until he got the masthead up ... 'Antrim Times, August 1845, how long ago is that then?'

'Fifteen months,' Reed answered, pouring cold water over his swollen foot that had taken on the colour and shape of a giant egg-plant, 'and sure enough by the time we left St Louis back in May we'd heard worse. It's a black blight affects the leaves but spoils the seed potatoes too. Not a potato to be had west of Wicklow, they were saying.'

'So what's the focking government doing about it? What's coming out of Doblin Castle?'

'Not their business. The laws are there, all they have to do is uphold them.'

'What laws would they be then?'

'Those that say the tenants must pay rent in specie or saleable goods. That means their barley and wheat. If they don't pay they're evicted. You grow grain for your rent and potatoes you eat.'

Paddy turned on the Irish Pole like a gale-force gust out of nowhere.

'You don't have to tell me that. I know all about that.' He banged the table and got hold of Reed's stock as if he meant to strangle him. Reed gave him a push, which, on account of the unsteadiness of his foot-shorn leg, almost floored him. Paddy recovered and stormed out to the yard, where he met Sutter coming in. Arguments, recrim-inations – for Paddy had it in his head that Sutter had heard of this famine and kept it from him, which maybe was the case – and Paddy all for setting out there and then with or without yours truly, he didn't care, he'd see his Mam in Tralee or in Heaven. Eventually Reed, whose physical strength matched the uprightness of his spirit, got him on his back on the big table, spread out like pig for the slaughter on St Andrew's Day, the old Toothpick at his throat, and spoke to him slowly and steadily, so he had to listen. Maybe Reed was a touch too ready to resort to the Big Knife.

'Patrick,' he growled, 'my family, whom I love as dearly as any man ever loved those closest to him, are up in those mountains, less than a hundred miles away, with little food and no proper shelter. Do you not think I would go to them now if I felt for one moment that I would help them by doing so? The trails are blocked. There is noth-ing to hunt, for all the game has moved into the valleys, the snow is ten feet. And you want to go not just through that, but then across plains and deserts almost as cold, across an ocean with no money to pay your passage, to find a woman on whose means of sustenance, be she still alive, you will merely be another burden.'

Slowly he let Paddy up into a sitting position, then turned to the Swiss.

'Captain,' he said, 'what's the earliest we can expect to make any headway into the mountains?'

'February, Mr Reed. End of February.'

'That's when I'll go then, Paddy, and if you've still a mind to it, I'll take you with me.'

That's not how it turned out. At the end of October, coming out of that first unseasonable storm, a small party led by a Mr R. P. Tucker had arrived at Johnson's Ranch, virtually in the Sierra Nevada, some fifty miles north of Sutter's Fort, but so bad was the rain and flooding and the distances big enough to add to the problem, we at Sutter's Fort knew nothing of this new arrival for some months. They had been part of the original Donner Party but back at the end of July, at Fort Bridger, had made the decision not to go with the main party through Harrison's Cut but to take the more traditional route north of the Great Salt Lake via Fort Hall. The advantage of the old trail was that it climbed river valleys out of the Great Basin into the Snake River Plain, thus minimising the amount of alkaline desert to be crossed. The disadvantage, of course, was that it was far longer. However, theirs was the correct decision and they arrived at Johnson's just as the weather broke. Tucker and his people, about a dozen of them as I remember, now decided to winter at Johnson's.

Then, in the last week of January, when the foothills and the Sacramento Plain had become an almost impassable quagmire from continuous rain and the run-off from the mountains, a skeletal pioneer called Rhodes, accompanied by an Indian who had looked after him, stumbled into Johnson's. He had a terrible story to tell.

The train had split into three. The main party was at Lake Truckee, completely snowed in, living in a leaky, barn-like shed and some outhouses that were now several feet below the surface of the snow. Most of these were connections of Stanton and Reed by family or friendship. Seven miles to the east, at a place called Alder Creek, was a second encampment, living in tents made from skins, also under snow, and mostly occupied by the Donners or their connections. With tents only to shelter them, it was the Donner Party that suffered most. The third party was a Forlorn Hope, which included this man Rhodes and had initially been led by Stanton, now dead, who had set out to cross the 'summit' and bring back help. It also included Sutter's two Indians, Lewis and Salvador, about whose fate Rhodes remained mulishly silent.

Tucker was stocky of build, dour of countenance, a severe, practical sort of a man. With a religious conviction regarding his duty to fellow men and women he now revised his plans, and resolved to go up into the mountains at least to rescue whomever of the Forlorn Hope might have survived, and if possible push on to Lake Truckee and Alder Creek. And this time, when Paddy heard of it, there was no stopping him. We left Johnson's Ranch in the first week of February – Tucker, about eight men he'd got together including Rhodes, all mounted, and Paddy on Rosinante, me on Paquita together with a couple of bags of jerk and flour, and a mule train loaded with lard and dried fruit as well as jerk and flour.

At first rain and its consequences, not snow or even cold, were the problem. It rained every day, in the afternoon and into the night, torrential, driving rain. Every mountain slope was a cascade of boiling mud sweeping down uprooted smaller shrubs as buckthorns and willows in impenetrable tangles which snagged around the feet of the forest giants, the majestic redwoods and sequoias. And some even of these were half torn up to expose the knotted masses of their roots while their crowns snagged and rocked against those of their neighbours.

For the most part we followed as closely as we could the twisting beds of rivers which thundered from pool to pool, thrashed through rapids in boiling whitewater. There was no peace: the waters roared, the skies thundered, the winds howled and whistled through the tree tops and between the crags, and everything, everywhere, was wet, wet, wet.

Needless to say, the combination of Paquita and Rosinante against the mules and horses of Tucker et al., the difficulties poor Paddy underwent when conditions forced us to dismount, were all such that within two days we were half a day behind the main party, and within three a whole day and we could no longer be sure we saw the smoke from their fires rising above the forested crags ahead and

359

above us. Paddy was not worried (I was . . . I usually do feel anxiety when I feel my survival is threatened): we had, he pointed out, plenty of jerk and flour in Paquita's saddlebags, and powder and shot for his old gun. 'Onwards and upwards,' he cried whenever I remonstrated or suggested that we should turn about. 'How can we fail either to meet them on their way down or catch up with them at Lake Truckee?' How indeed?

But before I describe the horrid outcome of this bullishness I must first recount an incident which occurred at dawn on our fourth morning. We had camped just as night fell, some way above the river, between two big humpback rocks part roofed by a fallen pine left there when the river had been even higher. I awoke at dawn after a fair night's sleep. No sign of Paddy. I stood, took a piss (forgive me, Mr Murray, but travellers are no more spared these inconveniences of the flesh than any other mortals) and hallooed as loud as I might for him.

No answer, so I buttoned up and made my way down to the riverside with my heart thudding with fears of bears, Indians, whatever, though reassured by the presence, still securely tethered, of our beasts scoffing a breakfast off an armful of leaves and grasses I presumed Paddy had already put out for them. They snorted a little, stamped, breathed clouds of vapour into the air as if to say: 'Not yet, dear friend, not yet, give us an hour more before you make us move.'

A turn or two round more boulders brought my old companion into view. He was standing with his back to me, on a big but flat rock lichened with lacy roundels, about which the heaving waters swirled. His arms were folded, his big duster coat trailed almost to his ankle, his hat was pushed to the back of his head, and his accoutrements and bits and bobs and, when he turned, the badge of the 88th gleamed in a sullen shaft of sunlight that had found a gap between the peaks above us. The valley, ending not a hundred yards above us in a magnificent cascade that made the air shake with its unceasing thunder as it dropped a clear two hundred feet or more before twisting and climbing down to us, was filled with mist and vapour some of which glistened in that paltry sunbeam.

He heard or sensed me coming and turned.

'Sure it's a magnificent sight, is it not Eddie? Harkee to what the Poet says,' and he struck a Thespian attitude.

                    The sounding cataract
Haunted me like a passion: the tall rock,
The mountain and the deep and gloomy wood,
Their colours and their forms were then to me
An appetite: a feeling and a love,
That had no need of a remoter charm,
By thought supplied, or any interest
Unborrowed from the eye. – That time is past,
And all its aching joys are now no more,
And all its dizzy raptures . . . For I have learned
To look on nature, not as in the hour
Of thoughtless youth, but hearing oftentimes
The still sad music of humanity . . .

I felt this could go on for some time since it is part of the late William Wordsworth's immensely long and some would say tedious effusion *The Prelude** and it was necessary to get a word in edgeways.

'Talking of appetite,' I interrupted, 'what can I get your worship for breakfast?'

He sighed, pushed his hands into his armpits, looked down at me.

'Eddie, there's a thrushes' nest in a patch of huckleberry just uphill from our camp. It's early days yet but from the way they carried on when I went near them, I reckon you may find a clutch of eggs. You can get some water to boil them in.'

'I haven't got the pan. It's back with the beasts.'

'Here, take my hat. It's soaked right t'rough so using it as a bucket won't make matters any worse.' He peeled it off by the brim, gave it a shake, and spun it across to me so the spray briefly rainbowed in that shaft of persistent sunlight. Then, aided by the stout hickory pole he used as a support, he swung himself off up the stream – perhaps to continue listening to the still sad music of humanity, perhaps to have a shit.

I hunkered down over the edge of the water with the hat between my knees, and for a moment I too was bewitched by the beauties of nature. The unrepentant sunbeam caught the surface ripples and

* No. Actually these lines, with a couple here omitted, are from 'Lines written a few miles above Tintern Abbey' and were first published in *Lyrical Ballads*. J. R.

made evanescent dancing sparkles of extraordinary brightness and even apparent hardness, which vanished as quickly as they appeared but were instantly replaced. Such was their brightness and beauty I reflected on the stupidity of men who value above the brightness of these transitory jewels the dull gleam of gold, the cruel hardness of gems.

Then, mindful of why I was there, I pushed Paddy's hat into the rush of it. Straightway it filled: it was heavy, the force of the current was like to pluck it out of my hands, and clumsily I heaved it up and dropped it beyond the edge. The water it took with it spilled out over the soggy brim leaving in the crown a debris of fine gravel, larger stones, and . . .

'Oh shit,' I said.

No eggs, but Paddy was back in twenty minutes or so, having deployed tickling techniques acquired in his Tralee childhood, with a brace of fine brown trout which he briskly gutted with his Toothpick while I got the fire going again. He used the ramrod of his hunting rifle as a skewer and broiled them over the flames and they ate as well as any fish I've ever had, gently scented as they were with pine smoke.

'You know,' he said, picking a hair-like bone out from between his teeth, 'Sutter ought to know about this creek.'

This made my heart thump I can tell you. Had he too stumbled on the secret of the place as I had? Was he, with his customary naïve generosity, ready to share it with others?

'You do? Why?'

'He's looking for a spot where good timber crowds down to the banks of a fast river, strong in current enough for him to set up a sawmill of his own and float the lumber down to his spread. I reckon this spot, or maybe one a little further downstream, would be ideal. In fact he has a millwright called Marshall coming over in the spring to prospect for just such a site.'

It occurred to me there might be profit to be had beyond that of knowing the likely site of a sawmill from knowing just where we were and this seemed an opportunity to ask.

'Colluma Valley,' he answered. Then, 'Where's my hat?'

I passed it to him, he gave it a shake and some gravel fell out. A crumb of yellow caught his eye. He picked it up, squinted at it on the ball of his thumb.

'Sulphuret of iron,' he said. 'Fool's gold,' and flicked it away as if it were so much nose snot. 'Well, we'd best be on our way.'

And soon we were, each on his usual mount, and the deep, right-hand, buttoned-up pocket of my trousers banged and shook against my thigh. A good half a handful, maybe two ounces in weight, of little bead-shaped excrescences the size of lentils, variegated in size and shape, almost perfectly smooth and bright, of pure gold.

42

By mid-afternoon of that day we were climbing through the snow line. For a time it was a winter wonderland of delight. Every giant tree shouldered magnificent capes of thick white snow. The sun, now behind us, struck fiery jewels out of this soft ore, jewels that were refractured prismatically into fiery ruby, bright orange and even emerald and sapphire points of light. Occasionally a tree, whether through the action of the raised temperature or prompted by a breath of air, shed a swathe of the stuff so it slipped, almost of a piece, to the ground below. The gorge narrowed and we had to leave the river bed and follow the escarpments above it and this meant an eery silence fell on our ears, as if they had been muffled, so it was not easy to distinguish the rush of blood in one's head from the now distant susurration of the waters. Below us mists gathered in the valley bottoms, above us real cloud shrouded the tops of the giant redwoods, as high as cathedral steeples, and let fall, so they drifted like giant white butterflies, huge flakes of snow.

The slope we were both crossing and climbing became steeper and steeper, the sides of the valley or gorge above narrowed over a fathomless chasm; we turned a corner, and faced, almost as the last glimmering light faded from the scene, a magical sight. Framed by the generally sheer walls of the gorge, white peaks climbed into the turquoise sky and caught the last rays of golden sunlight on their apparently pristine flanks. Above us, though, the sky was still leaden and snow continued to fall making a shifting veil between us and them, but this was not all. What conferred upon the landscape a magic beyond Nature's contriving, was an arched bridge, about the length and substance of the Venetian Bridge of Sighs, spanning the abyss below. This, I exclaimed, has not hitherto existed outside the imaginings of some spinner of fairy tales like Hans Andersen, or a maker of Gothick Mysteries. Its walls, compacted of ice thawed and frozen many times to an alabastine clearness and smoothness, were hung with stalactitic icicles, some as thick as a man's body at their source, but many too clearer and needle-like and no bigger than stilettos. The upper surface, which we could not yet see, was all fresh snow. And for a moment this wonderful structure was lit as if by stage lights cunningly set by a master of scenic effects, and then as quickly faded into a great shadow that continued through the night to float between us and the night sky and those distant peaks.

'Reckon we'd best bed down now,' Patrick grunted. 'We'll get across in the morning.'

Get across? In the morning? I should there and then, with my pocket full of gold, have turned round and headed back to Johnson's Ranch and Sutter's Fort, and filed a claim or whatever, whatever procedure was necessary.

Dawn, no, earlier than that, first light, I was wakened with the smell of charring flour and water twisted round a stick, cooking over a fire of small branches, and then the more attractive fragrance of coffee.

Paddy was leaning over me, his breath a touch sour with the mouthful of Kentucky bourbon he liked to start the day with.

'T'ere's no way beyond d' bridge dis side,' he said, once he was sure I was conscious, 'but I've had a look at it. Number one, the trail continues on the other side. Number two it was used within the last two days. A track has been hollowed out across the top, there are hoof prints and some droppings too under the trees where the new snow hasn't reached them. Must have been Tucker and his lot. The sooner we try it the better, before the warmth of the day can weaken it.'

'Paddy, I'm not crossing that thing,' I said, breaking a piece of twist off the stick he handed me and burning my fingers as I did. Hot though it was, it was uncooked paste in the middle.

'Then you find your own way back to Johnson's. Shouldn't be difficult. But I keep Paquita and the food bags. There's folk up there need them bad as we do or worse.'

Ten minutes to get the baggage all strapped up and on board the beasts again, finish the coffee, kick the fire out before he led us the last fifty yards or so to the end of the bridge. A fingernail of sun cleared the distant peaks and grew. I could feel its warmth on my cheeks, yet the vapour of my breath still froze on the stubble on my face and the brim of my fur cap. A couple of ravens cackled. I looked over the edge of the chasm. Christ, they were *below* us!

'Paddy, I get vertigo.'

'Don't look down.'

Yeah, and trip on a frozen yellow ball of horse poo.

He looked at me and made a decision.

'You go first. Then me, then the nag, then the donkey.'

Only way of getting me across.

The bridge was about four feet wide, soft, new snow lying over what was compacted in the middle, ridges of shovelled snow along the edges, sure sign someone had done it before us. But it was slippery. I skated at the second step.

'Here,' said Paddy, 'use this as a stick,' and he handed me his gun. He had his hickory.

It was no good. First, I couldn't move more than six inches at a time; then, there was a gust of wind and I swear the whole thing shifted. There was nothing for it. I had to get down on my hands and knees. Now the gun was no use, but with each movement forward I was able to pull it alongside me. About halfway I glanced back. Paddy was upright, a pace or two behind me, hickory in one hand, Rosinante's tether in the other.

'Get a fockin' move on, will yer?'

Another gust of wind blowing powder in my face, another lurch from the bridge, and this time a sort of tired groan as well. That made me move. I clawed my way across the last few yards and at last, with a flood of relief surging through my blood, my hands grasped rock. I scrabbled with my feet and hauled myself on to terra more or less firma. Not firma enough. In my panic I had set off a small cascade of snow and rocks tumbling down into the cloudy abyss, taking the rifle with it.

I looked round and up to see what Paddy thought of this but he had his own problems. There is one circumstance under which no horse will move, be it ever so broken down, old, biddable. No horse will move if it is having a piss. Rosinante was having a piss. Just beyond the halfway mark he had spread his back legs and was letting go. Golden streams beneath clouds of steam. Golden streams that cut through the snow like a hot knife through butter. Great lumps of it broke off and hurtled down: what was an arch became inverted. It was falling apart: the centre no longer held. At the far end Paquita backed off as far as the tether which linked her with the horse would let her. Both animals were bellowing or screaming now, Rosinante's head lifted, his teeth open and his tongue protruding, his hooves now scrabbling against the slope, then it went. The whole structure broke up and crashed, taking the horse with it, hooves flailing in the air before he was lost in the cloud and falling snow and debris below. But Paquita? The Spanish say you never see a poor lawyer or a dead donkey. The tether broke or came undone, and we could see her battling her way up against a small avalanche on the further side, back to the platform we had set out from. She trumpeted a last trio of eee-aws, and then was gone, down the trail up which we had come. Silence slowly returned, apart from the moan of the rising wind and the distant cackle of the big black birds.

'Well,' said Paddy at last, 'aint that just dandy? No food, no gun, nuttin' to ride on.'

And at that moment the last of the bridge fell away revealing just how insubstantial it was. One tall, thin spruce* pole, already dead and almost branchless, had been its core, and over the winter the massive structure of ice and snow had built up on it, collecting and coagulating, and occasionally compacted as humans and their beasts, and maybe animals too as bears and deer, had walked across it. To think I had allowed Paddy to trust my life to such a flimsy edifice! With that in mind I was not going to allow him to blame me for our losses, and we struggled on, heads down against the swelling icy blast, saying little but rather out of sorts with each other.

Throughout this account I have referred to the 'trail' but that gives a wrong impression. There was no established trail. There were paths frequented by Indians about their own affairs; there were tracks made by those animals which liked to follow a routine. There were

* Not a native to California. It was probably a dead ponderoso pine. J. R.

367

trails that held clear indications for a time that men had passed this way either down or up and occasionally both, but these would disappear under the snow in an open place or across scree or whatever and apparently not emerge again. The main valley up which we had started bifurcated again and again and all we could do was follow some approximate indication as to which prong bore signs of human use or simply which was the widest and deepest and therefore most likely to penetrate furthest into the mountain fastnesses. But Patrick, although he had never been in the Sierra Nevada before apart from when we came hither with Fremont and Carson, had lived for no one knew exactly how many years alone in the Rockies and he had a sense of how things went, where a col might be reached, or the side of a waterfall climbed, and so on. And of course, given a gun, when and where game might be taken. But now we had no gun. In fact, nothing.

'Our only hope,' he asserted, once we were again on speaking terms, 'is to find Tucker ahead of us, or come upon some other party whose straits are not as dire as ours.'

On the fourth day after the bridge, we crossed what he asserted was the highest col. Maybe he was right. Certainly for a time we were above the tree line clambering through a wasteland of boulders and scree, past frozen tarns, or trudging, our boots squeaking in the fresh snow, across occasional flats where one might guess that beneath the snowfields grassy roots, ground-hugging shrubs and alpine flowers waited patiently for the spring. One of these was bisected by a twisting line of dots and scrapes which, when we came up with it, turned out to be footholes filling with snow, the marks left by dragged feet, scraps of chewed leather, and a piece of meat kept pure by the cold, but also chewed on and spat out. There was also a yellow patch where one of the party had urinated.

'Seven people,' Paddy said after perusing all this for a minute or so. 'Most of them women, I'd say. And in a bad way. Heading west. Must be what's left of the Forlorn Hope that Rhodes and Stanton was a part of . . .'

'Good,' I said. 'Let's follow them. There's at least two parties out looking for them.'

But no. Paddy's course was set. It was east, always east, for Tralee. But we stayed with the tracks of these forlorn people, tracing in reverse their tragic journey.

Dear reader, I shall not distress you with too detailed an account of how we were, by then, suffering. Stomach cramps of excruciating ferocity set in on the third day. By the fourth we were suffering from both hallucinations and snow blindness. At times the landscape seemed dotted with a scattered crowd of people like us, moving to and fro across the snowfields, shadowy figures that never came quite near enough to be identified. But once a young girl, maybe seven years old, with golden curls, a thin cotton dress, and no shoes, overtook me, begged for water of which I had none, and ran on.

And then the snow blindness. The sun shone from a cloudless sky for at least three hours each day before the clouds began to gather, and for that time one felt one was progressing through a sphere of intensely bright white light that pierced the eyes like red-hot needles. When the sun was hidden by cloud or trees, or the mountains behind us, one walked through a grey gloom filled with shapeless masses over which drifted painfully bright after-images of green and red.

But now, following the tracks east we were indeed descending below the tree line again, though it was noticeable on this side that the trees were more etiolated, widely spaced and with few of the redwood giants of the west, just what seemed to my untutored and damaged eyes plain firs and pines.

As the gloom of evening fell we discovered two evidences that the suffering of the seven whose tracks we were on had intensified beyond endurance. First we came to a space between trees that still showed signs of having been cleared of snow. A tree, a hickory, possibly already dead, had been set alight and Paddy said the people beneath must have stood almost rapturously beneath its falling, flaming branches as night came on for them, as it now did for us.

'If you'll gather some wood,' he said at last, 'we'll get a fire going.'

So I scouted off down the track, picking up fallen branches, shaking the snow off them, and leaving them in piles to be gathered on my way back, and within two hundred yards came across the most awful sight we had yet seen, though plenty worse were to follow. Stooping to pull clear what I thought was a specially dry and probably friable end of a branch, I grasped a handful of twigs and pulled. There was resistance, then up it all came, rising out of the snow, the ghastly face and torso of a man, not a skeleton, though he was thin enough to have been described as such, and as I pulled

369

his head lolled forward and I saw how the top of it had been clumsily broken open and the brains within removed. Then there was a cracking sound and head and torso flopped back, leaving me with the hand and arm, peeling out of a buckskin sleeve, loosely hinged, flopping about me.

I screamed, of course, and shouted Paddy's name often enough to make him feel he should come and see what I was about in spite of his missing foot. Together we pulled the cadaver out into the snow and found another beneath it, but that was not the full horror by any means. Not only had the brains been taken from both but holes gouged too in their body cavities from which the livers, lights and hearts had been torn. And both were short a leg each cut from the pelvic region, though the knees, shins and shoeless feet had been tossed back.

'Well,' said Paddy, his voice laden with pity and some anger, 'it's clear what happened.'

'It is?'

'Aye. These are Lewis and Salvador, leastways that's the names Sutter gave them. The Indians he sent back with Stanton. Look, they have their beads and a feather or two about them yet. They have been abused, horribly abused . . .'

That seemed pretty evident but I waited to see what else he had to say.

'First their shoes, their boots are gone. Being soft and only partly tanned deerskin they would have boiled up into something almost edible. So first they made them go barefoot and you can see what that did to them.'

Indeed, the soles of their feet were a coagulated mass of blood and minced flesh.

'But since their survival depended on getting over the mountains they continued and these inhuman people followed them until the two brave warriors collapsed. The party walked beyond. Halted. Debated. Then one at least turned back and shot them. See?' And with his hickory he touched the holes just below the ear of each at the point where the jawbone joins the skull. 'Sustained by fresh meat next morning the party went on, and no doubt took a haunch from each to keep them going.'

He straightened, looked round at the trees which, in the near darkness, seemed almost to be closing in on us.

370

'This is an evil place,' he sighed. 'We'll go on a bit before we stop for the night.'

But we couldn't go far on account of the encroaching darkness, hardly more than a couple of hundred yards. We got a fire going and I set on it the saucepan which had been dangling from my belt when we crossed the bridge, filled it with snow, and wished we had a spoonful of coffee or a pinch of tea to go in it.

'Paddy,' I said, once the fire was certain enough to be left alone for a minute or so while we crouched as close to it as we could, 'hot water will not do. We must have some nourishment. And don't go on again about my losing your gun.'

'So what have you in mind, Eddie? Taking one of those haunches those murtherers left? Broiled Indian leg?'

'No, Paddy. But what about your spare boot?'

'Fock you, Eddie, I have no spare boot.'

'Sure you do, Paddy. Your right one does sterling service for your right foot. But all your left does is mask the fact you have no left foot, just a good, sound, solid bit of timber any man should be proud of.'

'Is dat so, Eddie?'

'Paddy, it is so. It's like what you might call . . . cosmetic. Like lipstick. Or a wig on an Anglo-Irish landowner.'

Silence for a moment or two, then he wheezed and chuckled, leant forward and began to unlace the surplus footwear which, you will remember, was a red cowboy boot only ankle-high.

'How long do you reckon?' he asked as he passed it to me.

'An hour on a rolling boil?'

'We'll see.'

I popped the article in the pan and the water immediately rose in a scummy froth around it.

'You should keep it skimmed,' he said.

At the end of the hour the cowhide was a shade floppier than before, but not in any real sense chewable. The long thong lace was more rewarding and we got down half each, winding it on the spoon like spaghetti.

Came first light and for once I was the first to awake. I looked around the small clearing we were in and sensed something familiar about it. Yes, there was one of the very few big redwoods on this side of the mountains. Yes, there was a drift of snow against its trunk, and yes, after I had scrabbled in it like a dog, a cairn of grit and small rocks . . .

I had the fire going again and the boot in the saucepan before Paddy woke up, I even managed to hack a few slices off the main body of the boot. We passed the saucepan between us, sharing too the one spoon we'd found in a pocket.

'Eddie, this is better than it was last night.'

'Stews usually improve if allowed to sit between heatings,' I replied.

'It has a meatier flavour, and even a whiskyish sort of a breath behind it.'

'Glad you like it, Paddy.'

He drank and chawed on and so did I, but as the fluid got lower, and the slices of leather which covered the bottom were taken out, it became clear to me that discovery was imminent.

'No need to finish it now, Paddy. Save some for this evening.'

'Now, what's this, Eddie? A couple of small bones.' He sucked the meat off them, and took a long slow look at them. Then he delved into the pan and came up with a bigger chunk.

'Shit, Eddie, this is a foot! One of them poor buggers' feet? Jesus, you're an evil son of a bitch making a cannibal of me. If I had my gun I'd blow your brains out, I swear to the Holy Mother I would, so help me . . . What's that you're saying?'

'Paddy, it's not a foot off one of those Indians, I swear.'

'So, whose foot is it?'

'Paddy . . . it's your foot. Your very own foot. And who I ask you has more right to draw sustenance from it than your very . . . Paddy? No. Oh no . . . !'

For the silly fool was sicking it all up, all that good nourishment, the best we'd had since the trout he'd caught in the brook, and worse than that he slung the contents of the pot way out as far as he could into the nearest snowdrift.

43

A gain, and without any justification at all to my way of thinking, he showed himself out of sorts with me, and lame though he was I was hard-pressed to keep up with him as he continued to dot and carry one down the trail the Forlorn Hope had made on their way up.

It was a nightmare journey, and, famished as we were, subject to illusions and fantasies. Most of what I remember I am sure actually occurred though I would not swear that my mind did not record some incidents as multiples of themselves. At times it seemed the trail was littered with bodies, though in fact it transpired there were not more than three or four on the way down. One, though, was Stanton, of that I am sure, propped against a silver birch, face almost as white as the bark, eye sockets empty from where the ravens had pecked them out, a coverlet of snow like a blanket on a cot pulled up to his chin, but with one hand clenched in a fist above it and in that fist a scrap of paper. It caused Paddy more distress than you would think possible, for the matter fed his obsession like that food the Bard speaks of that increases an appetite for itself, no matter how much of it you eat. He prised the paper from the dead Stanton's fingers, read it and wept, and then handed it to me.

Ah how that word my soul inspires
With holy, fond and pure desires!
   Maternal love, how bright the flame!
   For wealth of worlds I'd not profane
   Nor idly breathe thy sacred name
     My Mother.

When death shall close my sad career,
And I before my God appear,
   There to receive his last decree,
   My only prayer there will be
   Forever to remain with thee,
     My mother.

Of course I, who never knew my mother, could take a more rational and *critical* view of this effusion than Paddy could. For instance, in that second line why describe his desires for his mother as *pure*? Surely one could assume as much without being told? Does he protest too much? But these were thoughts I did not share with Patrick, who eventually folded the paper carefully and, brushing the snow away, thrust it inside Stanton's coat.

'Well,' he said at last, having recovered somewhat, 'at least he cannot be accused of having encompassed the deaths of the Indians Sutter lent him.'

'How's that then?'

'They were going up the mountain. To get help. They were further on than poor Stanton is. He died before they did.'

I supposed he was right. But there were others who showed signs of having been preyed upon not by the beasts and birds of the forest but by their companions.

'You cannot conceal the source of a wound made by a knife, especially if one edge is a saw,' Paddy remarked, 'nor how a bone has been shattered by an axe.'

However, he conceded that there were signs that these had died before being butchered, rather than, as was the case with the Indians, slaughtered for their meat.

Nevertheless, in spite of our condition, and urged on by the certainty we would come to where the main parties had holed out, and that with reasonable luck Tucker was still ahead of us and would have reached them with his mule train of supplies, we managed to press on, downhill now all the way, without resorting to the extreme measures taken by those whose path we were on. In this we were wonderfully helped by coming across the carcase of a bear, or at any rate the remains of one. It had already been well butchered but we were able to scrape enough frozen meat off what was left to make a better stew of it than that obtained from an old boot and a foot. I don't doubt it gave us the nourishment we needed to reach Lake Truckee, and a bit over, for we managed to hack out some scrag end of neck our predecessors had missed to take with us. As the old-timer said: 'Sometimes the bar eats you and sometimes you eat the bar.'

Next day – I think it was the next day – shortly after noon, we crossed a visual ridge and there below us, spread out, was a quite large, treeless snowfield which, on closer inspection, was seen to be for the most part a frozen lake on which snow had fallen intermittently for several weeks since it had iced up. There was an area around most of it where gentle slopes rose through sparse pine and spruce forest in such a way that one could imagine in spring through to autumn it was a meadow of grass cropped short by deer. And so we knew it to be, for we had passed it with Fremont and Carson some eighteen months earlier. Lake Truckee* at last.

We were still a mile away and three hundred feet or so above it and the first things we noticed, though they were by no means obvious, were humps of varying sizes, covered with enough snow to make their exact natures objects of speculation. They were placed between the lake and the main trail west, which was still, just, discernible, the one we had taken when we passed through with Fremont et al. but which the Forlorn Hope had ignored, possibly because they had known it to be blocked. One of these humps was quite large, as large as a small house; there was one similar but smaller abutting, and scattered around them some fifteen or so

* Since renamed Lake Donner. J. R.

smaller ones. Well, not to make too much a meal of it, these were respectively a cabin put up for the succour of travellers, a small annexe and the waggons of this part of the Donner Party. And for some time there was no sign of life, and then, as we watched, a tiny string of smoke twisted up into the air above the larger lump, blueish-white, hardly bending at all into the freezing, still air. Paddy sat on the trunk of a fallen pine and took up a pensive pose, chin on fist, elbow on knee.

'Well, should we not move down?' I asked, after a minute or so.

'Blessed if I know.'

'What's the problem?'

'There's no sign of Tucker. We're ahead of him. Whoever down there is still alive needs food. We have none to offer.'

I thought about that for a time during which a small cascade of snow fell from the side of the annexe to the biggest hump and two figures came out. At that distance we could make out very little of them: they were clad in brown stuff that could have been buckskin or fur, were hatted and gloved, and one carried an Arkansas Toothpick, the other a spade. They moved a short distance away from their abode and began to scrape snow back from something brown and red that lay in a shallow grave of snow. They hacked away weakly at it for some five minutes – clearly they were close to the end of any remaining store of energy they might have – and eventually managed to pull an arm clear from what we could now guess was a virtually dismembered body. Finally, with singular lack of conviction or real success, they attempted to rebury their colleague beneath a scattering of snow.

'None to offer?' I remarked at last. 'But plenty to take. They'll slaughter strangers as readily as they did Indians.'

Paddy looked up at me, eyes bloodshot and sad.

'Aye,' he said. 'Like as not. But maybe we should get a bit nearer. Nearer the trail anyway.' And he stood up.

The trail? He meant the trail east.

I followed him down the long slope for about ten minutes, which brought us to within a quarter of a mile of the encampment. We could see now how, in spite of recent but small falls of snow, the area around the hummocks was compacted, marked, and there were places where snow had been piled up in small heaps. There were coloured scraps – browns, greys, whites and reds – some of which one could not deny were bones and flesh. Four large crows, with beaks like the horns of anvils, squabbled over one of them. Every now and then one would rip away a shred and flap off thirty or forty paces to enjoy its prize unbothered by the others.

'It's a bummer,' said Paddy, shaking his head. 'We'll have to wait for Tucker.'

'Supposing he's turned back? Or lost?'

'We'll give him . . .' he gave it another moment's thought, 'a day. We have enough of Bruin to last us that long.' But he insisted we should withdraw back up the hill a bit to where the trees were thicker.

The next day was one of the longest of my life, bar those spent in sturrabins,* made worse by my private speculations as to what Patrick had in mind: did he mean to make contact with the starving wretches below us? Go up the trail to meet Tucker? Or press on downhill, back to the plains to the east? Although the last was clearly suicidal, I feared it was what he had in mind. Then, just as the sun was setting, and its rays in long, lance-like lines sifted through the darkening forest before shafting across the deep purpling gorges to the far distant summits of the Washoe Mountains, we heard a shout, and saw, winding down the trail, casting long shadows in front of them over the now lilac-tinted snow, a snaking line of men and horses. Tucker. I was straightway ready to rush down to meet them, but Paddy threw out a restraining hand.

'Hang about.' There was excitement in his voice. 'See what's at the back of them.'

I peered through the encroaching gloom and instantly saw what he was on about. For there, a hundred yards or so behind the last of the pack animals, was a donkey, still with the two big bundles strapped to each side of her back: Paquita! What a moke! As clever at getting through as I am.

'There's plenty of food for all of them on the other beasts. Paquita is ours, but if we want to get her to ourselves we must act with a touch of guile. For a start let's not join them till it's dark. There'll be confusion then, and plenty to occupy all their heads with what's down there already.'

* Cant for 'prisons'. J. R.

At this moment Tucker, still a couple of hundred yards short of the cabins, let out a shout, and quickly the effect was as if he had sounded the Last Trump on Judgement Day. As he and his party hurried ahead through the gloaming, the cabins opened up like graves, snow slid off the walls and eaves, doors creaked open, and figures as emaciated as skeletons long buried in tombs and graves staggered out, waving, gesticulating, falling on their knees, crying and moaning with joy and in some cases the pains of starvation. Presently a great fire was got going which the healthy men of Tucker's party were able to fuel with branches dragged from the wooded slopes, and above the flames a column of sparks rose into the night sky. The top layer of snow melted to slush around it and soon a couple of big pans were set on it to make a sort of thin gruel of cornflour and scraps of pemmican. Paddy and I edged closer and we could see the trouble Tucker and his men had keeping the poor wretches from scalding themselves or gorging themselves to a sudden death on unaccustomed food. Indeed, we too felt an almost irresistible urge to gorge ourselves though we had been partially starved for only a few days.

Into this maelstrom of self-absorbed activity Paddy and I merged and were scarce taken account of. Paddy quickly explained to Tucker, the flames of the fire playing over their faces, the pine twigs snapping and popping, the ghosts mopping and mowing around us, that we had been separated, and found ourselves on the track the Forlorn Hope had made, but high up in the mountains. Tucker told us how, much lower down, a mere twenty miles from Johnson's, they had found the seven survivors and sent them down with two of his men, before continuing up the main trail. He then added that he would be setting out for Alder Creek and the Donner faction at first light. The plan was that he would take all who were fit enough to travel back to Johnson's and Sutter's, leaving food for those who could not move easily until a second party could get up to them.

A little later we bedded down like sardines in the larger cabin, and, both warm and fed on civilised food, slept well. Nothing filtered through the foetid atmosphere save the snores of the healthy and the whimpering and occasional shouts of those plagued with the nightmares that would haunt them for the rest of their lives.

First light, and Tucker shouting instructions and giving orders. I shook Paddy's shoulder.

'Shouldn't we go with them?'

'No. We'll follow later. Go back to sleep.'

And then the slip-slop instead of clip-clop of horses pushing through the snow, the crack and creak of leather, and a short chorus of muted whoops and oaths as the riders mounted and got their beasts on the move.

A couple of hours later and this time it was Paddy shook my shoulder.

'O-K, Eddie, we'll get going now. No need to hurry though. Get some grub inside us first, get ourselves organised.'

Organised? What organising was there?

I stepped over the recumbent ghosts, wondering if any had died in the night, and followed him out on to the snow. A clear sky, and the crags and peaks like stage cutouts lit for a Drury Lane spectacular. The sunlight was blinding, the snow sparkling as if strewn with diamond dust, and I instantly feared a recurrence of that dreadful blindness we had suffered before, but Paddy was already striding up the slope and into the trees, and as he did, echoing from above us came that plaintive, once familiar and now welcome bellow of our faithful friend – eee-aw, eee-aw.

We came up to her, tethered to a tree, still with her packs attached to her back.

'How came she here?' I asked.

'Sure, was I brought her here. In the night.'

'Why?'

'You heard their plan, Eddie. They're going to take those that can walk back down to Sutter's. They'll need food for that. They're going to leave those that can't to take their chance here. They'll need food, too. They've been two weeks by my reckoning getting here and they've been eating all the way. It aint possible there's enough food left. So. They won't be ready to part with Paquita's load and we'll just have to take it.'

I gave it some thought. Paddy was driven, I knew, by his desire to get back to Tralee. I was driven by the thought of having only him to share Paquita's load with and not all Tucker's party and refugees.

'O-K', I said.

While all this was going on both outside and inside my head, Paddy was undoing one of Paqui's packs and took from it a Colt six-shooter, which he now stuck in his belt, beneath his coat.

'Where'd you get that from, Paddy?'

'Half-inched it off of one of Fremont's lot months ago. Glad to have it back, since you—'

'Since I lost your fucking rifle.'

Back at the larger shed we set about getting a fire going so we could brew us some coffee and grill a couple of twists.

By the time we had finished breakfast that limpid sky had filled with black cloud from the west and snow had begun to fall. Thick, heavy wodges of the stuff, so if you looked at what you could still see of the mountains beyond them, the illusion was that the flakes hung in the air and the mountains rose, with dizzying effect.

Clearly setting off now would be foolish, and indeed Tucker didn't return that day neither, nor night either, but it was not all bad news. Sitting in the bigger hut into the afternoon, with a candle going, two of Tucker's men, left behind by him to look after the invalids, brought out a pack of cards and suggested a game of euchre. Of course I joined in, and having extracted from the pack all the cards from six down and thereby given myself the chance to make some rearrangements in the order of things, proceeded to deal, asking as I did so: 'Well, gentlemen, what are the stakes?'

'Why, let's play for Mrs Graves's store of dollars. She has a couple of hundred in silver, I've heard say.'

'More, more,' came a voice from the steamy darkness beyond.

It was all a joke, but Mrs Graves, who was a tough-looking biddy, starving though she was, of about forty with long, black hair in ringlets, didn't take it as such and a little later pulled a beaver coat around her and shouldered her way out. I gave her three minutes then declared a need to have a piss, and, it still being daylight outside, though snowing, saw her three hundred yards or so off scrabbling at an outcrop of rocks beneath a broken pine near the lake. That'll do, I thought to myself, and before we set off in the morning I found her little cache and helped myself. Five hundred, to be honest, and a fat lot of use they were up there on the top of the Sierra Nevada.

We made a proper early start of it, though our progress was much hampered by the further foot or so of soft snow that had fallen. Many of the others had tried snowshoes, but few of them got the hang of them, and certainly not me, nor Paddy with his wooden stump. Still, with Paquita's help we managed without.

And, of course, Tucker too had got away from Alder Creek not long after dawn, and so it was just about halfway between the two camps that we met. The trail was serpentine and the edge of it away from the creek weaved its way round boulders, and what with that and the muffling effect of the snow, we were not aware of how close they were before they were upon us. Tucker, at the front, raised his palm in salutation.

'Well, lads,' he called, 'this is mighty generous thinking on your part, for I suppose that you thought we might run short and so you have come for us.'

He had five of his own men behind him and five or six from the Alder Creek camp, including women and children, one of whom was clearly very sick, and, if she had been left, once dead, was likely to be skewered and grilled like her cousins. Donner kebab.

'But we're O-K, you know?' he continued, 'and if you fall in with us we'll go back together.'

'No, Captain Tucker, that's not our intention,' said Patrick. 'Was made clear, was it not, we were to head on east after we had done what we could to help you?'

'Not with that moke and her cargo, you don't, Mr Coffey.'

And his hand began to swing towards the long-barrelled holstered pistol that hung from his saddle. However, Patrick surprised him, and me almost as much, by moving much quicker and coming up with his six-cylinder Colt, and shooting the army man's hat clean off without so much as grazing his scalp.

'I've five more shots in me locker, Tucker, so I guess you'll let us pass. And I see at the back of your train you have a saddled-up horse with no rider or load, so I'm thinking I'll be taking that too.' He turned to me. 'Ride on past them, Eddie, secure that nag and bring it back here.'

I did as I was told, gave Paquita a kick and a wallop, got to the end of the line, and then back. Paddy handed me the Colt and while he heaved himself up into the saddle I kept a bead on Tucker, then, with some relief handed it back to him.

'Women and children may starve because of this,' Tucker said, palms still stretched out on either side of his waist.

'But not us,' said Paddy, and spurred past him.

I followed, but as I went, I said: 'All he wants is to see his mother in Ireland before she dies of the potato famine.'

'His mother be fucked,' said Captain Tucker.*

* There are many accounts of the Donner Party, but the main source is *History of the Donner Party* by C. F. McGlashan, who, some twenty-five to thirty years after the event, interviewed all the survivors and printed their diaries, as well as reproducing relevant contemporary newspaper accounts and so on. A second revised edition was printed in 1880 of which a facsimile was produced by Stanford University Press, California, with introductions and other features by its editors George H. Hinkle and Bliss McGlashan Hinkle, in 1940, revised in 1947. I bought a copy at the Donner Museum in 1999.

Optimists still look for Mrs Graves's dollars by the lake; maybe if they read this they'll save themselves the bother.

There was a lot more to the whole affair than appears in Eddie's account, but what is here seems to be by and large accurate in so far as it refers to those parts of the tragedy he and Paddy apparently intruded upon. J. R.

44

'I aint no hand for trouble
But I'll die before I run . . .'

chortled Paddy, as our steeds slowed to a trot and then a walk to accommodate the slope which steepened for a hundred yards or so. Then he cocked his ear for a moment, checking there was no one careering behind us in pursuit before going on: 'Focking good shot, eh, Eddie?'

'You could've killed him.'

'But I didn't. You see, Eddie, in all those years I was a mountain man I had occasion more than once to shoot the head off a rattlesnake to save my life, so I learnt the art.'

We followed the trail and the creek for a couple of hours before passing the Alder Creek camp. It was still occupied by those Tucker had judged too ill to move. A wisp of smoke rose from a small fire burning and there was a pile of firewood too. A skeletal woman, grey hair wispy, eyes sunken, shawls and blankets wrapped round her scarecrow frame, poked her head out and watched us pass.

From then on the trail dropped quite steeply and as it did the vegetation slowly shifted from pine and fir, etiolated and scattered across the rocky mountainside, to scattered redwoods and evergreen oak and finally, as we neared the north-west corner of the big lake,*

* Lake Tahoe. J. R.

383

some broad leaf too and juniper in abundance. But it was different from the west side. The vegetation lower down was not as thick, there was less snow the lower we got, yet if anything it was colder.

We skirted the lake in a day or so and finally dropped out of the Sierra and back on to the plain, the Great Basin as it is called. We headed north across snowfields until we reached the Marias/Humboldt River which took us east. Ridge after ridge of mountains seemed to bar our way but the river always took us round them, crossing wide plains part filled with shallow, frozen lakes, but day by day it got better, the thaw slowly set in, the snow turned to slush and rain. Out on those plains, with the big mountains ten miles or more away but dominating the horizon, we watched, in the afternoons especially, the huge clouds gather, white marble palaces piled into the sky above, densely black below with curtains and pillars of rain beneath them, and then, as it swept over us, cold, thick and penetrating, with lightning and crashing thunder, we huddled into coats and pulled our hats down. But in the mornings the sun shone, the wet steamed a little, what had been grey and black the evening before took on hues of red soil and rock, meadows and the big rushes called tule greened up, sprouting feathery plumes for flowers, and patches of yellow sunlight floated over it all.

The birds were returning too. Crane, duck, geese, waterfowl of all sorts and again Patrick took to cursing me for losing his rifle: indeed, he had a point, our main, almost only diet being the jerk and maize flour Paquita carried in her two large sacks. However, as the spring continued to unfold and wildlife became more apparent and abundant, things got better. Paddy put together the means to make traps in the ways the Indians he had known in the Rockies had taught him, and once or twice a week he was successful and we dined royally off redhead or canvasback ducks and smaller birds as snipe and phalarope, and soon, by means of snares, there were fresh young rabbit as commons whenever we felt like it.

And people too. To begin with they had been around us in ways we had not observed or understood. Where there was timber, juniper mostly, the Indians, especially the Washoe, lived through the winter in quite large huts that were part subterranean: the floors were four feet or so beneath the surface and on them a timber frame was constructed, large enough to require vertical supports inside, which was then filled in with branches and in the upper parts brush and tule.

Finally, the whole structure was made weatherproof with clods and earth which also had the effect of rendering the structure almost invisible as such from a distance unless the fire within was emitting smoke.

We were invited into one such palace for a night and found it stuffily hot and humid. The Washoe go naked much of the time: out of prelapsarian or at any rate pre-evangelisation innocence. They gave us a feast of which the main component was a brace of Canada geese accompanied with a sort of mess of dried berries, ground acorn, nuts and pine kernels, kept over from the previous autumn. Dessert was crunchy ovals, the size of a small finger, very sweet and fragrant, made from the nectar-bearing parts of the tule flowers. I was disconcerted to find these intentionally harboured grasshoppers and the like. Paddy told me not to be so namby-pamby about them.

The evening concluded with a dance accompanied by flutes and drums to celebrate the return of spring. All very jolly and not untouched with mystery, too, in that cavern of a building, lit only by the fire and a few lamps, with the people painted up for the occasion in ochre, red, black and white swirls that lent their bodies and faces an expressive grace that was not always apparent in broad daylight. For all their nakedness they were decorous in their behaviour.

By the time we were rounding the northern end of the Shoshone Mountains the clans were already leaving these halls and moving out into the wide valleys where they built the smaller, domed huts we had seen on our way out.

They played a sort of football, too, the men that is, while waiting for the women to bring armfuls of rushes up from the lakeside, but not in a way that Paddy approved. For a start they only had one goal though they did have two teams of some fifteen or more young men and youths. These lined up in two parallel lines with about thirty yards between each player, so each line was not far off a mile long. Each team had its own ball, sewn buckskin stuffed with feathers. On a given signal the two players furthest from the goal each kicked his team's ball to the next who then brought it under control and kicked it to the next, and so on, down the line, to the last player who had to kick it through the goal. And the team whose ball went through the posts first was the winner. Those who had been stationed furthest from the goal followed the balls down the line so that when they reached the last two men all were there to cheer on their own kickers.

'This will not do,' Paddy cried, and dismounting limped amongst them, shouting and waving his arms, and suddenly I was put in mind of the way, back in 1812, this same man, then a young sergeant in the Connaughts, had organised a football tournament within the allied army, English, Germans, Irish, Scots, Spanish and Portuguese. Of course, he could not be understood but there were too a couple of braves who had ventured as far as Fort Laramie in the past and picked up a smattering of French and English which they mixed together like a pudding. Within half an hour they had the hang of it and were happy to kick the ball about to the manner born. I believe they really did rate this game better than their own since each player got many more than just the one go.

All of which was a distraction to what was happening a mere quarter of a mile away to the east.

It is a commonly held belief, fostered by such journals as the *Illustrated London News*, that waggon trains proceed in single file, one behind another. However, where the land is flat and uniform, they actually form up in line abreast, and they do this in order to avoid travelling in the dust of the waggons in front, to keep out of the ruts already made, or churned-up mud. And at the moment when the men of the Snow Goose tribelet had scored a decisive goal and were congratulating themselves with cartwheels and mutual embraces, just such a line of waggons was ploughing through their partially constructed summer village of some thirty or so huts. Clearly, to redeploy into line ahead to get round them would have been too much trouble.

The waggons, forty of them, drawn by teams of oxen, were moving at their customary pace over good ground, that is a steady two miles an hour, with scarce more than a yard between them, and were thus as irresistible and as calamitous as the god Jagganath or Juggernaut whose cart crushes willing pilgrims in Puri in Orissa. Some of the older women who were in or near the huts, looking after small children, were crushed, and the whole half-built village was levelled to the surface of the plain.

The waggon master, who was roughly in the middle, was drunk. He was Bavarian by origin I would guess, with short ginger hair and a huge moustache, but probably second-generation American since he was singing raucously, in a very deep voice, in an accented English.

The chief of the Snow Geese, whose name translated as He-who-shows-the-way, now stood firmly in front of this waggon, arms raised in a 'V' above his head, legs spread. The message was clear . . . Stop! I'd like a word with you! None of us was, as I thought, armed. Why should we be? You don't take bows and arrows with you to a football game.

The waggons rumbled on, wheels squealing. And the waggon master lifted up the rifle that was propped beside him, took brief aim, pulled back the pan and fired. He-who-shows-the-way dropped with a hole in his forehead and a splatter of blood, bone and brain blasted from the back.

Patrick, at least, was armed. He took the Washoe chief's place, feet apart, thumbs in his belt close to the butt of his Colt six-shooter. At the same time a lad on the driver's bench next to the Bavarian handed him a second rifle, took the first and began to reload it. The oxen came to a standstill a couple of yards in front of us and the rest of the line followed suit and pulled up too. Stand-off. I moved a yard or so to the side so as not to offer Patrick any distraction. He was angry, very angry. I knew the signs: his face pale in so far as it was visible through and around his great beard; his eyes narrowed; a very slight shake in his hands.

'What de fock did you do dat for?' he demanded of the Bavarian gentleman.

'Ah. A native of the Irish bogland. Out of my way . . . Mick! Trust a mick to go native.'

'What de fock did you do dat for?' Patrick repeated, and his right hand moved so it rested on the butt of the Colt.

'Does it matter? He was a naked heathen of a fucking Injun. The only good Injun is a dead Injun—'

Bang! Patrick's hand had moved like a snake's strike and the ball from the Colt smacked into waggon master's right shoulder.

'Dat was no accident,' he called, his voice carrying above the wounded man's scream. 'Make a gap in your line and let us through or the next one's in your head.'

Waggon master's sidekick got the message, took the reins and moved the waggon forward but to the side. At a gesture from Patrick those on each side followed suit. We all, Patrick, me, and the Washoe braves and their women, walked through the gap, four of the braves taking up the body of He-who-shows-the-way.

Some of the women moved through the ruined village, searching for children and grannies still missing. Presently a slow, high keening rose into the air as four or five bodies were found. Behind us waggon wheels began to squeal again and a long bank of rolling dust soon hid them from our sight. Paddy stood on his own, some hundred yards away, long coat flapping slightly in a breeze that had got up. His gaze seemed to be fixed on an undulating line of a hundred or so 'wavies', snow geese, white with black primaries, heading north, towards the Matterhorn-shaped mountain. You could, if you were so inclined, imagine that the spirit of He-who-shows-the-way was up there amongst them. Presumably near the front.

'Get the animals, Eddie. We'll be on our way.'

'Right now?'

'Right now. We're bad luck here. They won't want us around any longer than we have to be. Anyway . . .'

'Anyway?'

'I just want to get the fuck out of this fucking country as quick as I can.'

45

And move we did. Paddy drove us on so fast I scarcely noticed what we went through, what landscapes, what towns, what adventures, what people we met. Of course some impressions were so strong they do remain with me to this hour, and it is those I shall now relate as quickly as I can, for to be honest with you, Mr Murray, I am now a touch tired of this whole business especially following the rebuff decisive I received from your clerk this morning. I now have but one arrow left in my quiver, one shot in my locker, to save me from utter destitution – the Garth Papers. Tomorrow morning Mr Guppy of Henge and Carboy will take me to the place where he secretly deposited them on my behalf and I shall then see what I can do with them to raise the wind, and if not the wind, why then the whirlwind. Meanwhile . . .

Meanwhile, we crossed the Great Salt Lake Desert, then the Great Divide (Americans are exceedingly free with the word 'great' and would make everything about their country 'great' if they could) and so into the Great Plains, where, with the Rockies still in view behind us, the lower slopes colouring up with the vibrant not to say gaudy hues of autumn, the first event that marked my memory occurred.

We were crossing a hugely extensive but undulating prairie, des- iccated by the hot months preceding, the dry grasses rattling in the hot breeze, when we saw, rolling towards us, a long line of billowing, brick-coloured dust maybe a hundred feet high and still a clear league or more away.

'We should,' I called to Paddy, who was as usual fifty paces or more ahead of me, 'get out of the way.' I had in mind that this was yet another waggon train in line abreast.

He turned in his saddle, looked over his shoulder.

'The line is too long. They are coming too quick. An outcrop of rock would serve better to protect us.'

'What are they? What's happening?'

'Buffalo. There could be as many as five thousand.'

'Oh shit.'

By now the ground was trembling as if the earth quaked, and what had been a distant rumbling rose to something like a deep-throated roar. Paddy veered off to his right and I followed: he'd spotted a couple of thorn bushes on a rise, and yes there were some whale-backed rocks, mottled with yellow lichen, rising at their highest point to three feet or so above the earth around them. We sheltered in the midst of this natural defence and waited – but not for long. Almost immediately we could see the black-bearded, wedge-shaped faces, pulled in below their humps, the wicked curving though short horns coming out of the cloud.

'Dismount,' Paddy shouted, above the wrack of the storm, 'and tie your reins to the bush.'

I was loth to do so. Some irrational corner of my will insisted I was safer on Paquita's back than beside her, but my friend was already down and I followed suit. He was right of course. As soon as our animals were properly aware of what was bearing down on them, they pranced and kicked and shied, and did all they could to break free and run ahead of the onslaught.

Our little bastion served its purpose well enough and the flood of wild cattle parted in front of us save for maybe half a dozen, heifers and young males for the most part, which stumbled and bumbled into our sanctum. One, a cow, a mother perhaps, followed her offspring and swung her sharps at us, pummelled the ground with her hooves. Use your six-shooter, your Colt, I prayed at Patrick, but he would not – he merely spread his arms, flapped his long coat, pranced inso-far as his wooden foot would let him, took off his hat and semaphored with that, and she soon took fright and nudging her errant child with her forehead got it and herself back into the maelstrom.

That calf survived – and not because it was particularly fit (though it had shown intelligence in searching out our bolthole), but because its mother's soul was imbued with that sweetest and noblest of emotions, a mother's love. Considering this now, and in the light of what I have picked up from discourse with Mr Darwin, I would rewrite the engine of transmutation thus: it is not the fittest who survive but those whose fitness is most congruent with survival.

The first whose plight evidenced a foe behind them, and the nature of that foe, was a great bull, with a huge hump, and sweeping horns larger than most. His mask and shoulders were flecked with blood which, from some deep wound, he heaved in gouts over his protruding and dead-white tongue. He stumbled to his knees, raised his head and uttered one last, long, deep-throated challenge, choked off by a tide of dark, smoking blood, to the god which had brought him to this pass, before rolling over on his side. And now we could see what had brought him low – two gunshot wounds behind his shoulder, near his heart, no doubt penetrating his lungs. And I make no doubt it was his very fitness, his size, the glossy blackness of his furry hair, the magnificence of his horns and hump that had attracted the attention of his murderer.

Above the receding roar of thousands and thousands of hooves we heard the crack of rifle fire and could see, from the waist up, the torsos and heads of the buffaloes' tormentors and executioners. Hats, their brims flattened by speed, rifles and pistols flourished above their heads, grew sharp against the dust and then, like ghosts, were hazed again. Their banshee howls of triumph and blood-lust struck cold in our hearts, and as they came closer so too did their faces, twisted and contorted into expressions of ferocity and hellish delight.

There must have been thirty of them and they had a simple routine whereby those in front loosed off their pieces at point-blank range and then let their steeds drift back while they reloaded and those behind took their place. They surged past, paying us as little attention as their quarries had, and as the sounds and dust of the slaughter rolled away from us, left us facing a yet more horrid sight. Scattered over the prairie were their dead and dying victims, like the black rocks of a storm-tossed coast at low tide, receding into a distance of at least two miles where another cloud of dust marked the progress of the waggon train their killers had come from. Many buffaloes still bellowed with pain as they strove to get upright again, some bobbing and weaving and stumbling on broken limbs, and occasionally a calf, apparently unhurt, wandered through the carnage, wailing for its parent. Above this wide river of death the vultures and other carrion seekers circled the quadrants of a hazy sky and on its banks coyotes yapped and howled.

There were perhaps some four dozen waggons, spread out again in line abreast, and proceeding at their customary slow pace so it was possible for the women to run ahead into the field of death ahead of them. They did not linger long over the carcases. An arm thrust into the dead beast's mouth, a yank, and a slice were enough to free the flaccid muscle of the tongue which, with hands and forearms reeking as horribly as any Lady Macbeth's, they then folded into a basket or their capacious aprons before moving on to the next. None took more than three or four, and that was all they took, though we did see some older men using their Arkansas Toothpicks to cleave out the hump ribs of the smaller animals.

I feared a confrontation like the last, but the gaps were wide enough this time for us to slip through unmolested and leave us picking our way through the river of death that still extended a further mile or so back east across the prairie.

Interlude VI*

An Addendum to the Treasury Solicitor's Report on the Enquiry made into Darwinian Transmutation†

FOR ATTENTION AND EYES ONLY OF LORD PALMERSTON, HER MAJESTY'S SECRETARY OF STATE FOR HOME AFFAIRS

We have now read all of Charles Darwin's *Foundation*, which appears to be a draft of his theory of transmutation, and, placing it in the context of the many articles on similar and related themes that have appeared in the *Westminster Review* and other periodicals, together with many pamphlets and so forth issuing from the presses of the more extreme factions within the Working Classes, we feel we can assess the danger it represents with some confidence. We shall in due course present our findings in a full and proper manner but, herewith, at your request, is a digest or summary presented informally and for your Lordship's eyes only.

---

* I have placed this here for no better reason than that its contents cast a dark light over Eddie's speculations above concerning 'fitness' and 'survival'. J. R.

† This would appear to be the digest of a report submitted to Lord Palmerston by a small committee of civil servants, possibly aided by the advice of 'experts', with a remit to look into the nature and potential of transmutation theories. J. R.

Our main conclusion is this: that while the malcontents in our society who would ride on the backs of the Working Classes to positions of power with all the emoluments that go with them, point, amongst other concerns, to the current theories of transmutation to support their contention that a hierarchical form of society, based on property, manners, education and breeding, and sustained by a judiciary, a police force and, where necessary, a military loyal to its principles, is not God-given or sanctioned by God, it is our belief that these same theories of transmutation interpreted correctly, also offer support for the *status quo* rather than otherwise. Furthermore, we would suggest, that for reasons outlined below, the Queen's realm may well stand in need for such support.

There is no point, my lord, in denying the efficacy of the recent and continuing attacks on revealed religion, that appear almost daily in the proceedings of learned societies, most of them held correctly in the highest repute (we have in mind the Royal Society and the Royal Geographical Society to name but two). It is now very evident indeed that we can no longer look to religion or tradition as the bulwarks of an ordered society where all know their place and are happy to keep to it. Such are the effects over the last century or so first of identification of fossil finds, and their dating, followed by the work of geologists who place the distant origins of our planet at many thousands of millennia rather than the mere five thousand eight hundred and fifty-three years adduced by Bishop Ussher. We have also taken into consideration the questioning of the authenticity of miracles, the Virgin birth, the Resurrection, and even the deity of Christ, which in turn have spawned such dissenting sects as the Unitarians and Deists. We need not rehearse the consequences of all these, your Lordship is already well aware of them, but not least amongst them has been the undermining of both Church and Holy Writ as the unquestionable founts of knowledge and wisdom.

To be brief, it would do the State no harm if a whole new scheme of things could be put together which would as effectively support the way things are as Ecclesiastical Authority did in the past and it is our belief that just such a scheme might be constructed out of the current theories of transmutation, and that they may be used as readily on the side of law and order as against it.

As we understand it the first premise of transmutation theories is that all life, in all its multifarious forms, finds its root and origin in one (or a very small number) lowly single-celled life form, a sort of protozoic form, much like the scum on a pond, on the edge of a sea so rich in those minerals necessary for life as to have been a sort of *soup* or *protozoic slime*. Some of this slime then suffered a change in environment which threatened the extinction of all but those cells that had characteristics that enabled them to resist the new threat. The rest died, those remaining bred amongst themselves and thereby strengthened their life-preserving characteristics to such an extent that in time they could be seen to have become altogether new species. This transmutation eventually made the original a multi-celled creation, in which separate cells became dedicated to particular functions not available to the simpler forms, some perhaps being sensitive to light, others to the presence of nutritious elements in the surrounding soup, and yet others, through the production of microscopic hair or *cilia*, providing means of locomotion. And so on. It is proper then to call these later forms *higher* than their originals by reason not only of their greater complexity but also their ability to live longer, reproduce more certainly and so forth.

This process, according to the transmutationists' theories, endlessly repeated, caused the appearance of life forms ever higher until we reach MAN. With man the process stops, or rather undergoes a fundamental change. With man, in a broadly physical way the peak of what we may still call creation as readily as we call it transmutation, is achieved. The evolution of a higher being is inconceivable. Man is made in God's image. However, within the realm of man, there are gradations as clear cut as those that exist between the beasts and plants around us. The mechanisms of transmutation continue to exercise their influence. Some races of men are superior to others, some forms of society and even whole civilisations are clearly superior to those that are more primitive. No one can deny the superiority of the English over, say, the French, of the European over the African, of the white man over the jew and the jew over the negro.

Now let us focus on the English nation. It is divided and sub-divided again and again according to occupation and occupation is decided by innate ability. An Irish navvy is a lower being than a Yorkshire coal-miner; the coal-miner than the engineer who devises the tools used in a mine, the lifting gear and so forth; the engineer in turn gives way to the scholar and gentleman, who are as a class inferior to, though they are the begetters of, Holders of her Majesty's Commission. The Nobility and the Priesthood crown this pyramid, below Royalty alone. And we think we may now argue that this Chain of Being may equally be seen as the result of transmutation as readily as we ascribe it to God as revealed in Holy Writ, by Tradition, Heritage, and the Teachings of Our Mother the Church. Those who are superior are superior because transmutation inevitably causes those who may most suitably take their place at the High Table of Life to do just that. They are there because they are, of all men, the fittest to be there.

Further to this two of our members, the others dissenting, suggest that within transmutation lies justification for treating the natives of our colonies as different, lower life forms incapable of speculative thought or aesthetic discrimination, and therefore, quite properly, our servants. It was also pointed out that transmutation theory also suggests a rational plan for improving the stock of our nation by selective breeding and sterilisation of defective individuals.

We are conscious that this is all speculation, but speculation with a sound foundation until proved to be error, and on this basis we should recommend that for the time being at any rate, any move against the transmutationists in general and Mr Darwin in particular should be postponed *sine die*.

We remain your Lordship's humble and obedient servants,*

Accepted, P.

* No signatories appear at the end of this copy. J. R.

396

46

We left behind us those black, boulder-like lumps, over whose darkening blood, dull eyes, black mouths and nostrils the gilded flies of summer coalesced. Movement through time and distance brought an accelerated greening, a flowering up of the rolling prairies: there were still wide spaces in both dimensions when and where the bison floated like tubby dark caravels through grasses tall enough to hide their limbs; when small groups of braves in feathered bonnets trotted by with a single hand raised in greeting, where untouched woodland, filled first with blossom then rich foliage, sheltering antelope and deer, bears and wolves, climbed the hillsides or hemmed the rivers.

But as we approached the great waterway, how flat and insipid seemed the fields, some as big I should have thought as whole counties in England, of green wheat and, at the southern extremes of our pilgrimage, Indian corn or maize; how ravaged the hillsides which had been clear-felled for timber; how intrusive, in comparison with the low cones of teepees that melt into their surroundings, the squalid little villages of clapboard houses, rutted roads, shops each filled with precisely the same goods from the manufactories of the east, and the chapels old Billy Blake so aptly thought of as dark Satanic Mills,* clustered on the banks of the rivers.

* Eddie, surprisingly, is probably right. This is a disputed crux though Blake himself makes it clear enough. Later in the same poem, *Milton*, we have

We crossed at St Louis where I was saddened and gladdened by the memory of Kate all those years ago, but found little there to remind me of her. It was enormously changed not least because it was ten times larger! The immediate environs remained as messy, unfinished and generally nasty as the whole place had been ten years (or was it eleven?) earlier, and were circled with shantytowns where immigrants gathered and wondered how much further they had to go to find lives better than the ones they had left. However, the centre was now paved, there was an opera house or theatre, a city hall, big department stores, and hotels whose apparent luxury and grandeur, all gilded and framed with stuccoed statuary, aped those of Paris or London. The better sort rode in sprung carriages, and their ladies carried trimmed parasols somewhat comically above headgear and boas constructed from ostrich feathers more daring in their abundance than anything an Indian chief ever wore. And more barbaric.

Because we were determined to hold on to Mrs Graves's five hundred dollars to pay for our passages back to England and Ireland, we were in a situation Paddy particularly found bothersome. In the army forty years earlier he had been fed and clothed, while the pittance he was paid kept him in tobacco and spirits. Anything that was left he sent back to Mother in Tralee; later, as a mountain man, he had shot, caught or gathered what he needed to eat and even the materials for much of what he wore – his other necessaries he had bartered furs for. Consequently he found living in a cash economy without actually hiring himself out to work (and who would employ a man of sixty with a foot short of the full set?) deeply irksome and even humiliating. While I was happy to stand on a street corner with a penny whistle accompanying him as he sang 'The Wild Rover' or 'The Rose of Tralee', he was not. No question, it was time to sell my small handful of tiny gold nuggets.

'A. Finkelstein & Son – We buy anything!!!' was the legend across the dusty window of a pawnbroker in an alley, possibly originally a

'And the Mills of Satan . . . Where Satan, making to himself Laws from his own identity, / Compelled others to serve him in moral gratitude and submission, / Being call'd God, setting himself above all that is called God . . .' which is not to say Blake did not have the factories of industrialising England in mind, but he is using them as metaphors for the nonconformist chapels which condemned imagination, sexuality and so on. J. R.

mews, at the back of the opera house. Inside, a middle-aged man stood behind the counter in front of as weird an array of objects as you can imagine. There were Redskin artefacts, carved whalebones, framed lithographs and engravings, two huge piles of old clothes, guns with bent or blown barrels . . . The man himself wore an unusual sort of quarter moon-shaped cardboard shade above his eyes, spectacles and a striped apron over his white shirt. His hands were splayed on the counter-top on either side of the newspaper he was reading and within reach of them on one side was a single-shot, long-barrelled Colt, and on the other a hunting gun with most of the barrel shorn off. He looked up at me.

'Buying or selling?'

'Selling.'

'Take a running jump.'

Carefully I let the gold beads trickle out of my fist on to the counter. His lips tightened, perhaps his rate of respiration went up, but those were the only signs of excitement he allowed himself. From a drawer on his side of the counter he extracted a pair of fine tweezers and from a shelf a small glass saucer. Carefully he chose one of the smallest nuggets and put it on the saucer. Then he looked down at me.

'Take the rest with you. I'm going to test this by the fire method which will take an hour. Come back then and if the test has shown what I think it will then I'll buy the lot off you.'

So I went back out and Paddy and I went into the main square in front of the opera and busked for twenty minutes before some jumped-up job's worth in a uniform moved us on. Even so we got together seventy-three cents which bought me a glass of milk and Paddy a couple of shots of Van Winkel bourbon in a bar round the corner. When the hour was up I went back to the pawnbroker leaving Paddy negotiating a third tot on tick.

The first thing Finkelstein did was ask for the rest of the nuggets. This time he held out a small polished metal shovel and I tipped them into it. Then he fetched down a pair of balances, slipped the nuggets into one pan and, using tiny weights in the other, got them to rise and fall to almost the same level.

'A few grains under two ounces, fine, I'll give you thirty dollars.'*

* As usual, Eddie was done. The official price was $20.6 per fine ounce. J. R.

I agreed, and with some regrets watched him tip the tiny glittering shower into a small, soft leather bag. Then he counted out the dollars. As he did two men came through the door and stood behind me.

'Errgh! Naow isn't dis jus' d' ting. Me old friend Eddie the monkey man. I taut it must be your honour, from what young Finkelstein here tol' me of you, but I wud not believe it till I saw yer wi' me own eyes.'

Shit. Seamus.

'Turn around, Eddie, and look at me.'

I did as I was told.

He'd aged. Had not we all? His hair was now pure white, apart from the dirt and grease, though his eyebrows remained pitch black. His face was thinner with a red hectic on the cheekbones and hollows beneath, and not a lot of teeth. His frame too looked somehow slighter so I felt that if push came to shove I might physically match him, though not in the presence of his companion. This was a huge sombreroed Mexican with a big moustache, a pistol in his belt on one side and a knife sheath on the other. He was poking his nails with the knife, an evil-looking, daggerish sort of a weapon.

'Dis, Eddie, is your chance to pay me back for me gold yer took all those years ago. No, I am not a-goin' to take your dollars, for Mr Finkelstein here has said he'd rather I did not. But all I want to hear is where the gold you brought with you came from. Mind you, I want it exact. Exactly where it came from. Unnerstan'?'

Those huge eyebrows took a questioning walk up his forehead.

'For if you do not then Pedro here will help by cutting one of your ears off,' he added. 'Just for starters like.'

Pedro grinned at me, flashing as much gold from his mouth as I had just sold.

Well, I had no intention of going back to California and benefitting myself from the knowledge, so what did I have to lose more valuable than an ear?

'The far side of the Sierra Nevada. North-east of the bay. Look for Johnson's Ranch and Sutter's Fort. There's a river runs off the mountains called the Colluma, Colluma Valley. By now they're probably building a sawmill somewhere up it. Anyway, that's where I found it. The gold.'

Well, I don't know how Seamus improved his lot with this information. Maybe he went out there himself. Maybe he sold it. Maybe he got in with the waggon train masters who profited by it with promises to the immigrants. But that was the last I saw of him – he was headed, in mind at least, due west and I had no desire to go anywhere but east.

But I tell you one thing. I reckon it was there in that pawnbroker's I started the Great Californian Gold Rush and thereby ensured that California was populated with as scary a mass of rapscallions and scallywags as you'll find anywhere in the world . . . outside Whitechapel and Spitalfields.

I went back to the bar, settled Paddy's slate and ordered a half-pint of rotgut for us to share and a slice each of what was described as buffalo pie. While we were waiting to be served a lad dressed like a clown came in and left a throwaway on the counter. I pulled it towards me so I could read it. It was a blotchy presentation – different alphabets for each line, illustrations either crude or borrowed from one of the sets of small plates printers use to embellish posters, ballads and the like.

'Joshua Dawkins's Travelling Show, Marvels of derring-Do to escite [sic] and friten the Whole family. Full meenagerie, the strangest beats to be found in six incontinents. Last three days before we head east for the Xmass Facilities in Philly. Find us in Tom's Meadow on the Louisville Trail.'

Straight away I saw the possibilities.

'We should have a look at that,' I suggested.

'Eddie, you're a dumb idjit.'

'So you like to say. But don't you see? This is company for us all the way if we can get them to take us on. Food, accommodation, maybe some pay too. And protection.'

'All the way? As far as Louisville?'

'Paddy, can you not read? Facilities in Philly?'

'What the fuck is d' meaning of dat?' He was getting ratty the way you do when whatever you say is made to seem stupid.

'Festivities, Paddy. Christmas festivities in Philadelphia. We can get a boat out of Philly.'

'We can? I thought New York . . .'

'The river, Paddy. The Delaware. Whatever else it is, Philly is a port . . .'

He drank, ate, chewed it over along with the gristle in the pie.

'And what do we offer ourselves as?'

'I've seen you shoot. No one shoots like you do. I'd have been dead in the wars, I'd have been dead in the mountains if you didn't shoot the way you do.'

'Aye, Eddie. About that you're right, sure enough,' and he pulled the six-shooter from his belt and thumped it on the counter. Our neighbours all backed off.

'Steady boys,' the barman muttered.

'So what will *you* do while I come on like a gunslinger?' Patrick gave me a long, slow look. There was a hint of what? Something sardonic in his little blue eyes.

'Eddie,' he answered himself, 'we'll tink of sumting. Never you fear.'

We found them all right, a half-mile outside the city boundary, on the Louisville Trail, in a hay meadow already cut, six small tents, six waggons and six cages on wheels behind a circular enclosure of hurdles with flags of all nations and a pair of Old Glories flanking the entrance and a big swag of red, white and blue linking the posts. Inside this ring, which was about thirty-six feet* across, were two banks of benches, at twenty cents a place, and you could stand outside the hurdles and look over the heads of the moneyed classes inside for just five cents.

'First, we check it out,' said Patrick, and indicated I should find the ten cents that gave us standing room.

It was a sultry, late summer afternoon, thunder crackling behind the distant hills, the big evergreen oaks beyond the ring looking as heavy and solid as rock. There were few spectators, maybe thirty, mostly women and children, the men still out in the fields making a start on the harvest. The women gossipped, the children ran about screaming, a vendor walked about with a tray of toffee-apples and candies and another sold sarsaparilla from a pitcher, pouring the liquid into a small, communally shared cup. A preacher man handed out pamphlets declaring the show was obscene, an affront to Jehovah and a signpost to hell for poor sinners. He actually got two women, clearly already known to him, to turn back and go home.

The show started, twenty minutes late, with a bugle call from the tents pitched at the back of the ring. A couple of kids dressed as

* Just over eleven metres. J. R.

402

pierrots pulled back a hurdle and in came the parade led by Joshua Dawkins, no less, dressed in a top hat, a red frock coat, a high collar that was brushed by the points of a big waxed moustache, a huge black stock round his neck, white breeches and calf-high boots. A raggle-taggle of clowns with three genuine dwarfs ran round the inside of the ring, cartwheeling, wheelbarrowing each other, and generally tumbling about while an accordion joined the bugler and played 'The Stars and Stripes for Ever'. Then the show got under way.

A woman whom age had withered did some bareback riding on a white pony whose trot was the slowest we'd ever seen. A browned-up, turbanned imitation of an oriental made an elephant take in water from a bucket and blow it over the crowd. Then, encouraged by her mahout, she went down on her front knees to signify apology. A strongman bent iron bars. The clowns came back and fooled about with buckets of water, flour, ladders, planks and so forth. The finale had four genuine Cossack horsemen, wearing Redskin clothes and carrying tomahawks, careering around on black ponies, slicing withies held up for them by the clowns, one of whom we now noticed had lost a hand at the wrist. We could guess how. Then all the performers took a bow and Mr Dawkins invited us to parade along what he called the Street of Wonders, behind the tents. No extra fee.

This was the line of six cages. The fattest woman in the world – actually, we later learnt, a transvestite, the brother of the strongman who had performed; a two-headed donkey, dead, stuffed, and one had to look very closely to see the join; a Bengal tiger called Shiva pacing up and down his confined space and growling; two cougars, ditto; a pair of grey wolves curled up on each other, asleep; and an empty cage, empty apart from a large wooden bathtub, labelled Marisca, the Mermaid. In front of this Mr Dawkins doffed his hat, sighed, and addressed the reduced ring of about fifteen gawpers.

'Poor Marisca, she pined for the freedom of the waves, the song of her sister sirens,' he intoned. 'She departed this life ten days ago and has gone to swim in the great ocean in the sky.'

A lightning flash, a crack of thunder, and some heavy drops of rain plashed down on us.

'Which,' Paddy remarked, 'seems to have sprung a leak.'

What was left of the crowd drifted off and as it did the artistes began to dismantle the ring, strike the tents, gather in the mules that were grazing out in the meadow, and generally did what was necessary to get the show back on the road. Paddy and I stood on the edge of it all and watched. Eventually Mr Dawkins came up, jacket off now, and stock undone.

'Aint you two got homes to go to?' and he let loose a short stream of tobacco juice.

'Tell the truth, the answer is a straight no,' Paddy replied.

'I trust you don't have an idea of coming along with us.'

'Let me show you something,' said Paddy.

We were standing on the spot from which the ring had been mostly cleared, but there were still some posts that had supported the hurdles hammered into the ground. The toffee-apple vendor went by, Paddy scooped three of them off his tray and handed them to me.

'Put them on them there posts, Eddie.'

I took them, I had no choice.

I was hardly clear of the last post when Bang! Bang! Bang! All three seemed to explode into shards of crystallised caramel and apple, the third splattering juice and apple flesh on to my sleeve before the pieces of the first had hit the ground.

It wasn't only the good shooting. Those six-chambered Colts were still a thing of curiosity. Not many had been made and most had been distributed to the army. They were a novelty. And novelties are what travelling shows thrive on.

'And what about him,' growled Dawkins, once board and lodging, feed for Patrick's horse, powder, ball and percussion caps, and fifty cents per performance had been agreed on.

Was it coincidence we were back at Marisca's empty cage, or had Patrick steered us there?

'Eddie, take off your jacket and shirt and show Mr Dawkins what Nature gave you to keep you warm.'

I did as I was told, the rain incidentally still falling, turned away from Dawkins, and let him run his fingers through the hair on my back.

'Jesus,' he said.

'Oh shit,' said I.

So we were both taken on, and by and large found it a congenial way to travel, though slower than we would have liked. Our companions were tolerable – a mixed bunch but with one thing in common – they were all misfits in one way or another, either physically, mentally or emotionally at a tangent to your normal human being. The Cossacks, who had absconded at Vancouver from a Russian whaler, had no English at all. The fattest woman claimed he had a secret he would confide to no one and not just that he was actually a man, though in fact whispering in corners he admitted it to everyone: he was an unfulfilled madge-cove.* The bareback riding lady of a certain age, who was Josh's elder sister, was plagued with visions at night of devils that came to torment her; the dwarfs were dwarfs; and the four clowns, in common with most of their fraternity, suffered from a deep melancholia, so one would find a couple behind a waggon with their arms about each other sobbing their eyes out for no particular reason. But they all recognised Dawkins's Travelling Show was a haven, a stable point in a turning world, without which they would be cast out on the waves of a sea they would never be able to swim in, and so they worked like Trojans to keep the thing afloat.

At Louisville we picked up a runaway Negro called Atticus Clay, a prizefighter who guaranteed to floor within three minutes any man who had paid twenty-five cents for the privilege. He was young, very black, very big and practically a mute. Not deaf. He had simply lost the power of speech along with his tongue, which his owner had deprived him of on account, we were told, Atticus had given him lip. Paddy and he became the stars of the show in which I, billed as Monkey Man from Orandi-Pambi, the capital of Africa, assisted. Using the stooped mode of walking, swinging my arms as I had on the *Town-Ho*, and gibbering loudly the while, I made great play of refusing to allow Paddy to shoot an apple off my head, though I allowed him to draw a bead on an apple on a stick which I held out to my side. This he usually managed to hit with his first shot. I also performed mock fisticuffs with the Louisville Lip, which was our performing name for Atticus, he swinging his fist over my weaving head at which I would run round behind him and kick his bum.

Less to my liking was being made to sit in Marisca's bathtub at the end of the show even though Dawkins said I should wear a pair of cut-down pantaloons whilst in monkey mode, thus preserving both decorum, my finer feelings and the objections of any punter who knew what an ape's genitals look like.

* Homosexual. J. R.

After Louisville came Lexington, Kentucky,* whence we took a trail that ran due south rather than east. I questioned Dawkins about this. He explained that ahead of us were the Appalachian Mountains, a formidable five-hundred-mile barrier, and that the best way through them, although it constituted a quite major diversion, was the Cumberland Gap, which he assured me we would reach within a week. For those of us who had crossed the Rockies and the Sierra Nevada, the mountains themselves seemed nothing from a distance; however, an escarpment or a bluff, a narrow gorge with cascades and rapids, an undergrowth of brambles and dogwood, can impede a waggon train at two thousand feet as readily as at ten thousand, and the Cumberland Gap was the only one negotiable the whole way. Or so Dawkins claimed.

We started out from Middlesborough just as the sun began to gild the very tops of the mountains leaving us still, on the western side, in a sort of pre-dawn twilight. We ascended Cumberland Ridge from the top of which the bright luminary of the day appeared to our view in all its rising glory; the mists dispersed and the floating clouds hasted away at his appearing. The autumn colours burnished the air with the spinning yellow of the birches and the garish red of maple and on the lower slopes oak, hickory and chestnut.

Middlesborough, being a settlement in the western foothills, was surely named for the Tees-side town in England, for many of the settlers came from that area and the Borders to the north, and they still spoke those dialects and sang their songs. They were folk who kept themselves to themselves, rearing hogs because it was bad country for sheep, distilling corn mash to make the nastiest spirituous drink I ever came across, and playing their fiddles and banjoes whenever there was nothing else to do. Which seemed to be most of the time. The banjoes were fretless, and had five strings, one of which was a drone, and were played with considerable skill even if the result was jingle-jangle bedlam. Often two together would try to outdo each other in dexterity and speed, sort of duelling with each other, or they would accompany songs which seemed to carry a darker message than other versions of the same lyric.

* Not the Lexington which saw the opening shots of the American Revolution. That one is in Virginia. J. R.

When I was but a friendless boy
Just nineteen years of age
My father bound me to a miller
That I might learn the trade.

I fell in love with one dear girl
With dark and roving eyes,
I promised her I'd marry her
If me she'd not deny.

I asked her for to take a walk,
Over the blooming field so good
That we might have some secret talk
And name our wedding day.

We had not travelled very far
When I looked all around,
I picked up an old fence stick
And straightway knocked her down.

I took her by her little hand
And threw her round and round,
Then I drug her to the riverside
And threw her in to drown.

About three days and better
This damsel she was seen,
Floating by her sister's house
Down in old Knoxville Town.

We had a guide who warned us not to stray. These people had strange customs, he told us, as living like Indians whole families to a small dwelling, and having intercourse amongst themselves as fancy took them. They also, he said, shadowed trains like ours, invisibly flitting through the trees and undergrowth by tracks they alone knew, and always on the lookout for stragglers or even folk who had gone into a thicket to answer a call of Nature. These they took, and often were never seen again, being presumed to have been cannibalised.

Certainly they lacked civilisation – more than once we saw naked women washing each other by a stream or well and anointing their hair and bodies with buffalo grease.

Towards the eastern end of the Gap, just as we were beginning to think that our parting from the wild mountain folk was a sort of deliverance, we became aware that we were being followed – and not just by a handful of people but a sizeable raggle-taggle crowd led by two burly men, with slouch hats and big black beards carrying two poles that supported a huge banner on which were inscribed the words JESUS LIVES.

Jim, or Jemima, which he preferred, the fattest woman in the world, was walking alongside Paquita. So enormous was she, his head was just on a level with or higher than mine.

'What are they all up to, then?' I asked him.

'Same as us,' she squeaked. He often affected a high-pitched voice. 'Eh?'

'Heading for the annual camp meeting outside Knoxville.'

'What should we be doing at a camp meeting?' asked I, recalling how preachers generally made a point of putting down travelling shows, menageries and the like as the works of the devil.

'Five, six thousand come in every year to listen to the gospellers, but no one can't do nothing else but be preached at for four days long, so there's a fair, a harvest market, travelling shows like ours, all sorts. Dawkins takes us here every year.'

Which made me wonder that this might be the real reason we had come so far south out of our way, assuming Pennsylvania really was where we were heading.

47

August 1853

Well, this is a very fine thing and no mistake! The last shot in my
locker, the last arrow in my quiver, blown, all blown to kingdom
come. Most of the time I set no great store by them, indeed so little
store that I left them in a bag with other odds and sods of papers and
such like in the last room I had in Lambeth (not the first) before I
was pressed aboard the *Beagle* and made to sail to the Galápagos and
into all the adventures I have been narrating herein that followed.*
Then, when I was falsely arrested and incarcerated first in
Pentonville and then in Millbank, and had young William Guppy
acting for me in the Magistrates' and he demanding what assets I
might have to raise the wind to pay his masters Henge and Carboy,
Sols of the Inner Temple or wherever, I recalled them and sent him
round to my old address on the off-chance they might still be there,
and blow me they were! The landlady, a Mrs Murchison, being the
sort that always worries she might inadvertently break some law or
other, or be accused of a theft she had not intended, had kept the bag
all these twenty years against my return. Well, I told young Guppy to
put them somewhere safe, where they would not be thought to be,

---

* Not so, of course. He was not pressed on to the *Beagle*, he stowed away.
  J. R.

but always ready to be collected should the occasion arise, and also made it clear in passing that they represented a last resort towards squaring off his lawyer's fees, always an unwarrantably high expense, should his superiors press him on the matter.

Amongst them were copies of the Garth Papers, duly certified as such, which showed how the Duke of Cumberland (now King of Hanover since his niece, our gracious Queen, being female, was barred by her sex from claiming that throne as well as the one she most magnificently ornaments), when a lad, seduced or raped his sister Sophia, impregnating her, the outcome being a Captain Garth who took the name of a court equerry who had been the said princess's lover. How copies of these papers came into my possession I have narrated elsewhere.

Being now very hard pressed to raise the wind for next month's rent or, to be honest, a pound of apples just now come into season, I felt the time had come to realise the potential of these papers, perhaps by raising an auction between representatives of the more plebeian news sheets, and maybe the Lord Chamberlain's Office as well, and so sent a note by penny post to young Guppy, instructing him to retrieve them from wherever he had them hidden. His answer came back the same day, inviting me to meet him in a particular court in the vicinity of Lincoln's Inn that very evening and to prepare myself for bad news.

He's lost them, I thought, or they have been stolen by someone who has not recognised their worth. Maybe they have been torn up and the shreds used to hold some doxy's curls in place, to light a bailiff's pipe or wipe his bum . . . the truth was worse.

It being August and a hot spell, it was a fine steaming night to turn the slaughter houses and other unwholesome trades, the sewerage, bad water and burial grounds to account and give the Registrar of Deaths some extra business. The court itself was as dismal a place as any I've been in, its old, narrow houses being broken up into single rooms whose dim lights bore witness of draughtsmen and copiers toiling into the night, drawing up conveyances for the entanglement of real estate in meshes of sheepskin vellum at the rate of ten sheep to an acre of land. And the small space on this particular night was filled with a noxious, fatty smell as of burnt mutton chops cut from grandam ewes, the mothers maybe, I thought, quite wrongly as it turned out, of the lambs that supplied the parchment.

'Mr Bosham, are you there?' calls a voice from an entry.

'Mr Guppy?'

''Tis I. You come most carefully—'

'Upon my hour. So. Give me my papers or take me to them.'

He came out into the light of the one gas lamp that illuminated the area and a cat that had been rubbing up his trouser leg flitted away from him.

'I wish I could, Mr Bosham, I wish I could. Follow me, if you would be so kind.'

In the short time, with infrequent meetings, that I had known him he had always seemed to me a bright and cheerful young man and, in spite of a certain nonchalance in his way of talking and dress, not bad at his job in which I believe he took some pride. But now he had a hangdog look about him, walked with a stoop, head thrust out, holding the large tallow candle he had set a lucifer to, carbuncled like Bardolph with dripping wax, the candle I mean, drooping above its candle-holder. He followed the brindled cat, an emaciated little beast like most of those that haunted the neighbourhood, up two narrow flights of wooden stairs to a deal door which had been left on the latch. Here he paused for a moment.

'I asked you to come,' he said, 'because when a lawyer is the cause of a loss of valuables then it is natural to expect some chicanery, to believe he has got them into his own possession. And the truth of the matter in hand so beggars credibility, I fear that lacking ocular experience of the circumstances you would never believe me. Have you, sir, ever heard tell of a man called Krook?'

Well, at various times in my life I have had occasion to frequent the Inns, the law courts, and the theatres a little to the south round Covent Garden, and you pick up tittle and tattle in the snugs of the alehouses that are on every corner. I'd heard of Krook. How he collected documents which he could not read and stored them in their hundreds against the day when he would learn to read, and how he never did. Also how he drank prodigious amounts of gin and had grown prodigious fat. I rehearsed as much to young Guppy, on the tiny landing of that rookery.

'Aye,' he said, and the mournful tone in his voice deepened a little, 'you have it about right.'

He pushed the door open with his foot, and the cat like the fleetest of shadows slipped in ahead of him.

The smell of burnt mutton fat was now truly nauseous.

The room was small with bookcases all round, and tables laden not only with bundles of black ash that had been well doused with water and still steamed and smoked, but also much other useless bric-a-brac. In one corner a pile of empty gin bottles which no doubt sheltered a family of rodents, for Missee now scouted and sniffed about them the way cats do when they suspect the presence of a mouse. The coals in the fire, much of them reduced to clinker, also steamed sulphurically and on the boards in front of them, as if melted by the heat when they were in full blast, there was a wide pool of congealed animal fat.

I looked around while Guppy held his candle high. I poked into the bundles of ash and they crumbled as I did so, spinning flakes a little like tired, black snow in the draught from the door.

'And my papers were here?'

'I solemnly swear it.'

'Why?'

'I took it to be a safe hiding place. Krook was glad to have them. I told him a little of what they contained and he was wont to say they would be the first he'd study once he'd mastered the art.'

'Of reading?'

'Of reading. Meanwhile, he would, he said, keep them always near him, on the floor by the chair he mostly sat in. In front of the fire.'

'When did this all happen?'

'Last night. When it was even hotter than it is now.'

'And you did not tell me.'

'I did not want to cause you unnecessary distress, and nothing could be done. While I was able to identify the packet I was also able to establish the utter illegibility of the papers that made it up.'

'The weather hot. Yet he had a fire going?'

'He always kept a fire going, whatever the weather.'

I thought it through for a moment, looked again at that pool of grease which Missee now sniffed at tentatively, then growled, the way cats do when feeling some distress.

'He was sleeping and a coal fell out?'

'There is no evidence of that. The fire began inside him.'

'You know, Guppy, in spite of ocular evidence I am beginning to feel some doubt as to what is going on.'

'I said it beggared belief. But consider. It was a hot night. He was full of combustible spirits, he fell asleep . . . A doctor examined what was left and concurred with what had already been my guess.'

'Which is?'

'Mr Krook died of Spontaneous Combustion.'

Silence. Then the bell of the clock on St Paul's struck eleven and all the other clocks of the City followed suit.

'Oh shit,' I said, as the silence, as deep as the smell of burnt lard, once more enveloped us.

48

Blessed are they that do his commandments, that they might have the right to the tree of life, and may enter in through the gates unto the city. For without are dogs, and sorcerers, and whoremongers, and murderers, and idolaters, and whosoever loveth and maketh a lie. Revelation twenty-two, verses fourteen and fifteen. Brothers and sisters, let us begin with that first small lie . . .

A big, big field it was, maybe forty acres, almost flat but sloping on both sides down to the river that wound across its middle, dividing it into two. There were four bridges linking the two halves, and a wide ford as well, the whole curtained off by the edge of uncleared forest, out of which we came, down the trail from the Gap. By now we were part of a big procession of which the Hill-Billies (Jemima's name for them) were, along with us, only a small part. There were many who rode their animals, be they mules or horses, a few in carriages, but most walked, and as they walked they sang.

> *Am I a soldier of the cross?*
> *A follower of the lamb?*
> *And shall I fear to own his cause*
> *Or blush to speak his name?*
> *Shall I be carried to the skies*
> *On flowery beds of ease*

414

It would be comforting to think I could, I thought, flowery beds of ease don't come my way often, but apparently the answer was NO!

> *Sure I must fight, if I would reign;*
> *Increase my courage, Lord,*
> *To bear the cross, endure the shame,*
> *Supported by thy word.*

The trail wound through that half of the meadow to the south of the river and this seemed a jolly enough place to be. Although the sun had gone behind the mountains, the sky above them was still golden, yet already torches made from wound cloth soaked in bitumen were adding their shifting flames, while beneath them a thousand oil-lamps glowed with whiter light. For this was the profane, secular half of the meeting: there were stalls selling all manner of cheap foods, ground beef grilled and placed between buns or folded into tortillas, huge T-bone steaks, spiced ribs, candies, pancakes, charred sweet corn on the cob and toffee-apples. There were drink stalls, too, offering root beer, sarsaparilla, lemonade and moonshine whisky.

Banjoes fought not duels but battles, fiddles sang of the pleasures of dancing, even in Hell. Smoke from the *barbacoas*, redolent with the odours of charred food, drifted through the pools of light, and through the throng urchins and Negroes passed handing out more throwaways giving notice of where, on the north side, and when, which great and famous preachers would be sermonising, according to the revelations of their particular sects or cults. There were Baptists and Anabaptists, Lapsarians and Sub-Lapsarians, Methodists and Wesleyans, Presbyterians and Adventists, the last of whom having been let down by God regarding the date of the Day of Judgement in 1831 and then again in 1843 were now looking towards the sixties for the fulfilment of the Law and the Prophets . . .

Whosoever maketh a lie, brothers and sisters, are the words of the Revelation. Let us in God's name first look at such sinners amongst us who have ever, by one jot or tittle, by as little as an 'i' with its

415

dot, stepped aside from the path of truth. Which of you did not, as a small child, betray the innocence the Lord gave you at birth by denying it was you who took the last cookie from the cookie jar, or left the door of the hen-coop open the night the fox got in . . . Brothers and sisters, maybe that fox was the devil himself, for he is most apt to assume such shapes, not to catch the unwary fowl, but in his most devious way to set the trap by which your mortal soul might take its first step along the path to everlasting damnation . . .

'This'll do,' declared Dawkins, giving his bravo moustache a twist, and pointing at a space not far from one of the bridges across the river with the ford almost behind us, a space between a group of Indians in full fig who alternated displays of horsemanship on their palominos with exotic dancing round a bison-head totem, and a kitchen where a couple of Negro slaves turned huge spits on which roasted a whole ox and a whole hog, and smaller ones loaded with fowl, and all supervised by a hugely fat Nashville farmer and his even stouter wife. We knew they were from Nashville because they had a big banner proclaiming they were 'The Famous and Very Exselent Nashville Traveling Roasting Kitchen, Prop: Mrs Daisy Parton'. And also because they had slaves. Tennessee west of the mountains was slave-owners, to the east it was not.

The carnivores in Dawkins's menagerie became even more restless at the smell of raw and cooking meat and once we were more or less settled Dawkins sent me next door to buy shanks and heads and such like, with Atticus and Tom the Strong by my side to lend weight and substance to my mission. Mother Parton tried to take advantage, considering herself to be in a seller's market, but the sight of Atticus using a hanging beeve carcase as a punchbag and the way Tom lifted the back of her parked waggon and gave it a shake so the pans and such like inside tumbled about persuaded her that butcher's prices with a heavy discount for quantity purchased was a fair deal. They heaped up six heads and twenty-four shanks in a blanket we'd brought with us, and soon our animals were quietly gnawing away at them.

And, oh, my friends, if that first little lie was the first step, then what was the next? Whosoever LOVETH and maketh a lie, is what the Holy Book says. Sure, this means those men who look on

women not their wives with lustful carnal thoughts of fornication
or adultery, and worse still, those women who likewise look on
men. But then, add to the first sin against the Lord Thy God, as
proscribed on the tablets Moses took down from the mountain,
Thou shalt NOT commit adultery, add to that evil the greater evil
of False Witness . . . Oh, brothers and sisters, how the evil con-
cupiscence of the flesh leads us into even greater sin, for such are
the wiles of Satan!

Once we were pitched there was now a moment to look across to
the other side of the river. A big, wide-open space of mowed grass was
edged with tents, their sides furled so one could see into them and
each had a stage at the back, and placards or banners, the tabernacle
of this, the chapel of that, the holy church of the other. At the back
was the biggest tent of all, a pavilion supported on a row of four redwood trunks maybe a hundred feet high and spreading wings of
canvas out from just below their peaks which were held in place by
as many stays and shrouds as you might find on a four-master ship of
the line. And above it all, fixed to the tallest pole, just stirring in the
breeze, Old Glory, The Stars and Stripes.

Josh Dawkins reckoned upwards of five thousand could get under
the shelter of it all, and it was reserved for the four greatest and most
universally renowned preachers who were billed, just one for each
night. The stage was maybe fifteen or twenty feet high and was
backed by a huge curved screen of polished wood, which we were to
discover served as a sounding board and magnified the physical power
of the preacher's voice so it could be heard not only throughout the
interior of the tent but way back to the riverbank too. The whole was
lit by a constellation of small candelabra which hung on halyards
slung over various horizontal beams so the many candles filled the
spaces about ten feet above the heads of the congregation leaving the
vastnesses of the roof in smoky, mysterious shadow. There were also
torches burning at the corners of the stage and at the entrances to the
smaller tents, set like chapels round the periphery of the interior of a
cathedral. The effect was of shifting light, dancing shadows and pools
of deep darkness, especially between the lesser tents.

As I was taking this all in, the area was still scarcely a quarter filled
with men, women and children who stood about in groups, some
single families, others congregations with their pastors, making up

their minds which preacher to hear first, while others continued to pick their way through our side, heading for the bridges and scarcely giving us a glance. One group, maybe Baptists of some sort or another, stood on the bank of the river on our side and sang:

> *There is a land of pure delight*
> *Where saints immortal reign*
> *Infinite day excludes the night*
> *And pleasures banish pain.*

> *There everlasting spring abides*
> *And never withering flowers –*
> *Death, like a narrow sea, divides*
> *This heavenly land from ours.*

> *Sweet fields beyond the swelling flood*
> *Stand dressed in living green,*
> *So to the Jews old Canaan stood*
> *While Jordan rolled between . . .**

Suiting their actions to the words they all now plunged into the flood and, scorning the nearby bridge, waded across.

'Don't worry,' murmured Madge Dawkins in my ear, 'we'll do better and better business each night as they tire of the sermonising and run out of what food they brought with them. First they'll gorge at Ma Parton's, then they'll come to us.'

And sure enough, towards midnight with a three-quarter waxing moon high and south of us, the crowds began to filter back over the bridges and through the ford. Our clowns raced amongst them, mopping and mowing at them, thrusting their throwaways under their noses, and even, the larger ones anyway, blocking people's way so they moved perforce towards our ring. It was not long before we had an audience some fifty strong and rising, many chewing on Mrs Parton's steaks, ground meat, pancakes and the rest or slurping from upraised bottles of root beer or moonshine.

---

* By Isaac Watts, 1674–1748. It is said he was inspired by the view west across Southampton Water to what is now a noxious chemicals disposal facility at Marchwood. J. R.

At what he judged was the optimum moment, and following a bugle fanfare, Dawkins led out the parade, himself in front, then Madge and Patrick, next the Cossacks, then Tom the Strong, and finally the clowns, those that were not out in the crowd, but including yours truly with my clout round my privates, walking bow-legged, banging my chest and swaying and grimacing to the manner born. This and my comic encounter with The Lip were my moments of glory, for once out of the ring I hurried back into my cage and waited for the gawpers.

Which was when things got difficult, for here we were not alone, isolated in a field of our own, but surrounded with rival attractions, having entertained an audience now definitely very reluctant to part with cash for what they had seen. The clowns were instantly among them with hats and bags for coins, while Tom, Atticus, and the Cossacks cajoled and then threatened the more recalcitrant with the possibility of unhinged joints or severed limbs.

Outside the City, my fellow lovers of Christ, are dogs, sorcerers, whoremongers, murderers and idolaters, for so says The Disciple Christ loved, and behold, I say unto you, indeed it is true for behold, there they are on the far side of the river they will never cross, holding court with the Devil himself, tempting you with evil sights and profane food and drink, yea I say unto you, abhor and avoid such temptations and stay here in the City the Good Lord has brought you to . . .

And so forth, though very few paid heed, for having done their duty to God all they now wanted was a good time, even the Baptists, who waded back just as we were beginning our second performance, or, as we Thespians call it, the 'second house'.

49

But all this was nothing to the fourth evening, when the moon hung like an orange lantern above the trees, the smoke from the fires and torches rose like the pillar of smoke and then the pillar of fire as the moonstruck night descended, and the crowd poured in, some from as far as a hundred miles away. There were five thousand, at least, and all were now very conscious that this was the last night for a year and there was much to make the most of and on top of that the preacher with the greatest reputation for carrying a crowd, for gathering the largest number of souls for the Lord, and generally stimulating excessive enthusiasm, was to be the top of the bill.

The Blood, my Sisters and Brothers, the Blood. Let me take you by the hands and shew it to you. Close your eyes and come with me to the foot, yea, the very base of the old wooden cross. And what you ask, with your eyes firmly shut, what you ask is what is this strange fluid that falls upon my face? It is warm, is it not? If it is warm, say . . . Yes!

Yes Lord, Yes!

Lift up your faces, my Sisters and Brothers, let that holy fluid fall into your mouths, catch it on your tongue, it tastes . . . how does it taste? The way iron tasted when you licked the barrel of your

*Daddy's pistol, the way his big knife tasted if he gave you a pre-
cious morsel he had cut from the Lamb for you to take off the
blade with your tongue? Taste it, taste it, taste it for it is yours by
right, dear Sisters and Brothers, and what makes it so? You know,
YOU KNOW. It is yours by right because it was shed for you, for
you Little Sisters, to WASH YOUR SINS AWAY!*

His name? The Reverend Doctor Samuel Sabbath, DD, MA,
M.Litt., etc., etc.

I didn't recognise him, not at first, not for some time. Why should
I? Thirteen years had passed, eleven since my last brief glimpse before
he carried away my Kate. No longer was he wearing a high white hat
with a curly brim, a long-tailed black coat, stovepipe striped trousers
and a waistcoat whose front was the Stars and Stripes. His white
moustache was no longer curled at the ends but met what had been a
neat white goatee and now looked like a polished spade to make a hir-
sute ensemble worthy of a patriarch. His skin too had paled with age
to a corpse-like pallor beneath the yellowish pale brown it had been,
so no one, not in the know, would credit he was a man of colour. And
instead of the cane and the thin cigar, he held a shepherd's crook in his
right hand and in his left a bible bound in soft black leather. He wore
a conventional black morning coat and trousers, but over his shoulders, fastened with a gold chain, a long, full cape that reached down to
the ground and on his head a black skull-cap floating, as it were, on
waves of white hair. So much could I see from our side of the river.

*For your sins, my Sisters and Brothers, your sins, THAT is why
you kneel beneath the arms of the Cross and taste His Blood.*

And from somewhere behind him a choir of angelic voices sang:

> *There is a fountain filled with blood*
> *Drawn from Emmanuel's veins*
> *And sinners plunged beneath that flood*
> *Lose all their guilty stains.*

'Paddy,' I said, 'I'm going across the river.'

We were relaxing after the 'first house', and I was still stripped
down to my cache-sexe clout. Atticus and Tom were sparring nearby,

421

keeping the cold out of their limbs. It had not been an easy perform-ance, for the onlookers, conscious that this was the last night of the camp meeting, had heckled us a lot, had been less ready to lie down once Atticus had hit them, scoffed at Tom's antics with the dumb-bells and even insisted they could outshoot Patrick. He now looked up from his six-shooter which he was cleaning most meticulously, always his practice after a performance.

'Whoi?'

'Get a closer look at the preacher man. I reckon I've seen him before, a long time ago. Coming?'

'It's not in my nature to listen to a Prod preacher.'

'That's a "no", then.'

'Reckon so,' and having pulled an oily rag through one of the chambers he moved on to the next.

So I crossed the river on my own, filtering in at the end of the bridge which the people behind objected to, even though they were supposed to think I was an escaped monkey man or something of the sort. I'd already noticed during the previous three days that strictly absent from the snatches of sermons I'd heard was any reference to Christian charity and indeed precious few of the vast congregation showed much. Moreover, on this the last night, emotions were run-ning high already, not the least of which was a mood of irritation flaring into anger for an imagined or real slight. At the best of times I dislike being part of a crowd and to be part of this one made me feel doubly insecure, so as soon as I could I moved to the side, slipped between two of the lesser tents and by this clandestine route approached the main one, pausing only to look through the gaps to see what effect the preacher was having on his audience.

Considerable, was the answer. For instance, at the end of the pas-sage between the first two tents I could see a young man whose arm circled the neck of a young girl who knelt beside him, with her hair hanging dishevelled upon her shoulders and her features working with the most violent agitation. Then both fell forward on the tram-pled stalks of grass, as if unable to endure in any other attitude the burning eloquence of the tall, grim figure in black who was uttering with incredible vehemence an oration that seemed to hover between preaching and exhortation. By angling myself somewhat I could see how he looked like an ill-constructed machine moving with such violence as to threaten its own destruction. His words tumbled out painfully, rapidly, while the kneeling throng called on the name of Jesus with sobs, groans and a sort of low howling inexpressibly painful to listen to.

Beyond the couple on the floor was another figure, young too, wild and terrible; his large eyes glared frightfully and he screamed without an instant's intermission the word 'Glory' with a violence that seemed to swell every vein to bursting. It was too dreadful to look upon long and I turned away shuddering.

For your sins Brothers and Sisters, yea your sins, for I say unto you, you are a generation of vipers, a concourse of Gadarene swine, housels for all the imps and devils of Hell, and until you approach the bleeding feet of your Saviour, clasp your hands and arms round the central timber of the cross, reach up and kiss those bleeding feet, it is to hell that these infesting devils will drag you.

But now casting my eyes beyond the poor man who cried 'Glory' they fell on the first woman to be afflicted with the 'jerks'. She was one of the mountain women, who wore little, just the skirts and shirt which they pulled in lewdly so they might just as well have gone naked for all they hid. First her head jerked back and forth then as the rhythm quickened, her shoulders and then her breasts, and finally her whole body except her feet which remained attached to the ground beneath them, jerked forward and back as the convulsions took her. The affliction swiftly spread to those around her, by a sort of invisible contagion it seemed, until she was the centre of a throng of women and some men, all spasmodically jerking, eyes shut, fists clenched while the voice thundered on.

Reach up now with your hands, cradle those feet, Oh how beautiful are those feet that walked the halls of Heaven before they scuffed the dust of this damned earth, are these the toes, the ankles of your God? Yea verily they are, and is this the head of the roofing nail that pierces them, and this the blood? Are these the calves, the taut lean muscles of the man that strode in hunger over desert and mountain for your sake?

And now I could hear a terrible cacophony of noise, much as you would expect to issue from the flaming caverns that are the entrances to Pandæmonium, the capital of Hell, a terrible mixture of barking, howling, grunting, and many began to dance, that is their feet now moved back and forth, their eyes open or glazed, and their hands and arms waved slowly and alternately up and down in front of them, just as if they were indeed stroking the calves, the knees, the thighs of their dying Saviour.

Reach up higher, my dear friends, my dearest friends, and stroke the muscles of the divine torso, reach with your fingers and find the wounds the centurion left, leaking blood and ichor, probe them with your fingers the way the doubting Thomas did, discover them and know them as the sign He died for your sins . . . your lecheries, your wantonness, your bearing of false witness . . . FOR THIS IS THE ROCK THAT WAS CLEFT FOR THEE . . .

And at that very instant, for surely he had given them a cue, a quire of women dressed in white, with white hoods over their heads, which had filed on to the stage behind him began to sing, to sing like angels, at which he raised his long arms spread above his head and . . .

> *Rock of Ages, cleft for me,*
> *let me hide myself in thee;*
> *let the water and the blood,*
> *from thy wounded side which flowed,*
> *be of sin the double cure;*
> *save from wrath and make me pure.*
>
> *Nothing in my hand I bring,*
> *simply to the cross I cling;*
> *naked, come to thee for dress;*
> *helpless, look to thee for grace;*
> *foul, I to the fountain fly;*
> *wash me, Saviour, or I die.*

Many of the crowd joined in this lugubrious hymn but others wailed, and rolled about, and some, taking their cue from the second verse, tore off all their clothes and rushed towards the stage. That this was expected and prepared for now became evident for women from the celestial quire came forward and wrapped them in scarlet blankets, and, leading them by the hand, took them up the steps on to the stage where Baron Samedi, Nuncle Sam, the Rev. Samuel Sabbath greeted them with a kiss while an acolyte, a huge man built like a blacksmith, and wielding a huge bullhorn, bellowed out their names, declaring they had declared for Christ and were reborn, as indicated by their coming naked into a new world. Brave new world I thought, that has such people in it.

I was near the front now, in a small patch of shadow between the tent of the Followers of the Redeeming Spirit and the stage itself, and at this moment fate if not God took a hand and nearly cost me my life. First, through what cause I do not know, maybe a candle flaring to catch the line above it, or a badly tied knot, a candelabra carrying six candles on branched candlesticks fell on my head. Spilling hot wax on my shoulders and setting the hair on my head on fire, it then tumbled into a patch of dried grass that had not been mown or trodden down, which also caught.

Now at the time I did not concern myself with the apparition I must have presented to those nearby, but pray consider it as I do now: a small, hairy, dark monkey man with flames on his head, rising out of flames and dancing a very merry, eccentric jig and yelling and screaming his head off.

'The devil,' screamed a woman old enough to know better, a few yards away from me, 'the devil is come amongst us . . .'

Well, when you think about it, she would, would she not? And as I danced or rather scampered way from the burning grass, smacking at my head and still screaming, the cry went up all round me, and worse still the clout I was wearing came undone and slipped away from me, exposing me in my full devilishness. Small I am in a general sort of a way, but not undersized in certain respects . . . Of course, the shout went up all round me: 'The devil, Beelzebub, Old Nick, nay he's naught but an imp . . . but evil for all that, brood of Lucifer, Belial, Mammon and Lilith . . .' and 'Just look at that donger!'

For obvious reasons I do not often inspire fear in others, but this occasion was the exception. While men as large and obviously strong as the giant with the bullhorn, indeed he may have been one of them, came close-ish, and armed with a sturdy intent to thrust me back to the halls of Tartarus whence I came, at a space of some three or four yards they hesitated, moderated their pace to that of mine which was

425

now cautious, with my head constantly swinging to eye any surprise attack on my flank or rear, and thus for some fifty yards I made my weaving way within a circle of brutes or brutish men who contented themselves with abuse both scatological and eschatological.

This was too much for the Reverend Samuel, not because he believed the sanctuary of his pavilion had been questioned by my sudden appearance but rather from a sense that he was left out of it all, was no longer in control, the centre of attention. Whatever. With a train of his white-clad Amazons streaming behind him, like the tresses of a comet, he launched himself off the platform, and still with shepherd's crook and holy book came surging down the centre, parting the throng much as Achilles and his Myrmidons had done when, filled with wrath at the death of his bummer boy, Patroclus, he returned to the battle on the field before Troy.

Pausing a pace or two in front of me he lifted his crook up high and, with a look more akin to that of an angry Moses than an Achaean hero, launched into a chant of improvised dog Latin and preacher's English, something on these lines: 'Oh Maleus malorum, infecit crucem omnipotentatem, hence foul Beelzebub, be you a minion of Old Satan or his offspring hence in vincula vinculorum, begone I say unto the steamy halls of Hades . . .' and so on, twenty-four-carat, dyed-in-the-wool mumbo-jumbo but with enough in plain-speaking English to convince his followers that the force was with him rather than me. I had no inclination to stay and now made the psychological error of moving more quickly and with more determination towards the river – a signal to the mob that I was in retreat, defeated, and could be approached and handled with impunity.

In a moment they were on me, and I was scooped up above the heads of seven or eight of the most fervent men and women and carried thus above the throng, still of course screaming and writhing, with Samedi and his white-shrouded Bacchantes just behind me. At first I was not much bothered by this: the worst I expected was to be thrown into the river and allowed to swim or wade across it back into Vanity Fair but as we approached the threshold of the main concourse I saw ahead of me, lit by the flares and candles and swinging a little in the draught, a hangman's noose. Some bastard, perhaps instructed to do so by the Baron, had dropped the largest centred candelabra, removed it, and retied its rope into an instrument of judicial murder.

'I'm fifty-nine,' I screamed, 'too young to die,' as the Very Reverend Saturday reached up with his crook, hooked the noose and brought it down into the hands of the biggest of his roughs, who, without lowering me nearer the ground at all, fixed it round my neck, and pulled the knot tight. The reverend came close up to me, I was almost upside down now with my head on a level with his. I could smell his breath – metallic like blood and with far more in the way of sulphur about it than there was about me.

'Why, Nuncle, why?' I whimpered.

'To be honest with you,' came the hoarsely whispered reply, 'I'm not too sure. Mainly I think because you know what I once was. I sat upon a hornet's nest, did I not? I danced upon the dead, I tied a viper round my neck and then I went to bed.' And he stepped back, signalling that I should swing.

Such was the length of the rope, soaring up into the roof above, and the height they were holding me at, there was no drop and so no chance of my neck breaking and no sudden asphyxiation either, just a slow tightening of the noose as my weight exerted its pressure on it. But it had other effects, such as you may have read of, even experienced for all I know, namely a surge of blood to my 'donger' followed by an ejaculatory spasm. My hands, of course, were free, though pulling at the noose, but now I briefly lowered them to cover my shame, but too late: what had happened was to the simple onlookers a final proof they had a devil on their hands and once again they shrank back in horror and terror.

Or maybe they did that because a Bengal tiger had sauntered through the parting crowd and now stood below my feet which he proceeded to lick.

Not a lot more to tell. Paddy was behind the tiger to which he was attached by a collar and a rope. He was on his horse and he looked quite magnificent, his hat pulled over his eyes, his big white moustache, his long coat; all his silvery accoutrements and the brass badge of the Connaughts caught and reflected candles, the moon, and, I'll tell you now for it is not in my nature as a narrator to use art to create suspense or surprise by not revealing to the reader what was becoming apparent to most of the actors and onlookers in this scene, the flames that were beginning to consume the canvas walls and the stage at the back of the pavilion.

Meanwhile, however, I could feel my eyes popping and my tongue swelling, and was grateful when he took prompt action. He drew his six-gun from his belt and with one shot hit the cord above my head. Thus weakened my weight did the rest, the cord parted and dropped me in front of the tiger who turned his tongue's attentions to my face.

Baron Samedi now made the last serious mistake of his life. Patrick had one pistol and had fired one shot. That was all pistols could fire in those days. The huge majority of pistols. Quickly, but with no undue hurry, Nuncle Sam now delved beneath his cloak and produced his own, normal, single-chamber Colt.

'I get up on the flatboat,' he chanted, but not loud, just enough for Paddy to hear, 'For I am Uncle Sam, Den I went to see de place, Dey killed de Packenham.'

Patrick allowed him to begin to level the pistol, so there would be no doubt at all that he was firing in self-defence, and shot him three times, and, so close did they come, all three shots hit the reverend's heart before he had even begun to fall.

A woman, one of the first behind him, pushed past, stepped over his dying body. Her fingers, thin, apart from slight arthritis, struggled to loosen the noose. She was hidden by her robe but now pushed back the hood revealing grey hair which yet carried hints of the rich amber it had once been. Her figure was slight, her stature small. She was wearing spectacles which, once the noose had given a little and was slipping wider, she removed. She was Kate.

And she was looking up at Patrick.

'That man,' she said, 'is a god.' She paused as if struck by lightning, then looked down at me. 'Eddie, if we can get to it, and I'm sure he'll manage it, there's a chest with quite a lot of money in it in Samedi's waggon.'

Behind Patrick, still on his horse, Eleanor the elephant lifted her trunk and blew a fanfare of assent.

Twenty minutes later we were back on the safe side of the river, Tom the Strong having carried the chest for us from the park area to the side of the pavilion, which was now burning well. Huge sheets of canvas billowed above it, flames blazing at their edges, like tops'ls coming adrift in a storm, a bending, spiralling column of sparks and smoke climbed the heaventree and obscured the moon. Hot air, funnelled into a gale that blew across the concourse, roared like a railroad locomotive. A huge crowd spilled across the river, one of the bridges collapsed, some children and old folk no doubt drowned or were trampled, but in front of us they eddied, much as the buffalo had done, but this time on account of Shiva and Eleanor who stood guard between the bank and our camp.

The chest, trunk really, was large and heavy and even Tom had begun to sweat under the weight, his perspiration gleaming on his shoulders in the light from the flames. Gold is heavy. Kate found a key, warm from her breasts, and threw it open. Gold there was, and bills, and deeds showing shares in hotels, banks, ships, railroads and mines, many of which turned out to be forgeries. Patrick, Kate and I had taken three hundred dollars each from the chest, mostly in gold, and had handed the rest, at Patrick's insistence, to be shared by the entire Dawkins Travelling Show. Kate kept the certificates. There was plenty of cash for all of them. Enough to persuade Dawkins that he had no further need for caged animals. Released, the two wolves howled at the moon from the forest nearby, while the cougars hunted deer. Shiva lingered for a time, his tail swinging behind him, then he too loped off into the dark.

The pavilion burned on as if it were the citadel the devils built in Mr Milton's poem. Old Glory, the Stars and Stripes, billowing high above the rest, was the last to catch, ending in a shower of sparks as if the stars were falling out of its folds.

'The tigers of wrath are wiser than the horses of instruction,'* I intoned, for want of anything else to say.

'Sure, they both have their uses,' Patrick replied. Kate squeezed his arm and led him away into the darkness where she befriended him and both found a garden of delight.

They got decently married in the Catholic church in Philadelphia. I didn't attend. I went and had a look at the Declaration instead.

> We hold these truths to be self-evident, that all men are
> created equal, that they are endowed by their Creator
> with certain unalienable Rights, that among these are
> Life, Liberty and the pursuit of Happiness.

* From *The Marriage of Heaven and Hell* . . . oh, sod it; if you know, you won't be arsed to read this, and if you don't, what difference will it make to you to know where Eddie found it? J. R.

Dream on.

In a bar afterwards I was accosted by a stranger, a very old man who congratulated me on not being eaten by a bear. I offered him a drink and he asked for a sarsaparilla. It was only after I had left that I recalled who he was.

Patrick and Kate went to Boston. Her plan was to use the money and other assets they had taken from Samedi's treasure chest and Patrick's share of Mrs Graves's hoard to buy fifty of Mr Singer's new sewing machines, a suitable building, and set up a clothes factory. After all, it was a line she and her mother had been in long ago when they first arrived in Vicksburg, but now she'd do it properly, that is getting young girls to do the hard, sweated work for her. It seemed Tralee no longer figured much in Patrick's view of things, nor his no doubt long-passed-on Ma.

> Kate's a dear delicious creature,
> Merry as a sunny elf,
> Beautiful in form and feature,
> Smiling mould of beauty's self;
> When she laughs, her silken tresses
> Fall upon her gentle breast;
> And her eyes as dark as midnight,
> Never seem to be at rest.
>
> Kate's a sweet but saucy creature,
> With a lip of scarlet bloom,
> Woodbines sipping golden sunlight,
> Roses drinking rich perfume,
> Voice as dainty as the whisper
> Founts give in their crystal shrine,
> Saucy Kate, so full of mischief,
> Would that I could call thee mine.
>
> Kate's a dear and merry creature,
> Sprightly as a fleet gazelle,
> Fondness dwells in every dimple,
> Surely love has marked her well.
> Many hearts have strove to win her,
> Bowed with disappointment low;

430

Saucy Kate, I fear to say it,
Winsome – always tells them No!

I caught a ship belonging to the Rathbone Line, carrying a cargo of cotton and sugar to Liverpool. She'd called at Philly for a consignment of furs, and, would you believe, a barrel of processed whale shit.

Epilogue

Fragment of a letter written by Charles Darwin to an unknown correspondent, possibly Thomas Huxley. Internal evidence suggests a date close to 28 May 1876 as the reflections on religion echo those in the *Autobiography* which was begun on that date.

I was intrigued by your suggestion, indeed prophecy, that religion in all its forms will have passed away by 2003. I suppose this thought, or hope, must have come to you as long ago as 1853, being a century and a half before the date you suggested. Well, let us hope you are right; the earth will indeed be a happier place if your prophecy is fulfilled, though I cannot say that much progress has been made up to now. Those Protestant churches of moderate views and practice (I exclude most of the dissenters) have grown used to scientific rationality, and by fudging it manage to incorporate its findings within their own mutilated creeds. The Romans simply ignore it all, believing that in time it will go away. However, it is not religion that concerns me now. You have suggested that my personal response to the uncovering of Natural Selection as the mechanism by which new species come into existence has undergone a shift in feeling over the last two decades. You are right, of course.

An event occurred in that same year (I am speaking of 1853) that set off a train of thought which grew in my mind if not like a mighty oak from an acorn, at least like a briar that climbs a hawthorn bush and late in summer adorns it with what looks like a second season of blossom, though with very different flowers than the natural may.

You will recall perhaps that at that time, at the very beginning of our acquaintance and possibly before it had matured into the friendship we now enjoy, my outlook on life was sensibly darkened by four circumstances. These were, in descending order of importance, the still recent death of my dear daughter Annie; continuing ill health which I had not at that time learnt to accept as a burden I should have to support for the rest of my life; the horrors, often reported pictorially, of the war in the Crimea; and the influence of such works as *The Principle of Population* by Thomas Malthus and Mayhew's *London Labour and the London Poor*. The result was that as the shape of my theories on the origin of species took on an almost palpable form, looming out of the mist of obscurantism like a mighty mountain, I read that threatening shape as something black and bleak. Nature seemed at that time to be a seething slum like that depicted by Mayhew, out of which only a few survived to become new species, the rest doomed to futile struggle, neighbours elbowing one another aside, the weak trampled underfoot. Nature was an evil, negligent mother, aborting her failures like the breeder's runts on some domestic dump. She was depraved as when hermaphroditic jellyfish fertilise themselves with their own sperm, and profligate as when a sea slug produces six hundred thousand eggs which, had they all survived, would soon have filled the ocean.

Well, at just this time, as if out of the darkness that precedes the dawn, I chanced to renew the acquaintance of a man, perhaps I should say *homunculus*, who, although quite unaware that he was doing so, cast a little light in the darkest places, opened the door, albeit only a crack, on to a better world.

I was first acquainted with him on the *Beagle*. He was not a member of the crew but a stowaway, escaping who knows what fate at the hands of Justice. Once Fitzroy was aware of his presence he ordered that he should remain with us until our first port of call under the English flag. Now this was three-quarters of the way round the globe, at the Sydney Penal Station in Australia. Until then it was also Fitzroy's order that this man, Edward Bosham, should be required to work his passage assisting in the galley. I also made use of him as a porter during my forays and lengthier explorations on various islands and on the continent of South America. Eventually, while we were at work on and around the Galápagos Islands, he took his fate into his own hands and absconded, no doubt aware that our next port of call of any significance would be Sydney which, for all we knew, could bring him into the shadow of the gallows. We therefore deemed it a mercy to him not to pursue him, but chose instead to leave him to take his chances where he had chosen to take them.

Imagine my surprise therefore when, some eighteen years later, he turned up at a public alehouse, south of the river, where I was quizzing certain pigeon fanciers on their breeding methods, and later actually at Down. On one of these occasions I picked up on a turn of phrase he had used, namely: *the survival of the fittest.* I did not for the time being put these words into writing, but Herbert,* having heard me use them, did.

Apparently this Bosham returned to Down some weeks later and was discovered by Parslow in the little lobby by the glass doors to the garden. He resisted Parslow's attempts to apprehend him and a short bout of fisticuffs followed, at the end of which he managed to escape. A week later he wrote to me asserting that his call had been entirely innocent and at my invitation, which, as I remember it, was not quite true, and that as a result of Parslow's attentions he had suffered a blinding headache for several days, indeed was still suffering, and had consequently been unable to work, resulting in an important loss of income which he hoped I would reimburse. The sum of fifty pounds was mentioned.

I had occasion to be in town that week and, having, quite early in the morning, concluded my business at the offices of the Royal Society, took a cab to Bosham's address in Lambeth. I found him in his nightshirt with a cap, looking like Wee Willie Winkie, and sipping slowly at a glass of gin with hot water which he said was the only thing that effected any amelioration of his condition, though Collis Browne also helped. One eye was slightly discoloured and he claimed a lasting stiffness in one arm which he said Parslow had twisted with unusual force. It was not the limb he used when raising a bottle to his glass or a glass to his lips. His accommodation was a single room, but well enough appointed.

'I am ready to defray any expense you may have been put to,' I began, speaking as severely as I could, 'as a result of Parslow's actions,

---

* The philosopher Herbert Spencer is generally credited with inventing the phrase. J. R.

which, however, I must advise you I cannot condemn. The man was doing his duty.'

He replied that he had been commissioned by Mr Murray of Albemarle Street to write a book of his travels across the United States of America, and that he had been unable to proceed with this task since the incident at Down. I desisted from telling him that I was very well acquainted indeed with Mr Murray* as I sensed there was more to come and I saw no reason to dam the flow. I had arranged to stay the night with Erasmus since I had another appointment the following morning, and nothing to interest me for the rest of the day, at least until suppertime when my brother would return home, so I decided to stay a little longer and hear more of this strange little hairy man's adventures. I then asked him what places in the United States he had been fortunate enough to visit.

'The whole gamut,' he declared, 'from south to north and east to west and back again. The Girth of a Nation, you might say, which is my preferred title,' and with scarcely any prompting from me he embarked on a long and entertaining tale which would rival those of Baron Münchausen, I assure you. And one theme ran through it seamlessly: that of survival. It appears he survived being marooned, as he put it, on Albemarle, a voyage in a whaler, a trek (to use the South African term) across Mexico, the War of Texian Independence, and countless other adventures up the Mississippi and into the Far West. He survived. And why? How? Out of a deep desire, born of the pleasure he took in the process, of being alive. He never said so in so many words, but such was the power and relish of his account, that was clearly what drove him. He, however, had another answer which I shall reveal at the appropriate time.

And out of all this came the germ of a deeper understanding of what Survival of the Fittest really means, which has only really been borne in on me with its fullest force, in these last few years of my declining life.

In recent years the word 'fit' has come to mean (and I believe this to be largely due to a misunderstanding of what I meant by it, though it is much how Spencer uses it) 'in a suitable condition, prepared, ready' and by extension 'in good form or condition', hence 'strong',

* Murray had already published Darwin's *Journal*, and was to be the publisher of the *Origin*. J. R.

435

'healthy'; thus the 'fittest' are the 'strongest', 'the most powerful', the 'healthiest' and so forth. Now in many cases where Natural Selection operates, but by no means all, these are indeed the case, and one tends to focus on these to the exclusion of others when one's view of the matter is coloured by a general perception of the world of nature as a field of battle, competition, struggle, waste and so forth. In such a world it is indeed the most powerful, the strongest, who will survive.

However, many species survive not only because they produce individuals who are stronger than their fellows, but because they are broadly social, from termites, some bee species, through cattle and related mammals living in herds and colonies, to man himself, especially at his happiest and most fortunate. And most of these species also depend on an extended period of nurture by their parents, a practice which brings its own rewards. I would take this argument further and say, too, that most species continue to exist in symbiosis, understood in its widest sense, with all the species that surround them, in a harmonious balance which, if I may use a recent neologism, is œcological, a symbiosis prescribed by Natural Selection.

And here is one further factor: if the general rule for a species was that the lives of all its members were blighted with the constant misery and unhappiness pertaining to an existence of unending struggle, surely they would neglect the propagation of their kind?

There are, however, other considerations that lead to the belief that all sentient beings have been formed so as to enjoy, as a general rule, happiness. For, while I accept that an animal may be led to pursue that course of action which is the most beneficial to the species by suffering, such as pain, hunger or thirst, and fear, or by pleasure, as in eating, drinking, and in the propagation of the species, I should add that pain and suffering cause depression and lessen the power of action, while pleasurable sensations stimulate the whole system to increase action. We see this in the pleasure from exertion, both physical and mental, in the pleasure from our daily meals, and especially in the pleasure derived from sociability and most especially from loving our families.*

---

* A slightly fuller version of this passage, in particular, appears in *The Life and Letters of Charles Darwin, including an Autobiographical Chapter*, ed. Frank Darwin, Murray, publ. 1887. Darwin was no doubt working on it when he wrote this letter. J. R.

But (and as I get older, it happens more often) I digress: the meanings of 'fit' and 'fittest' were my text. I do not need to tell you what the real meanings of 'fit' are, but nevertheless here they are and they are at bottom what both Herbert and I meant by them: 'suited to the circumstances of the case, answering the purpose, proper, appropriate, in a suitable condition, prepared, ready'. Thus, the 'fittest', those that survive, are those that are simply, and, in nature contingently, best prepared for survival. Or, put it another way, those that survive are the ones most fitted for survival, in whatever way that may be, which is getting perilously close to circular argument if not tautology.

At all events, as the shadows lengthened in that upstairs room in Lambeth, and Eddie Bosham concluded by candlelight his tale of survival, it occurred to me to ask him, before I left, to what he himself attributed his survival through so many difficult and occasionally dire experiences.

He gave the question long and ruminative pause, hummed a little to himself, closed his eyes. At last he spoke.

'The kindness of other people,' he said. 'And, though not as often as should have been the case, the kindness I have shown in return.'

Grateful for such wisdom, albeit from an unlikely source, I wrote out a banker's order for ten pounds, which he accepted gratefully, as a gentleman should, not obsequiously, but as if it were his due.

Acknowledgements

I took some trouble over this book and a full list of all the sources I have used, borrowed from or downright cribbed would be pages long. Here are the main ones – apologies to the rest. Some are credited in footnotes to the text.

Barrett, Samuel A. and Gifford, Edward W., *Indian Life of the Yosemite Region – Miwok Material Culture*, Milwaukee, Wi., 1933

Beale, Thomas, *The Natural History of the Sperm Whale*, London, 1839 (Herman Melville acknowledged *The Natural History* as a major source, and if you compare certain passages in the two texts you will see he was right to do so)

Browning, Robert, *Dramatis Personae*, London, 1864

Cooper, James Fenimore, *The Prairie*, New York, 1850

Darwin, Charles, *The Voyage of the Beagle*, London, 1839

Desmond, Adrian and Moore, James, *Darwin*, London, 1991

Dickens, Charles, *American Notes*, London, 1851; *Bleak House*, London, 1853

Keynes, Randal, *Darwin, His Daughter & Human Evolution*, New York, 2002 (of all the books listed here, this was the one I loved most)

Larson, Edward J., *Evolution's Workshop*, New York, 2001

Lewis, Jon E., *The Mammoth Book of the West*, London, 1996

McGlashan, C. F., *History of the Donner Party*, Stanford, Ca., 1947

McLynn, Frank, *Wagons West*, London, 2002

Melville, Herman, *Moby Dick*, New York, 1851

Nofi, Albert A., *The Alamo and the Texas War of Independence*, New York, 2001

Petite, Mary Deborah, *1836 Facts about the Alamo & the Texas War for Independence*, Mason City, Iowa, 1999

Severin, Tim, *In Search of Moby Dick*, London, 1999

Shakespeare, William, *Mr William Shakespeare's Comedies, Histories and Tragedies*, London, 1623

Tebbel, John and Jennison, Keith, *The American Indian Wars*, New York, 1960

Townsend, John Kirk, *Narrative of a Journey across the Rocky Mountains 1834–36*

Twain, Mark, *The Adventures of Huckleberry Finn*, New York, 1884

Among the museums I visited (in the flesh, not just virtually) the most useful and entertaining were the State Indian Museum, Sacramento, Ca., which incorporates the last surviving fragment of Sutter's Fort; the Donner Memorial State Park, west of Truckee, Ca., which amongst much else has an immigrants' waggon; Down House, Down, Kent, England, where Darwin's study has been furbished as it was when he used it, and his garden preserved.

Of course I have used the web and visited probably more than a hundred sites, including the home pages of every town mentioned. Special thanks are due to Lee Jackson who runs *victorianlondon.org*, a huge and indispensable resource for anyone interested in the period. Most of the song lyrics were taken or adapted from Public Domain Music (www.pdmusic.org/1800s), or The Lyric Storage Center (LyricDepot.com).

William Pembroke Mulchinock (1820–64) wrote 'The Rose of Tralee'. The original Rose was a Mary O'Connor, who died in 1849, that is at least two years after Paddy first sings the song. Don't ask.

You can now order superb titles directly from Abacus

☐	Joseph	Julian Rathbone	£8.99
☐	The Last English King	Julian Rathbone	£7.99
☐	The Kings of Albion	Julian Rathbone	£7.99
☐	A Very English Agent	Julian Rathbone	£7.99

The prices shown above are correct at time of going to press. However, the publishers reserve the right to increase prices on covers from those previously advertised, without further notice.

──────────────── ⟨ABACUS⟩ ────────────────

Please allow for postage and packing: **Free UK delivery.**
Europe: add 25% of retail price; Rest of World: 45% of retail price.

To order any of the above or any other Abacus titles, please call our credit card orderline or fill in this coupon and send/fax it to:

Abacus, PO Box 121, Kettering, Northants NN14 4ZQ
Fax: 01832 733076   Tel: 01832 737527
Email: aspenhouse@FSBDial.co.uk

☐ I enclose a UK bank cheque made payable to Abacus for £ . . . . .
☐ Please charge £ . . . . to my Visa/Access/Mastercard/Eurocard

☐☐☐☐☐☐☐☐☐☐☐☐☐☐☐☐☐☐☐

Expiry Date ☐☐☐☐   Switch Issue No.   ☐☐

NAME (BLOCK LETTERS please) . . . .

ADDRESS . . . .

. . . .

. . . .

Postcode . . . . Telephone . . . .

Signature . . . .

Please allow 28 days for delivery within the UK. Offer subject to price and availability.
Please do not send any further mailings from companies carefully selected by Abacus ☐